LORD OF
SLAUGHTER

M.D. LACHLAN

The right of M.D. Lachlan to be identified as the author of
this work has been asserted by him in accordance with the
Copyright, Designs and Patents Act 1988.

First published in Great Britain in 2012 by
Gollancz
An imprint of the Orion Publishing Group
Orion House, 5 Upper St Martin's Lane,
London WC2H 9EA
An Hachette UK Company

This edition published in Great Britain in 2013
by Gollancz

1 3 5 7 9 10 8 6 4 2

A CIP catalogue record for this book
is available from the British Library

ISBN 978 0 575 08969 3

Typeset by Deltatype Ltd, Birkenhead, Merseyside

Printed in Great Britain by Clays Ltd, St Ives plc

The Orion Publishing Group's policy is to use papers that are
natural, renewable and recyclable products and made from wood
grown in sustainable forests. The logging and manufacturing
processes are expected to conform to the environmental
regulations of the country of origin.

www.orionbooks.co.uk
www.gollancz.co.uk

To Julie Gibson
For friendship and because the idea of her having a book
called *Lord of Slaughter* dedicated to her makes me laugh.

Hades I call thee Numera, and even worse than Hades,
For in its horror it surpasses even Hades.
In this murky and most deep dungeon
There is no light to the eyes, nor any conversation,
For the constant smoke, and the thickness of the darkness
Suffer us not to see or recognise each other.
But bonds and tortures, and guards and towers
And the shouting **Varangoi**; and terror keeps you awake.

MICHAEL GLYCAS, BYZANTINE HISTORIAN, 12TH CENTURY

Through hunger and thirst,
Through heat and bitter frost.
By never avoiding the hardships of weather thou didst purify
thyself as gold in the furnace.

KONTAKION OF THE EASTERN ORTHODOX CHURCH, TONE 4,
DATE UNKNOWN

From there come the maidens
mighty in wisdom,
Three from the well
down beneath the tree.
Uthr is one named,
Verthani the next —
On wood they scored —
and Skuld the third.
Laws they made there,
and life allotted
To the sons of men,
and set their fates.

THE POETIC EDDA, 10TH CENTURY

1 The Rain

Under a dead moon, on a field of the dead, a wolf moved unseen beneath the rain's great shadow.

The downpour had started with nightfall as the battle ended. There was too much blood for Christ to bear, said the victorious Greeks, and he had decided to wash it away.

The wolf slipped through the ranks of dead and dying, past the little cocoons of light where men nurtured lamps or candles in their sagging tents. Even there it was just a smudge in the darkness, a spectre made by the rain.

The boy Snake in the Eye looked out of the imperial tent for signs of a break in the weather. Any moon would have made looting possible but its slim crescent had faded the previous evening and the clouds had rolled in. He saw nothing in the sodden night beyond the weak glow of the lamps.

He was sure men would try to claim what plunder they could, even in that black deluge. The ground was a mire, though, and not all the wounded were beyond defending themselves. Why die ingloriously in the dark to the knife of one of the rebel's half-dead Normans or Arabs? If you were going to die, better to do it where your fellows would see you and credit you for your warrior's heart.

Snake in the Eye often dreamed of a famous death — surrounded by a press of enemies, their spears bright under a cold sun, his sword flashing arcs of sunlight and crimson — filled with the elation of killing and dying.

'Twenty faced him and twenty went with him to the halls of the dead, to cheer him to the mead bench at the All Father's side.' So the skalds would sing for him one day.

He had never feared death and thought it a fine thing to die well and live for ever in the tales of his kin at the fireside and in the marketplace, though he would not throw his life away. For now he would sit tight behind the ditches of the camp and begin searching the bodies and the baggage train with the crows in the morning light. After that, he would go dancing with his loot to Abydos, to see the grateful town throw open its gates to the men who had lifted its siege. Then he would enjoy all the pleasures available to the liberator, including that of watching the rebel leaders impaled on the walls.

The rain fell so hard that no lamp or fire could be had outside and men huddled in their soaking tents waiting for dawn — those who had tents. In the summer most of the army slept in the open. When the rain had come in, fast, cold, unseasonable and heavy, the soldiers had crammed into any available shelter, fighting for cover before the blind blackness fell. The unlucky and the weak stood shivering and stamping in the bare scrub, clinging together for warmth in the sightless dark.

The horses of the cavalry moaned under the onslaught of the water and the warriors sang in the night to keep up their spirits. Snake in the Eye heard the songs of the Rus, of how Helgi won the battle at Kiev. He heard those of the Greeks, who called themselves Romans and sang of how Constantine had raised the greatest city in the world. And he heard those he loved the most — old songs of the north, from the Viking warriors, his people. Songs of heroes, dragons and battles against incredible odds. He understood each language. He'd been a market boy at Birka in Skania and it had paid him to be able to speak to as many varieties of men as he could.

He heard more than songs under the beating rain. Men and animals still lay dying in the storm and, to Snake in the Eye, their cries were a sort of music too. They filled him with a physical joy that tingled from his boots to his tongue.

'Any sign of this weather clearing, boy?' A voice from inside the tent.

'No, lord.'

'I thought not. Come back in here. I need to talk to you.'

Snake in the Eye turned away from the guard who sat

shivering at the tent's dripping entrance despite his three cloaks.

The emperor was alone, his war council having finished digesting the events of the day. He gestured for Snake in the Eye to sit next to a small and ornate brazier. The boy did so. The brazier fascinated him. The basket that held the fire was wrought with little lizards that seemed to wriggle in the heat, black against the light of the coals. At the emperor's feet lay something equally as fascinating – the head of the rebel Phokas, scarcely recognisable as human – the rebel had fallen from his horse and been trampled by his own cavalry – but Snake in the Eye knew it was him. He had been there when Bollason, the famous Viking, had found the body and decapitated it.

The emperor's eyes flicked momentarily to a trickle of water dropping from a corner of the tent.

'You did us good service today in translating my commands. You are a Varangian but you speak Greek like a true Roman. How did you learn our language?'

'I make it my study, sir. I have travelled this way with my father trading furs, and your countrymen come to our market.'

'You speak impressively.'

'I find all tongues easy, sir. I can converse with the Arabs as well, enough to trade anyway.'

'Then you can be useful to us. I should order you castrated so you can attend me formally at court.'

The boy paled.

'Don't look so terrified. Many poorer sons have made that career choice. The chamberlain who rules in my place in Constantinople when I am on campaign is a eunuch and not of good family. Do you think he could have risen to be so mighty had he stayed intact? Of course not. He would not have been allowed as close to the purple.'

Again, the boy said nothing.

'Don't worry, I shan't command it but it's an option you should consider. You handled yourself well under the pressure of the battle today. You would benefit by ongoing access to my presence. It's not so much to give up. You're not even a proper man yet, it's apparent to any who look at you.'

'I am a man, sir.'

'Listen to your voice. Look at the smoothness of your chin. I'm a Roman emperor, boy, I've seen enough eunuchs and ordered enough cut to know the difference between a man and a boy. You can't miss what you've never had. What is your name?'

'Snake in the Eye.'

'Why so?'

The boy pointed to his left eye. The emperor beckoned him forward. Snake in the Eye held the eye open wide and the emperor peered into it. Around the pupil curled a second blackness, a deformity of the eye.

'It does look like a snake,' said the emperor. 'What is its meaning?'

'Death,' said Snake in the Eye, 'so my mother told me.'

The emperor pursed his lips, impressed.

'I have always paid attention to things like this. It is an important mark, something from God.'

'Our people say it is an image of the world snake – a serpent whose coils stretch across the whole earth. When it shakes, the seas boil and the land splits.'

'Would you shake the earth and boil the seas, Snake in the Eye?'

'I would, sir, on your behalf.'

The emperor touched his tongue to his upper lip.

'A snake in a boy's eye. One thing among many strange ones recently. Two days ago – you saw the fireball in the sky?'

'It was a good omen.'

'We made sure it was. I had to drum up a legion of fortune tellers and wonder workers to convince the men it was a sign God was with us.'

'He surely was, sir.'

'Who knows what these things mean? Men call comets the terror of kings. I tell you for nothing, it put the wind up me.

Must have been a good sign, I suppose. We won, didn't we?'

Snake in the Eye stayed silent. He sensed the emperor just wanted to voice his concerns. Snake in the Eye's one purpose was to provide a pair of ears so Basileios could talk out loud without considering himself mad.

'The rebel drops dead in front of me, then this downpour arrives out of nowhere in high summer in a land that hasn't seen rain in a year. What do you think of that?'

'The land is grateful. You have removed the rebel and reset the natural order. Perhaps the rebellion caused the drought.'

'You speak like a man twice your age. Are all the Varangians like you?'

'I come from a line of wise men and have been brought up in their company but I am wise enough to know that I know only a little of the world. This is why I spend my time listening, when I can, to people who know more.'

'A good policy. It is better to listen than to speak, even for kings. Only the king who keeps his secrets to himself knows he can never be betrayed.'

He took a sip of his wine and swirled the remaining liquid around in the bottom of his cup, staring into it as if he expected it to reveal the answer to some troubling question.

'There are envious men working against me by supernatural means, I am sure, envious men in league with envious demons. *Fascinus*, St Jerome called it, so says my chamberlain. Envy turned to hurt. Harm in the gaze. Was it Christ who came to our aid? I hope so. But this will excite the envy of demons even more. If the rebel can be struck down in such a way, why not me? These past years I have ...'

He stopped speaking.

Snake in the Eye had spent his time in the Greek camp learning everything he could about the emperor and the organisation of the Byzantine forces. Basileios had not had a woman in five years. His closest advisers insisted he had no time for such things. He thought of conquest, not women. The soldiers whispered that an Anatolian witch had cursed his cock to limpness for the ravages of his armies. That explained why he didn't marry. But there again his mother had been a murderous witch – she killed her husband, the emperor Romanos, with poison and married his successor. When she grew tired of him she had him killed too and would have married a third emperor if the Church hadn't interceded. With a mother like her, Basileios had learned to be wary of women. He was known to be a superstitious man and may have seen wives as bad luck.

The emperor seemed to get irritated with his own deliberations. He pointed to the boy's eye.

'An interesting mark. Perhaps a sign of great fortune.'

'Not for my enemies,' said the boy.

Basileios laughed. 'Ah, let's hope not. You amuse me, Snake in the Eye, and that in itself is a great fortune.'

'I hope to be of greater service than making you laugh, lord. I am a man now, just, and my axe is restless in my hand. I would kill for you. That is my destiny. I was raised as a merchant but in the northern way – as a warrior too. I have a skill at arms unmatched by my fellows and one day it will be unmatched by men throughout the world. Your enemies are my enemies and I would watch them fall.'

Snake in the Eye believed the words as he said them. He beat most older boys in their fighting games, despite his size. Would it be so different to face a grown man with sharp steel? Not if you kept your wits, he thought.

'Perhaps you will, one day. If you get some hairs on your chin and a sword, I think that would be a start. First, tell me about these Norsemen, their customs and their ways. To command them, I must know them.'

So Snake in the Eye told the stories of his people – of battles, journeys by ship, incredible hardships. The emperor listened with conspicuous pleasure – happy he had secured the services of unusually violent and hardy men. One fact particularly pleased him.

'When we give an oath it is our solemn bond,' said Snake in

the Eye. 'We will not break it for anything – not starvation, not death or poverty. A man, to us, is only as good as his word.'

'That is your boast, but is it your practice?' said the emperor. 'Many men who swear loyalty to Christ do not act as Christians when their betters are not looking.'

'If our men swear, they swear in earnest,' said the boy. 'In the market at Birka I have never known a man of my people fail to keep a promise. When a Norseman says he will pay you in ten days, you will be paid in ten days, even if he has to cut another merchant's throat to do it.'

The emperor glanced at the cloaked back of the Hetaereian guard who sat cross-legged in the rain at the small open entrance to the tent.

'Romans have no such code,' he said. 'They live in terror of the emperor or they slit his throat. They have known no other way since the beginnings of the empire.'

'Our men are not like that,' said Snake in the Eye, who had not mistaken the direction of the emperor's thoughts. 'If we pledge allegiance to a lord, we will die rather than betray him. We are dependable. Above all else, we are dependable.'

The emperor took a fig from a silver bowl at his side and toyed with it in his hand. 'Did you take an oath to Vladimir before you deserted him?'

'We did but he released us from it to send us to you.'

'He never paid you. Six thousand of you and no attempt at rebellion?'

'Our leaders had sworn. That was the end of the matter.'

'I will think on it,' said the emperor. He replaced the fig and fell to silence.

The rain kept coming, harder and harder. Eventually the emperor grew tired and ordered the flap of the tent closed to the minimum necessary for ventilation, and had the coals in the brazier reduced to just a couple. The soaking eunuch guard ducked into the tent and went to shoo the boy out but the emperor raised a hand.

7

'He has earned a dry night,' he said.

Snake in the Eye lay down to sleep on a silk cushion, pulling a blanket of fine goat wool about him, and staring up at the tent's roof by what remained of the brazier's glow. He glanced across at the head of the rebel. He smiled to see the swollen slits of eyes watching him in the dim light.

You were greater than me, he thought, *but now look at you. The poets will sing of me, not you.*

His limbs were sore from the day's exertions but he was not sleepy. His mind hummed with the thrill of battle. He ached to do it all again, but this time, this time at least, to get in on the kill. At the great northern market at Birka Snake in the Eye met many foreigners and saw many remarkable sights but nothing like he had seen that day.

He'd stood next to the emperor, translating his commands for the Varangians as the armies engaged, right by his standard and the portrait of St Helena exhibited on a pole to face the oncoming enemy. The emperor's Greeks, foot soldiers at the front, slammed into the rebel's iron-armoured Armenians with a sound like the fall of a million metal plates and the battle started. Images from the day came back to him – the rain of arrows from both sides, the strangeness of the enemy's Bedouin camel riders, the grace of the Anatolian cavalry as they harried the infantry with arrows dispatched at full gallop, the similarity of the troops as Greek fought Greek in tight and ordered lines. With the fighting at its fiercest, the rebel led a charge with his heavy cavalry into the emperor's flank.

Snake in the Eye found the horsemen fascinating – kilbanophoroi, they were called – the men all swathed in scale armour, their faces invisible beneath masks of mail, the horses covered in thick felt skirts so they seemed almost to move without legs. They rumbled forward at the trot, a rolling wave, slow but irresistible. But as the rebel had come on at their head, his pennant streaming from his lance, he had fallen, gone straight down as if hit by an arrow. No arrow had been fired. The Greek infantry had fled before the lances of the horsemen, trampling through their own archers in their desperation to get away. The bowmen, shoved down and aside, caught the panic and ran themselves. No one had fired an arrow — it was obvious from the vantage point Snake in the Eye shared with the emperor — and yet the rebel had gone down.

The charge faltered and then the cavalry fled, spreading panic through the rebel forces. So the emperor let loose his Varangians — the Vikings. No solid Roman lines there but six thousand men with long axes and spears howling like wolves into the fight.

Snake in the Eye went with them and he waved his axe and screamed his insults, but something held him back from killing. What? Other boys of his age took part in the battle. He defied anyone to call him a coward. He placed himself before the enemy's spears; it was just that the enemy ran before he could engage them. Snake in the Eye told himself this was no honourable way to kill. He wanted to face his opponent, equally armed and armoured, and to best him one on one. He would not take part in slaughter.

But as the visions of the day returned to him as he waited for sleep, he wished he had at least killed one. A fantasy came upon him in which an Armenian had come for him.

'Fancy your chances, do you, boy?'

'I'm no boy, foreigner,' he'd said. They'd swung and cut, hacked and blocked in the mud. He imagined the thrill as he threw himself aside to dodge a lethal thrust, felt the tearing of the fabric of his tunic as the sword grazed his belly. He relished the panic on the face of his enemy as he realised he had committed too far, the thump as a backhanded blow of Snake in the Eye's axe took away half the Armenian's head. Then they'd all come at him, all the ironclad Armenian hordes, and he had been a scythe and they the barley.

It hadn't happened, but Snake in the Eye hoped one day it would. It must. He was hungry for stories to tell.

He had tried to test himself ever since he was old enough to hold an axe, seeking fights with men, offering them insults and anger. They had never taken him seriously. Too small, too much a boy to be considered worth killing. When his hand went to his axe to make them take him seriously or die, something would come over him. His hand would not move; his feet were rooted. He'd been beaten, humiliated on many occasions, longing to kill but paralysed in the face of his enemies. His father had been kind to him, wanting to believe his son would eventually emulate his ancestors.

'It's the battle fetter,' he had said. 'It strikes the best of warriors. It's a gift. Only Odin can impose it. He's saving you for something special. He won't let you waste yourself in a pointless scrap with a man twice your size. You will grow and you will become mighty, believe me.'

Snake in the Eye shifted on his pillow and touched the stone he wore at his neck on a thong of leather, asking it for luck − blood luck, fine enemies and glory kills. It was not an expensive piece of jewellery, just a triangular pebble marked with the head of a wolf. His grandfather had owned it, an amulet for the blessing of the gods, and his mother gave it to Snake in the Eye when the boy was five. He'd worn it ever since.

A slinking shame crawled through his mind when he thought of his grandfather, Thiörek, son of Thetmar. Sometimes called the fat warrior, he had killed so many men it was said ravens followed him where ever he went and fell from the skies they became so fat. But his grandfather had been a head taller than other men by his thirteenth year. Snake in the Eye was short for his age, his stature slight, and his skin was like a girl's.

He would kill, he would kill. Not soon, though. The Armenians had fled or died − at least the ones who fought for the rebel − the Normans and the Turks too; the camels had run and the Greeks lay bleeding. In Constantinople, he thought, Miklagard, the world city, he would find his cure. There he would throw off the battle fetter.

He tried to sleep but his mind was wild with memories and fantasies. He remembered the mad delight that had followed the victory, recalled the coming of the rain − rain, said the

Greeks, like Noah saw. Snake in the Eye knew that story, he had been at many campfires and heard tales from all over the world. Looking up at the wet cloth of the tent, he had the idea he had called the rain himself, to blot out his shame.

The images and sensations of the day played out again and again in his thoughts and eventually began to fade, as if his mind was heavy with blood and torpid like a gorged leech. Snake in the Eye dreamed of a rain-black night and a field of the slain where a wolf came nosing towards where he lay.

Then the wolf was at the tent and it had never been a wolf — just the idea of a wolf, an idea you could catch by looking at it. It was a man. The rain-blind guard at the tent's rear was taken down in silence, his neck broken. The killer drew a sword that shone even in the dream's dark night like the cold crescent of the moon tumbled to earth, a wicked talon of silver, a razor curve shaped and sharpened by death.

Snake in the Eye stirred, opened his eyes and knew his dream was over. Above him was a man who was not a man, a wolf who was not a wolf, and in his hand was a cruel curved sword that the boy sensed was an ancient killer.

His thoughts cleared and, in the brazier's faint light, he saw standing over the emperor a man wrapped in little more than a wolfskin, which he wore with the head over his own. At first he thought it was a legionary because one of the Greeks had worn the skin of a great cat like that. But this wasn't a legionary. It was a wild man, stained with mud, his skin dyed grey like a wolf's, the water dripping from him.

Snake in the Eye shouted and leaped foward. The man caught him with one hand and held him by the throat with a terrible strength. The boy squirmed and choked, desperate fingers unable to prise away the crushing grip.

No one came, the boy's choking unheard beneath the rush of the rain, the songs of the camp and the screams of the dying.

The emperor woke, his eyes wide with surprise. He gave a snort, almost resigned, more like a man cursing his luck the

11

last wineskin had gone from a market stall than someone about to die.

He looked at the weapon.

'I am a Roman emperor, born in the purple, friend, so if you are of some conquered people and expect to see me beg, you will be disappointed. You are unwelcome but not unexpected. Do what you have to.'

Snake in the Eye fought against unconsciousness. The tent blurred and the brazier's light cut trails in front of his eyes. The wolfman released his grip, dropping the boy to the floor. Then he threw his sword at the emperor's feet and spoke two words in hacking, guttural Greek.

'Kill me,' he said.

2   The Lovers

'I ingest your eyes. I drink your blood. I eat your liver. I put on your skin.'

'What are you talking about, Loys?'

The young woman propped herself up by one elbow on the bed, gazing down at the man who lay beside her in the dawn light. She nibbled on a little figure of a man made from bread while her companion gently twisted a strand of her long blonde hair between his fingers and gazed up at her, smiling.

'It's a charm – I heard it in the market. It's to make you love me. That's what the bread people are for. That's me—' He tapped his finger on the bread in her hand, 'and this in my tummy was you.'

'Idolatry!'

'It would be if we believed it. As we don't, it's just bread.'

'You don't need a charm, I already love you.'

'But you wish you did not, don't you, Lady Beatrice?'

He drew her to him and kissed her. Then they broke and she turned her eyes from his gaze.

'I wish I did not.'

'So serious.' He took her hand and held it to his mouth.

'Intemperate love is serious, so the Church tells us,' she said.

'It is a woman's weakness to be governed by unruly passions. But I love you immoderately too and I do not have the excuse of my sex to hide behind.'

'I had hoped when we married, it might fade and be replaced by proper feelings of charity and tender unity. That's what's meant to happen, isn't it, to good people?'

'We tried our best. We drank the honey wine at our wedding.'

'Not enough, maybe. I am in the grip of a vicious love.

When you are here, the idea of us parting fills me with a dread like grief. I burn for you.' The woman's eyes were wet. He let go of her hair and put his hand to her cheek to comfort her.

'And I for you. It is regrettable, but we have prayed against it and still it remains.'

'All holy teaching tells us such desire is base and unworthy of marriage.'

They spoke French, her voice noticeably accented with the harder consonants of the Norman court. His pronunciation was softer, indicative of a more humble upbringing.

'What would you do if you did not love me?' he said.

'Our marriage would be happier. I would sit here with my embroidery, content, not restless and longing for you to come back so much that I sit hating the sunlight and calling the dusk down like a country witch. Or I would have married an equal and still be sitting outside some fine hall, watching the grapes ripen in the sun and my husband work his hawks.'

'Yet this little room holds more pleasures than all the fields of Francia.'

'So that was my fortune, to love and to starve.'

'We are not starving, Bea.'

'Only while I have my bits of jewels and gold to sell. What if we are robbed again? We need a better place than this, Loys, more secure.'

'It is secure while you're here.'

'Sat on three cheap rings in this wooden hutch like a hen on her eggs. They will never hatch, Loys. I want to go out to see the streets. This is the most marvellous city on earth. I can't spend all day looking at the four walls.'

'You'd be exhausted in half an hour.'

'I'm not as weak as you think I am.'

He sat up on the bed and patted her belly. She was visibly pregnant.

'You mustn't wear yourself out. Not with him in here.'

'Let's hope it is a him.'

'Do you really think it would give us the chance to return?'

'He'd be my father's only heir. If I can make him vow not to harm you, then, yes, he might accept you. I'm sure you could drag up a noble ancestor from somewhere. You're of his blood, sort of. Your father came over on the same longships that he did.'

'Not quite the same. Mine crewed the cargo ship, not a warship.'

'He has to respect your heritage.'

'If you have a son.'

'If I don't?'

'Then, when I am established at the university we will live at the court. You'll be able to move freely there. I've offered to hire a eunuch to escort you while I'm not here.'

'We can't afford to waste money like that. I wish there was another way for us to live but by studying.'

'I must work for free until I am offered lodgings and a stipend. You know this – we've been over it.'

'Yes. I'm sorry, I just ...' She turned her face to the wall.

He held her hand. 'I am a scholar; I can do nothing else. I have no lands; I have no other skill. I will come home as quickly as I can and then I will take you walking by the palace.'

For the first time she smiled.

'If my father could hear me. My life dependent on a tradesman.'

'Is a monk a tradesman?'

'You're no longer a monk, Loys.'

He kissed her.

'Whose fault is that? Your father's people are tradesmen, though they trade as much in blood as furs. If your father could hear you I'd be worried. Do you fancy the idea of him lurking behind the door with his axe?'

He sprang off the bed and tapped the bolt home in the door.

'A noble man disdains to show fear,' she said.

'A scholar checks twice if he wants to keep his head. This place is safer for you than almost anywhere else. Your father won't look here. I know his mind. It's impossible for him to even think of you in a place like this.'

'So why do you check the door?'

'I know enough of the arts of learning to beware of certainty in all its forms. Your father would not look here. What of chance, though? What if God punishes us for our loving each other rather than him?'

'Will God punish us?'

Loys put a hand to the mouldy wooden wall of the little room.

'Perhaps he already has.'

He pulled on a pair of linen under trousers then opened the shutters wide.

The street was filling up with traders setting out their stalls — below a man with a tray of Persian apples, the Greek name for peaches, paraded back and forth. He'd buy her one before he left for the university, he thought, and hope it would please her.

Loys gazed out towards the east, over the vast sea of Constantinople. The sky was dark, rain clouds scarring the sunrise with bands of purple. It was July but the air bore the edge of a chill.

They had two rooms, one for her, one for him, in the Greek way. The woman who rented them to them pointed out that the female chamber, though cramped, was comfortable and light. Bea hadn't spent a second in it since they'd arrived in the early summer. When at home, they lay together in each other's arms.

Loys hoped to secure some lodgings at the university before winter. He had no idea how cold it might get in this part of the world but, if it was anything like Normandy, these little rooms would be nowhere near warm enough. The Greeks in the university had told him the winters could be bitter. It was cold in their room that morning and it was July. Beatrice was susceptible to fevers too. In a way he was thankful for that because it was through a fever he had come to know her.

It really did seem like the will of God they were together. She had been ill, consumed with a fever, and he had gone with an ordained monk to see what they could do to help her but expecting to administer the viaticum to commend her soul to heaven.

They had found her very likely to die, terribly agitated and hot, screaming that she should be left alone, not pursued. None of the servants would attend her because they said she was possessed.

Loys was with old Father Paul, a good doctor in his day but who now drank too much wine and was fat and red in the face. He reminded Loys of a big round blood blister and he wondered that his colleague didn't burst at any minute. They sat with the girl and Paul – whose age and holiness had made the presence of a chaperone unnecessary – actually fell asleep. Loys hated to see Beatrice so sick, not because she would die – plenty died younger – but for the torment she was suffering. He took her hand and told her God was with her and loved her. The gesture calmed her. Loys kept holding her hand, half an eye on Father Paul to see if he woke. He whispered to her: 'I am at your side and I will not leave you. You won't die, see, how can you die when I hold you to life so securely?' He sat like that for an hour before she opened her eyes and asked for a drink. When he fetched her one, she sipped at it, took his hand and lay back to doze some more.

Lord Richard heard she had recovered and came to the chamber. Loys would never forget his grim presence. He was so brusque and short-tempered he seemed a breath away from punching you to the floor even in the moment of his delight. He didn't thank the monks; just swept into the room, put his hand to Beatrice's brow and said, 'Glad to see you sitting up. I knew you were of tough stuff.' Then he left them.

Even though Beatrice quickly recovered, Loys persuaded Paul they needed to check she didn't relapse. The lady was troubled by dreams and there was a possibility she was still haunted by demons.

So they went back and heard how in her fever she'd had a dream so vivid it now seemed more like the memory of something real. She was in the woods in the evening and she sensed something far inside the shadow of the trees – more of the darkness than in it. It was as if all the darkness of the world, the shadows of the forest and those that lurked beneath the church gables, the ancient and hungry darks of childhood that brooded beneath beds and in cupboards, that skulked under stairs and in attics, flowed in to the body of the creature that pursued her. Instead of fleeing from it and hiding, she called to it, speaking in a voice it understood – the howl of a wolf in the hills.

Paul simply said she had been frightened by her fever and that she would soon be well again. So it seemed. Beatrice became happy and began to look forward to seeing the monks. With Loys she forgot her dreams. For three visits the fat doctor dozed while Loys and Beatrice laughed and talked. When Loys made an excuse to visit alone, Beatrice always made sure her chaperone was old Marie, so deaf and so in awe of monks that she sat with her face buried in her embroidery, oblivious to the couple flirting. Of course, both knew the danger they faced. As a monk who had taken his vows Loys was not free to marry her, and as a low-born man he was no sort of match for a duke's daughter.

Loys and Beatrice prayed for their affection to pass and agreed not to see each other. But she knew he collected firewood in the forest on a Wednesday morning and she – who had always loved to go out alone on her horse to greet the dawn –suddenly found it necessary to exercise her horse in those woods at that time – despite the winter cold. They had met, away from chaperones, away from the dozing Paul. She told him what she feared. She saw a man in her dreams who she was convinced meant her harm. She needed to go where he could not find her.

'He can't find you in your father's keep,' said Loys. 'He has a hundred warriors to defend you there.'

'He will find me,' said Beatrice, 'because I have seen him. He is here.'

'Then identify him to your father and that is the end of it,' said Loys.

'It won't do any good,' said Beatrice. 'I'm not even sure he is one person or a demon that inhabits many people, as he chooses. He watches me and I know he will not rest until he has me.'

'Then ask to go to your cousins,' said Loys.

'No. I would be with you. I want you to take me away from this place.'

'I have my vows, lady,' he said. 'What will I do if I break them?'

'I will give you new ones,' she said, and he understood she was asking him to marry her. He looked into her eyes and knew he bore a passion for her before which his monastic vows, his studies, his security, were pale and insubstantial things, mere candles to the light of the sun. It had led to where it had to lead – a little room somewhere away from the vengeful gaze of her father and away from the monastery.

Now they were in that little room, in Constantinople, the city chosen because they both knew Greek, he as a serious student, she because there had been a fashion for learning among the ladies of the court, who had taken it up as a pastime while their husbands were away at the wars. He came to her and said, 'One day this love will fade, I promise it, and we will live properly and free of unreasonable passion. Free of love. Until that day we can only pray. Let me kiss you.'

She put up her mouth to him and he bent to take a long kiss.

'Behind me,' he said, 'is dawn in a city of marvels. The mighty churches, the domes, the spires and the schools, the statues and the Hippodrome, ships and galleys from a hundred lands bobbing on the bright water, all I have longed to see for all my life. In front of me, you naked in the morning light. I cannot turn around and, it is my shame before God to say it, but neither do I want to.'

She drew him to her and he put his hand to her breast.

'You have to go,' she said.

'Yes,' he said, 'but in the offices and schoolrooms, when I sit with grand philosophers and debate the nature of God's earth, it is of you I shall be thinking.'

'Think on your philosophies and your work,' she said, 'the sooner you might be with me in something resembling our former comfort.'

He broke from her. Then he dressed.

'Come to the window,' he said when he was done, 'and watch me go.'

He held her again, her human warmth like a current pulling him into the comfort of the bed. He tore free of it and went to the door.

'Bolt it behind me.'

'Yes, Loys, I'm not stupid.' She smiled at him and gave a little wave of goodbye.

He blundered his way down the dark stairs, careful with his hand on the splintery wooden wall, and then stepped out into the light of the summer morning, the jabber of the streets. His put his hand up to shield his eyes and was jostled by a gaggle of high-hatted priests who squeezed past him to avoid a cart that rattled by, its horses at the trot. If unreasonable passions governed him, then how much more did they govern Constantinople? So different even to Rouen. Men moved about their everyday business here at the pace of a Norman responding to a fire.

He went to the man selling peaches and bought one. Beatrice leaned out of the window. She had dressed and had her wimple on now, as demure as any wife emptying a piss pot into the street. He laughed to himself as the thought occurred to him. They'd received a visit from the neighbour the first time they'd done that. It was against the law in Constantinople. It still seemed odd to him to make the wives of the town parade along with pots of shit to throw into the sea when they could have kept their dignity and saved their efforts by just pitching them outside.

'Here!' he shouted and threw the peach to her.

It flew up through the chilly dawn light, a little sun rising to noon in her hands as she caught it.

A line from a psalm came into his head.

'You send forth your spirit. They are created and you renew the face of the earth.'

'An apple!' she shouted. 'Thank you, serpent!'

He smiled and waved and then went on his way to the university.

3 Profitable Murder

The emperor picked up the sword. The wolfman went down
onto his haunches while the boy lay limp on the ground. The
sound of the rain and the singing of soldiers filled the tent.
The emperor turned to his right. The back of his guard was
just visible through the slit in the tent flap.

Basileios walked to it and opened it. The man jerked around,
his soaking face staring up in surprise at the emperor's sudden
appearance. He shook with cold. The emperor beheaded him.

Then he turned back inside the tent.

'It's a fine slave who tells the Roman ruler what to do,' he
said to the crouching figure. 'Look at you, in your mud and
your dye. Why should I do anything you ask me?'

'Kill me,' said the wolfman, 'or kill you.'

The man's Greek was appalling and Basileios hardly understood what he was trying to say. On the floor the boy coughed
and hacked, sucking breath back into his lungs.

'How did you get in here?'

The wolfman's face was uncomprehending.

The emperor studied the wolfman in the glow of the weak
coals. He was gaunt, almost starved in appearance, but wiry
and strong-looking, smeared with mud on his belly, chest and
knees from where he had crawled through the night. Matted
black hair stuck wet to his face and a soaking wolfskin lay
across his shoulders, its head sitting on top of his.

'Kill me. Kill you.'

A shout from outside. The Hetaereia had found the head of
their companion. A man poked his head into the tent. He had
the smooth skin and delicate features of a eunuch. His short
sword was free in his hand.

'Alarm!'

'Stand down, soldier,' said the emperor. 'The moment for alarm is long past. Remain at the entrance to prevent people coming in: I don't want the tent demolished by men rushing to make themselves my protector. On your present showing it would be better if I guarded you.'

'You know this foreigner, sir?'

'No, but I intend to, and the task will be made much harder if your men kill him.'

'One of us is dead here already, sir. I—'

'By my hand. If you are more vigilant you will not suffer the same fate, now do as I say!'

The man disappeared outside. Shouting, footsteps nearly indistinguishable from the fall of the mighty rain. The wolfman stood and the emperor backed away.

'Kill me. Kill you,' he said again.

Snake in the Eye sat up. He said several words, separate, staccato. Basileios heard Greek, Roman and some in a language he didn't recognise. The boy was saying one word in different tongues – 'brother'. He was appealing to the wolfman, trying to become his friend.

The wolfman spoke slowly to the boy.

Snake in the Eye translated. 'He is a wildman of the Varangian people. He says you have to kill him. He is deadly bad luck to you. Use that sword. It is poisoned with the dreams of witches and can end your trouble.'

'Is he Bollason's man?'

Bollason was chief of the Varangians. Snake in the Eye wanted to make himself important to the emperor for the moment so he thought not to involve Bollason. He just asked the wolfman if he could speak Greek any better. The man shook his head and waved his arms.

'He is working alone, sir, and despises Bollason.'

'Ask him when wildmen became so interested in the emperor's health. Why does he value my life above his own? Ask him why.'

The man spoke again.

'A wolf is coming for you. You are a god but a wolf is coming to kill you.'

The boy translated, his voice hoarse.

'Well, it's a tame wolf who bends down and asks you to chop off his head,' said the emperor.

'You are part of a great magic. A very great magic. Your part in the spell is to kill him. He must die, and by your hand. Otherwise you are in mortal peril.'

The emperor paled when he heard this translation and his lips pursed in anger, not fear.

'I've had enough of sorceries and witch work,' he said, 'and I will take part in no spell, nor be a conjurer's fool. Is this the price, Satan, of what happened today, the death of my enemy, a human sacrifice? Is this some trick to obtain my soul?'

'He says he will kill you if you do not strike him down,' said Snake in the Eye.

Basileios sneered at the wolfman then threw the strange curved sword so it landed flat beside him.

'Tell him to go on then,' said the emperor. 'He had the chance while I was lying asleep. Tell him to do it.'

The boy repeated the words to the wolfman, who trembled, violently shaking his head. 'Kill me! Kill me!'

'Guardsmen!' shouted the emperor.

Eight men crashed inside the tent, crowding around the emperor, threatening to knock down the whole sodden structure.

'Take the pagan. Don't harm him. I need to get more learned men than me to speak to him and I want to have him in a fit state to answer their questions. Those scholars sit on their arses all day doing nothing; let them earn their keep for once and get to the bottom of this. Tie him, watch him and, when we get back to that stinking shit hole of a capital city of ours, chuck him in the Numera and await further instructions. Take him, go on!'

The men advanced on the wolfman, who offered no resistance as they dragged him outside.

The emperor dismissed his guards and again only Snake in the Eye remained.

'The guards are incompetent,' said the Emperor, 'or rather treacherous. They must have let him in. I cannot trust my own people any more, nor any Greek because all of them are eligible to take my throne if they can get the army's backing. Yet, if I move against the Hetaereians it may spark them into rebellion.'

Snake in the Eye said nothing. He looked out of the tent. A weak dawn – the damp light of a hidden sun. The rain had stopped. No more singing but the cries of the untended wounded, the squabbling of the soldiers as they looted.

'What would you do?' the emperor asked the boy.

'You got your answer on the battlefield today – kill the leaders and their men will not oppose you. Cut off the head and the snake cannot bite.'

The emperor stretched out his neck.

'No need to send for the chamberlain when you're here, eh?'

'Shall I send for him?'

'He's going ahead of the army and very likely moving already. He doesn't like life in the field, that one. He mourns a week without a bath in the way most men do the loss of a limb.'

'Then how shall I serve you?'

'Send for your Bollason. Alert him that the Hetaereian generals will be brought here. When they enter the tent, his men should surround it and he should come to me. Your counsel is apt.'

'Yes.'

'Good. Then after that you can take a message to the chamberlain. Take my banner and fly it from one of your ships. You'll bring news of the victory. It's important you Varangians do so; you must take the credit.'

Heat came to Snake in the Eye's cheeks. Here was his chance. 'Will you need a man to kill for you? I could do that work if you require it.'

'You truly do have a snake in your eye, don't you, boy? You are a venomous creature.'

'So my mother told me. Men like me are useful to kings, are we not?'

The emperor nodded. 'Very useful. Though do not fool yourself into thinking you are in short supply. All men can do all things if required. The only difference is the level of enthusiasm they bring to each task. Do not take pride when I confide in you. I only speak to you as I would speak to a monkey, no more. You are too young to scheme and plot, too naive and foreign and stupid. You imagine yourself subtle, Snake in the Eye – I read it in your face – but you are not. That is why your company is pleasant to me. I tire of subtle men.'

'Yes, sir.'

'Get Bollason, and when you've brought him here you can sail on after the chamberlain. There are too many odd doings for my liking and I want them stopped. Tell him I'll brook no resistance this time: these things are to be investigated and investigated properly, no matter the stir it causes. I want him to look into them in person. Fireballs, unexplained deaths, wolfmen babbling of prophecies – I want to know what it's about and I want an end to it, you tell him that. Speak no word of this man coming to the tent tonight to anyone but the chamberlain. I don't want people thinking they can walk in here as easy as into a church on a Sunday. Here.' The emperor took something from a bag at his side. He passed it to Snake in the Eye. It was a small medal marked with the emperor's head and some writing. It meant nothing to the boy. He could speak many languages but read none.

'This will give you safe passage if you are questioned more closely. The chamberlain, as quick as you can.'

'Yes, sir.'

Snake in the Eye left the tent. The guard outside the flap gave him a simmering stare. Snake in the Eye ignored it and ran to bring the Viking chief to a profitable murder.

4   A Reluctant Assassin

From the moment the two monks arrived at the lighthouse sea gate it was a race between the mildly dishonest, the very fraudulent and the plain violent to secure their trust. Both men were clearly foreigners by the leggings they wore; no Greek bothered with such things beneath his robe.

'Lodgings, sirs, lodgings. You are monks, yes, monks of the north. I can help you here. What are you, my friends, what is your tongue?'

The man was short and thin and a tiger's smile lit up his face. He spoke Latin, which was a rare language in those parts, known only to scholars and those who wished to part them from their money.

The younger of the two monks spoke: 'We are from Neustria, friend.'

'I have met many men from there,' said the man, instantly sliding into French. 'We have many of your mercenaries here. They are like brothers to me. Please, come with me. I have very good lodgings at a very good price. I will be your guide to Constantinople, your friend in this new Rome.'

'How much?'

'See the room and then see what you think. You have money to pay?'

'We have money.'

'Come on then.

The young monk glanced at the older one, who lowered his eyes in assent. They followed the little man.

The monks were of different orders, it appeared. They both wore black robes but the younger one had his head tonsured with the familiar circular baldness of the western Church, his hair reduced to a band about his temples. The other, however, had his white hair cut short at the back but left longer on top. A tattoo of a dragon's head leered from the back of his neck. The con men and thieves of the dockside thought nothing of this – they were used to seeing all sorts on their quay and used to taking their money.

The monks walked, shaking off their sea legs as they passed into the hubbub of the streets, quickly moving out of the broad plaza of the port and towards the tumble of back alleys. The one with the white hair shouldered a rolled blanket, while the younger man carried a bag on his back. At the opening of a narrow alley the monks hesitated.

Their guide reassured them: 'Don't worry, friends, this is Constantinople. It is the world's city and it can frighten the mightiest man, but come, let me guide you. You have a friend here in me. What are your names?'

'I am Azémar,' said the young monk, 'and this is Mauger.'

'Welcome, then, Azémar and Mauger! Let me take your bags.'

'You leave our bags,' said Mauger. His accent was thick, not like the younger monk's.

'Very wise, very wise. It's good to hold on to your valuable things. But you have nothing to fear from me. Come on.'

The two monks exchanged a glance. Mauger put his hand on Azémar's arm. 'We have to sleep somewhere.'

They followed the man into the lighthouse quarter, through the root-mass of backstreets that insinuated its way down the hill.

'The houses are so strange,' said Azémar. 'One on top of another. Why do they do that?'

'They build them up into the air to save space,' said Mauger. 'Not all is as it is at home. You may one day think these tall houses as common as any in Francia.'

Azémar crossed himself.

'Down here.' The alley would have been dark even on a bright day. It was scarcely wide enough for two people to pass each other.

They went in, the big scholar first, the Greek behind him, the young monk bringing up the rear.

'I fear I shall never find my way out from here,' said Azémar.

'That won't be a problem.' The Greek grabbed a knife from his belt and plunged it into the older monk's back. Screams from the dark and men leaped at them. One bore a club, another just a plank of wood, a third a rough spear.

The knife went through Mauger's robe with a crack. The Greek stepped back, his eyes wide as he looked down at his shattered blade.

Mauger span and punched the robber hard in the face, a pulverising blow that collapsed him limp as a coshed eel to the cobbles. Azémar stepped back against the wall, quickly crossing himself. Mauger's thoughts were not on piety. He strode towards their attackers, coming between them and his companion.

The club swung at the monk's head but too slow. Mauger stepped into the arc of the swing, enveloped the arm that held the weapon, seized the Greek's throat and drove his head into the wall.

The man slumped lifeless. Mauger didn't let him go; he charged at the men behind, using the robber as a shield to block a swinging blow from the plank of wood. The monk threw the dead man into the remaining two robbers and followed him in, smashing another hideous punch into the face of the first, dropping him to the stones. The final man let his spear fall and fled, but Mauger took a small axe from his belt, hidden beneath his robes, and hurled it through the gloom of the narrow street. It caught the robber on the back of the head and sent him flailing to the floor. Then Mauger was on him, wrapping his arms around the man's head, pulling and twisting to break his neck.

Azémar lowered his arms from around his head, where he'd put them like a young boy anticipating a blow from his father. 'You've killed them all.' His tone was flat, as if he was commenting his comrade looked well that day.

Mauger dropped the dead robber and stood up, offering no reply.

'Four is an impressive tally.' Azémar moved forward to the first body to inspect it. He felt for a pulse but there was none.

'They were not warlike men and they were surprised to meet resistance. Any of Duke Richard's warriors could have done it,' said Mauger.

'They looked warlike enough from where I was standing.' The young man moved on to the next corpse, checking that too.

'It's easy to look warlike,' said Mauger, 'but to be it is harder work. A sword is put into the true warrior's hand on the day he is born. Such men as we are not to be bested by vagabonds.'

Already curious people watched them, the adults too wary to come near, children running to examine the bodies at their feet.

'You didn't use a sword.' Azémar checked the remaining robbers for signs of life. None. He crouched and muttered a prayer over the dead men.

Mauger shrugged. Then he crouched beside Azémar and spoke quietly to him, wary of being overheard. 'Better to be thought a hardy monk than a warrior, if word of this spreads. These Greeks who call themselves Romans are famous for their spies, and the fewer men who know our purpose the safer we will be.' He picked up his roll of bedding from the ground and hoisted it to his shoulder. 'We'll save the sword for times of greater need.'

'What might constitute greater need than being attacked by four armed men?'

The warrior, for he was a warrior, leaned down to the monk's ear and whispered, 'The need to cut off the head of the scholar Loys. Now let's move.'

Azémar got to his feet. 'He stabbed you. I thought you were dead.'

Mauger patted his side, which chinked like a purse full of

coins. 'A wise man wears his hauberk in new company,' he said. 'So my father told me.'

The young scholar looked down at the bodies. The man the warrior had punched first was unrecognisable. His nose and mouth were almost as one, a bloody crater.

'Did you know that was going to happen?'

'In these places it's always a possibility.'

'You seem to relish hurting people. Is it the same with everyone from the old country?'

'My country is your country now. I am a Norman. I left my old life behind me when I took my new name and learned your language.'

'You got off the boat from the north six months ago. You are a Viking to your bones. They love to kill and plunder.'

'My feelings about what I do don't matter. I have a duty to oppose my enemies and those of my lord.'

'Does Loys deserve his fate?'

'The end is the same if he deserves it or not. Duke Richard has commanded he will have his daughter back and the scholar will die.'

'If we find him.'

'We will find him. Or rather, you will, Master Azémar. If you want your family to prosper.'

The young man shrugged deeply and put out his hands.

'You could do this alone.'

'No. You will identify the scholar. I want no possibility of a mistake.'

'It is an evil thing you make me do.'

'Not so. The scholar is a rebel against his lord and so against God. You are doing Christ's work.'

'Or Judas's. Loys was my friend.'

'I will shed no tears for him. Is friendship a higher calling than your duty to your lord? Or to your family, whose safety and health depend on our success here? Come on.' He headed off down the alley.

Azémar recalled the furore at the monastery when it was

realised Beatrice and Loys had gone, recalled the duke's men sweeping through the cloisters, Richard's boiling rage as he told the abbot he was lucky not to see his abbey burned to the ground.

Luckily for the monks Beatrice had confided to her sister they were sailing for Constantinople. After a few days of pressure the girl told what she knew. The hope of recapturing his daughter took the edge off Richard's anger as he threw himself into plans to get her back. They'd sought a monk who could identify without question the disobedient scholar. Azémar saw no way to protect Loys but to volunteer for the journey. If he was charged with identifying Loys to Mauger then at least he could warn his friend and give him time to get away.

He'd expected to travel with a company of men and had asked Mauger why Duke Richard had not sent more. 'It's an assassination, not an invasion,' said Mauger. 'A mighty king rules in Constantinople and he has eyes like God's. The less notice we draw the better.'

Azémar had toyed with the idea of killing Mauger in his sleep and going on alone. He was not a killer, though. He was a Christian man who couldn't commit such a sin. Even escape was impossible. Mauger held all their money and kept it close. Azémar wouldn't get far without silver to speed his journey and the knight would soon be on his trail.

Of course, he'd tried reasoning with Mauger. On the ship he'd put many plans to him.

'Can you not just say you killed him, say his daughter killed herself with grief when you did? That should satisfy him.'

'He wants the scholar's head. I have sworn to deliver it. There is nothing more to say.'

Azémar had directed his future arguments to the gulls and the waves. He knew he had a better chance of success with them. His father had been just such a man – still a Viking and a pagan at heart, despite his new religion and his even newer fancy Frankish manners.

When Azémar knew Mauger would not be moved by

argument he decided his best plan was to wait until he actually found Loys. Then he would desert Mauger and warn him.

Azémar looked to the sky. It bore a haze of grey over the blue. He crossed himself, praying they weren't ready for another soaking like they'd had on the way down. The ship's pilot had stretched the sail across as shelter and they'd spent nearly two days under driving, windless rain.

He would not betray his friend, he knew that. If he and Mauger didn't return at all then perhaps Richard would spare Azémar's family. Mauger was loyal as a dog and would never betray his lord. Only disaster would prevent him from completing his task. So Azémar would have to engineer a disaster.

'If it must be so, it must. First let's find somewhere to sleep. I've had my fill of being tossed out of my bed by storms and I'm tired enough to drop.'

'Agreed,' said Mauger. 'Let's go back to the port. Thieves are lazy; only honest men will be left by now. We'll bed down for the night and then start looking for your friend in the morning.'

He pulled his robe about him and headed out of the dark alley towards brighter, wider streets.

5   The Chamberlain

Loys set off on his long walk to the Magnaura. Like many immigrants to the city, he and Beatrice had settled very near to where they'd first entered – the lighthouse gate just north of the aqueduct on the Golden Horn. Scores of people offering lodgings greeted the incoming boats and it was impossible to choose between them. The couple had allowed themselves to be led away by the first man who'd approached them and been lucky he wasn't a thief or too much of a fraud.

The thicket of backstreets wasn't too dangerous at that time of day but he was glad to turn into the main street, wide, broad and bright with its splendid granite porches supported by elegant columns, some faded to white, some still in the colours the city's founders had painted them. No ramshackle and stinking wooden buildings here, nothing crammed or cramped. Loys had been raised in a well-to-do family in Rouen, a cathedral town. But on this road more than any other he was as wide-eyed as a farm boy with straw in his hair – a barbarian, as the Roman natives of the town called him. He liked the feeling, really. All his life he had been the cleverest person he knew, the best read, the most worldly. Here he felt unsophisticated, daunted and naive. It would be a challenge to leave his mark on this city.

He passed soap makers, their stalls smelling of violets and roses, candle makers, linen sellers with their wares laid out in scarlet, blue and white, silk men – their fabrics in vibrant colours too, a flash of gorgeous purple poking from a chest to indicate they served royalty, not that the common people could buy silk of that colour even if they could afford it. Leather workers offered fine belts and boots; swords were arranged on one stall with two small shields above them, looking to Loys like a terrible beast of staring eyes and giant teeth. Wine was on sale, beer and olives, oil and pottery, some in practical fired white earth, some decorated in vivid greens, reds and blues.

Fishmongers declared the quality of their wares, their catch laid out like treasure, iridescent in the cold light. Saddlers and grocers challenged the crowds to find a better price anywhere on Middle Way. Jewellers sat flanked by scowling eunuchs, a bullion dealer stood by his scales, six fully mailed Norman mercenaries around him. They made Loys shiver, though they were not Beatrice's father's men, he would have recognised them. Next to the bullion dealer was a row of coin changers, less impressively protected by native Greeks and hard-eyed easterners. Loys longed to take Beatrice here, to buy her jewels to make up for the ones she'd lost to robbers in Montpellier before they'd boarded the ship for Constantinople.

The streets were busy, and he fought against a tide of people heading towards the Golden Gate – the city's main ceremonial entrance. 'What's happening?' he asked a boy who passed him.

'The emperor's back! He's leading a triumph. He's got the Varangians with him! Northern giants! They have a savage who attacked him in his tent with them!'

Loys had no time for that, he had to be at his studies.

He pushed on, past the emperor Marcian's granite column and into the squabble of the Bull Market – where bulls and virtually everything else were on sale. It was less busy than usual but still busier than any other market he had ever attended in his life. He shoved his way through, thinking it the one blessing of poverty that you lacked a rich purse to steal.

From there he went under Theodosian's Arch, decorated with images of victorious Roman soldiers – still gaudy in yellow, red and pink after all these years - and on down the Middle Way to the Forum of Constantine, where, thank God, the market was closed. He strode past the statue of the Roman emperor who had founded the city, only glancing at the other marvellous bronzes that decorated the wide square. At the exit of the forum were two keystones in the wall in the shape of huge blank-eyed heads, both taller than he was. Their brutal, heavy features stared out with expressions of ancient animosity. They made him shiver. Pagan gods or heroes, he thought, their names now forgotten. Loys saw eternity in their stares and his own life seemed fragile and fleeting.

Once through the forum, the magnificent hippodrome appeared – a massive building in pink cement supported by marble columns that stretched like a parade of trees out to the south-west. He had seen a chariot race there but it had all been too rough for him – the rival factions of Blues and Greens brawling on the terraces. He'd winkled his way out of the crush when a brute of a man behind him had pissed up the back of his trousers.

Past the hippodrome to the north-east shone the bright white walls of the palace and, beyond that, the most marvellous thing he had ever seen, the great dome of the mother church of Eastern Christendom, Hagia Sophia. He'd known God in that place among the ribbons of incense smoke that climbed from the gold of the altar through the sunbeams beneath the huge vault of the ceiling. The building was beyond mortal dreams, it was infused with God's glory, its architects divinely inspired.

He walked on, following the Middle Way past the Numera. He never liked this part of the trip. The Numera was the city's prison – built over one of Constantinople's ancient cisterns. The most disturbing thing about it was its silence in the midst of such a busy city. Every other building in that area burst with noise, from the beggars and traders on the steps of Hagia Sophia to the clucking officials coming and going from the palace and the young men of the Magnaura laughing and fooling their way to their studies. Not so the Numera. Even the relatives of the prisoners, straining at the bars of its gates to offer food for the inmates and bribes to the guards, were cowed and subdued. The building itself was utterly quiet, its walls thick and the labyrinth of cells and tunnels, man-made or natural, that sprawled beneath it so deep that no sound of torment ever escaped.

The Numera was the plainest building on the road, a square block of unfaced brick in dirty yellow, like a stubby bad tooth in the mouth of a beautiful woman, thought Loys. At dawn it sat directly in the shadow of the great church, squatting silent in darkness as if the sun feared it. He guessed it would be getting a few more inmates with the emperor's return.

He arrived at the steps of the Magnaura, its vast columned porch looming above him. He went up, nodding to the guard at the scholars' gate, and passed through into the cloistered garden that led to the Senate House – which is what the school was still called, though the senators had long gone.

The scent of olive trees hit him. In the streets no tree would survive a moment – firewood and building materials being precious commodities. Here they stood in smart lines, their branches heavy with the green and purple fruit. He picked one and sucked off its flesh. 'Agh!' Bitter. He smiled to himself, wondering if they always tasted that way straight off the tree. He imagined Beatrice by his side, laughing and saying, 'Well, there's something you didn't know, you with all your learning.'

Birdsong filled the air but it came from no natural birds. At the bottom of the line of olive trees was one of the wonders of the city – another olive tree, life-size and cast in bronze, with splendid birds in its branches, their glass feathers catching the light in spangles of colour. Their song piped high and sweet, backed by a sound like rain from the water that powered the machine. He would never get used to this, he thought. In some ways he considered it unholy and recalled the passage from the Bible: 'Thou shalt not make unto thee any graven image, or any likeness of any thing that is in heaven above, or that is in the earth beneath, or that is in the water under the earth.'

God forbade such things. But could God begrudge man such beauty? Loys would have loved to have shown the singing tree to Beatrice, though that was impossible. No woman was allowed in the precincts of the university. He moved on.

The Senate House had an exterior of light yellow cement

with three big arches of windows sitting beneath a dome. He still felt a thrill entering the exalted halls of the Magnaura. Today he had just a couple of teaching jobs – rhetoric and philosophy to the dense sons of some nobles. They weren't inclined to learn much so he wasn't inclined to teach much, and beyond giving them a few philosophers' names to drop when questioned by their families, he spent his time with them talking of the many curiosities of the earth – the dragons of the east and the sand seas of Arabia.

Then he would take a class on law himself and – the highlight of his day – join the formal debate in the afternoon. That day he was speaking on the energies of God as separate from the essence of God – how we can know what God does but never what he is. Loys had also prepared a speech on the practice of hesychasm – a hermitage of the soul, withdrawing and stripping away all sensory perception until the eye of the soul awakens and an intuitive knowledge of God is developed. Loys was a theoretical rather than a practical student of this discipline.

He reached the door of the building and stepped inside to be met by the doorkeeper. He waved and went to walk through into the teaching cells but the man put up a hand to stop him.

'Visitor for you.'

The doorkeeper's face was pale.

'Who?'

'Go to the master's rooms. He's there.'

'Who?'

The man said nothing, just scuttled into the little office behind his table. Loys went across the wide atrium, glancing down at the mosaic beneath his feet. Perseus slaying the Medusa, the snake-haired monster whose gaze turned men to stone. The way the doorman had acted you'd think there was one waiting for him in the master's study.

He walked to the back of the building, passed the turn into the debating arena and went along a corridor to a single door on the left. He had been here only once before – when he gained admission by interview to the school. Well, actually an appearance before the faculty, at which he had to win through in a debate. It had not been easy – Rouen didn't have that sort of competition – but he had done it. One debate on a subject of his choosing, one on theirs. Thank God they hadn't picked the law.

He knocked on the door and a voice he didn't recognise said, 'Come.' He thought it was a woman, but when he opened the door the master was on one of the guest chairs in his own room and behind the study table, in the master's normal place, sat an exceptionally finely dressed and – no other word would do – beautiful man of around thirty. He shimmered in white silk and gold and, most tellingly, a bright purple sash worn left to right over his scarlet and brocade tunic. Only the emperor, his family and their very nearest associates had the right to wear that colour.

Behind him stood two enormous men, one clearly Greek by his short hair and beard, the other an African, his skin a deep black. Both had golden whips at their belts, along with a club and a sword. The whips, Loys knew, were for clearing a way through crowds for their master.

Loys instantly prostrated himself. He had no idea who this man was, but that sash, combined with the fact he'd turned the university's master out of his own most comfortable seat, meant it was better to overdo the formalities rather than risk any appearance of arrogance.

'Stand up, scholar, stand up.' The sing-song voice was of an unusual timbre. The man had smooth skin like a woman's, beardless; his limbs were long and his hands thin and grace- ful. His fingers bore three gold rings, one of which looked heavy enough to be an official seal. Certainly a eunuch, thought Loys.

He stood up.

'Do you know me?'

'No, sir, I do not.'

The man put his tongue into his lower lip in contemplation.

Loys noticed the master had his eyes firmly on the eunuch, a static smile cut into his face like a scar into the skin of an orange.

'I am the chamberlain. The parakoimomeno.'

Loys instinctively bowed. The parakoimomeno – he who sleeps beside the emperor – was the second most powerful man in the empire after the emperor; some would say more powerful even than he. Basileios was always away fighting his wars. The emperor didn't enjoy court life even when he wasn't fighting, and stayed at his estate up the coast. The chamberlain remained in Constantinople and was responsible for all the day-to-day running of the city.

'He doesn't look clever,' said the chamberlain to the master.

'He is the best man for the work you describe, sir,' said the master. 'I have none better.'

'You're not just giving him to me because he is a foreigner and you fear to lose a native scholar?'

'This man is steeped in occult lore, sir.'

A long silence. The chamberlain's expression was as blank as the moon's. Loys and the master waited for the chamberlain to speak, and they waited a good while.

Eventually he said, 'You are a foreigner. You live here at the school?'

'No, I live—'

'By the lighthouse gate.'

Loys said nothing, just gave a little bow. The eunuch was trying to intimidate him, and the wise course of action was to let him. No point standing up to such men. Better to allow them to intimidate you with long silences than with their soldiers.

'With your wife. Who is higher born than you, it appears.'

Loys remained silent still.

The chamberlain puckered his lips.

'I'm impressed,' he said. 'Silence is a talent and a precious one.'

After that Loys didn't really feel he could speak until asked a direct question.

'What do you think of magic, scholar?'

'Sir?'

'Your theory of magic, what is it?'

Loys rocked from foot to foot.

'The Church tells us it is the devil working through malicious and envious men.'

'But what do you think?'

'I am bound to think the same. Though I can consider and understand heresies, even rehearse their arguments the better to prepare our priests to know them, then—'

The chamberlain held up his hand to silence Loys. He reached inside his tunic, took a coin out of a pocket and laid it on the table.

'Study it and tell me what you think.'

Loys picked it up. It was an ancient Roman coin from the time of the founding of the city. On one side it showed Constantine along with his mother St Helena, on the other a picture of Christ on the Cross. It had been drilled to allow it to be worn as an amulet.

'It is a charm, sir,' said Loys, 'probably for good luck or power.'

'Yes, it is. And I would say it's an effective one. From where does it derive its power?'

'From the image of the True Cross.'

'Is that the same as from God?'

'A difficult question, sir. There are many drunken old women who babble the name of Christ in their spells. It would depend how it was used. And, of course, by whom. Contemplation, proper contemplation, of the image of Christ can lead us closer to God, whatever the iconoclasts would have had us believe. The Cross is an inspiration to faith, and it is through faith miracles are achieved. Yet the devil has many disguises.'

'Spoken like a philosopher,' said the chamberlain. 'Which is to say you have given no answer at all. What if I told you the power of the coin came from the image of the emperor?'

'Then that would make it no more than a pagan icon. A channel for the evildoing of demons.'

'Our founder and ancestor Constantine a channel for demons?'

'I did not mean to imply ...' Loys was very hot. 'It is the image of a man. The likeness of a good man, an excellent man, can still be used for evil. I refer only to what the saints and scholars tell us. There are sympathies and antipathies in nature. The image of a powerful man might be able to manipulate these. Demons might fear him and so the amulet might bring good luck. Sorcerers could use it to do more.'

'To alter the future?'

'Anyone can alter the future, sir — it's as simple as choosing to buy an apple at the market or to pass by the stall.'

The chamberlain smiled. 'Don't be clever with me, scholar. Could it be used to magical effect?'

'I believe so, yes, if my reading is correct. But it would not be holy to do so. That is the province of wonder workers and I curse their names.'

The chamberlain tapped the table. 'Could you tell a sorcerer from a saint, scholar? Their actions are often very similar.'

'I believe I could.'

'How?'

'The saint's powers come from his faith. The image of the Cross, as on the coin, simply provides a focus for that faith. So it is not exactly true to say the image of the Cross holds power in itself. It is, rather, the power of faith it unlocks inside us, as we see in the Gospel of St Mark. There a woman touches Christ's robe and is cured of the affliction of the issue of the blood. But Christ tells her it is her faith, not the touch of his robe, that has made her well. A sorcerer works through demon-infested objects, not faith. And a sorcerer must fail. Any attempt to control demons is doomed to disaster.'

'Yet our saints have been nailed up, drowned, eaten by lions, burned, beaten and buggered for all I know. A funny sort of success.'

The profanity shocked Loys. The chamberlain's words weren't blasphemous though they sat on the bench right next to it, so to speak. But of course nothing the chamberlain said was blasphemy, simply because it was he who had said it. Anyone pointing the finger at a man like that was likely to lose the finger and more besides.

The chamberlain spoke again: 'Where do you get these ideas from? Do you invent them or is there a foundation in the work of learned scholars?'

'From Proclus, mainly, a man of this city in ancient times, though Proclus brings with him one hundred other philosophers back to Plato.'

'Proclus was a heathen, was he not?'

'No, a Christian, but he followed other religions besides. He wanted to become a priest of the whole universe.'

'A pretentious sort of sacrilege. And do you follow other religions?'

'No. Proclus was wrong to be promiscuous in his faith. I am a true Christian.'

'Not after our fashion, though? You follow the Pope.'

'I follow Christ,' said Loys.

'But you do not accept the teachings of the Eastern Church.'

'The Eastern Church has great wisdom. I am honoured to attend its services.'

'But the Pope commands you.'

Loys was on difficult ground here. He didn't want the chamberlain to extract a confession that he was effectively controlled by a foreign power. This was no place for fine distinctions, to say the Pope controlled his spiritual life but that in Constantinople Loys was a loyal subject of the emperor. Powerful men might not choose to see the difference.

'My master is the art of learning, sir. There is right and there is wrong, and an appreciation of the difference is all that is required of the godly man.'

The chamberlain leaned back in his seat. For a while he said nothing and Loys felt himself frying beneath the man's gaze.

Finally: 'You won't prosper in Constantinople with that attitude.'

Another long pause. Then the chamberlain did something extraordinary. He smiled. Loys glanced at the master. He still wore a fixed smile, like he'd taken too close a look at the Medusa.

The chamberlain gave a little chuckle. 'It was a joke, friends. You could allow yourself to laugh.'

Loys forced out a laugh and the master was seized by a fit of hysteria, beating his hand on his knee and wheezing as if about to die. The guards behind the chamberlain were impassive.

When the laughter ended, which was not soon, the chamberlain turned to the master. 'I would like to speak with the scholar alone.'

That stopped the old man's mirth. For a moment he looked as though he might say something. Then the chamberlain pointed to the door. The master stood and went to it, hesitating in front of it.

'You put your hand to the door, push and walk through. Do they not teach that in your philosophy, old man?'

The master went out. The big black man followed him, shooed him away down the corridor and returned to stand behind the chamberlain. The black man frightened Loys. The Arabs wrote that the blacks were the first of men, intellectually, physically and spiritually superior to other races in every way. This man looked it, with his quick eyes and gleaming muscles. He had a presence that made Loys want to take a pace back.

'I need to speak to you frankly and in confidence. Only you, I and one other know what I am about to tell you. If these secrets escape there will only be you to blame. You know what that would mean.' Loys' eyes flicked to the guards.

'The guards are trustworthy, but if it pleases you we can communicate in this way and they cannot understand us,' said the chamberlain in Latin.

'The master?' said Loys in the same language.

'He only knows a little of my purpose.'

'I am ready to serve.' Loys bowed and then bowed again, against himself. He wanted to show respect but he didn't want to look like a serf.

'I have a problem,' said the chamberlain, 'and you are its solution. Dark forces are at work in this city. The emperor himself is under magical attack and has been tempted by demons.'

'This was the savage who broke through to the emperor's tent?'

'Hardly. Lazy guards rather than magic, I think. No more than a madman wanting alms, whatever the gossip you might here to the contrary.'

'I'm glad there was no attempt on the emperor's life.'

'The emperor has more to fear than deranged men and drunken guards. This is much more serious.'

Loys kept his eyes forward, determined to show no reaction that could spark the chamberlain's disapproval.

'Furthermore, there is reason to suspect certain other high men face these assaults. Some may even lose their position because of them. Putting it straightforwardly, the emperor has been afflicted in the body, so he may also be attacked in his humours and attitudes. No one in this empire can afford Basileios to come under the sway of evil forces.'

'No,' said Loys.

'The master says you are his best student. I need you to set out clearly for me the nature of magical attacks and how they might be countered.'

'The solution is plain for Christian men, sir. By prayer.'

'We have tried that and to no avail. Christ clearly wants us to take another course. This is no different to the way we would conduct any battle. We send out scouts to assess the enemy in his strengths and various weaknesses. You are our scout, our magical scout.'

'I'd be honoured to make a study, sir.'

'It is more than a study. The emperor expects his problems to end. The dark fate of great men must be averted. We want to know how that might be achieved.'

'You are asking me to discover how to cast a magical spell?'

'Exactly so.'

'That is not Christian.' Loys heard the words pop out of him. It was as if they trailed pennants behind them through the air, pennants he wished he could grasp in order to pull them back.

The chamberlain pursed his lips. 'Oh come on, scholar. How many heathen practices do we study? Your philosophers of Athens never knew Christ. How much heathenism surrounds us, just under the surface of our Christian life? You quote the learned pagans with no fear to your mortal soul; you take pleasure from statues of false gods, you walk upon mosaics showing all manner of unchristian things. Look to the star and sickle moon that is our city's symbol. Do you know how that came to be? Why we mark it on our walls and gates?'

'I do not, sir.' Loys, remarkably for him, had never even considered it.

'It is the symbol of the goddess Hecate. "At my will the planets of the air, the wholesome winds of the seas, and the silences of hell be disposed; my name, my divinity is adored throughout all the world in diverse manners, in variable customs and in many names. Some call me Juno, others Bellona of the Battles, and still others Hecate. Principally the Ethiopians which dwell in the Orient, and the Egyptians which are excellent in all kind of ancient doctrine, and by their proper ceremonies accustomed to worship me, do call me Queen Isis."'

'Apuleius's *Metamorphoses*,' said Loys, recognising the quotation.

'Correct,' said the chamberlain. 'How much of our wisdom and art is taken from the pagans? Half the masses on their knees to Mary are secretly praying to Hecate in their hearts and the other half pray to her without knowing it. Paganism surrounds us. We are the fish; religion is our sea but cold and old tides are within it.'

Loys summoned his courage. 'I must have a care for my immortal soul, sir.'

'That sounds like defiance, scholar.'

'No, sir, it is not.'

'Then what do you call it?'

Loys said nothing.

'It is an academic study,' said the chamberlain. 'I am not asking you to perform these sorceries, just to describe them and to tell us how they might be done. I am sick of frauds and ragged prophets. This requires the attention of serious men. You will be rewarded.'

Loys' tongue came to his lips. The chamberlain smiled at that.

'You will have rooms in the palace, where your wife will be able to wander freely among its many marvels. Has she seen the metal birds that sing beneath the fountains? You see them every day in the Magnaura but a woman cannot walk here, can she? And remember, as an honoured lady of the court, she need only command a court eunuch to come with her if she wants to take to the streets. Your food will be paid for and proper garments too, so you don't offend the eyes of courtiers. Baths will be available and warm rooms – they say this winter is going to be a cold one and if the summer is anything to go by they're right. Scholar, do you want to spend the months of true cold in that little pile of wood down by the water?'

Loys shifted. He felt like a mouse who suddenly realises a cat has been watching it. And he knew, as the chamberlain knew, he had no alternative but to accept.

The chamberlain clicked his fingers at the huge Greek eunuch and the man slid a wrap of cloth across the table.

'There's a pound of gold. Seventy-two solidi. That should keep the lady happy, I think.'

'You know a lot about me, sir.' Loys wondered who among the scholars had been spying for the chamberlain.

'Pick up the gold.'

Loys did as he was told. It felt heavier than a pound. Four

years' wages for a soldier. There sat the chamberlain, richly dressed, delicate in features and movement. Was that how Satan had appeared to Christ in the wilderness?

The chamberlain watched Loys weighing the gold in his hand. 'We have men who are paid to know all about you. The Office of Barbarians, as men call them, though they dislike the title themselves. They dislike any title, in fact. With so many foreigners we need someone to keep an eye on them all. Though in truth their time would be better spent watching our native Romans nowadays. Come to the door of the palace as soon as you can and mention my name. They will be expecting you.'

Loys bowed. He wanted to give the gold back but that was impossible. Another part of him wanted to kiss the little bundle, to hug it and to cheer.

'I will expect your report by the end of winter. A working and efficacious spell to cure the emperor of his malaise and to protect him and the high men of this city against further attack.'

'What is the emperor's malaise?'

'That need not concern you. Now stay here as we leave.'

Loys almost wanted to laugh, though he had no idea why.

The chamberlain left and, after a short while, the master returned. He had a cowed look to him. Loys had seen it before. It was the look of a boy who has been beaten in a fight, a man who has been made to appear foolish in front of a girl, a losing gambler creeping home to his wife. Humiliation, surprise even that life still went on after such a loss of status.

'You can go, Loys,' he said, returning to his chair behind the desk.

'I will not be at the debate?'

'No. You are the chamberlain's now.'

'Will my place at the school be open when he finishes with me?'

The master turned down his mouth and shook his head.

'Succeed or fail, he will never be finished with you. You are his, for bad or for good.'

'But why did he pay me so well? Why raise me up to live in the palace? He could have just commanded me to do his will and left me in that barn by the river at no cost to himself.'

'You don't understand our powerful men. You are his: you represent him, you will use his name to aid your researches. His enemies will discover what you are doing, too, be sure of that. So you must be a fit representative. His glory shines on you and he expects to see it reflected. His servants can't go dressed in rags; they themselves must seem like important men. He is a terror, Loys, a terror, and you are now his mirror. Rejoice. You could be on your way to great riches.'

Loys smiled. 'But to get there I must have commerce with demons.'

The master pointed at the pouch in Loys' hand. 'You already have,' he said.

6 Taken

Beatrice only picked at her embroidery that morning. She was a northern woman, just one generation from the people who had settled the lands of the Franks in Neustria, and was not used to her life being so closed in.

She put down the thread and frame and went to the window. The streets were so full of bustle and interesting people, but the Greeks would never tolerate her walking on her own. The smells of the market drifted up towards her – the frying omelettes, the little fires that had been set to cook them, a waft of cheese, the more pervasive note of fish. Just down the street a fisherman sat at a brazier taking live mackerel from a net of fluttering silver, coshing them on the pavement, then gutting and cooking them while a queue of people waited.

She needed to walk, to get out of that freezing little room and stretch her legs a while.

Pregnancy was gruelling. How long had it been? Six months? Seven? Her body seemed full and heavy as if she'd taken an enormous drink of water. She was beginning to waddle when she walked.

Beatrice lay on the bed, hoping Loys would come home early and they could go to see the markets. She had a great desire to eat figs, which she took in itself for evidence of her condition. She should have asked him to get her some.

She had told him her dreams had receded since she had come to Constantinople. In fact they had grown worse. She was always wandering that riverbank where the trees stood like things of pale stone, where the moon silvered the water, where something blundered and snuffled in the woods that stretched away from the bank. The thing in the trees seemed closer now. It sought her. To do what? Harm her. Yes, harm her, but without intention, like the smashing power of the sea, like the tree that falls to crush and kill, as destructive and inhuman as the wind. She did not forget the fear of her dreams when she woke, it was always there, like the bell that tolled the hours.

Only Loys made her feel better. When she woke from her nightmares to find him at her side, she wrapped her arm around him and felt safer in his human warmth.

She got off the bed and returned to the window. Down the hill, stretched the houses of the lighthouse quarter, falling in a ramshackle tumble to the edge of the bright blue waters of the Golden Horn and the lighthouse gate – the only sea gate where they admitted unlicensed foreigners. Sitting at this window was her sole entertainment, though it was good entertainment. The city streets fascinated her, the people so varied and so many – the Moors with their skin like ink, the easterners in their desert wraps, the many colours of the bureaucrats' robes, who seemed to be everywhere. She watched the squabbles of the market traders, the little children sneaking in to steal fruit or a loaf, the world travellers disembarking among the press of frauds and thieves.

Over the water the blue hills rose up towards the big white church of St Dimitri. A faint haze smudged the horizon and she wondered if that was usual in the city at that time of year.

She did miss the court, her family and the familiar faces of Rouen. She longed to hear how her little sisters Emma and Hawis were getting on. The memory of them running in the woods playing hoodman's blind made her laugh but brought a tear to her eye too. Her maids said ladies shouldn't play such rough games, but they were Franks, employed by her father to teach his girls nice manners. Little Hawis had told her maid that she was a Viking's daughter and, as such, needed to toughen up because northern women were not like the fainting Frankish ladies. When their husbands beat them they didn't weep and whine but picked up a stick and thrashed them back.

'That is not a natural way to behave,' said the maid Barza.

'Neither is pissing in your husband's soup, but that's what my auntie Freydis did when my uncle beat her,' said Hawis.

Beatrice wondered if she would ever see her sisters again. If the child inside her was a boy, then perhaps. She bowed her head. And if it wasn't a boy? Then she'd just have to try again and again until one appeared. Maybe she should even buy a child in a market and present him to her father as his heir. The more she thought about the idea the better it seemed.

And what of her mother? Now tears came down her face in great gouts. There had to be a way back. But not while she dreamed those dreams. She had run away with Loys for love, true, but that that wasn't her only reason – she wasn't so stupid.

Plenty of noble ladies had their loves and managed to keep them close despite the husbands their families had chosen. Minstrels, tutors, advisers, merchants even, all had a legitimate claim to regularly attend on a lady. An old, sleepy or bribable chaperone made everything possible, particularly if you had a warlike husband who was always away fighting.

No, she knew why she had fled. The dreams. Something sought her and at Rouen it found her. She needed to move, to hide. She loved Loys dearly but she would have found him a place in her life in Rouen had she been able.

She remembered that morning – the frosty predawn when she had crept out of the hall to saddle her horse and slip off to meet Loys. She had looked for him in the woods but then had noticed something strange – the dawn was not coming and the moon was still high. It was the middle of the night. Why had her father's guards not at least questioned her? Had she woken no one, not even a dog, as she left?

It was cold, very cold. She turned her horse for home but around her the hoar frost seemed to glow, her horse's breath clouding the air under the sickle moon. The woods felt full of eyes and she dearly wished to be home. She spurred the horse, but the animal wouldn't budge.

A noise behind her in the trees.

'Loys?'

'Loys is not here but the night is cold. Won't you share my fire?'

An extraordinary man stood twenty paces from her. He was tall and his hair rose in a red shock. Stranger, he was scandalously underdressed, just the skin of a wolf tied around his midriff to cover his shame, a long feather cloak on his back. A fire burned further away in the woods. How had she not seen that?

Beatrice kicked the horse again but it didn't move, standing as if entranced.

'Come, lady, the ice is cold and my fire is warm. Though you, I think, have a chill in you no flame can dispel.'

'It's not seemly for me to be here with a man on my own. Go away from me, sir. My father does not like to hear of vagabonds on his lands, let alone ones who approach his daughter so boldly.'

'You are a beauty. The god always wants beauty and lives that are painful to lose. He could go to the starving, to the sick and the imprisoned and take them — and take them he does — but it is the lovely life he wants the most, the life like yours. Dismount.'

Beatrice did so, though she didn't want to, as if her body was not her own to command.

'Who do you speak of?'

'Why, who else? Old man death himself. Lord Slaughter. King Kill. The back-stabbing, front-stabbing, anywhere-you-like-and-plenty-of-places-you-don't-stabbing murder god. Odin, one-eyed corpse lord, corrosive and malignant in his schemes and his stratagems. But of course you know all this, you've met him before.'

'I don't know who you're talking about. It sounds like idolatry.'

'Funny,' he said. 'They call us idol worshippers, while they are on their knees before their painted saints. And what do the saints ever bring them? Misery and death at every turn.' He clicked his fingers and pointed at her. 'Ask what I bring you.'

'What do you bring me?'

'Why, me,' said the man. He bowed and walked forward to take Beatrice's hand. 'And, lady, there is no richer gift.'

Beatrice felt very odd indeed. Was this another fever? She had seen this fellow in her fevers before, she was sure, but this seemed so real.

She walked with him through the wood towards the little fire. Beside it he spread his feather cloak and lay down. Beatrice did not think it odd that it surrounded the fire in thick down for twenty paces about. It looked so warm and wonderful. She dearly wanted to test the comfort of the feathers. She lay down too, next to the man, all fear of him gone. The feathers were truly very comfortable, more comfortable than any bed she had ever lain on. Beatrice gazed into the man's eyes and thought they were the green eyes of a wolf. She wanted to confide in him.

'I have dreams.'

'So do I,' he said, 'and sometimes it's easy to fall in love with a dream. I did once.'

'Am I a dream?' She didn't know quite what she said.

'The very idea! You, lady, are reality. You are to where the dreams of gods fall with a thump.'

'I go to a place by a river and there is a wall full of candles. I cannot touch them.'

'Are you the only one there?'

'There are others.'

'What others?'

'A boy who seems lost and a thing in the darkness. I cannot see it but I know it is there.'

'It is a wolf and it hunts you.'

'Why is the wolf hunting me?'

'To love you and to kill you.'

'Why would he kill someone he loved?'

'Well I don't think he means to. It's just that he always associates with such disreputable types.'

Beatrice breathed in the aroma of the man's skin – like incense and smoke, like the freshness of rain, like iron in the hand.

'Why does he follow me?'

'For what you have inside you. The thing that howls and calls. The wolf trap rune. You are a mighty bait, lady, irresistible to a creature of such palate.' Something seemed to stir within her and she saw a shape, a long thin line with a sharp slash through it. She heard a howl in her mind and a shiver went through her flesh. The shape was calling to the wolf, however odd that seemed.

'What can I do to escape him?'

'I have told you enough. For that, lady, I require something more from you.'

'What is it?'

'You have been too long a maiden.'

The threat was clear but Beatrice did not feel scared. The man's statement felt curiously reasonable.

'Can you truly tell me how I can escape him?'

'I can.'

'How do I know you are telling the truth?'

'I am a god.'

'There is but one god.'

'So forcefully stated,' he said, 'and so obviously untrue.'

The air danced with points of light, like the silver shimmers that appear in the eyes on rising too quickly, but unfading. Snowflakes fell, as big as saucers, and yet she was warm.

'Tell me and I will give you what you want.'

'Give me what I want and I will tell you,' he said .

'Tell me a little, so I may know if you are trying to deceive me.'

'Give me a little, so I may know if you are trying to deceive me.'

He undid the brooch that held the neck of her tunic together and dropped it onto the feathers. Then slid his hand inside the robe's neck onto her breast. Her body tingled, her skin tightened, a delicious chill like going out into the frost after too long in a stuffy room.

'If he insists on following you,' he said, 'take him to the place he would least like to go.'

He kissed her and she inhaled his scent. It seemed so complex – like a bright stream, like wet grass and like earth, like the sea on a sunny day, but under it all the odour of burning. The moon was a sharp crescent, the morning star sparkling like a jewel next to it.

'Where is that place?'

'You will know it. Now I will know you.'

He lifted up her skirts and did what he had asked to do and it seemed to Beatrice that, in her pleasure and her abandon, the world opened to her, gave up its secrets. She felt the lives of everything around her, of the trees with their questing roots, of the swallows never still, of all creation in its tumult and uproar, its wild delight. And when it was done she slept. The sun and the shouts woke her.

'Beatrice! Beatrice!

The winter sun was bright. The man, with the feather cloak had gone, taking the night with him. Loys bent over her, his bundle of firewood at his side.

'What happened to me?'

'You fell from your horse! Are you all right?'

'I think so.' She hugged him, and he kissed and comforted her.

So it had been a dream, a vision brought on by a faint. But it didn't feel like a dream.

In the blue evenings of the weeks that followed, walking the earthen ramparts of her father's fortress, she heard the voice of a wolf in the hills and something inside her trembled. She understood what the wolf was saying, or rather caught the message in its voice. It was lonely and calling for its friends. But when she dreamed, the same voice called for her and she found herself standing in her father's hall at midnight, wandering outside to look at the hills.

Something was coming for her and the idea had assumed an unreasonable importance in her mind. In sleep she went back to the river where she had been in her fever, back to the wall where little lamps burned and where something crawled and crept towards her in her bed. But someone else waited unseen, someone who wanted to help her. When she woke she'd seen Loys and felt that with him the dream demons could not harm her.

The instinct to leave Rouen had been just that – an instinct. 'You will know,' the strange man had said. She did know. The thing that sought to harm her was there and she had to run from it.

A disturbance in the street, men's voices, Greeks. She craned from the window to see what it was, but couldn't. Boots tramped on her stairs – a man's footfall. It wasn't Loys. This fellow jingled like a shook purse. She recognised the sound. A hauberk of mail. A warrior was outside her door.

She went to the back room to hide, not knowing what to do. The door was bolted but any man who wanted to have it down could do so in a second. She had only the little knife she used to cut her thread. She took it up as a voice, thick and foreign, spoke loudly in Greek.

'Open. Lady Beatrice, we know you and your station. Open the door and we will do you no harm.'

Beatrice crossed herself. She came back into the main room and ran to the window. The street was too far to jump.

'No man enters here without a chaperone!'

Too late. A heavy blow, the door smashed in and she stood facing the soldiers.

7 The Road to the Dark

The wolfman trembled before the walls of Constantinople. They were vast, stretching from the water up the hill as far as he could see, almost too bright to look at in the morning sun, burning like he imagined the walls of the city of the gods would burn. Could Asgard be so vast?

The army had disembarked at a port ten miles down the coast so it could march into the city and receive the accolades of its people. The Varangians – Vikings and their kin from the Russian steppes – led the column. The wolfman was behind, with the emperor's Greek guard, who marched leaderless and subdued. He had watched their great men hang.

It had been a weak and yellow dawn, the sun trapped beneath deep cloud, burning like a poor candle seen through the vellum of a window. The light had come up but the rain had not relented. They hanged them on a plum tree, one after the other. Everything was wet through and the hanging ropes were swollen and would not slip, so they'd tied the ropes as tight as they could, thrown them over a branch and pulled, leaving the men to dance and throttle. None of the victims said a word and none of their men made any protest. It was, said the soldiers, the Roman way.

Their job was to guard the emperor, and someone had got through. There was no excuse. Many among the Hetaeriean ranks thought Basileios was being lenient. Other emperors might have ordered the regiment decimated – every tenth man killed.

Now the army had outrun the bad weather and the day was bright under a sharp sun. The wolfman, though, scented something on the horizon. Smoke. A sooty rain had fallen on the battle and the wolfman tasted it here, even under the heat of the Greek autumn sun.

The front of the column burst into clamour as the army passed through the shanty town that spilled from the city walls like litter from the back of a house. Already hostile eyes were on him; a crowd jeered and a couple of bystanders threw mud and stones. The guards barked at them to stop and, dazzled by the exotic sight of the emperor and his new northern army, they forgot the wolfman as they poured forward to acclaim the victors.

The army arrived at the city gates. The wolfman looked to the head of the procession, where the emperor rode his white horse. On the journey home the emperor had put on plain soldier's clothes but now he wore a sparkling crown and a great collar flashing with emeralds and rubies.

The emperor addressed the Varangians. The wolfman couldn't understand what he said. He knew only a handful of words in Greek and he'd used all of them when he'd asked the emperor to kill him. The boy who had been in the tent translated into Norse. The Vikings would be guests outside the city walls for a while. When proper accommodation had been arranged for them they would enter. In the meantime, their every need would be met and all services provided. The northerners grumbled and moaned – some saying they had been tricked – but then a big Viking dressed all in red spoke.

He said the emperor honoured his promises and the Vikings would be well rewarded. As a gesture of goodwill, the Varangians would be paid within a week for the work they had done for Vladimir even though they had fought for Constantinople for less than a month. And tents would be delivered to them.

This assuaged their anger and the men pulled off the road and down the slope towards the sea, dragging their baggage with them, women, children, dogs and flocks of goats and sheep all trailing alongside. The Norsemen travelled light, used to sleeping on their ships, stretching the sail across as a canopy. Few had tents. Much of their treasure was in their ships, under guard down the coast, and so there were few carts or horses to move – just their personal possessions and weapons, their families and their livestock.

The Hetaereia advanced to the gate and the wolfman found himself near the front of the army behind the standard bearers, one carrying an image of St Helena, the other the sickle and star banner of Constantinople.

Past him came two riders, one in blue and one in green. They went up to the gates and hammered on them with gold-tipped staves.

'Open in the name of the emperor!'

'There is only one emperor, that is Basileios, born in the purple, king of all the world! The gates open for none but he!' It wasn't one man who spoke but hundreds, it seemed to the wolfman.

'It is the king of all the world who is here!' shouted both riders together. 'Basileios Porphyrogenitus, autokrator, ordained by God on high. Bow down before him.'

'We bow down!'

The gates swung open, and it was as if some great weight of waters swept down on the wolfman. He had been on the Ever-Violent Rapids on the Dneiper on his way from Kiev and been awed by their force. Here it was similar, a great roar sweeping out of the city and over him. He could suppress his fear, tell himself that his fate did not matter and that not one twist in the skein of his destiny would be different for worrying about it, but he could not control his wonder. This place was like nothing he had seen and, though he sat bound on an open cart, he forgot his discomfort, forgot the menace that faced him and just gaped at the spectacle.

The horses of the outriders lurched forward and the Greeks filed into the city. They walked through the gates, the crowd howling and clapping, people pushing out of the city to greet the strange northerners, to touch their hair and beards, feel their muscles – kiss them, even, in the case of some of the more excitable women. The Vikings weren't slow to respond, hugging the women and crying out to more to join them. The column halted, pressed in by the throng coming out of the town – merchants carrying silks, food and tents, doctors rushing out waving bandages to advertise their trade, men with great pots of what the wolfman thought must be beer.

His cart jolted forwards and he really did start to feel a little afraid. The whiteness of the streets dazzled him and the noise of the great mass of people was almost unbearable. Giants looked down on him and a seething growl rose within him, but then he realised these were men of stone or metal – statues, though much bigger than any he had ever seen.

Alongside the column merchants ran, tugging on the tunics of the Greek warriors, trying to get them to buy fish, bread, candles, gaming pieces, weapons and many things the wolfman just didn't recognise. It was an uproar the equal of any battle. A man ran along with a table twice his height, poking a hand out from beneath it to tug at the warriors. It reminded him of a creature he had once seen in the possession of a southern merchant – a tortoise.

The procession moved on, down the avenue of porches, through splendid squares, past huge and gaudy columns, beside what appeared to be an endless bridge following the route of the road. These things seemed monstrous to the wolfman, his head pounded and he was covered in sweat. The biggest town he had been in was Kiev – a village compared to this place.

He had to endure. His first mission to be killed by the emperor had failed; the harder route now opened to him, the one that would require all his courage. There was a reason for the splendour of Constantinople, Miklagard, the world city. It lay below it, in the waters that flowed under its streets – in the flooded caves that had been made to serve as cisterns to hold water for the fountains, drinking troughs and baths, and beyond them, deeper, to where older waters lay.

People spat at him and a few threw dung and stones. His

guards warned them away, shouting that this was the emperor's prisoner and whatever harm was to come to him was not for commoners to decide. The warnings proved useless and the crowd continued to curse and throw things. In the end two of the Hetaereia jumped up alongside him and protected him with their shields. They had been instructed by the emperor to deliver the prisoner to the Numera alive, and they knew Basileios' tolerance for mistakes had evaporated at Abydos.

The wolfman steeled himself. He'd put up with worse, much worse – with freezing mountain winters, with the hardships of the lone hunter, with weeks spent starving and chanting beneath the harsh sun and the cold moon, singing the song his wolf brother had put into his head.

He once had a name: Elifr. He remembered it but it had no emotional connection to him now. He'd lived with a family in the north, by the great cliff of the Troll Wall. He'd never felt part of them. While his brothers were broad, tall and blond, he was smaller, thin, but with strong arms as spare and lean as the roots of a tree. Though his mother cared for him, she did not love him as she did her natural sons. He had been taken in as a child, as the return for a favour from a healer who had saved his father from a fever that looked set to kill him.

So Elifr had grown up lonely, wandering the hills, volunteering to take the sheep to the furthest pastures.

He remembered the night his wolf brother had come to him. It was summer and he slept only lightly. In the day he had found fresh wolf spoor and he knew the predators must be close by. He'd brought the sheep into a natural bowl in the hillside and lay down on one of its sides, watching over them. He kept his fire going, though the night was warm, to make the wolves more wary.

Its heat lulled him and he slept. When he woke the fire was dead and a fog lay low on the land, filling up the bowl in the hillside like a milky broth. The sheep had come near and stood beside him, out of the mist. The sky was clear. It wasn't full dark, but the washed-out light of the northern midnight, and only the moon and the morning star beside it were visible.

He gazed over the fog, up to the mountains of the north, to the mighty cliff of the Troll Wall looming like something too big for the horizon, as if it should be nearer.

The wolf appeared on the other side of the bowl of fog almost exactly at his level. The big black creature sat as if upon a cloud. Elifr picked up his spear and scanned for others, his vision swimming in the floating light.

He shook the spear as if to throw it at the wolf.

'Go! Go on!'

The wolf didn't move, just sat watching him.

Elifr put the spear down, picked up his sling and fitted a stone. Still the wolf stayed. The boy raised an arm to take aim at the wolf but didn't release the stone. There was something odd about the wolf. It didn't behave like a normal animal. Wolves were not stupid and didn't sit still while shepherds aimed slings at them.

'Are you a ghost?' he said.

Then he heard himself say: 'You are the ghost of a wolf.'

He spoke again, but not with quite his own voice. It was lower and slower, as if he didn't fully command his tongue and his lips: 'You are waiting in a wolf.' What did he mean by that? Elifr thought he really should know what his own words meant.

A voice seemed to speak in his mind and he mumbled along with the words: 'You are the rocks and the stream and the rain on the mountain and the light through the rain. You are the movement of the shadow, a shape cut by moonlight, and you are the gold of the sun on the summer grass. You lie still beneath the frosts of winter and are set free by summer's heat. You are me, as I was.'

The wolf kept watching him across the bowl of mist.

A restless feeling came over Elifr – no, more than restlessness, a feeling of cold torment. The wolf was trying to express something. Elifr mouthed some words: 'Until the act is done.'

'What act? What ...'

But the voice in his head went quiet and the wolf turned back up the hill. Elifr abandoned his sheep and set out after it, on the journey to magic and misery.

The cart stopped, and Elifr, the wolfman who had been Elifr, was in front of a squat block of a building that sat in the shadow of a great domed cathedral. Elifr peered up. A gold structure sat on top of the dome, a bulbous pillar supporting a crescent moon. It seemed to shimmer in the hazy air. Again, Elifr tasted smoke.

Elifr had no time to sit and wonder. The Hetaereia lifted him from the cart and set him down on the ground. His limbs ached from the age he had spent sitting.

'Prisoner of the emperor!' shouted one of the Hetaereia.

'Stand forward with the emperor's prisoner!' shouted a tall Greek guard with a bushy black beard and a short whip at his belt.

They pulled him in front of a doorway which sat like a square of blackness cut out of the bright day.

'Emperor's prisoner is forward!' said the man at the side.

'We will receive the prisoner!'

The guard with the beard took Elifr by the arm and pushed him through the doorway. Other guards within took him on into the prison. It really was very dark inside, only the weak light of an oil lamp in a niche in the wall to see by. He was in a short corridor that led to another door. The stress and stink of the jail was in his nostrils, blood, piss, shit and vomit and more – subtle secretions undetectable to ordinary men. Only someone who had earned magic from the gods in ritual and privation could have smelled the iron in the sweat, the sour scent of ashes on the breath: the tiny leakings and excretions of human misery.

Elifr couldn't understand what the men said and it would have given him no comfort if he could have.

'No torture,' said a voice behind him.

'None?'

'Not by us. This is one for the Office of Barbarians.' The man put his hand on Elifr's shoulder.

'You're in luck, friend. You're not going to have to suffer one of our ham-fisted beatings; they're sending the professionals to deal with you.'

The wolfman caught the threat in the man's voice and turned to look into the Greek's eyes. Then he faced forward again.

The men opened the door at the end of the corridor and a waft of incense hit him, though human filth was still powerful beneath it. A meandering pipe and rhythmic clapping sounded from inside.

He couldn't work out what it was, but he told himself it didn't matter. His second plan was now under way and he was where he needed to be.

8 The Chamberlain's Man

Loys strode back to his lodgings, along one of the top streets to avoid the crush caused by the incoming army. The bulge where he'd hidden the gold inside his tunic seemed as conspicuous as if he'd stuffed a live goat up there, but he had no choice other than to take the back way.

With the return of the army the whole city was in ferment, more even than normal, so he didn't draw particular attention to himself by the briskness of his pace, which broke into a run at points where he felt particularly threatened.

The weather did nothing to settle him. The sky was strange – a curious and delicate shade of yellow had come over it while he had been with the chamberlain and the sun seemed wrapped in gauze. The light was like dusk and it wasn't yet past noon.

He hurried through the backstreets. There were no tall porches here, no merchants selling gold and silk. Constantinople was shot with bright avenues straight as flower stems that bloomed into rich corollas of forums and squares. Here was the tangled mass of alleys that supported them: narrow, winding and – even on brighter days than this one – dim. The backstreets were the province of street hawkers, gangs of hungry-eyed youths who loitered full of simmering intent, unwashed women and drunken men. They sold leather on the Middle Way. Here, flea-raw children scuttled in the gutters, picking up animal dung or even dead dogs to sell to the tanneries beyond the walls. Better-fed and more pious people crossed themselves and prayed or hurried to chapels and churches. The odd sky, combined with the cold, had set men's nerves jangling and they went to confess their sins and pray.

He calmed himself. *Look at it with other eyes, Loys.* There was a man, clearly a doctor in a good saffron gown, walking along. Three priests hurried on through the gloom, children and adults pulling at the holy men's hands as they walked, asking for blessings to protect them on this strange day. The Numeri – soldiers from the city's permanent garrison, so called because they were the ones who brought prisoners to the Numera – were a reassuring presence, idling on a corner. Mind you, they seemed more intent on looking up at the sky than guarding the streets.

Normally he would have enjoyed the mild frisson of danger the backstreets offered but, laden with the chamberlain's gold and frightened by the task he had been set, he felt vulnerable and conspicuous.

Loys forced himself to walk more slowly. His fear was nothing to do with the sky or even with the gold he was carrying. It was fear of what the chamberlain had asked him to do – to create a working and efficacious spell in three months. Was it possible? He had no idea. Was it holy? No.

He would find Beatrice and get out of Constantinople immediately. Ships sailed every day for the north or down to Arabia. The Caliphate was a centre of learning and might welcome a man of his skills. He would not defy God for the chamberlain or for anyone.

He cut up past the huge brick building of the Cistern of Aetios, a source of drinking water for much of the city, skirting its olive gardens – whose trees enjoyed the emperor's protection – and towards his lodgings.

He dived into the even narrower streets of the lighthouse quarter.

They were curiously empty. People were inside, with the shutters drawn. He looked up to the sky. The yellow was deepening and darkening, the sun becoming a blur. Something between light rain and snow wet the street. He shivered, and not just with the cold. The sky was unnatural, he was sure.

He went into the building that housed his rooms, up the

gloomy wooden passage and stairs. When he got to the top he had to feel his way, the light was so bad.

'Beatrice, Bea?'

No reply. He felt for the door and knocked at it, knowing it would be locked from the inside. Silence. He pushed at the door and it fell open.

The light of the gloomy day cast a feeble glow through the open window. The room was freezing. Beatrice was not there, nor any of their possessions. In rising panic Loys ran forward into the separate chamber set aside for his wife. That too was empty.

He came back out into the main bedroom. There was the mattress on the bed, the chamber pot and the small table which bore a blob of red wax. They had not been able to afford wax candles. He went to it. It was marked with a seal. He picked up the table and carried it to the window. The wax bore a crescent and a star and some words he couldn't make out in Latin.

Loys put his hand on the window ledge. The crescent and the star was the sign of the city and so of the emperor and chamberlain. In one way he was relieved. She'd neither left him nor been taken by her father. But now he knew the master of the Magnaura had spoken truly when he'd said he belonged to the chamberlain.

The sky had darkened even further and great black clouds loomed over the sea, the sun gilding their edges with fire, plumes of inky black backed by burning gold like monstrous cinders. They turned the sea to a field of shining tar and cast a stark blue light on the harbour front.

A dread was inside him. This weather was not natural – it couldn't be, the stamp of sorcery was all over it. And rather than fleeing, rather than taking Bea and running from it, he was expected to investigate. Looking at that sky, he could believe the demons had come to meet him.

He held his hand out of the window. Dirty snow fell upon

it. He put his fingers to his mouth and licked at them. They had a fine grit in them and tasted of ash.

He'd seen a play in the marketplace, the mouth of hell gaping, hungry for sinners to fall into it. Some trickery had allowed smoke to belch out of the gaping maw. Was this it? Were the gates of hell open, smoking and stinking of cinders? Had the day of judgement come?

Words from the Revelation of St John came to him: 'And the angel took the censer, and filled it with fire of the altar, and cast it into the earth: and there were voices, and thunderings, and lightnings, and an earthquake.'

There had been a comet only days before. Was that the censer?

Then his speculation fell in on itself and he thought only of her.

'Beatrice!' he said.

He thumped down the stairs and ran back to the palace.

9   The Numera

Elifr's eyes became accustomed to the torchlight as they pushed him into the Numera. Four men guarded him, two in front, two behind. They paused at the open door at the end of the corridor. Hot air, stale and fetid, breathed out, but it was scented with incense and he heard music, a pipe with a high nasal sound weaving a sinuous reel, clapping in an alien, unfamiliar rhythm. A man's voice sang what sounded like a song of joy.

The butt of a spear prodded his back and he stumbled on into a lighter space, a large vaulted room lit by reed torches. People swarmed everywhere, women, children, some men in rich dress. To Elifr's left a merchant in green and yellow silks was sitting on a fine chair eating a bunch of grapes, while a woman knelt beside him holding a goblet of wine. It could have been a scene from any rich man's house apart from one detail — the man wore manacles on his feet and his hands were bound together by an iron chain.

The piper sat cross-legged in the corner with others around him clapping out a stuttering beat. Some people even seemed to be trading, and a couple had parchment and styluses with them. This was not what Elifr had imagined. It was more like a marketplace.

The spearman shoved him in the back again and said something to him in Greek. Elifr didn't understand a word but the meaning was plain enough. This is not where we are taking you. Move on.

They walked across the vaulted chamber to another door, where a guard stood nodding to the music. The spearman took a small black disc from a string at his waist and presented it to the man on the door. The doorman added it to a string of similar counters at his own waist. Then he unlocked the door and they moved through.

A long line of pillars stretched away, leaving a narrow walkway between them and the wall on Elifr's right. In the dappling light of the reed torches they reminded Elifr of a forest in autumn. The smell was far from that of the fresh woods, though. Here it was rank, a thick human stench.

They walked along the row of columns. Eyes were in the dark and people cried out.

'Have you come for me, Michael, my son?'

'Bread. I am hungry.'

Someone sang in a high clear voice. It was a hymn, Elifr realised, like the Christians sang and, though he understood not a word, it carried a feeling of great sadness. He sensed it was a song about death.

Other men just hummed or babbled to themselves. And yet Elifr sniffed food on the air. These were not the worst off here, he felt sure.

They came to stone steps cut into the floor, which dropped away into darkness. Elifr tested his bonds. He had been working at them since the moment they were put on. Now they were loose enough. He muttered to himself under his breath – ancient rhymes that had come to him in his visions on the mountainside.

'The grey wolf is gazing upon the abodes of the gods.'

One of the guards glanced at him but said nothing. Elifr repeated the phrase again and again in his head, concentrating on the rhythm of the words, the pattern of their contractions and expansions, their grindings and deep sounds that to him began to take on the quality of natural things – rock on rock, wind on water.

The men went on down with their torches fluttering against the darkness. Elifr heard groaning, muttered prayers and terrible wheezing. The stink of shit was overpowering.

The steps turned and dropped again into a large natural cave leading off into black-mouthed tunnels.

The darkness teemed. There must have been a thousand men down there, but room enough for only half that number. No one ate grapes in his fetters here; the prisoners were secured to the floor with short chains. They blinked into the torchlight, some pale as creatures found beneath a stone, some still relatively healthy-looking. Here and there men lay dead in their irons, wasted almost to skeletons, still pressed against the living who lay beside them.

'A rain of blood is pouring.' Elifr was drifting away now, his mind freeing itself from the bonds of his humanity. He said the words aloud without thinking.

A guard said something to one of the others. The man glanced at Elifr and shrugged.

'A loom has been set up, stretching afar and portending
    slaughter.
Upon it has been stretched a weft of human beings
A warp grey with spears that the valkyries are filling
    with threads of crimson.'

The words pounded in Elifr's head like a rising tide of blood. A guard put his hand to his mouth, a gesture that the wolfman should be quiet. He was not.

'We are weaving the web of the spear
We are weaving the web of the spear
We are weaving the web of the spear.'

Elifr rocked back and forwards where he stood. One of the guards laughed. The man with the bushy beard smiled and held up the manacles and made what sounded like a harsh joke, for the laughter it brought from his colleagues. Elifr was indifferent to it.

The song went on.

'Blood-red clouds are gathering in the sky
And the maidens of death are singing.'

Elifr's limbs felt loose and lithe, his joints supple. The chant seeped into his mind, raising the wolf, numbing the human until all that was left of the man were the words.

A guard reached towards him to put his hand over Elifr's mouth but there was no need. The words stopped and his humanity fell away from him like a flower into a river in flood. He split the guard's nose with a vicious headbutt, a thump like a cleaver hitting a butcher's block. The man's knees went from under him. He collapsed, grasping at the wolfman for support, receiving only a knee driven at force into his face. The man fell back, his head hitting the ground with a wet smack. The other guards drew their swords, but the torch had fallen to the floor, where it guttered, its light failing.

Elifr's hands came free of the bonds and he was on a guard, past the sword before the man had time to raise it. He drove his thumbs into his opponent's eyes, and his teeth ripped into his neck, biting away a hunk of flesh and sending a spray of black blood across the torchlight. The guard dropped as the other two came on, but Elifr had the fallen man's sword and punched it backhand straight through the bushy-bearded man's chest. Howling, he leaped towards the only standing guard, who fell back over the bodies of the screaming and groaning prisoners, struggling to get away. Elifr leaped again and choked the life from his remaining opponent.

Prisoners shouted out, some protesting at the men falling on them, others just shrieking and gibbering in the madness of despair.

Elifr sat on his haunches. The rhyme had come back to him now and he used it to anchor his human thoughts. He controlled his breathing.

'The maidens of death are singing.' He withdrew from his battle frenzy. Men sobbed in the dark, calling out the names of wives, friends or children.

He could do nothing for them. Even if he released them they would be butchered by the guards above.

He said a name under his breath: 'Adisla.' The name of a girl he had never seen outside a trance-induced vision. He pictured her face on the mountainside and offered a prayer to the gods of the stream and the snows that he would never see her in real life. He had loved her before, in lives before, died for her before. He would die again but this time for ever. She, he and others had been toys of the gods – their deaths, their misery offered as a sacrifice to the fates to forestall the day when the gods themselves would go to their final slaughter.

No more.

He said another word: 'Ragnarok.' The twilight of the gods, when the old mad gods would die, the slaughter-fond lords of blood and battle would fall and the world would be returned to peace. *It is coming*, he thought, *it is coming*. His visions had led him to this place and they had so far proved true. The end of the gods was near. He had seen it in the comet that had lit up the sky, the yellow haze that hung on the dome of the cathedral, smelled it in the sooty rain of the battle. He had work to do. The end depended on him. Odin, the chief of the gods, master of sorcery, of poetry, of death, war and madness, had given him a part to play in averting the death of the gods and the wolfman would need to struggle if he was not to play it.

He remembered the hills, the Troll Wall and its caves, how the echoing earth had called to him and how he travelled down into the deep dark, losing himself as he descended, following the ghost wolf. The caves were empty and sightless but he had felt his way down as an animal feels its way. He found cold pools where it seemed right to sit and to freeze, found sharp rocks which had invited him as if they were a bed. In starvation, in freezing and in agonies, the god's plan for him had been revealed.

When he had crawled from those tunnels where the air seemed to move and whisper as if through the lungs of a sleeping giant, he was half an animal. He hunted as an animal, stalking his prey without spear or sling to take it by stealth and surprise; he fought as an animal, coming down to rob travellers of food and clothing, disdaining their gold and their jewels. But the man who remained in him would not surrender to his fate like an animal. He had seen her, in his dreams, the girl by the water with the light in her hair, and he was linked to her for ever, a link of pain, misery and death that stretched back over lifetimes.

He saw himself in those visions too, or rather not himself, but his brother who looked like him. His brother was a wolf, a true wolf, not a man who had sought for the wolf inside him by listening to the singing spirits of the mountain, by following them through the agonies of ritual. His brother was a hunter too and he hunted Elifr and the girl and he brought them to death again and again over many lives. Odin had found his way to earth as a man and died at the teeth of the wolf to please the fates and put off the day when he would die for real. But as he did so, he sucked others down with him to death and dejection again and again. The god was a river whirlpool and mortals were leaves caught in its pull.

The girl's face troubled his dreams and he knew his bond was one of love but stronger than love, one of destiny and fate. He would deny it. He would frustrate the gods, run from her and from his brother, take up the strands of his own fate and weave a skein himself.

Elifr had gone to the mountain for a year, chilled by the cold and baked by the sun, starving and thirsting to find out what to do. He had seen his destiny was to die at the teeth of his brother, the wolf. If he avoided that destiny, if the god himself killed Elifr, then the pattern might be broken, and he, his brother and the girl would be reborn free of each other, free of the god.

But his dreams had led him to that tent on the field of the slain, and the god had put down the sword and refused to kill him. So now he would go to the earth to find what he sensed was down there – Mimir's Well, the wisdom-imparting waters that the god Odin had drunk in exchange for his eye. The god came from the east, it was known, and now Elifr believed he had seen the location of the well. It lay, below the Numera, somewhere in the old tunnels that led from the lowest part of the prison. In there he would gain the wisdom and insight to bring about the death of the gods.

In the shifting light of the torch he searched the guards. The one who had carried the torch had flint and tinder. He took them. Then he stubbed the torch onto the ground to extinguish it and returned the prison to blackness. Men groaned and cursed as the light disappeared, but he did not resore it. A wolf needs the light much less than those who pursue it.

He moved forward through the dark, guided by senses enhanced by his rituals and his trances, by smell, by the echo of the cries of the prisoners on the walls, by the lightest of touches.

When the Hetaereia finally missed their guards and came running down with lights and shouts to find the bodies of their comrades, Elifr was gone, down into the tunnels to face his destiny, like Odin, seeking death.

10   The Office of Barbarians

Loys ran himself to breathlessness down the Middle Way. The yellow of the sky was giving way to black, the dark clouds he had seen over the sea now blooming like ink into a saucer of water above the city. A gritty sleet stung his face. When fatigue made him slow, the sweat chilled on his shirt, which stuck to his arms like a cold poultice.

Foreboding filled him as he rounded the Numera and ran towards the palace. The sun was invisible now and cast the streets in a blue half-light. The clouds were an unnatural deep grey, almost black, so heavy they looked as if they might fall and kill him. Even in Normandy the rain clouds didn't look like that. He shivered, and not with the cold. Was this a further magical attack? Would he be called on to explain and counter it?

Concern for Beatrice welled up in him, swamping all other fear. *Where was she?* Had she been taken by the chamberlain? Or by someone else? He breathed deep to try to calm himself. It had to be the chamberlain. No normal abductor would have left a seal.

He ran up the palace steps, under the great portico with its frieze of battles and conquest. Two guards – Greeks – barred his way.

'I am the chamberlain's man,' he said. 'I am to report here.'

The guards looked him up and down.

'You are a scholar, and a poor one at that.'

'I am the chamberlain's scholar.'

'So where is your silk and your fine shoes? Why do you smell of the docks rather than of perfume and oil?'

Loys stood tall.

'I am the scholar Loys, appointed by the chamberlain to do

his most valued work. I am to report here for my lodgings and my clothing. The work is pressing, and if you want to frustrate it that is up to you. When the chamberlain asks me why I have not done as he asks, I shall say you stood in my way and defied his will.'

The two guards said nothing but one stepped inside. When he returned he was with a short man dressed in a yellow silk gown and a three-cornered blue hat.

'This is not the poor door,' said the man. 'If you wish to apply for alms go to the kitchens at the rear of the palace.'

'I am the chamberlain's man,' said Loys, 'the scholar Loys.'

'My God, are you really?' said the man, as if he'd just been informed a toothpick he'd discarded at dinner was part of Christ's True Cross.

'Proper ...' Loys tried to find fine words, 'proper raiment has been provided. Take me to my wife. I think she has been brought here.'

'I know nothing about that.'

'She should have been brought here not an hour ago.'

'My shift has only just begun.' The man examined his tablet. 'You are listed here,' he said, 'and expected. Come in and pass quickly through the room.'

Loys stepped inside and the world was transformed. Outside, under the bubbling clouds, the light cast the buildings in blues and greys. Here, a thousand lustrous colours shimmered under the lamplight.

Few people had been on the streets but though this room was very large, it was crowded. It was a wonder to Loys – lit with oil lamps that gave off a soft golden light. Every surface seemed alive. The floor was a mosaic of flowers and lilies with the representation of a pond, complete with shining copper fish at its centre. The walls were lined with trees but no tree that had ever grown in a forest. They were rendered in gold and silver with berries of rubies and leaves of green glass. The branches threw a canopy over the ceiling, silver moons and twinkling stars – diamonds or glass, he couldn't tell – peeping between them. Rich and beautiful people sat or lay on couches, and servants dressed in tunics laced with gold and emerald green served drinks and food from silver cups and plates.

The room fell completely silent when he entered and everyone turned to look at him. Loys suddenly had a sense of himself standing in the same clothes he'd grabbed as he'd run from Normandy, save for a fourth-hand scholars' gown, breathless in front of these people who moved like fabulous fish through the waters of a beautiful fountain.

Another man came forward. He was short, bald and dark and wore a robe of green velvet.

The man in the silk showed him the tablet. 'The scholar is to go to his rooms here,' he said, 'as quickly as possible.'

The dark man smiled. 'This way, sir,' he said.

As he led Loys across the room the man said: 'The Room of the Nineteen Couches. They wait here to see the emperor. It's become rather more popular since the mouth of hell spewed out all this brimstone across the sky. People imagine the emperor will defend them from the devil's legions.'

'You know what is causing this sky?'

'That's your job, isn't it?'

'What do you know of my job?'

'This is Contantinople, my friend. The ancient city of By-zan-ti-um.' He enunciated every syllable of the city's old name in a way that was far from friendly. 'Everyone knows everything about everyone here. And if they don't, they make it up.'

Loys swallowed. 'It is the mouth of hell? You know this?'

'A figure of speech. Surely you should tell me what it is.'

'I don't know. At the moment my only concern is for my wife. Is she here?'

The man did not reply, just led Loys out of the Room of Nineteen Couches through a bronze door struck with the sickle and star of the city's emblem. They went down a short corridor.

Loys studied the figure beside him. He had been so keen to

find Beatrice that he hadn't really paid any attention to the man. He'd taken him for a servant but he didn't talk like a servant. And he wore velvet, a deep green. No one dressed their servants so richly, no one.

This corridor was as splendid as the couch room, the walls glittering with greens and blues showing an undersea scene, complete with images of the sea god Poseidon with his chariot of wave-horses. The light came from lamps arranged all the way down the wall and a big window at the end. It was uncovered and opened on to a lovely garden of orange trees. Loys shivered as the draught blew in.

They walked down corridors and through rooms glittering with decoration. Loys would have liked to have seen more Christian symbols, but he knew the emperor and his retinue for holy men so could find nothing to object to in them mimicking the art of previous generations. Men love stories and, as long as they saw them as stories, there was no harm in them. But where was Beatrice?

They came to a corridor plainer than the rest but still hardly simple. Here the mosaic was only on the floor – scenes of rural life, children feeding donkeys, men collecting hay from the fields.

'You're aware your appointment has caused a stir in the palace.'

'What sort of stir?'

'There are those who say it shows a lack of faith in the abilities of the existing intelligence services.'

Bronze doors led off the passage. Was Beatrice behind one of them?

'I have nothing to do with the investigation of foreigners.'

'Then you think your evil magicians could be Romans? You're in our city for a blink and already you're slandering us. '

'No. I don't know. I haven't started investigating.'

'No, you haven't, because you don't know what you're doing. Let me point out where you might start.'

'I'd be grateful.'

They had stopped and the man faced Loys directly. He had the appearance of being made of something more solid than flesh, some weighty marble, maybe.

'The Varangians. It doesn't take a great scholar to work it out. A clear blue day – no problems. The Varangians march in – the sky darkens. So work back. The rebel Phokas is struck dead by magic. Who was there? The Varangians. The emperor fought three battles without them and the outcome was decided by sword and shield. This one by sorcery. Their arrival is heralded by a comet.'

'That wouldn't explain the emperor's ongoing illness.'

'The emperor has an illness?'

'No, I—'

'Dear, dear, you need to control your tongue, scholar. That is treason, did you know that?'

'I said nothing.'

The man glanced around him.

'Indeed not. But you are a northern oaf and may well make such a mistake again one day, and in front of witnesses, at which point you will need friends. I could be one of those friends. Let me give you a word of advice. The Varangians are to blame for this. No question. Make them the focus of your investigation. Limit the deaths this causes.'

'What deaths?'

'Well, for a start we'll be purging the street magicians as soon as we receive an edict from the emperor.'

'You said the Varangians were to blame.'

'And so I believe. But this is a serious situation. The Varangians are six thousand armed fighters, and it will take time to undermine them, isolate their leaders and bring them to task for their crimes. The sky is boiling and the mob is restless. The street magicians are but two hundred jabbering men and wild women. God is angry with them. What else could this sky mean?'

'But you know they're innocent.'

'I suspect they're innocent of this, but who knows what other guilts they hide? They are enemies of Christ, and in times such as these we need only the Saviour's friends around us. The chamberlain has opposed this action before but now he will sanction it, I'm sure.'

'I'll see to it that he doesn't.'

The man smiled. 'Don't make me your enemy, scholar Loys.'

'That is not my intention.'

'Our intentions matter little in life. It is what we do that counts. Just by being here you are a threat to the authority of some of the great offices of state. When people find out you are conducting this investigation – which many already have – they will think those in charge don't trust those offices, and if those offices do not have the emperor's confidence then they are a little less respected, a little less feared. Killing the soothsayers has a practical benefit. It restores the fear.'

'At the cost to your immortal soul.'

'These people consort with devils. If Christ came back today he would be the first to shed their blood. Now excuse me. What you're looking for is within.'

He tapped the door then walked back the way they had come.

'I will oppose you,' said Loys to his retreating back. The man stopped and turned.

'You could stop me immediately if you chose.'

'How?'

'Resign.'

'That would be my death.'

The man tilted his head, a sarcastic smile on his face. 'So there's a limit to your compassion and love for the low people, I see.'

'I am not a martyr,' said Loys.

'Not yet,' said the man. 'If you need to leave this city in a hurry, stain your left-hand thumb and small finger with ink. My men will contact you. You may need us. You and your wife.'

'Who are you?' Loys felt the blood leave his face at the mention of Beatrice.

But the man walked away, disappearing around a corner.

Loys watched him go with the certainty that his destination, should he take up the man's offer, would be the next world and his mode of conveyance a dagger to the back.

Loys knocked at the door. After a few moments it was opened a crack by a eunuch, tall and old. 'Come in, master.'

He opened the door wide to a vision. Beatrice sat in a long dress of deep and lustrous blue. At her neck was a collar in cloth of gold and behind her a maidservant combed out her golden hair. Next to her was a table and on it a silver goblet and a plate of grapes.

'Loys! You've been so long; they said you'd come immediately. Look at you. You're soaked and you're covered in dirt. Have you been attacked?'

'No, gosh, no. You know me. No one crosses me and gets away with it.' He put up his fists and gave a little growl, trying to be light, trying to reassure her.

'Oh, Loys, come here and hug me.'

He did, and as he put his arms around her felt a huge need to protect her.

'Did you see the sky?' he said.

'What about the sky?'

'They brought you here before it happened?'

'What happened?'

'Never mind. Just bad weather.'

'It was a fine day when I arrived.'

'Who brought you?'

'Men from the chamberlain's office. I was afraid of them at first, but they were finely dressed and bore seals so I went with them.'

'I was worried about you.'

'They said you'd know I'd come.'

'No matter. You seem to have settled in.'

'I should say so! Isn't it wonderful in here? It's so lovely.

The floor's as warm as a kitten and look, they've laid out clothes for you. Even my father has never dreamed of luxury like this. My clever, clever, husband. I knew they'd reward you one day!'

Beatrice gestured towards a couch. Loys too had been given a rich robe of blue, though without a collar. That was only allowed to those of royal status. He was pleased Beatrice's rank had been recognised. There were undergarments of linen, slippers too, in fine blue silk decorated with gold brocade.

'What are these?' said Loys to the eunuch.

'A badge of office, sir, the mark of the chamberlain's men.'

'You can bathe,' Beatrice said. 'Down the corridor there's a wonderful heated bath. You should try it, Loys.'

'I will. I've heard about such things but I've never seen one.'

He studied the robe. Picked out in fine embroidery on its back was a picture of Christ casting out demons and sending them into a herd of swine. The message from the chamberlain about what was required was clear enough.

'Can you get a message to the chamberlain?' he said to his servant.

'Yes, sir.'

'Can you tell him I need to see him at his earliest convenience?'

'Yes, sir.'

'Your mind is always on your labours, Loys,' said Beatrice. 'Look at all this lovely stuff. Think how lucky we've been, how clever you are to bring us all this.'

'Well,' he said, coming over to Beatrice and picking a grape, 'let's hope I can live up to it.' He smiled for her benefit.

'You can. I know you can, Loys,' said Beatrice. She looked so alive, so relieved to be out of that stinking woodpile by the water. He kissed her, careless of the servant in the room.

'For you,' he said, 'I will make sure that I do.'

11 A Fight for Snake in the Eye

Snake in the Eye felt strong and powerful in his Armenian armour, with his Greek sword at his side and his horse archer's shield proudly on his back. He'd scarcely taken the armour off since he won it. The emperor had spent nearly no time at all in Constantinople and departed for Bithynia in the east almost as soon as he had finished his triumphal march. His attentions had shifted from the rebel to the threat from the Arabs.

Arabic translators were now in greater demand than Norse ones, and Snake in the Eye found himself left with the bulk of the Varangian force, camped outside the walls, waiting for the emperor's instructions when the great man had made an appraisal of where the Vikings might be needed. At first Snake in the Eye enjoyed his privileged status as a go-between, running from Bollason and his men to the various offices of the city to strike deals on food and supplies. The problem was that Bollason's army was large, restless and feeling short-changed. They had been promised the gleaming streets of Constantinople, an earthly Asgard, a home fit for gods, let alone men. Instead they were camped out on a freezing shore under a black sky.

Snake in the Eye soon found that his position – having the ear of the emperor and of Bollason – brought its own problems. Men overestimated his influence and asked him why they had not been allowed into the city, why wine was in short supply and so on. One even told him he should insist on a prettier sort of whore for the brave victors of Abydos and offered to accompany the boy to ensure he made the right choice.

And then the rain had come in, another violent downpour like the one that had swept the field at Abydos. Warriors who had only grumbled before now began to complain bitterly, to blame even. By the time the rain passed, the campsite had turned into a mire. Snake in the Eye had been both lucky and unlucky. He was in the city securing a supply of pork for the Varangians when the flood descended. He couldn't see five paces in the deluge and he had stayed there, a merchant allowing him to bed down in a storeroom.

So he returned to the camp the next morning dry and clean. He made his way to the tent next to which his father had set up his small forge – no more, really, than a hole in the ground. A big Viking waited while the head of his axe was sharpened. Next to him stood his son – Snake in the Eye's age but already with a wispy beard, an axe of his own at his side and a cut to his ear that suggested he knew what it was to be in a battle.

'You look dry enough,' said his father.

'I got caught in Miklagard. A merchant let me bed down in his store. '

The big Viking snorted. Snake in the Eye caught his disapproval.

'You think I should have sat out in the rain?'

The man said nothing.

Snake in the Eye put his hand to his sword.

'That is a foolish way to proceed,' said the big Viking.

'It's a fool who looks down his nose and is too cowardly to say what he thinks!'

'Cowardly' fell loud from his lips. Its effect was like a magic spell. Around him the sounds of the camp faded. Men stopped their talk. People who had been walking past stopped to stare. A woman who had been beating out a carpet let it fall to her knees and stared at him.

'The bigger fool is he that calls a man a coward for no more than a glance. You go to your Greek masters; you take luxuries that are denied to your fellows, shelter when your kin freeze and soak under Hel's own skies. I will say nothing. Call me a coward and that moves me to correct you.'

Snake in the Eye drew his sword. Now the man's son had his axe free, though the Viking himself just laughed at Snake in the Eye.

'You are a boy and so some foolishness is allowed. Apologise now and I will take only the compensation of free service from your smith father here. Otherwise you will die.'

'An apology is in order,' said the smith.

'I will not apologise!' said Snake in the Eye. 'Come on, both of you, and I'll make this a sad day for the whore you married to beget him.'

The big Viking lunged at him. His movements seemed slow to Snake in the Eye, and it would have been easy to strike him down with his sword. But, yet again, his arm failed him; his will to fight was not there. A fist smashed into Snake in the Eye's jaw, snapping his head sideways and putting him down.

Snake in the Eye tried to stand and took a good kick to the chin. He recalled nothing after that until he was pulled up to sitting, a blond Viking staring into his face. Someone shouted, 'I will kill him! I will kill him! Let me free!'

'What have you done?'

Snake in the Eye's father lay dead on the ground, the boy with the axe too, the right side of his head caved in. Snake in the Eye's father had clearly hit him with his smith's hammer but had paid the price. A scrum of men held the big Viking back.

'Get up, get up!' A blond Viking he had never seen before shook Snake in the Eye by the tunic.

'I want vengeance! He called me a coward and his father killed my son. He provokes a fight and backs down from it. I want vengeance!'

The hullaballoo had the whole camp straining to see what was happening. Through the press of people a huge figure dressed all in red pushed his way forward. It was Bollason.

Snake in the Eye felt for his sword, determined to prove himself, but the blond-haired man snatched it away.

Bollason pointed at the corpses. 'Explain.'

The big Viking shouted that he had been insulted and denied justice, that his son was dead and he was owed revenge.

'Calm yourself, Arnulf,' said Bollason. 'Justice will be done, you have my word. You, boy, what have you got to say for yourself?'

'I want to fight him,' said Snake in the Eye. He got to his feet, shaky.

'Come to me then, you snivelling little bastard, and I'll cut your throat,' said Arnulf.

Bollason stood in front of Snake in the Eye. 'I hear reports of you,' he said. 'I hear you're trouble. If it wasn't for your usefulness with the emperor I'd let Arnulf here pin you to this shitty shore with his spear.'

'Let him try.'

Snake in the Eye's head ached where he'd been punched and kicked. Why had the man only sought to hit him? Why not kill him? Because he hadn't taken him seriously, because he held him in contempt as a boy.

His father would never see him triumph as a famous warrior now. He had been a smith, a profession that exempted him from fighting unless in dire need, too valuable to risk putting in harm's way. Smiths were honoured, seen as magical even, so there was no question of his father being accused of coming too slow to the fight. Yet, Snake in the Eye now felt curiously free. His grandfather on his mother's side had been the famous killer Thiörek. Had his father's line brought the curse of cowardice to the family?

He would not mourn his father; he would avenge him.

'Let me fight him,' he said to Bollason.

'You're a boy. You cannot and you will not,' said Bollason.

'I am a man the same as the one who is dead on the floor here,' said Snake in the Eye.

'Do you want me to have your trousers stripped off to prove my point? You're not yet a man and anyone can see it. You try to act like one but you fail.' He addressed Arnulf. 'The boy is not ready to face you in *hölmgang*. He is still a child by my reckoning and it would dishonour you to fight him.'

'Then let him provide an uncle, or even a friend. I will have vengeance for the death of my son.'

'His father lies dead.'

'As does my boy. The original insult, the slur of cowardice, has not been answered yet. I demand redress. It is my right under the law.'

Bollason shrugged. 'He's right. Have you an uncle who can fight for you?'

'I was here only with my father.'

'Do you have friends here?'

'He has no friends, that one,' said a woman. 'He's a nasty piece of work who has been lucky to live so long.'

'Then he must face me!' shouted Arnulf.

Bollason shook his head.

'No,' he said, 'there's a whole stack of trouble if we kill him. The emperor favours him and he translates our words, which we'll need when the emperor returns. But it is dishonourable to think only of the convenience of having him here when he has deeply dishonoured you, Arnulf, and caused you so much grief. There is a middle way.'

He pointed at Snake in the Eye.

'You are banished from this camp, translator or no,' he said. 'You will return here only when you are a man and can fight Arnulf on equal terms or with someone who will fight for you. While you are away, try to grow up a little. The world sends us enough battles without us seeking them with each other.'

'That is a shame to me,' said Snake in the Eye. 'I cannot stand such an injustice.'

'Then I'll gut you here and now myself,' said Bollason.

'I welcome it,' said Snake in the Eye.

Bollason rolled his eyes to the heavens. Then his patience suddenly snapped. The Viking leader was famous for his short temper and now it seemed he had come to the end of it.

'Get your sword,' he said, 'and let's you and I do the old dance together. Hedin, give him his sword!' He roared the last words into Snake in the Eye's face so hard that the boy took several paces backwards and everyone around laughed.

The blond man passed Snake in the Eye his sword and he

tried to strike Bollason, but the battle fetter still held him — he couldn't make his arm do what he wanted it to. He came forward in a ridiculous way, his sword forward but his arm limp so the weapon's point trailed on the ground. As he advanced, it caught in the mud, jolting the hilt up in his hand. Bollason, two heads taller than the boy, closed the distance in a blink and stepped on the sword with his left foot, his weight levering it out of the boy's hand, flattening it into the mud. He shoved Snake in the Eye hard and sent him sprawling back. The Viking didn't pause, walking forward to put his foot in the centre of Snake in the Eye's chest, pinning him to the ground. Snake in the Eye put his hands around Bollason's foot but the man was as immovable as one of the statues from the Middle Way.

'Like I said,' said Bollason, his face now impassive, 'you are a boy. Come back when you have become a man, should that ever happen, and I will grant you your *hölmgang*.'

All around Snake in the Eye people laughed and pointed. Only Arnulf continued to rage. Dying did not bother the boy at all, but the scorn wounded him deeply.

Bollason released his foot and pointed to Snake in the Eye's sword. 'Use that to attack me and I shall use it to spank your bottom.'

Snake in the Eye boiled with embarrassment, his face red, his limbs stiff and tense. He picked up the sword and left the camp, heading in the direction of the city, taunts and jeers at his back. He wanted to turn and hack his mockers to the floor but knew he couldn't. He may as well have been carrying a Byzantine lady's fan as a sword. An enchantment lay on him, he was certain. One day he would break it and return to write his name in the blood of those who had mocked him. He just had to find out how.

12 An Invitation

The chamberlain had not answered Loys' request to see him, and the scholar sat at his desk with his head in his hands. He'd heard nothing about any slaughter, and the guards on the palace doors had said no one had moved against the soothsayers. The streets were dangerous enough, purge or no purge. Venturing outdoors had become an unsettling proposition. Some were convinced the last days were at hand and had abandoned all pretence of civility, robbing and even killing. The city guard was struggling to keep anarchy at bay. In the palace, at least, he and Beatrice were safe. For the moment.

Loys tapped at the parchment. He needed to order his thoughts. In other circumstances he might have been excited by the project. He had been sponsored to undertake a great work, to bend his mind to one of the big questions of philosophy. There was nothing wrong with investigating occult and magical practices, as long as you kept to theory, but the chamberlain wanted a working spell. Did that blur the division between the theoretical and the practical? Loys felt in his heart that it did. Christ allowed no fudge or compromise. For or against, right or wrong? Which side of that divide was he on?

On top of this a more immediate anxiety gripped him. The penalty for failure would be severe. He could end up damning himself to hell and being dispatched there by the chamberlain in short order. He needed to go, to get away from this horrible city. Beatrice was a sensible woman and would bury her disappointment at having to leave the luxurious palace if he explained their peril. But could he leave? Everything was done for him here – everything: his food laid out, his bed freshened, books he requested delivered and scented herbs changed daily.

He knew enough of men like the chamberlain to understand they would not invest time and money in him and then allow him to walk away. The man had known everything about him when he was living in a shack by the lighthouse; how much more would he know now he had him under his nose?

Loys had a chariot race of anxieties going on in his head. He had enemies, that much was obvious, and within the ranks of the palace bureaucrats too but he had merely been threatened as yet. And he had a protector. He thought of the chamberlain with his thin sleepy face, those eyes which seemed only half awake but missed nothing. He would not believe in chance if Loys was found dead in an alley.

Loys was inclined to begin his investigation by studying the demons, through the works of the learned men who had categorised and named them. He had always been taught to move from first principles, so he turned to astrology to begin with. Proclus said there were sympathies and antipathies in nature. Men's destinies were connected to those of the constellations, to those of plants and animals, even tides. Astrology was Loys' particular expertise, though he found it more useful for describing tempers and dispositions than he did for actually predicting the future. Still, he would need to consider all influences on the emperor before he could advise on how those influences might be dealt with. Books of ancient wisdom – the works of the Greeks, the Arabs and the Persians – were scattered about him.

He consulted his charts. The moon, Mars and Mercury were in conjunction. He took up a Latin translation of Haephestio of Thebes. 'A conjunction between the moon, Mars and Mercury will produce men who are steeped in magic, knowers of secret things.' He gave a dry laugh. He wished he knew where to find one of those now. He considered the planets: mother moon, Mars the warrior and Mercury the messenger and carrier of dreams. *The Vikings!* There were enough of those in Normandy – savage cousins of the local Norman nobility getting off their boats wet behind the ears, comically dressed but no less violent for it. They worshipped a form of Mercury – Odin – a mad god according to them. Mercury was coming to the ascendant. As were the northerners outside the walls. Mercury was the planet that ruled magic.

So what correspondence had afflicted the emperor? Loys used Basileios' birth information to cast his horoscope, consulting the books for the position of the stars. It took him nearly all evening and revealed nothing. The emperor was blessed, according to the planets. Then Loys examined the last five years, to judge the particular influences and pulls of the stars there. Nothing. Fluctuations, difficulties but no grave disasters were apparent.

He began to read another book – *Ancient Blasphemies* – a record of the beliefs that had been discovered during local purges. He browsed through, turning up nothing in particular until he reached a certain page. Hecate, the goddess of the Constantinople. Was it possible she was a demon and God had struck at the city for worshipping her? He read on – goddess of crossroads, of the dead, of walls and borders, of the borders between the living and the dead – she was associated with dogs and with poison and poetry. As if by command two of the palace dogs set off barking, making Loys jump. She was worshipped at the end of each month, when the people sacrificed black lambs at crossroads and at holy sites.

So much information, so little use.

By the time Beatrice came back from visiting the women of the lower court, parchment lay all over the room and she asked him if she could tidy it up. He let her, then he held her hand as she stood behind him to look at his work.

'Is the sky still dark?'

'Still dark,' she said.

'What do the ladies say about it?'

'It's an ill omen, what else could they say? First the comet, now this.'

'What do you think?'

'Our fortunes have improved since its appearance. But God

93

is angry with the earth, it must be so. Lady Styliane says so. The comet is a sign of that, according to the wisdom of the Arabs.'

'Who is Lady Styliane?'

'A lady of the court. The chamberlain's sister, no less.'

Loys concealed his fear. 'And she is wise in astrology?'

'Her late husband took an interest,' she said.

Loys smiled. 'I hope you haven't been consorting with witches, Beatrice.'

'She is no witch. Astrology is the study of nature, don't you always tell me?'

'Yes. In the hands of learned men. Not bored and credulous ladies. There it can slide into sorcery.'

'Lady Styliane is neither bored nor credulous. She is an amusing woman. You should meet her. Or perhaps not. She's very beautiful and I would not wish her to meet you when dark stars are governing our fate.'

She kissed him.

He thought of the comet and shivered. That had heralded nothing good for sure – the disappearance of the sun and the birth of a lasting darkness. But that was not the cause of the emperor's malaise. The darkness had happened only recently, and the emperor suffered from a long-standing condition.

Beatrice went to bed and he continued his studies through three candles. His head ached with the mental effort. Perhaps if he addressed the influence of the comet, then he would see something?

He consulted his books and worked his chart, tracing the comet's path across the sky as best he recalled it. Abu Mash'r – an Arab mathematician – was very helpful here, and Loys calculated his angles and drew his charts according to the wise man's prescription. He cast the seven hermetic lots, his pen marking the lines against the ruler in quick and fevered swipes. In the lot of fortune he saw minor problems, in the lot of spirit some difficulties. Nothing pointed to an illness striking at Basileios.

Beatrice stirred in her sleep. For a second he longed to join her but he had gone beyond tiredness in his desperation for an answer. *So work backwards.* When he did, he found nothing again.

Beatrice woke him at his desk the next morning, a pool of wax from the candles at his elbow.

'How are you getting on?'

'Well,' he said, not wishing to alarm her.

There was a knock at the door and the eunuch servant entered.

'Hello,' Loys said.

Beatrice put her hand to his head. 'You're very nice, Loys, but this is a court. If you behave like that no one will respect you.' He had forgotten it was bad form to greet slaves.

'I have a message, sir,' said the eunuch.

Loys glanced at Beatrice.

'You can reply to that.' She laughed and stroked his hair.

'What is it?' said Loys with exaggerated formality.

'The Lady Styliane would see the Lady Beatrice in her rooms at noon tomorrow.'

'Sounds like you've made a friend,' said Loys.

'It is a formal occasion for the lady's particular friends,' said the servant.

Beatrice glanced at Loys. 'Do you think I should go?'

'If you want.'

'It could be a worthwhile association for us.'

Loys smiled. Beatrice had been brought up at a court and it was as natural for her to think that way as it was for Loys to overlook it. His wife would prove a big asset to his career – were he not mired in this magic business. She understood instinctively how things worked. He was wary of great people; she was drawn to them.

'The invitation extends to you too, sir,' said the eunuch.

Loys and Beatrice exchanged a glance.

'Me?'

The eunuch lowered his eyes in assent.

'What could she want with me? Is it normal for the ladies of the court to take their men with them?' he said.

Beatrice coloured slightly. 'I don't know if I did the right thing, but I mentioned your task to her.'

Loys swallowed, trying to think before speaking. Panic rose in him and anger too – for the danger in which Beatrice had placed them both.

'I said nothing about the emperor,' said Beatrice, 'just that you were researching magic on the chamberlain's behalf.'

Loys brought his hands together as if readying himself to pray. He saw what had happened. Beatrice had come to trust this woman and had made a casual remark that had rebounded to haunt her. He couldn't blame his wife. He had put her in danger by telling her anything at all. Were they in danger from Styliane? Who knew? But he had seen already the court had its sectional interests and was certain he was about to encounter another.

'Well,' he said, glancing back at the useless results of his night's scribbling, 'let's see what she has to say. She may be able to help.'

And at least he could mention the soothsayers to her to see if any sort of protection could be offered to them.

He squeezed Beatrice's hand and gave her his best smile.

13 Help for the Hunters

Mauger and Azémar walked through the umber light beneath the great dome of Hagia Sophia. Its windows were bright despite the dim day outside. Shining archways ringed the base of the dome, and the scholar imagined for a second they were the windows of heaven, with God and the saints gazing down at him.

It was an incredible building, raised to the glory of God – whose commandments Azémar was obliged to break. He imagined his soul standing where he was standing, surrounded by those windows, with God on his throne on the final day, judging him for helping Mauger to murder his friend.

'The scholars come here?' said Mauger.

'I think this is the best place to start,' said Azémar. 'It's the church of Holy Wisdom. Where better to search for a scholar?'

'You know about these things,' said Mauger, 'so I will trust you.'

Azémar eyed the long roll of thick cloth the knight wore on his back. It was his bedding but also contained his sword.

'You don't intend to chop off his head here on the cathedral flagstones?'

'If you see him, identify him and leave the rest to me.'

'You'll need to follow him to find the lady.'

Mauger gave Azémar a look that suggested he'd thought of that already.

Azémar shivered. The sky had frightened him, the sun reducing to a pale yellow disc like a dog's eye and then vanishing entirely. A half-hearted snow fell and the cobbled streets were slick and slippy, the unpaved ones muddy and filthy. The rich kept inside while the poor wailed and prayed, huddled beneath the porticoes or crammed into the churches.

The only good thing to come of it was that Loys was likely to stay indoors. The cathedral contained its share of the poor now and their voices echoed to the ceiling. One voice sang above the rabble, sounding a kontakion loud and clear: 'Though thou didst descend into the grave, O Immortal One, yet didst thou destroy the power of Hades.'

Azémar crossed himself.

'Ask.' Mauger touched Azémar on the elbow.

'What?'

'Ask one of those scholars.' A group of monks stood whispering by a pillar

Azémar swallowed. At least Mauger couldn't speak Greek. He would never know what had been asked.

Azémar approached them.

'Hello, dear friends in Christ. Foul weather we're having, isn't it?'

The monks ceased their conversation.

'You are a foreigner,' said one, a tall man with thin lips and nose like a big crab apple.

'Yes.'

'Then perhaps you can tell us where this weather has come from. Did you bring it with you?'

'No. That is ... no. We don't have its like in my lands.'

'And where are your lands?'

'Normandy, near Francia.'

'I hear that it is overrun by barbarians.'

'There are many fierce northern men there, it is true, and our dukes—'

One of the monks held up his hand to interrupt him. 'Then why don't you go back to your fierce northern men and your dukes and take your weather with you?'

Azémar smiled. This response gladdened him and he hoped he would meet its like every time he asked anyone anything. The harder it was to find Loys the happier he would be.

He walked back to Mauger.

'Well, I hope you saw that.'

'What did you ask them?'

'Just as you asked, Lord Mauger. For the whereabouts of our scholar Loys.'

'I am not a fool, Azémar.'

'Nor do I take you for one, but you note the response I got.'

Mauger stood close to Azémar. 'I can find him without you. With you it will be easier by far, but I have money enough to hire a translator who will do my work honestly. Let me be clear, Azémar. If I do not have an idea where this scholar is staying by the end of the week then I'll kill you and go on alone. You choose.'

Azémar felt the blood drain from his face. 'I treat you honestly and fairly, Mauger; you do the same to me.'

'So I shall. But I want to see you working hard for me.'

Azémar held up his hands. 'You shall see it, you shall see it!' he said.

For the next hour he busied himself in the cathedral, approaching people and asking them questions about everything but where Loys was staying. He tried to think of a way out of his predicament but he'd been trying that since Rouen and hadn't come up with one yet. Eventually the subdued light of the church and the mingled odours of the poor sheltering from the weather, the incense and the reed lights began to make his head spin and he headed outside. Mauger followed five paces behind.

Even the beggars had deserted the area outside the great church and the ground was wet under the sleet. Sitting by the wall on a huge black wolfskin was a boy − or not quite a boy, a youth − huddled in a rich blue cloak trimmed with gold. He was talking, and as Azémar breathed in the fresh air he found himself listening. The boy spoke in Norse, a language Azémar knew well. His grandfather had been a Norseman and his parents had used the language at home.

'In the time of the famed King Ingvar lived a slave who was a precious jewel to her masters. For this slave was mute, which is a rare gift to a master, and she had lived a long, long time – longer than anyone else, and yet she had never grown old. In this way she was like an heirloom to be passed from generation to generation. Now know that she came to travel east with the princess daughter of her master to be married to a Wendish king. All was easy in the travelling but, on arriving at a certain port, a rich traveller claimed the slave for his own, saying he had bought her many years before. But the princess would not give up the slave and took her east.

'Coming to a certain river, they travelled down it, but a fever struck among the crew until none but the princess and the slave was alive. Fearing for her life, the princess asked what might be done. The slave, throwing off her silence, replied that there was nothing to be done and her master was coming for her.

'Then the princess died and the fever stepped out of her and became a man, the rich traveller who had—'

'A good enough tale, boy.' Mauger cast a coin in his direction.

'Thank you for your compliment but not your coin,' said the boy. 'I am seeking things other than alms.'

'I apologise for not seeing that you are richly dressed. What do you seek?' Azémar noticed that Mauger spoke formally to the boy, giving him respect.

The boy stood up. 'The blessing of the gods. A man told me if I recited this story here then fortune would come to me.'

'Has it?'

'I haven't finished the tale yet,' said the boy.

'You know this city?' said Mauger.

'Well enough.'

'You speak Greek?'

'Many languages.'

'Then great fortune may have attended you. I want to keep my scholar friend here honest. I'd like your help.'

The boy glanced Mauger up and down. 'To what purpose?'

Mauger seemed to think for a second. 'I need to find some-one.'

'To what purpose?'

Again Mauger took his time. 'Revenge on an enemy.'

'Should not a monk pray to find forgiveness in his heart?'

Mauger said nothing, but the boy caught the meaning in his silence.

'Since I have no better employment for the moment, I will help you.' He stood and bowed to Mauger and Azémar.

'You'll be paid well,' said Mauger.

'I seek no pay,' said the boy. 'I am a warrior and a killer. To share the joy of your revenge will be enough.'

'You speak like a warrior because our Norse tongue is the tongue of warriors,' said Mauger. 'I am Mauger and this Azémar.'

'I am Snake in the Eye,' said the boy. 'Now, how shall we find your enemy?'

14 The Lower Caves

When Elifr sensed water he thought it might be safe to light the torch. He got out the tinder and flint and set to work.

His eyes adjusted to the light. He had come to a narrow shelf of rock at the side of a cave of black water – the ceiling supported by elegant pillars. He had no idea what this place was – that the Greeks used it to supply water to the palaces. Nor did he know the connection to the tunnels of the Numera had come about as the result of a rockfall, and since it was said the water spirits had been seeking a way to the surface, the hole that had opened had not been closed. His dream-sharpened senses told him this way led down.

The route to this cave was not easily found or reached – just a split in the ceiling of the cavern. But Elifr, his wolf senses sharpened by hunger, sensed the deep water that lay beyond. Elifr had earned many meals in the mountains by taking birds' eggs from perilous ledges and he climbed the rough wall to squeeze his way through.

Could the prisoners get out this way? Which of them could get free of his manacles? Even if they did, the dark itself was as effective as any irons.

Elifr peered out into the flooded cavern. He gave a start – there were faces staring up at him from the torchlit water. He calmed himself. They were not real. At the base of two of the pillars were the carved heads of snake-haired women, gazing blankly up. He tried to see further out, the swimming torchlight making a ghost of his reflection.

Words came to him, just the echo of a memory. *I am a wolf.* He'd spoken those words before, unimaginable years ago. Another word. *Mother.*

He remembered his family, the hearth, the little house on the hill with its turf roof and low walls, lying next to his brothers and sisters in the night, breathing in the smell of their hair, listening to the push and pull of their breath. The spirits had called him and he had given up that life without regret but here it seemed precious again. No hearth, no home. *Just this black water.*

A dry terror seized his throat, a terror not of death but of the ordeal that would precede it.

No point delaying. He put a foot into the water. It was cold but he would get used to that. He had endured worse and knew he could survive a long time in there. The waters of this land were cold but nothing compared to the ones of his northern home.

He propped the torch against a rock, swallowed as if gulping down his fear and offered a prayer to his spirits.

> 'You that roar in the mountain winds
> You that sparkle in the waters
> Spirits of sunlight and moonlight
> Find your servant in this darkness.'

The prayer gave scant reassurance. The realm he was moving in was not governed by the spirits of rock and stream. This was the realm of the dark god Odin, the magical, the mad.

He threw off the loincloth the Greeks had put on him, wishing he still had the pelt that had been torn from him in the emperor's tent. He would have been more a wolf in that, an animal that did not feel the creeping dread in that place.

He walked forward into the pool, fighting down an urge to gasp as the water came up to his thighs. The torch stretched its shadows over his head as he went. The pillars seemed a city themselves, stretching out to the limit of the light.

Each pillar had at its top a carving of a mythological beast, things of bursting eyes and ravening mouths. Reflected in the torchlight, they loomed below him like monsters from a dream.

Elifr moved forward on instinct, not sure what to do. The

pillars went on and on. Tear shapes were carved into some of them, ruder than the carvings at the tops. A strong sense of their meaning came to him. People had died here, lots of them, constructing this place. The tears were the only record of the slaves who had worked to build it.

The ceiling dipped to meet the pool and he could go no further. Carved eyes, hundreds of them, watched him from the rock there. The water was colder. He walked the width of the wall. Yes, colder streams flowed in at two places. He felt beneath the water. There were inlets in the wall. Big enough to swim through? What to do?

Again, one of those voices from the dark of his mind: *Magic is a puzzle, not a recipe.*

He trembled with the cold. He did not have long. He needed to act.

Elifr could see nothing beyond twenty paces back in to the cave, the limit of his torchlight. This place hated the light. And light was no use down there where he needed to go. *Then what? Only faith. Only belief in the purpose.*

He put out his hands. Childish stories came into his head, of the trolls and monsters who were said to lurk in dark pools such as these. His mother had sung a rhyme to her children in the bleak winter nights.

> *Born before, of spirits obscure,*
> *Where the mountain stream plunges into the dark*
> *The mere stands, there you will the marvel foul behold*
> *The heath stepper, fen dweller, war creature*
> *His talons ungentle, his teeth the heroes' bane.*

At the time he'd been frightened, then later thought it a tale to warn children away from dark waters. Now it seemed to stir something inside him, a fear in his bones that sparked imaginings of bloody claws reaching out to grab him from the unseen depths of the pool. The fear comforted him. It was familiar. In his rituals on the mountainside the greatest terror had always led to the greatest insights, to an awakening of the senses and the mind of a wolf. *Is there anything beyond this wall?* He had to know what would be asked of him. A little sacrifice, a little bravery to prepare the way for the great sacrifice to come. This first sacrifice didn't seem small, though.

He had to do it, had to risk it. This was the place that had been revealed to him. The torch guttered and went out. Now the dark was absolute and his mind made up. He cast away the useless brand, gulped in three quick breaths of air and kicked down to the smaller of the two inlets, pushing himself into the blind black waters.

The cold gripped him, his breath left him and he returned gasping to the surface. He tried again and again, but with the same result. He knew this was the way – he had learned that in his visions – but he could not go on, not with his human powers. To continue he would need to summon a wolf inside him, as he had summoned one when he freed himself from the guards. But for that he would need an enemy, a threat to trigger his fury. He would need to draw the guards after him. The wolfman sniffed the air, gaining his bearings in the darkness. Then he started back, up towards the Numera.

15 An Ambush

Azémar, Mauger and Snake in the Eye made their way down the steps of Hagia Sophia.

'Here's someone we can ask,' said Snake in the Eye. He spoke in Norse, his accent thick, and Azémar felt at a disadvantage. He only knew the language through his parents. He wasn't as fluent as the boy or as Mauger, who spoke it as natives.

Snake in the Eye pointed out a monk in dark robes and full beard who hurried up the stairs. From somewhere a lament sounded: 'Having foolishly abandoned thy paternal glory, I squandered on vices the wealth which thou gavest me. Wherefore, I cry unto thee with the voice of the prodigal: I have sinned before thee, O compassionate father. Receive me as one repentant, and make me as one of thy hired servants.' The people were asking forgiveness for their sins, convinced the terrible sky was a punishment from God.

'Fellow,' Snake in the Eye called to the monk in Greek.

The monk stopped and his eyes darted from man to man. He clearly wanted to be away.

'Do not give my friend the answer he seeks,' said Azémar in Greek. 'No good will come of it for any of us.'

Snake in the Eye ignored him. 'Where might we find the scholars of this town?'

'You are not the sort for scholarship,' said the monk. 'Now let me on my way.'

'It would be a convenience to you to die so near to the house of your god,' said Snake in the Eye, touching the handle of his sword. 'I ask a simple question and seek no money or food or anything else it can pain you to part with. Be civil, and we will remain so.'

The monk glanced about him. No one around, not even a beggar.

'Try the Magnaura,' he said, 'for the good it will do you.'

He moved around them and all but ran up the steps to the great church.

'Do not reveal this to my companion,' said Azémar, still in Greek. 'I will pay you to keep this secret.'

'I don't seek pay,' said Snake in the Eye, in Norse, 'but adventure and sword work.'

Azémar looked to the ground. Why did he have the luck to meet an earnest idiot like this?

'Where do we have to go?' said Mauger.

'The Magnaura. I have no idea where that is, but it won't take us a moment to find out. Look, here comes a man of the palace now.'

Down the street came a man in a scribe's white tunic.

Mauger glanced at Azémar and smiled.

'It seems our work here might be shorter than we thought, scholar,' he said.

The scribe directed them where they needed to go, and two hundred paces later they came to the door to the compound of the Magnaura.

'Do we go in?' said Azémar. He really couldn't think what to do if Mauger saw Loys. Throw himself in front of the knight's sword, he supposed. But he knew what Mauger was capable of. Azémar would only be putting off the inevitable.

'We watch,' said Mauger.

'Why?'

'Because I need to know this place, its weaknesses and its strengths, before deciding on my course of action. I intend to survive my encounter with your friend, and it seems unlikely I will do that if I act too rashly. The soldiers of this land are no fools and there are enough of them. When I strike it must be quickly and in secret.'

'I would take a thousand men,' said Snake in the Eye.

Mauger laughed. 'Perhaps, but we who have seen more wars cannot be so confident.'

Azémar waited with the two men, not knowing what to do. The sun laboured under the heavy clouds, the light was weak and he was cold. They had been there a long time when he noticed men gathering around them. The weather had kept people indoors but now there was a crowd outside the Magnaura – twenty men at least behind them, in front of them the same number. This was very odd because the streets were otherwise almost deserted.

'Hello, lads. A word, please.'

A short bald man in pale blue robes spoke. He took Azémar by the arm. Another man tried to grab Mauger but the warrior threw him down, and was running almost as he struck the ground.

Azémar tried to shake free, but a third man had his other arm. Men went streaming after Mauger, but the knight had a good start on them and ducked into an alleyway.

'What is this?' said Azémar.

'We just need to talk.'

'And you are?'

'Forty strong,' said the man, 'and you are one, so I will ask the questions if you don't mind.'

Snake in the Eye had not been approached. 'Is he a spy?' said Azémar.

The man drove a solid punch into Azémar's guts. The scholar retched, his knees wobbled and he had to sit down on the ground.

'I am the emperor's man,' said Snake in the Eye, 'and no spy. These men are not my equals so would not dare touch me.'

One of the mob, a heavy man who wore a smith's apron, pointed at Snake in the Eye. 'You're his favourite for now. But when that changes, you'll get a visit from us, don't you worry.'

Snake in the Eye was silent, just stood looking up towards Hagia Sophia as if nothing was happening.

'With us,' said the bald man. The mob swept Azémar through the backstreets leading him on at the trot up the hill away from the cathedral.

'Where are we going?'

Another meaty blow struck him in the belly, staggering him sideways as he ran.

'Save your energy for answering questions, sorcerer,' said the man who had hit him, 'because you are going to need it.'

16 The Lady Styliane

Loys had been honoured to be given his own chamber with access to a bath and a slave to tend him. In the salon of the Lady Styliane, however, he felt as though he had been short-changed.

The room was immense and decorated like a vine grove – creepers in mosaics rising to the ceiling, great pendulous bunches rendered vivid in purple and red. Slaves were everywhere, bringing food on silver plates, decanters of wine, parchments and books to courtiers on couches and chairs. One slave carried a little brush with which he swept the seat of anyone who rose and bowed their way into the lady's presence.

The lady herself was striking. She was in her early twenties, quite small and dark, impeccably dressed in light yellow silk with a permanent marionette's smile on her face. Beatrice had described her as beautiful, and she was certainly that with her clear complexion and vivid green eyes.

Loys sat next to Beatrice on a couch, where they were kept waiting interminably while the lady received her guests, who seemed mainly to comprise rich merchants, ladies of the court and various bureaucrats – all in couples. He sat self-consciously still, not quite knowing how to hold himself but glad he had bathed and dressed in fine robes. Here it was safer to be seen as an official than as a distinct person, particularly a foreigner. The court seemed to understand officials. It understood foreigners too – once it had incorporated them, given them their shoes of blue, red or gold and marked them as its own.

They had watched eight separate audiences when the doors opened and a new person was announced: 'Logothetes Isais, master of the public post, and his wife the Lady Eudocia.' Loys fought to control his surprise. It was the man who had accosted him in the corridor, the one who had offered him a way out of the city. Master of the public post? The postal service doubled as the emperor's intelligence-gathering agency. So this was the head of the Office of Barbarians, the chief spy of the empire, standing so close he could touch him.

Isais bowed deeply, though he couldn't help a glance towards Loys. Loys wondered if Isais was here for his benefit or if he was here for Isais'. His feet shifted on the carpet. He wanted to get out of there.

The lady spoke to Isais and his wife briefly and waved them away. Then she took a little water poured from a golden jug into a fine glass beaker as Isais backed out of the room. If Loys had had any illusions about the power of the woman he was about to meet, he had none now.

They had waited so long that the call, when it came, took Loys by surprise. 'The scholar Loys of the Lord Chamberlain's Office and his wife the Lady Beatrice of Normandy.' Loys noted a slight hesitancy over 'Lady', as if nowhere in the servant's experience had that ever been linked to 'scholar' before. He got to his feet and bowed deeply, all flustered. Beatrice rose effortlessly behind him.

'You bow in front of her,' whispered Beatrice.

Loys' legs seemed made of stone and he approached the lady like a country clot before a king, which was not far from the truth. When he came level with her couch he bowed again, bending his knees and tipping forward at the waist. Beatrice, he noted, did not bow but merely inclined her head.

'Welcome,' said Styliane. 'Please, lady, allow your husband to sit beside me. I have heard so very much about him that I'm fascinated to meet him.'

Beatrice sat down, leaving space for Loys on the couch, but her husband still stood.

'Come, don't look as if I've asked you to sit on an ants' nest. The rules of plebeian society do not apply to the elite. A man can sit next to a lady without being consumed by lust and a lady can sit next to a man without being a whore. Sit.' She patted the couch next to her.

Loys sat down by degrees, lowering himself slowly as if he expected a servant to run him through for his presumption at any moment.

'There you are,' said Styliane. 'Still alive and no devils leaping out to punish you.'

'No, lady.'

She raised a finger, and a slave brought them glasses of wine on a silver plate. Beatrice took hers elegantly, but when Loys picked up his glass, his hand shook and he rested it on his lap to steady it.

'Devils are your speciality, are they not?'

'Lady?'

'The chamberlain has set you to investigate them.' Around the room people withdrew, the servants melting away, the remaining people on the couches following them.

'I ...' The chamberlain had given him no indication his mission was secret but Loys had no idea how much he was allowed to reveal.

'It concerns the emperor's affliction, does it not?'

'Those matters are above my station, lady.'

She waved her hand. 'I give you permission to speak freely. No one can hear us here.' It was true: the room was now empty, though a servant stood directly behind him.

'The servants—'

'Are mutes and illiterate. And they are stupid. I am always served by stupid men; I find them more reliable than the intelligent variety.'

There was a long silence and Loys noticed a slight fading of the lady's smile.

'Do not make me ask you again, scholar. Perhaps I should ask your pretty wife. She seems amenable to frank conversation. You have said much, haven't you, lady, but I think your Norman court is more open than is wise or safe here.'

Beatrice said nothing, just sipped at her wine and smiled. If she was intimidated, she didn't show it. The threat to Beatrice brought a sharp pain to Loys' stomach.

He kept his voice pleasant enough. 'If you have spoken to my wife then you have no need of me.'

'Your wife told me you were an intelligent man. You don't speak like one.'

'I am clever enough to stay out of politics.' Loys was surprised at his sudden sharpness.

The lady's smile brightened again.

'You stand up for yourself. I like that. I didn't bring you here to quiz you, anyway. The problem with this city is there is sometimes too much information. I confess I don't know what to make of half of it. Your friends are interesting fellows.'

She spoke the last sentence almost as a throwaway but, however light her manner, this woman said nothing without calculation.

'I have no friends here.'

The lady took a sip of her water.

'Really?' She turned to her servant. 'That fellow we took today by the Magnaura. He is not a friend of dear Loys here. So he is lying. He will be punished for that.'

Styliane put her hand on the rear of the couch, almost scandalously close to Loys' back. He supressed the impulse to writhe away. She went on, 'I would be your friend. If you tell me a little of your endeavours then I may be able to help you. My husband took a great interest in matters of magic and divination, though it didn't enable him to predict his death by poison. He was a student of the old religion of this city, that of Hecate – in order to combat the pagan menace, naturally. I have a little knowledge in that area myself. But then, what can my knowledge avail you? Your master the chamberlain knows all about these things. After all, his mother was a witch.'

Loys actually felt his jaw drop.

'Our mother was a soothsayer, a disciple of the dark lady. Did he not tell you? Don't look so surprised. Constantinople has always been open to men of ability, no matter how low their birth – though very few from where he and I began. The chamberlain is a remarkable man to rise so high. He was not always so favoured. He's done his time in the Numera, believe me.'

Loys did not respond to this. The mention of soothsayers made him recall Isais' threat to the street magicians.

'I would ask a favour, lady.'

'You who have given so little?'

'Logothetes Isais has mentioned he intends to purge the fortune tellers and amulet sellers. I would ask you to prevent that from happening.'

'I am a noble lady, not a bureaucrat – how can I help?'

Loys recalled the way Styliane had dismissed Isais with a wave of her hand. She could act if she wanted, he knew.

'I thought you might ...' he searched for the right words '... speak to someone.'

'Why not ask your master my brother? Although perhaps not. He has little tolerance for magicians.'

'Even though his mother was a soothsayer?'

'Some say because. Our mother died, you know. Don't pay attention to any of the silly rumours surrounding that; she died as a result of her devil worship. Seeking oracles in the earth, so they say. The rumours concerning my brother's role in it are just that. More rubbish from magicians and witches. No one wise pays attention to them. Would you like more wine? Come, you must drink. You're hardly sipping.'

Loys took a swig of wine. He needed to – his mouth had become very dry.

'My brother is plagued by rumours. His opposition to any investigation has always been on the grounds it would give credence to silly market talk.'

Loys swallowed. So the chamberlain had been forced into commissioning him. Right.

'What talk?'

'The sort that attends any man who rises quickly. People can't believe a man rises on talent. There must always be someone to suggest something untoward. Half of this stuff is spread by his enemies and the other half by idiots. He and the emperor came up together to each other's mutual benefit. The chamberlain is a holy and devout man. It's what everyone says.'

'I see.'

'In fact, it might be argued they overthrew a witch to obtain power. You know our emperor's dear mother Theophano seemed to have secured the throne through her lover the former emperor John. And then by God's grace – it must have been God, who else could it have been? – John took ill suddenly and died.'

She smiled directly at Loys and took a sip of her water.

'It was huge good fortune that the death brought a bitter, bitter dispute between the chamberlain and Basileios and Emperor John to an end. There is no doubt the death was natural. Why, none at all! People have said all sorts of treason – that Basileios and the chamberlain consorted with demons and are now paying the price. Rot, of course.'

The lady smiled again.

'So I expect you have been told to direct your attentions to the foreigners.'

'Yes.'

'An excellent plan. It must be they who have caused all this fuss. Though they weren't here at the start of Basileios' illness. I am confident you'll work out how they conjured something up five years before they got here. There are many powerful men in the palace who will sleep safer once blame has been apportioned.'

'Yes.' Loys felt like a puppet who had until that moment been under the illusion that he moved of his own accord but who had finally worked out what the strings were for.

The lady leaned forward and said very quietly, 'Because if the sky and the comet and the death of the rebel and the emperor's lamentable condition were shown to be the work of men in this palace ... Well, imagine what their enemies would pay for such information. Imagine the privileges and position the scholar who presented such evidence would accrue.'

Loys was struck dumb. He had no idea of how to deal with this, no notion of how to survive caught between this woman and the chamberlain.

Beatrice looked at Styliane but past her, conspicuously making no effort to catch what the lady was saying to her husband.

'Be careful,' said Styliane in a low voice. 'Many eyes are on you but you have a powerful protector in me. The time will come soon, scholar, when you will need to choose your friends from your enemies. Already people talk about the rightness of a lady being married to a scholar. Can her father have been happy with that marriage? Choose well and wisely.'

Loys bowed his head.

Styliane sat back. 'Now, my dears, I have detained you long enough. Please, Lady Beatrice, you must attend me next week. I have a Bible study group and it's quite the place to catch up on court gossip.'

Beatrice thanked the lady. The scholar stood, not knowing what to do with his glass. Beatrice took it from him and put it on a little table. She led him away. A eunuch opened the door and the couple went through. Their servant was waiting outside.

Loys could see no immediate way of handling the competing pressures he was under. Instead he concentrated on his discomfort in such high company. He didn't want to show Beatrice he was concerned by the clear threat to him.

'I'm sorry I embarrassed you in there,' he said in Norman, 'I'm not used to court niceties.'

'You didn't embarrass me.' Beatrice used their native language too. 'This place has ridiculous protocols. They're only there to embarrass you – that's why they exist.'

'I don't understand.'

'They make insiders feel more like insiders and outsiders feel more like outsiders. It's a very elaborate way of looking down their noses. And listen to her with her veiled threats and clunking great hints. That was insupportable behaviour, Loys, I'm surprised she dared be so bold.'

'We are in danger,' he said.

'A courtier is always in danger,' said Beatrice. 'It's the price of opportunity. Escort us back to our room,' she said to their eunuch, returning to Greek.

They made their way back through the corridors, stopping to exchange the formal greetings and replies required by the guards at each door. Loys was weary with it all. Even to a former monk whose life had been ruled by ritual, the demands of the Byzantine court seemed heavy and unnecessary.

They arrived at their room and went within. Loys immediately noticed all his papers and books were gone.

'Did you clean this chamber?' he asked the servant.

'No, sir.' The man didn't seem quite sorry enough about the burglary for Loys' tastes. He was about to shout at him, to ask him how this had been allowed to happen but, as he began to speak, he lost the thread of what he was saying and instead concentrated on seeing what had been stolen.

'Is anything else missing?' said Loys. Beatrice went to the small chest she kept by the bed. The lock had been prised apart.

'My rings are still here,' she said.

Loys leaned for support on the wall. Whoever had taken his papers had not even paid him the courtesy of pretending it was a robbery. Beatrice sat quiet and thoughtful on the bed. Loys wondered what her father would do in a situation like this. He would seize the initiative. But how? He had an idea.

'We have been buffeted by hostile winds for long enough. It's about time we created a storm of our own.'

'What will you do?'

'I am the chamberlain's man, ordered to perform an investigation,' said Loys, 'so I will investigate and I will accuse, and we will see what fear brings us that pleasantness did not.'

17 The Vala

Bollason sat by the sea's edge, watching the dark horizon. Behind him stretched the tents of his army, their pennants of ravens and wolves snapping in the breeze. The light was like nothing he had ever seen, the black ocean shining, the sky iron and the air silver-blue.

The dogs of the camp seemed restless, barking and grumbling at the falling sleet. Two gulls tumbled and brawled over the ocean, crying and screaming as if one said it was day and the other night. Nearby a child howled and would not be comforted.

'Could this be it, Vala?'

'Don't call me that.'

The woman beside him was not young but she was very beautiful in the weak blue light.

'It's true. I know no one wiser than you.'

'I have no art, Bolli. Your mother had the runes in her heart, not me.'

'And yet you saw.'

'With borrowed eyes. Yes, I saw.'

'This could be the end time, happening here.'

'I don't know, Bolli.'

When she turned to him, she revealed an ugly scar covering most of the right side of her face. It was a burn; no knife or sword destroyed flesh like that.

'If the god dies here, then what?'

She waved her hand, a gesture between exasperation and dismissal. 'What always happens. Death, agony, rebirth. Always.'

'Elifr has tried to stop it.'

'Elifr is a man. He acts first and thinks later,' she said.

'He is seeking to protect you.'

'I cannot be protected,' she said. 'Elifr has a place in the schemes of the gods, and though he moves to frustrate them, he will only bring destruction on himself and those he seeks to keep from harm.'

'I could protect you, if you'd let me.'

'I am not the one who needs protection. This is where Odin earned wisdom. This is where he went mad. If he returns here then the city will fall.'

'Suits me,' said Bollason. 'There'll be riches for us all then.'

'It must stop, Bolli. I cannot go on.'

'Go on with what?'

'Losing my sons for ever. Putting them away, hiding them to keep them from the mad god's gaze.'

'Your sons are dead, Vala.'

The woman looked out to sea.

'I have lived too long,' she said. 'The gods think they bless me but I carry a heavy curse.'

'They do bless you. You are the same today as when I first remember you.'

'In my appearance, perhaps,' she said, 'but I'm tired. I need to do this.'

'You're sure the well is where you say?'

'We saw as much.'

'Then let me bribe us into this prison and do your work.'

She shook her head. 'The ritual is long and could bring notice. We need to take control of that place Bolli.'

'You talk of ritual but you say you have no art.'

'I have art enough for what I need to do.' She wouldn't tell him what would be required of her because he would try to stop her, as the wolfman was trying to stop her. Death – the god's old price.

Bollason leaned forward and looked up to the black skies. 'Your answer will be there?'

'It is as your mother showed me. We are near to the end, Bolli. It will just take a little courage.'

'If that is all it took then I could ask any of my men to do it. I would do it.'

'But you cannot.'

'No.'

'Only me.'

'Could my mother have done this?'

'That was a lore-wise woman. But no. This was not her destiny. It is mine, so she told me when ...'

The woman's voice faltered.

'She died, Vala. I have been a warrior these fifteen years. I am not so tender as you think.'

She smiled and touched his shoulder. 'I knew you when you were at your mother's breast. Your heart is not as hard as you want people to believe.'

'It is hard enough.'

'But you follow me out of tenderness.'

'Yes. And by my mother's command.'

'And if your mother had not commanded it?'

'I would still follow you, Saitada.' He sat quiet for a while and then: 'How will you know you are at the place? If we can take command of the prison and you go down into the earth, how will you recognise the well when you see it?'

'I will know, I'm sure.'

Bollason said under his breath, 'Mimir's Well. Odin gave his eye for lore in those waters.'

'And the fates sit there spinning the fates of men.'

'That well is called Urtharbrunnr.'

'They are the same. And different. One magic well has many manifestations, just as the gods themselves take many bodies in the form of men.'

'So Odin gave his eye. What will you give?'

'More than that. I am a woman, not a god; the waters will want more from me.'

'Will you survive?' he said.

'My destiny is here. The destiny of the gods is here. I have my part to play.'

'In death?'

'Consider the sky, Bolli. Odin's magic is unfolding. He will come here to die on the teeth of the wolf so the fates may spare him in the realm of the gods. He must not be allowed to do that. He must die in the realm of the gods. The mad reign of Odin must end. It's as your mother saw.'

'And it's the girl we will find at the palace who must die?'

'If it was that simple Elifr could have killed her. I don't know what needs to happen to her. We need to bring her to the waters.'

She watched the dark sea and recalled the rhyme that had been born in her mind when the old vala had died. She said the rhyme. She didn't want to burden Bollason with it but she needed to speak her fears to someone. And besides, he had a right to know what was happening.

'In the east did the old one sit
She bred the bad brood of Fenrir
One of these, in a wolf's fell guise,
Will soon steal the sun from the sky
Now he feeds full on dead men's flesh
And the sky is reddened with gore
Dark grows the sun and in summer
Come weather woe, would you know more?'

'So said my mother,' said Bollason. 'Is the prophecy coming true?'

'Fimbulwinter,' said the woman, 'when the summer departs and great harm comes to men. This is the sign the death of the gods approaches. This is the sign Ragnarok is here. Look – snow in summer, unexplained deaths on the battlefield.'

'So Odin is riding to meet his fate at the teeth of the wolf?'

'Yes. In this world. So he might live in his own. We will suffer; the world will suffer, but he will live.'

'If the god is on his way to death then what can stop him?'

Saitada glanced at Bollason and he was a little boy again,

caught acting foolishly. No one could tame him when he was a child, not with beating, not with shouting, not with denying him dinner or sending him to bed. Saitada, though, could silence him with just a look, leave him creeping in shame from the scene of his naughtiness.

He had that feeling now, stupid, desperate to please her but despairing of how it might be done. He'd loved her since he was a child, first as an aunt, later with all the ardour he should have held for women of his age. He hadn't wanted them. He had travelled the world, become a great war leader, killed many men in battle, forged his destiny with sword and spear. But when he returned home and looked into her eyes he felt unmanned and unworthy of her. Her spirit was greater than his, and in front of her he was only ever a child.

Saitada threw a pebble down towards the ocean. She remembered the raw dawn, the standing stones stark against a sky of slate. The prophetess had gone seeking an explanation for Saitada's tormented dreams that had come upon her when her husband died.

Saitada had watched him go, wasting to nothing in his bed, he who had sailed the world and brought the gold he had won with axe and shield back to their hearth. The disease took him, her sons too.

The night the third boy died Saitada had wept by his bed until not sleep but a sensation of falling had come to her. She heard names shouted through the darkness, strange but with an echo of familiarity: Vali, Feileg, Jehan, Aelis and her own. Visions sparked in her mind – a leering smith, naked from the waist down, the hot iron with which she had spited her beauty and ruined her face so he would look on her with pleasure no more. She saw a white-haired warrior, his sword a talon of fire; she saw a demented child; and she saw the god, the one who had come to her three times now. The bright, beautiful, burning god who came to her as a wolf, or who stepped from the corpse of a princess, his skin pale in the moonlight, or who had found her adrift at sea and rescued her in a boat made of dead men's nails and lain with her on a silver beach under the morning star.

Three times he had given her sons that she had tried to hide from the notice of the All Father. Twice she had failed. This time she would protect them – her boys, the twins, the ones she kept secret from her husband and kin, the ones she had hidden in the hills and over the sea.

She'd hoped to make a life away from the notice and schemes of the gods, had gone back to the land of the white-haired king, raised a family and tried to forget. But he wouldn't let her rest – him, her lover, the father of the twins.

After that night when she had buried her last son by the farmer she had never slept well again. Always in her sleep strange voices spoke half-remembered names. In her dreams she went to a cave, a low and dark place where something was pinioned and tied, something that seethed and shook, something that longed to be free. An ancient torment was awaking inside her.

Bolli's mother, the vala, the prophetess, had said she might help free her from her nightmares. They'd gone to the standing stones, where the iron clouds cast a grey veil of rain upon the hills to perform the ritual.

Saitada had helped the old woman, lit the fire and sprinkled on the herbs, kept her awake through nine days and nights on that storm-blown hill. The visions came and they had killed her.

As the sorceress died Saitada had seen too – the magic well, the font of all knowledge, a comet rising above it in the east. She told Bollason his men would win fortune in Kiev and sailed with them there, where they had sold their services to the prince. She spent ten years in the hills, while Bollason fought his wars. With her goats, her staff and her cloak she was happy in her solitude.

She sat by the streams and in the mouths of caves, her mind floating on the vast emptiness of the evening. She watched shooting stars like swift fish in the vast purple ocean of the night, watched the low sun of dusk ignite the storm clouds, turning them to lumbering dragons with bellies of fire, and saw the dawn make its diamonds from the snows. In the winter she took to a cabin and, in solitude and privation, looked for answers. The east, always the east drew her eyes. She had no fire herbs, she had no training or guide to help her. She proceeded by instinct, starving and thirsting the visions from herself, sitting in the cold, wakeful for days until the truth came to her. She needed to know how to find the well, to take her wisdom to the next stage.

The wolfman found her in the eighth year, sent, he said, by dreams. He had seen her in a high place, overlooking the land. She was important to the gods, important to him too. She'd asked him if he was a god and he said he was not, just a man who had dreamed her. She told him she had dreamed him too, every day since she had given him up to the family in the hills. She had dreamed him because she was his mother.

She held him and called him son but wept because in her visions she sensed what the gods intended for him.

In her dreams she was always in that cave, where the thing she could not see shivered and groaned in its bonds. She had a role to play. Was she waiting for something? For someone? With the wolfman at her side no revelation would come.

They shared their rituals, their starvations and thirsts. And then she had seen more than she had ever seen when alone: the city of the moon and star and, under the moon and star, the well, its silver waters glimmering beneath the star-bright sky.

The words had come to her and never left her since.

In Mimir's well I gave my eye for lore
And on the storm-blown tree
I hung for nights full nine
Wounded by the spear, offered I was
To Odin, myself to myself
I took up the runes

Shrieking I took them
And from there did I fall back.

She knew what she saw – the well that sat beneath the world
tree and whose waters impart all wisdom to those who pay the
price to drink from them – the well that is every magical well
in every world, where the fates sit, where Odin gave his eye
for lore. The wolfman perhaps saw even more. He ran from her
vowing to save her, though she begged him not to go.

'You will only damn yourself,' she said.

But he was gone and she was in the wilderness, weeping for
his loss. In her misery she remembered – years before, lifetimes
before, how her son, in the form of a wolf, had hungered for
a woman and how that woman had led him to kill the hanged
god. Saitada had performed her role in a ritual set out by a god
to draw his killer to him.

She had welcomed the wolf then. Not now. She thought she
had revenged herself on the god for taking her children. No.
She had done his bidding without knowing it – killed him on
earth so he might live on in his heaven.

As Elifr had gone from her, her despair had deepened,
opening doors to knowledge in her mind. She had seen the
howling rune, the slinking and crawling rune, the rune of the
wolf, of the trap and the storm. That was the fetter that held
down the wolf god, prevented him from rising and slaying the
old deceiver Odin. It lived within a woman, always within a
woman. She had seen her before when she lived before. Saitada
wept to know how her sons had been drawn on by love. That
couldn't be allowed to happen again. The rune would have
to be dug out of the woman who carried it. By death? Very
likely. But only the waters could tell her, so the woman who
bore the rune inside her would have to be brought to the well.

She had gone into Kiev and Bollason had welcomed her.

'At the moon and the star is our fortune,' she had said.

A day later the Prince of Kiev had offered the Varangians to
the Emperor of Byzantium and she was on her way down the

Dneiper with six thousand men. They would take possession of the Numera when they had worked out the lie of the land. There would be a battle, and it was fitting men should spill blood to oppose the will of the gods, a sacrifice and a statement of will.

'I do not pretend to understand this,' said Bollason.

'There is no understanding it,' said Saitada, 'there is only the water. Down there in the earth, where Odin went. We find the girl and we take her there.'

'How will you recognise her?'

'I have seen her before.'

'And what of Elifr?'

'He must be opposed. I know what is required of me in there, and he will also oppose me. He means me to live.'

'Don't you mean to live?'

'I hope to live. But above all I mean to play my part. That is all I am required to do.'

'If we find the wolfman, I will kill him. It will strengthen your purpose. You cannot go forward to fight with gods while you have ties to bind you in this realm.'

She shook her head. 'If anyone is to kill him, it is me.'

'Why?'

'You asked what I could give more than my eye. I can give him.'

'Can you do it?'

'I don't know.'

'Don't shirk from your purpose through too soft a heart.'

'I won't. But everything must be done according to what I find in the well. There is one clear way forward and around it – thorns and briars.'

'I would kill him.'

Her face became stern. 'From boyish jealousy that he has more of my affections than you do. He is my son; you cannot think I would love you more. When I told you there was fortune in the east, you took on the enterprise like a man. See it through as one.'

126

'My courage is fine. For myself I will face a thousand enemies. But for you, as you face this magic, I am a coward. I fear for you and I confess I am fond enough of you.'

Saitada smiled.

'Stem what tender feelings you have. They are a snare to you. I cannot be loved, Bolli. The dead god's shadow is on me. Don't let it fall on you too.'

'My mother gave her life for you. I am ready to do the same.'

'Then give it well. Do not throw it away through too soft a heart.'

The man laughed. 'You would have made a fine wife. You are a warrior, Saitada, though your sword is your tongue and your spear your beauty.'

'I am old, Bolli.'

'And finer than a girl. You are beautiful.'

'I am death to you, and any man who gives himself to me.'

'It's fifteen years since I first killed a man in battle, and I have sent many to the All Father's halls in that time. Odin is impatient for my company at the mead bench, I feel it. Warriors know when their time is upon them. So did my father. One day soon I must die – I can't be lucky for ever. I will give up my life for you. It is no great thing.'

The woman swallowed and stood.

'It is,' she said, 'but I think it leads to peace.'

'You would find peace with me. I have treasures many and gold enough to please any woman. Marry me, Saitada, for I will place an otter's ransom at your feet.'

Saitada smiled at Bollason's attempt to use fine language. She thought of the myth in which the god Loki kills an otter who is not an otter but a man in that form. The man's father captures Loki and makes him swear to pay weregild for his son's death. Loki steals a ring from a dwarf, but the dwarf curses the ring and it brings only misery to the mortals when Loki passes it on.

'I am the otter's ransom, Bolli. I am the cursed gift. The fates have wed me to the gods not men.'

'Then divorce them. It can be done with a word.'

'No word I know how to speak.' She reached to touch his hair. 'Who knows, I may find it in the well.'

'When will you go to the water?'

'When can you get me in?'

'My men are ready. I have deals to do first, but I think in two or three days we should take this place.'

'Deals?'

'With the emperor. I have sent messengers. His troops are not up to the job – they're losing control. Even now people are fleeing. We're working on him to let us replace his bodyguard. Then the city is ours.'

'The Greek guard will resist.'

Bollason tapped his sword. 'I said I was ready to die for you.'

'Just get me in to the building that sits in the shadow of the dome. Your death is not required. We need to hold that place until the time is right.'

'When will the time be right?'

'When I have summoned the courage.'

'Then it will not be long, Vala.'

The woman smiled at him. 'No, it will not be long.'

18 A Wolf

Azémar tested the bonds behind his back. They were firm, and tight enough to render his fingers numb. He was in some sort of cellar, he thought. It was very dark, though a weak light came through the floorboards that made up its ceiling.

No one had given him any explanation of why he was there or who had taken him.

Then, when the sickly light of the day had faded and the cellar dropped into complete darkness, he heard footsteps. Azémar mentally crossed himself and prayed for deliverance. He knew he had not fallen into the hands of common robbers because he – in his monk's habit and tonsure – clearly had nothing to steal. Kidnappers then? It wasn't unheard of for monks to be ransomed back to their monasteries, but he was so far from home that it could take years for a messenger to reach the abbey at Rouen. And Lord Richard certainly wouldn't pay for his release, not after failing in his mission.

His captors had mentioned sorcery. Perhaps they were just superstitious men seeking to blame foreigners for the strange weather that had afflicted their city. In that case he gave himself no hope at all. They'd kill him just in case he was guilty.

The door opened and light reached out in a sharp triangle across the wall. Azémar came out of his slump and straightened his back. Footsteps on the stairs: two people descended, the taller one behind with a candle. He made out a small figure in a cowled robe attended by the much larger man, who was heavily built, wore a whip at his belt and carried a stool in addition to the candle. The man set the stool on the floor in front of Azémar and the person in the cowl sat down. It was a woman, small and richly dressed, her robe sparkling with gold thread, the elegant hands adorned with glittering rings.

'Why are you here?' The woman spoke in Greek.

'I was captured.'

'Why are you here in Constantinople?'

Azémar swallowed. In his fear he'd imagined the woman was asking him what he was doing tied up in a house, almost that she might let him go.

'I'm looking for a friend.'

'If you don't reveal the whole truth of your purpose here with your next breath I'll have you beaten,' she said. Her voice was neutral, pleasant almost, but Azémar did not want to test her threat.

'I am here to find the scholar Loys. I was sent by the father of his wife.'

The lady raised her finger and the man hit Azémar across the face with his whip.

A bolt of pain went right through him from his cheek to his boots and he cried out.

'Sent for what? Don't make me ask questions of you, monk; volunteer all that you know.'

Azémar saw no reason for any concealment that might bring death closer or make it more painful. He was scared but not as scared as he had expected. His mission was finally at an end, he wouldn't be responsible for his friend's death and for that he was glad. Sweat soaked his body and he panted heavily though he had run nowhere.

'I am here to direct an assassin. I was a friend and confidant of the scholar Loys and I have been told by my lord to find him.'

The guard raised his whip.

Azémar gabbled out everything he could think of: 'He has eloped with the Lady Beatrice and her father wants me to bring her back to him. Along with the scholar's head.'

'Why didn't he apply to the emperor to have her sent back, along with the scholar for him to behead at his pleasure?'

'Lord Richard is not a man who enjoys refusal or being in another ruler's debt. Better we kill the scholar here than he has to go cap in hand to the emperor.'

'Your friend the assassin, where is he now?'

'I don't know.'

The lady raised her finger and the man hit Azémar again with the whip, this time across the other cheek. Azémar screamed and lurched forward on the chair in a hopeless bid to break his bonds.

'Until he tells us,' said the lady, and the whip came down on Azémar's back, then the top of his head, across his legs and his head again, flashes of agony lighting up his skin.

'I don't know where he's gone! He ran away! Our lodgings are by the lighthouse gate, but beyond that he could be anywhere!'

The beating stopped. Azémar coughed. He tasted blood. He was sure his nose was broken.

'He killed two of my men,' said the lady.

'I am sorry, lady, but I do not control him! He is a wildman, a northern cousin of our lord. I can hardly talk to him, let alone account for his actions!'

'Is he with the Varangians?'

'No, lady. We're working alone, I swear.'

'You were consorting with the emperor's translator.'

'We met him on the steps. Mauger asked his help in finding Loys, that's all.'

'Again.'

The whip cut into the top of Azemar's head and he blacked out with the pain. When he recovered his senses, the cowled lady sat very near to him.

'Have you anything more to tell us?'

'I'm speaking the truth, I swear.'

'We will find out. I have seen your face before, scholar – know that.'

'I have never left my monastery before this, lady.'

'I have seen you. In places you do not choose to go.'

'I don't understand you.'

'The feeling is mutual.'

She clapped her hands and another man appeared on the

stairs wearing a thick glove and carrying a bucket of hot coals and a small brazier.

'No, lady, no!' Azémar writhed away.

'Put it in front of him.'

They put the bucket close to his face. Its heat was horrible.

'I need a closer look at you,' said the woman. 'I need to know what you are. Your arrival was foreseen.'

'How foreseen?'

'The comet that eats up the sky. It is your sign, I think. The chart was cast that you would be here, and it is too much a coincidence that I recognised you in the church so well.'

'I am a monk, a simple monk.'

'Perhaps. But I think not. I think you are worth the effort of divination. And, as you will see, the effort is very great.'

Another servant brought in a small chest, set it on the floor and opened it. It contained nothing sinister – just powders and small bottles. For a mad moment Azémar thought she had brought out her make-up. One of the servants poured the glowing coals into the brazier.

'The third day,' said the woman, 'not before. At the second bell come in and revive me.'

The two men bowed and left.

The woman took off her robe. Underneath it she wore a shift that exposed her shoulders. Even in the poor light the mass of scars made Azémar gasp.

Now she lifted something from the chest – a sort of tray containing the bottles and the powders. From underneath she took a jewelled knife and then replaced the tray. Azémar wriggled but he was held fast.

She took some powder and sprinkled it onto the coals. A noxious smoke filled the little room. She unstoppered a bottle, anointed Azémar's forehead with the contents and did the same to herself. Then she sat in front of Azémar, almost within touching distance.

She breathed in the smoke and chanted:

'Mistress of corpses. Entrapper. Reveal here. Reveal and

show all the things that have happened, are happening and are to come. Reveal here, corpse mistress, cold lady of the earth's great deeps, she who rises as the moon and whose light shines out over the lands of the dead. Mistress of the dead, lady of the dead, she who stands at the gateway of death, reveal here. Reveal.'

She took the knife in her right hand and cut herself on her left shoulder. Then she put the knife into her left and cut herself on the other shoulder. She showed no sign of pain, though the cuts were quite deep. Blood flowed out over her white shift.

'I have honoured you with my blood, lady of the dead. Blood drinker and blood bather, lady of slaughter and death. Reveal, reveal.'

The lady slumped forward, though she continued to mumble.

Time seemed to lose definition for Azémar. He became very sleepy and despite the discomfort of his bonds began to doze. He woke. The lady remained in the same position, but her wounds no longer bled. How long had he been there? A long time, he thought.

He dozed again and this time he dreamed.

He walked in some strange woods by a river at night. They were beautiful and wet, hung in night colours of silver and grey with a fresh scent of growth and decay that he found intoxicating. He wandered, looking for something. A light shone through the trees and he went towards it. What was it? A little brazier just like the one the lady had thrown the powder onto.

He felt cold so he decided to go to it to warm himself. The lady sat next to the brazier, slumped as she had been slumped in the cellar.

Azémar thought he would go to her, tell her he meant no threat, ask for her protection even.

He put his hand to her shoulder. But when he took it away again, it was covered in blood. He licked at his fingers. The taste was delicious. He put his hand back on her shoulder, smeared on more blood and licked at that too. Then he couldn't stop himself. He bent to the lady and licked at the wound on her shoulder, drinking in its beautiful and strange aroma.

The lady shoved him away, her face contorted in terror. She said one word. 'Wolf!' And then there were other presences about him. Other words. 'He's broken his bonds!'

Someone unseen struck him across the face and he fell back. He was half in the forest, half in the cellar, it seemed. Or rather the forest was a cellar, a cellar containing a forest. The strangeness of those thoughts struck him and he giggled. His arms were pulled behind his back and he was tied again.

He heard a voice in Greek: 'Should I kill him, Lady Styliane?'

The woman panted and coughed. She regained her breath and said, 'That won't be possible. Get him to the Numera.'

19 Descent

The chamberlain had thought himself safe in his gilded apartment, where he lay — a thing of status on a couch, its hands perfumed with frankincense, its face softened with oil, its body wrapped in a silk robe. But the magic sparked inside him, kindling memories as bright as the fire in his hearth; memories that, like the fire, lived and burned.

In his mind he heard voices and saw people. Two figures in a field of boulders on a hill overlooking the great town below. They began to move, the story began to move in his head, little patters of words coming back to him as a walker in the hills feels the rain of dirt that heralds a rockfall.

'I'm afraid, mother.' He saw a young girl peering down into a black space between boulders. He was there, on the hillside, watching — the magic inside him forcing him to see.

'The fear is part of it. Strengthen yourself, Elai. Nothing is won without effort.'

The taller figure, the mother, held a fish-oil lamp in her hand, though the moon was nearly full and shone bright. She sat on a big boulder at the centre of a wide field of them.

Below, two or three summer hours' walk away, the lamps and candles of Constantinople twinkled. The city seemed to hang like two shimmering pools of light separated by the deep and encroaching darkness of the invisible sea that surrounded and divided it.

The woman pointed to the huge church of Hagia Sofia. The moon turned its dome to shining metal and the windows that sat beneath it were white in its light. The woman's thoughts opened to the chamberlain like a flower and he saw how the church reminded her of a squat giant, his helmet pulled low on his forehead, scanning the land for intruders. Well, she thought, it was looking in the wrong place if that's what it was doing. They would approach by one of the unseen roads that ran for miles through the hills and under the city.

'That is where we are going,' she said, 'under there.'

'It's so far,' said Elai. She was thirteen years old but still a little girl in her fear; the chamberlain sensed as he watched her. He shuddered at the intimacy, the depth to which he knew her heart.

'I made the journey when I was your age,' said the mother. 'Your grandmother made it too, and hers before her. The goddess is in there and will grant you her sight. You just need courage. The tunnels are marked and we have enough lamps and oil. The way is straight enough if you know what you're doing. The worst we will encounter is a wasps' nest, and none of those when we've gone fifty paces into the dark.'

'And the dogs of Hecate?'

'The dogs won't come for us. We are the goddess's servants. They wait only for trespassers.'

The girl nodded. 'Is Karas coming?'

Karas. The chamberlain crossed himself. It was his own name, though no one had called him that in fifteen years. What did he share with the child? A body? Yes, in some ways, but grown and altered. A mind? No, not any more. Then what? The deeds. The actions that now unfolded in his magic-stewed brain. In that way alone, he thought, he was the same person as the boy he now saw in his vision, the boy he had been. He was fettered to the past by memories that refused to fade.

He saw the woman turn her eyes to the boy poking about at the bottom of the rocks. Karas was ten years old, brother to Elai. The chamberlain, restless on his couch, wanted to reach out, to take him by the hand and lead him away to his games in the slum.

'I have dreams too,' called Karas. 'I should complete the ritual.'

'Go back and look after Styliane, as I've asked you to do,' said his mother.

'She's right enough with her aunties. Let me come. I want to know the secret of my dreams.' He came climbing towards them over the rocks.

'You're young, Karas, and haven't come fully into the world. You have a memory of what you were before, in lives gone, that's all. When you become a man properly such things will go. Men are made to do and to fight. They can't hold magic inside them.'

The boy sat down next to his mother. 'I would hold magic.'

'Be content with what you have. You have no natural harmony with that –' she jabbed a finger at the moon '– or the tides that surround us.'

'What do my dreams mean, then?'

'What dreams?' The woman had hitherto paid little attention to Karas. The boy was full of mischief and full of questions about things he did not need to know. Magic was a woman's gift, given from mother to daughter. Her son's fascination with it struck her as strange, and not a little effeminate.

'I've told you a thousand times.'

'Tell me again.'

'There is a wolf.'

'Yes.'

'And he's waiting for me.'

'Yes?'

'That's it.'

'That's not much of a dream, is it? You'd build no reputation as a seer based on that, would you?' His mother and his sister glanced at each other and laughed.

'Well, what does it mean? He's in a forest of big strange trees and he's waiting for me.'

'Perhaps it means a wolf is waiting for you,' said Elai, 'in some trees.'

'Don't tease me; no one teases you over your dreams.'

'No.' The girl turned her eyes to the ground. 'But you don't dream as I dream.'

'How do you know?'

Their mother raised her hand.

'Stop quarrelling. Karas, look. I'll interpret your dream if it means so much to you. You know we are descended from the Heruli, who broke the empire in the west. Your know your forefathers were great men of the northern tribes, and one of them, Odoacer, overthrew the emperor Romulus Augustulus.'

'I know this.'

'I'm telling you you know it – and that means if you had any insight at all you'd be able to work it out for yourself. You asked for the interpretation, now hear it out. Odoacer took his wolf warriors to the temples of Rome and made the emperor bow down before him. Perhaps you can hear your ancestors calling to you. They worshipped the wolf. They were wolves, some of them, if you listen to the myths. Perhaps it's you as you were who you see.'

'Well, if I'm getting messages from ghosts, that shows that men can hold magic. I should be able to go with you.'

'You have an echo of magic, and you are as near to it as those lights of the town are to the stars.'

'Please let me come with you.'

The woman pushed her toe into a space between the rocks, almost like a bather testing the water for temperature.

'It does feel right you should come. You might be of use,' she said.

'Come on then, let's go!' The enthusiasm of his childish self filled the chamberlain with dread.

'Listen first. When we reach the appointed place, your sister and I will work a magic to allow us to speak to the goddess. There is normally very little danger but, for a while, we will not be as ourselves and – being in the world of the gods – will not be aware of what happens in this world. You watch over us and make sure neither of us falls into the waters.'

The boy smiled. 'Right. Shall I go first?'

'You'll go last and not yet.'

His mother took some rolled cloth from her pack, along with some twine.

'Tie this around your knees, both of you, and wrap some around your hands. The way is long and you won't make it unless you protect yourself.'

The children followed their mother's example with the cloth. Then they were ready.

The woman peered into the gap between the rocks. Nothing marked it as special or worthy of exploration, but she lowered her pack into it and wriggled in afterwards, careful with the lamp.

'Follow.' She looked out at them, her face a pale mask in the moonlight. She disappeared inside, and the boy and the girl clambered down after her.

'Is there a wasps' nest?' said Elai.

'No,' her mother called back to her, 'so the dangerous part is done. Come on.'

The chamberlain watched in his vision as they crawled down a low tunnel that opened into a little cavern, just tall enough for the woman to stand in if she stooped. It stretched out twenty paces and led into a deeper darkness at its far end. They went towards it, the light of the lamp wobbling on the walls. The rocks were not even and it wasn't easy to make their way on them, so progress was slow.

The passage dropped quite steeply at first but quickly became a long gently sloping tunnel. The children had to bend double and their mother went on her hands and knees. Karas was at the rear. He glanced behind him. The lamp-light cast shadows that seemed to stretch away at one instant and rush back towards him the next, like grasping hands snatching at him. The chamberlain was the boy again, no longer an observer but lost to the story, back there, Karas once more.

All separation dissolved. He was ten years old, imagining himself already a magician, the shadows an enchanted cloak he could pull about him to disappear in a breath. He remembered a story his mother had told him, 'The cloak that was cut from the night.' Perhaps, he thought, he would gain magical insight and take his own shears made of moonbeams to the heavens to bring his mother a fold of darkness to stitch into a cloak of shadows with her needles of starlight. He wasn't scared; he was excited, but his sister was silent and pale. He couldn't understand it. If his mother was correct, then Elai was going to be offered a great gift. Why did she seem so nervous?

They bent and crawled, walked and slithered through the passages for hours. The wall bore marks at points along the way – the moon and a star, the symbol of Hecate, goddess of Byzantium, the old name for Constantinople. The city was now under Christ's sway, but plenty of people still found time for the old gods, particularly in hardship or when in need of insight into the future. These marks, though, had not been made by the common people. Even if they found the entrance to the caves, they would never go within. The marks, in a rough ochre, had been daubed by generations of priestesses who had kept the secrets of the caves and visited them only to find their insight.

'What are these?'

They had stopped to rest and to eat and Karas had found some more marks on the wall – no more than a few rough scratches but clearly made by humans.

'Old symbols of our kin,' said the woman, 'from years before.'

'Made by the wolf warriors?'

'Or people like them.'

'Did they worship the goddess?'

'I don't know, Karas. The goddess has many forms and appears in different ways to different people.'

'How different?'

'She is called Isis, and she is called Hecate. In the north they say she is not a woman at all and call her Odin or Wodanaz or Mercury.'

'How can she be male and female at the same time?'

'A person looks different when you approach them from the back to the way they look when you see them face on. How many more ways of being seen do gods possess?'

'She is a god. She can do what she chooses. That is what makes someone a god,' said Elai. 'They form the world according to their wishes.'

'Then the emperor in Constantinople is a god,' said Karas.

'Of a sort,' said his mother.

Karas wanted to talk more on this subject. His mother and sister would never discuss this sort of thing with him normally. Here, he was gaining the knowledge that he so craved. But his mother just put the remains of the bread and olives into her pack and said it was time to go on.

First Karas smelled the damp in the air, then he felt it on the walls. Now the rocks took on a different character. They were more like the roots of trees, or the melted bodies of candles, than anything he had seen before. He imagined himself crawling inside the root of a great tree, seeking the water from which it drank.

They seemed to be in there for days, though he had no real sense of time. His mother had brought little food – she said it was better to starve to prepare for the ritual. Now rest was not pleasant. Their bodies cooled quickly and their wet clothes stuck to them.

'You have never told me your dreams,' said Karas to Elai when they stopped again. 'What are they?'

The girl shook her head.

'Tell me,' he said.

'I cannot tell you.'

'Tell me.'

'Mother?'

'He won't know what to make of them, so why not?'

Karas had never seen his mother in a mood like this before. She wasn't exactly scared but there was a resignation to her, as if the things she normally cared about no longer mattered in the face of their task in that place under the ground.

The boy glanced around at the dripping walls. The rocks fell in layers like gigantic mushrooms and twisted faces seemed to leer from the walls through the candlelight.

Elai spoke: 'Something is looking for me. It has always been looking for me. It hunted me down in lives before because of what I have inside me.'

'What do you have inside you?'

'Things that whisper. Signs and symbols that unlock things. I can see them, I can hear them, but I can't touch them.'

'So what use are they to you?'

She waved her hand in irritation. Karas caught the implication. He wouldn't understand.

'What use are they?'

'They are part of something.'

'Of what?'

'A god.'

'So you're a little bit of a god.'

'We're all a little bit of a god,' said his mother.

'This is rubbish. She's just a silly girl,' said Karas.

'She carries an aspect of the goddess within her. That's what I believe. Hecate faces three ways. Virgin, mother, crone. Your sister is the virgin.'

'And what good is it to her?'

'That is what we're here to find out.'

'Well, if she's a goddess, can she magic us up some food and fine clothes? "I'm part of a god." Where did you learn to talk like that, Elai?'

'In my dreams. Anyway I never said that, exactly.'

She was so serious he stopped his mockery. She had something else she wanted to say, he was sure.

'Is there more?'

'I don't know. I hope to find out in the well. It will tell me what to do about what's following me.'

'And what follows you?'

'A wolf,' said Elai.

'Ha!' He pointed at her. 'I dream of a wolf and it's nothing; she dreams of a wolf and she's taken to the earth to be given magical insights!'

'Not given,' said her mother.

'Then what?'

'She is here to earn them, or pay for them. Nothing is given at the well; things are only exchanged. And not everyone wants to give what is asked of them. I didn't, nor will I.'

'But you have a power of prophecy.'

'A weak one, and the one I was born with. I would not answer the bargain that was put to me.'

'I would answer any bargain,' said the boy.

'Good that you won't be asked then.'

They ate the last of their bread and olives and pushed further down. When they stopped they froze; when they moved they sweated until they were soaked. Down, down into the lower caves. Finally they came to a stream that dropped in steps into blackness.

Careful with the lamp, they sat and bumped their way forward until Karas, peering ahead, saw something that sent a cold chill through him.

Their lamp wasn't the only light down there. Ahead of them was a chamber and the rock was glowing.

His mother wriggled forward through the stream on her behind. When she reached the chamber, she set the lamp on a rock. Karas and Elai followed her in.

Nearest to the lamp the rocks glowed with an intense red; further away the light shone softer and more diffuse. The glow was like a reflection of the lamplight, thought Karas, not on the surface of the rock but deep within. He was in a sort of crucible, a wide and shallow cave only a man's height above the water shaped like an open hand. The rocks in the pool stretched up like fingers, the water sitting in the palm as if the earth was offering it. The water glittered in the light of the rocks. Karas thought of the bloody hand of Christ, pierced by the nails of Romans, thought of his mother's words: 'Not everyone is prepared to give what is asked.' What had Christ given on his cross? His life and his agony. And what had he become? A god.

'Why do the rocks glow, Mother?' he asked.

'It's not magic as I understand it. They only borrow the light of our lamp,' she said. 'If we were to put it out, they would die too.'

'Don't put out the light,' said Elai. She had fear in her voice.

'I have no intention of doing that.'

His mother moved further in, climbing over the huge fingers of rock. Shelves of stone edged the chamber, some bearing the remains of candles. Karas counted. There were eight such level places, two large ones near the water and several smaller ones. He was reminded of when he'd sneaked into the hippodrome to see the chariot racing. It was like that, he thought, a tiny stadium.

His mother found a ledge and gestured for Elai to sit beside her.

'Come on. The way is easy, and if you fall in, the pool is not deep here. I can fish you out easily.'

'I thought it was a well,' said Karas.

'And so it is, but wells are only deep to reach the water. This is the bottom and it is fed by three good streams.'

Karas only saw one.

Elai made her way around the rocks, climbing carefully, pausing to ask for her mother's help twice, to be directed to a hold or just encouraged to come on. Finally the girl was beside her.

'This will take a while, Karas,' said his mother, 'but remember it was you who asked to come.'

'I am in no hurry,' said Karas. His bravery had left him, though, in the blood-red well, and he had the strong urge to cry.

He waited while his mother prepared Elai for the ritual. She fed her herbs from her pack, then took some herself. She also took out a long ladle and set it beside her. Then she sang:

'Lady of the moon,
Lady of gateways and leavetakings,
Lady of those who step through and depart,

Lady of the dead and the lands of the dead,
Lady of magic and song,
Here at the meeting of three ways,
Here in the waters where the ways are tied,
Avenging spirit put your eyes upon your daughters.'

The chant went on and on and Karas shivered deeply. He was cold and could not imagine his sister and mother were any warmer. They sat with their feet in the water.

Her mother took the ladle and held it up in both hands. Chanting all the time, she bowed three times in three directions, then dipped the ladle into the water and lifted it to offer to Elai.

Elai drank it down. Karas watched, fascinated. His sister's eyes had become glazed and she rocked back and forth where she sat.

Still the chant, unceasing. Eventually his mother began to rock on her seat too, her eyes vacant. Both of them mumbled words under their breath.

'Hecate, goddess, moonblind where the waters meet, lady of the death and the journey of death, she who guards the threshold and the gateway of death, she who admits only the dead, Hecate, goddess, at whose disposal are the starry chambers of the night, the black void of the cold oceans, lady of hidden places, she who guards the threshold and the gateway of death.'

Karas lost focus in the cold. He wanted to go back to the surface for the warmth movement would bring, but the ritual held a fascination for him. It was as if he was an ocean and inside him stirred unseen and depthless tides.

A scream, almost unbearably loud in the tight little cavern. His sister: 'How will I be free of him? I will not become him, I will not die by those teeth as she died!' Her eyes were wide and glassy.

'I will not. That way I cannot go. I will not. No!'

Karas wanted to go to her, to help her, but he did not.

'I will not give what is asked. It is too much! Too much.'

Karas watched her in the lamplight and the soft glow of the rocks. So she would reject what the waters offered while he would not be even given a chance. Why?

His mother's chant went on, but Elai cast about her as if blind and searching for the direction of a sound.

Why should she refuse what he would take in a breath? He clambered around the fingers of rock towards where his mother and sister sat. His muscles writhed on his bones with the cold, a deep tremor within him. He squeezed in beside them. Then he ate the herbs. Their taste was bitter and earthy – more than earthy – bits of grit and stone grinding on his teeth as he chewed. He forced them down. His mouth was full of dirt. He took up the ladle beside his mother and dipped it into the waters. He drank.

He lost all idea of how long he had been listening to the chant. His nose ran, and he blew the snot from it. He couldn't be sure he had it all out and blew and blew again. He was salivating heavily and became strangely conscious of the muscles of his face. They didn't quite seem to be under his control. He stretched his mouth and moved his head from side to side.

His mother's chanting took on a strange quality like the words were physical things that didn't disappear as they were spoken but came floating out of her mouth to settle like petals on the water. He couldn't see them, but he had the strong sensation they were there, these word-petals, dropping from her mouth.

He heard voices calling him. The words were in no language he knew, but they rustled in his mind like leaves disturbed by footsteps in a wood.

Then they became clearer and intelligible. *This is the place.*

'What place?'

He looked around him to see who spoke. It was a woman's voice, but none he recognised.

The place where you are lost.

'I am not lost. I know my way back.'

Can you see what you have drunk?

The waters were no longer red with the light of the rocks but clear and grey. Within them shone symbols – some silver, like quick fish in the pool, some copper and shimmering as if picked out in spangles of sunlight, some solid and hard, barnacled and green like the ribs of a sunken ship.

'What are these?'

The needful symbols.

'What need?'

The need of magic.

He knew what these things were – keys, keys to making the world in the image of his will, keys to godhood.

'What is asked of me?'

You know what is asked.

He fell to giggling. He was convinced there was a hair in his mouth, irritating his palate and tongue. He dipped the ladle in the water again and drank. But there was no hair, or if there was he could not wash it away. His face burned on the right-hand side. He was having difficulty thinking, as if waking from a deep sleep – that moment when the self is forgotten and the apparatus of eyes, brain and ears merely detects the world without interpreting or making sense of it.

Then something like his self returned, though altered. All the ragged, unfinished, deliberately set-aside and overlooked desires in his mind came loping to the fore, and all the tenderness, the love and the kindness shrank back before its advance.

A shape played and wriggled on his sister's skin, three triangles interlocking. And then there was only one triangle, but, in seeing it, he understood that it was not meant to stand alone. It wanted the other two for company. He saw battles, banners streaming in the sun, red and gold and another, blacker, that was the banner of death – a broad sweep of flies above a field of the slain. A story he had heard came into his mind. The goddess Hecate went to a feast and a rich and spiteful king set out to trick her, to test her powers of insight and knowledge, so he served her up a dismembered child in a stew. The goddess, to punish him, condemned him to turn into a wolf and eat his twenty sons. A man who became a wolf. He was a fellow to fear. The man-wolf's anger was so deep, his hungers like the sucking tides of the ocean, always there, never sated.

Karas's thoughts returned to himself and his family's life outside the walls. What was it? No more than the existence of rats. They lived in a slum with no hope of advancement. Down here, in the well, was hope. Up there, in the living forms of his sisters and his mother, restraint, tradition. No father, three women to care for. He was anchored to poverty. There could be no great school for him, no bureaucrat's position in the palace, while he was responsible for them. Resentment bubbled inside him.

He drank the waters again and this time felt the symbols enter him — chiming and breathing and filling him with wild visions of battles, of mountains and woods and wide blue seas. They grew in him, as if he were the land and they a tree springing from him, as if he was a tree and they an encircling vine, as if he was the vine and they the land that was nurtured by its fall of leaves and fruit. He felt their power — to control men, to sway them, even to kill them. But then they left him. The symbols would not stay.

'What is asked of me?'

He knew what.

He stepped into the waters. Here they came up to his chest, though he felt the floor dropping away under his feet. He reached up for his mother's feet and pulled her in. Entranced, weak and cold, she put up no resistance as he drowned her.

He drank again and the symbols flooded into him. But again they would not stay.

He pulled at his sister's feet and dragged her in, holding her under. For a second she fought, and then all strength left her and she drowned as easily as her mother had done.

Once more he drank. This time the symbols came into him like a tempest, blowing the everyday and the mundane away, letting him see the true relations of things, driving him mad.

148

He coughed, choked, laughed. Everything was clear to him – the way to the surface, to the light, but more than that, his future – what he needed to do to achieve all the things he had dreamed of.

He turned, disturbed by... by what? Something followed him. *What?* Nothing but a movement in the shadow cast by the lamp. Was it behind him again. *What?* Was that the dream wolf, slinking in the dark?

He kissed his sister, lifting her to a shelf of rock in the pool so she sat as if bathing.

'The symbols are here,' he said, 'in me now. They needed to leave this place and you would not take them. They had to leave; there was no choice. If he finds them here, he'll be born again. We must hide them from him.'

He pulled his mother through the water to the shelf and sat her beside his sister, kissed her too.

'I have given what you could not,' he said, 'and now a great magic dwells within me. But it is only mine for a little time, so I must never be a man. I do this to honour the goddess and you are with her now. I am good and I have acted for good.'

He pulled himself out of the pool up towards the lamp. As he took it the shadows made wolves on the walls which seemed to stretch eager jaws towards him, but he was not afraid. The symbols protected him. But how long would they stay?

He climbed up the tunnel, towards the light, towards the hillside. He would run to Constantinople and go to the administrator of the palace to ask to be apprenticed to him as a eunuch and servant of the emperor. A symbol expressed itself inside him and said its name in a strange language that seemed magical and beautiful to Karas. *Fehu.* The name brought images of the bountiful baskets of the harvest, of sunshine, of gold, and it brought the thought of good luck. The palace would not refuse him. He would be cut, he would be prosperous and he would never be a man, so he would keep the magic he had earned at the well.

In his bedchamber the chamberlain put his hands to his face and wept.

'I'm so sorry,' he said. 'I'm so sorry.'

He recalled the dream that had come to him after the incident at the pool, after he was cut and entered the Office of the Palace. In it, he flew over clouds that stretched out like silver cities in the moonlight, cities that burst into flame with the red dawn. He was pursued. By what? A wolf. He saw it sometimes, no more than a shape made by the rising plumes of storm clouds, white teeth that snapped towards him as the moonbeams split in the sodden air.

A wolf really had come – the wolfman who had been taken to the Numera – like a dream made flesh. The chamberlain had ordered him killed by another inmate – it was dangerous to move against one of the emperor's prisoners directly – but the man had escaped before that plan had been put into effect. Now he was down in the caves below the prison doing who knew what? Could he find his way to the chamber where the rocks sweated red light and where the hungry waters sparkled like blood? Of course not. It was too far, the route too difficult to find from that side. The spirits that haunted those depths, that kept the curious guards away, that led prisoners to deaths of starvation and thirst in places unseen, would protect him.

But the presence of Norsemen at all worried him. He was a learned man and knew what the symbols he'd taken from the well were, or rather how they appeared to him. Runes, the Norsemen's magic writing. He shared a common ancestry with the Vikings, he thought, through Odoacer who burned the forum. Perhaps that was why the shapes appeared that way to him.

Karas tried to think of a way forwards. He'd resisted an investigation for so long but the emperor, who had taken it he was born to greatness and never thought to question where his remarkable good fortune came from, had now insisted. It seemed wise to employ the Magnaura's greenest and least

150

qualified student for the task – the master of the university was no fool and had inferred exactly what sort of man he sought for the job – 'fresh, unencumbered by too much detailed knowledge of the town, able to provide a new perspective, not tied to any faction'. An idiot, in other words. But now the chamberlain almost wanted to confide in Loys, to see if he really could suggest a way forward, a road other than the goddess' old road – the road of blood, of death, of misery. He would not confide in him, of course. Instead he would wait, pray and hope no further sacrifice would be required.

He wiped the tears from his face, rang his little bell and called for his servant to dress him for bed.

20   A Champion for Snake in the Eye

Mauger had killed two of his attackers and now fled through the tight backstreets as quickly as he could. The time for subterfuge was over and he needed to put a good distance between him and the people who had taken Azémar.

The streets were not crowded – only the poor stayed outside now, huddled into porches or doorways, fearful faces watching him as he ran, his naked sword drawing too much attention. All of them were potential informants, he thought. He had to hide before either the men who had been chasing him caught him or the city guard noticed him. The light was dropping, the dim day giving up its struggle with the engulfing black clouds. All he had to do was keep moving until night fell.

He ducked around a corner into a narrow alley. It was deserted, so he took the opportunity to put his sword back into his sleeping roll.

He stood still to listen for a while. No sounds of pursuit, just some voices from the houses, a woman and a man arguing and children shouting as they played.

Then steps. And more steps. He put his hand to the hilt of his sword, ready to pull it from the roll.

His pursuers came to the top of the alley. There were two of them.

One of the men spoke. Mauger couldn't understand what he said but could tell the words were designed to soothe him. The speaker was a slight man but in his hand he carried a sling. Mauger glanced behind him. Another man, this one with an axe. His way out was blocked, no way of telling how many men stood behind those he could see.

Mauger gestured for the sling man to come forward. The man fitted a lead shot to his weapon. Two swings of the sling and Mauger barged through the door of the house at his side as the bullet whistled past his head.

The room burst into uproar as he crashed in – three families all together, children and animals. Two men grabbed him, a small dog bit at his heels. He threw them off but then others had him – the men from outside and everyone who lived in the house. He kicked and fought but he was hopelessly out-numbered in the tiny space. His legs began to buckle. The dog at his feet would not relent and five men held him, though he would not let them take him down.

'Hold!'

The voice was in Greek but Mauger recognised it – the boy Snake in the Eye.

No one paid any attention to him whatever.

'Hold in the name of Basileios, who is king of all the world!'

Snake in the Eye held up something in his hand, a medal of some sort.

The Greeks shouted at the youth. Although Mauger did not understand what they said, he guessed they were unwilling to release such a violent man, fearful of what he might do to them.

'If I make them let you go will you vouch not to harm them?' said Snake in the Eye.

'I swear it,' said Mauger.

Snake in the Eye spoke again in Greek. Three of the men let him go, one pulling the dog free. The two from the group who had taken Azémar, however, clung on – rough-looking Greeks, one tall and muscular the other short and squat.

Mauger was no oathbreaker but he had sworn not to harm anyone who let him go. He stamped down on the side of the tall man's knee, snapping it like kindling wood. The man fell screaming and Mauger drove his shoulder into the squat man's side, shoving him back over a stool and sending him crashing down. The man stood quickly, drawing a knife, but Mauger had picked up a chair and thrust it at his opponent, catching him in the eye with the chair's foot and putting him down again. Mauger stepped on the man's throat on his way to the door. The sling man, who had stayed out of the fight in the doorway, bolted away down the alley.

The combination of Snake in the Eye's medal and Mauger's belligerence meant none of the householders tried to intervene and the warrior made the street easily, Snake in the Eye close behind. Mauger looked around. No sign of the sling man.

'Other men can't be far away,' said Mauger. 'Is there a place I can go that's beyond their reach?'

'Come to our camp outside the walls. You are a brother northerner and a mighty man. You will be welcomed there.'

'Very well,' said Mauger. For the moment it seemed the wisest option. He was known in the city. He couldn't hope to stage an attack on Loys at the university or the palace now. So a subterfuge was called for, and the boy who had rescued him could be useful.

'Take me to the camp,' said Mauger, 'and you have my thanks for making those low men release me.'

Snake in the Eye grinned. 'We may yet perform for each other many services,' he said. 'Follow me. These Greeks cannot harm you there.'

Mauger glanced back at the house, where the fearful inhabitants watched them leave. He would remember their faces, though they would also remember his. Should he return and kill the injured men who had attacked him? No time. He had been seen by their companions anyway.

It was night now, and few lights shone from the windows and doors of the alleys. The clouds were a shroud, blanking out the stars and the moon, reducing vision to no more than twenty paces where lamps or candlelight broke through doorways or windows, to nothing where it did not. Some people lingered on the streets – soldiers carrying torches in the main. Here and there a whore sat by a window, nearer or further from its light as her age or beauty made advisable.

154

Mauger followed Snake in the Eye towards the walls, glad of the dark.

'You're worried, friend,' said Snake in the Eye.

'It's not your concern,' said Mauger, 'but I think it best if I do not use my true name in this camp. I will be accepted as a Norseman more quickly, and if Azémar gives up my name they will not find me as easily.'

'Then what is your name?'

'Ragnar,' said Mauger. It was his real name – the one his father had given him, and not the one he had adopted when he came to Normandy, and a common one.

'I still want to help you,' said Snake in the Eye. 'I'm eager for honour. Let me be your friend. I can find this man, surely I can kill him for you.'

'No,' said Mauger, 'that must be done by me. I need to know I have the right man, and it's a matter of honour that I do it with my own hand. I have vowed to my lord to kill him and I can't let another do it for me.'

'You still want me to find out where he is?'

'Yes. The university may still be the best place to look. He used to be a monk but that profession has closed to him.'

'What is his name?'

'Loys, the scholar Loys. He is with a woman, a noble lady. They may not be travelling under their own names, though I think they will. It would be too shameful for a high born woman to disguise her rank.'

'Let me look into it,' said Snake in the Eye.

'I will. But why are you so eager to help me?'

'I have something I need you to do for me,' said Snake in the Eye.

21 Friend Fear

Loys had decided on a two-pronged approach — the first of which would be to spread fear.

He began by calling in members of the postal service — Isais' men. That risked invoking the spymaster's displeasure — a possibly lethal course of action — but he would be buffeted no longer. In Constantinople, he had realised, you either pushed or got pushed.

The work wearied him. He interviewed a variety of men from straightforward courtiers to hardened spymasters who smiled too much and drank too much of his wine while he spoke to them. The interviews were painstaking and had to be conducted according to strict court protocol. Loys, on the advice of his eunuch servant, had ordered a fan of office and learned a five-minute official greeting. His visitors had to bring fans appropriate to their rank and station, and there were four chairs in the room — one for himself, one for low men and one for high men. The most splendid chair sat beside him, empty. It was for the emperor and a signal to those who visited that the investigation took place on his behalf.

At first no one gave up anything, and Loys began to see the whole process as simply an exercise in marking out his territory, showing the court he was a man to be reckoned with. Then, after a month of wearying interviews, he summoned one of the palace ostiarioi, the ceremonial doorkeepers who kept the lists of people to be admitted to the palace and saw to it that the proper protocols of greeting and introduction were observed.

The man reminded Loys of a richly embroidered cushion, he was so fat and so colourful.

'Do you know or have you ever known of anyone striking

bargains with devils, demons or other maleficent powers?' said Loys.

'No one at all,' said the ostiarios. He smiled in a jolly way.

'Do you know, or have you ever known, of anyone involved in the production of magical amulets, charms or spells?' said Loys.

'No one,' he said, again with a smile. 'If you are looking to trap me, you shall fail.'

Loys glanced down at his notepaper and scribbled 'defensive' on it. Then he looked up.

'Why would I be looking to trap you? Surely if you have nothing to hide you cannot be trapped.'

'Well, quite so, but all the same. You know. It's quite nerveracking being questioned like this. One wrong word and all that.'

'One wrong word about what?'

The man gave a loud 'hem!'. 'I don't know. I mean, that's the problem with wrong words, isn't it? You don't know they're wrong until you've said them.'

Loys fixed the man with a stare.

'Have you ever prayed for the health of the emperor?'

'Yes. Often.'

'Have you ever kissed the emperor's image and asked for his blessing?'

The ostiarios seemed not to know quite how to answer. He sat and gulped for a moment like a frog wondering if it was a fly or a bee he had swallowed.

'I would be disloyal if I said I had not.'

Loys linked his fingers and leaned forward, his elbows on the table. 'You are aware that is conjuring?'

'Oh come on, everyone does it.'

'Really?' said Loys. 'Could you furnish me with their names?'

'No, I . . .'

'You are unwilling to reveal your accomplices?'

'This is ridiculous. You might as well say that when the people call for the saint of the walls to bless the emperor they are casting spells. They carve the symbol of the moon and the star, and we all know that began when the names of the saints were unknown.'

Loys looked at the ostiarios with hard eyes. Really he pitied him. The man was no more a devil worshipper than he was. He was naive, a little conceited about his own intelligence but harmless enough. However, Loys needed to build a reputation in the palace, to be known as a man who should not be crossed.

'Have you done these things?'

'No, I—'

'If I were to call at your house now I would find no evidence of idolatry or anything similar?'

The ostiarios coloured. 'We are simple people,' he said, 'and the affliction of the sky troubles us greatly. We sometimes turn to the old ways, not to harm but to help the emperor and the city. A thousand men have carved the star and the moon on their walls. It is a protection for us and the emperor. What can be wrong with that, when it is the symbol of the city?'

'But you have just admitted you carved it for the purposes of sorcery. You imperil your soul. Do you not know of the sermon of St Andrew the Fool?'

'I do not listen to the sermons of fools,' said the man, trying to regain his dignity.

'He was a wise fellow,' said Loys, 'who feigned madness and drew the scorn of all men for his love of God. He told the story of Vigrinos, a magician whom a lady asked to give her a spell to make her cheating husband love her.'

'I have no interest in the stupidity of women.'

Loys smiled a tight smile.

'There is a wider point here. The magician cast his spell and the husband became faithful. But demons afflicted the woman in her dreams – a black dog that caressed her like a lover and kissed her on the mouth, an Ethiopian inflamed by lust and other manifestations. She fasted and prayed, and it was revealed to her that to make his magic the magician had defiled holy icons with shit, filled a magic lamp he had given her full of dog's urine and carved the name of the Antichrist on the wick's base along with the words "Demon Sacrifice". This was the price she had paid to return her husband to her. Her soul. St Andrew says demons often use magic for apparent good with the aim of making unsuspecting persons subject to their influence. Is this what has happened to you? Have you fallen in with demons?'

'Your knowledge of these matters is very great, sir, but, no. I ... No.'

Loys scribbled some notes again – nonsense, really. He was simply trying to be intimidating, though he suspected he wasn't very good at it. He imagined the man a mouse and himself a cat eyeing it. That idea made him laugh when the doorkeeper tried to speak but only came out with something resembling a squeak.

'You will be recalled to answer at a future time,' said Loys.

'When?'

'I cannot say. You'll have to wait.

'I am not in league with devils.'

'I will decide that,' said Loys. 'I am charged with discovering the source of this unnatural weather, the reason for fireballs and other phenomena that do not concern you. So unless I find greater evidence of devil worship then I shall have to conclude that even the slightest evidence is enough to justify suspicion. I suggest you and anyone who wishes to avoid such suspicion does his best to bring anything unusual to my attention.'

'There are a thousand magicians and soothsayers not fifty strides from the palace gates.'

'They are low people and could not have worked the magic to cause this sky. We are looking for someone within the court, I am sure of it.'

'I will make every endeavour to be watchful,' said the gate-keeper.

'Good,' said Loys. 'You may expect to see me again some-time soon. The chances are that I will need to commit you to the Numera for a period.' Loys had no intention of doing this but was prepared at least to threaten it.

'Sir.'

'Yes.'

'I have a family.'

'Then endeavour to keep it,' said Loys.

The man sat for a few seconds looking at his shoes.

'Have you thought of interviewing the prisoners in the Numera?' he said.

'Why should I do that?'

'It would seem politic to start with known criminals and enemies of the state.'

'Do you know something, Ostiarios?'

'No,' he said, 'I do not. Just that I think the Numera's list of prisoners might be a good place to start. There are sorcerers in there for sure. The chamberlain stuck one in there just the other day – one of the Arabs they captured in Abydos – right by the emperor's tent, I heard.'

'Which Arab?'

'I don't know. I just heard it mentioned over a cup of wine.'

'By whom?'

'By ...' The fat doorkeeper was suddenly wary of incriminating anyone. Loys held his silence and let the man fill it with his own fears. 'Meletios the warder would know.'

Loys didn't find it too surprising a sorcerer had been imprisoned, as sorcerers and heretics had a habit of finding themselves locked up. But the ostiarios thought it worthy of mention. No one else had mentioned a sorcerer. That in itself was odd. *Idiot Loys.* Circles existed within the court, codes and secret understandings of which he knew nothing. Perhaps knowledge of the sorcerer's existence had been limited to a very few. Perhaps it wasn't common knowledge that the savage who had attacked the emperor was also a sorcerer. Loys wanted to question the ostiarios further. He knew he wrote on delicate parchment, so to speak. It would be all too easy to put a pen through it and ruin the work completely. Better to proceed slowly. And besides, he'd heard enough rumours to build a bridge of them back to Neustria.

'I thank you for your advice.'

The man bowed and Loys put down his fan to signify he was dismissed. When he had gone, Loys scribbled a note to Meletios saying he had been mentioned as part of investigations into sorcery and must to report to be interviewed within a week. He then lay back in his seat and looked up at the ceiling. Beatrice, who had been behind a screen at the rear of the room, came out. She was bigger now – very pregnant.

'You did well.'

'It's unfair to treat these fellows this way.'

'Anxiety is a condition of a courtier's life. You are just speaking to them in a way they respect and can understand. This will yield dividends more quickly than poring over all the books in the world.'

Loys took her hand. 'I know. I don't have to be comfortable with it, though.'

'No. But you have to do it. It's a matter of survival for us. We'll get ourselves in a position where we can prosper here or at least survive. How long now until the chamberlain wants his report?'

'Two months. And how long until the baby?'

'The physician thinks a month.'

'Good timing,' he said.

'Why?'

'Because if it looks like I'm not going to get to the bottom of this and God grants us a boy, we can make our escape back to your father before I have to face the chamberlain.'

'You will get to the bottom of it, Loys. I have faith in you.'

He lowered his voice and drew her close. 'And what if the bottom of it is at the top?'

She knew to whom he referred – the chamberlain. Styliane had hinted as much.

'Then know all you can. If our friends are truly our enemies then perhaps some who appear our enemies might be our friends. She has said as much.'

'That is a dangerous game.'

'More dangerous to blunder blindly. Has there been nothing from your interviews?'

'All too wise and too scared to mention his name, if indeed he's complicit in this. And I am too wise and too scared to ask them to.'

'But it's important to have all the information you can get. Might you find an excuse to look into the chamberlain's past? And Styliane's too.'

'You think she could be responsible?'

'Of course not. But a prince looks at the lie of the land before deploying his troops. You need to do the same.'

Her voice was just a whisper in his ear, scarcely audible.

He was sick of interviewing, that was for sure. It had served his purpose of making him feared. But he wanted to know more about his master, who seemed to have so much to do with sorcery in one way or another — if only his seemingly fervent interest in its eradication. And why hadn't the chamberlain told him he'd locked a sorcerer up?

Beatrice was right. It might, he thought, be worth a trip outside the walls. He would please Isais by seemingly investigating the Varangians and delve into the chamberlain's past while he did it.

'I'll go first thing tomorrow,' he said.

22   The Pale God

I have died, thought Azémar. *I have died and this is hell*. He could not bear the heat of the Numera, nor the darkness, nor the smell. His irons afflicted him terribly and skinned his ankles raw.

They'd taken him down to the lowest level, given him no food and left him in that black hole – to die, he was sure.

The stench was obscene, the floor rough and uneven, offering no comfort, and the moans of the sick and the dying really did make him think of the cries of the souls of the damned in their torment.

The darkness was terrible to bear, that and the hatred of the other inmates. Occasionally, perhaps once a day, the guards came to give him water – no food – and those around him who still had the sanity to realise what was happening would scream and beg for a drink or curse him for his luck.

He tried to save some for his fellow prisoners, gulping down as much as he could and taking a big last mouthful. A man lay next to him, and he found his mouth and dribbled the water in. It gave the man strength enough to weep. Azémar sat with him, holding him, trying to bring comfort where there was none.

Rats scuttled about them, tormenting them as they slept. He would feel a movement on his foot and he learned to kick quickly and hard before the animal bit him.

The rats weren't the only ones on the lookout for food. Hunger and thirst did bad things to men. The darkness of the Numera was a darkness of the soul and they fell on the dead and fed upon them. When the guards with the water came with their lights Azémar saw terrible things, sights like something from a church painting designed to terrify people into belief. Yes, it was like hell, and men had become devils there.

When the woman had said she needed him but that he could rot a while, he had thought he would be left in that horror for a day, a week. How long had he been imprisoned? He lost all track of time. Only the coming of the water and the death of the man in his arms told him he was moving from moment to moment at all.

The hunger became acute and Azémar hallucinated. He was in a pit of wolves who sat watching him with unblinking eyes, some of yellow, some of blue and some of a terrible red. One wolf above all others seemed to watch him. At first Azémar thought it was a pagan idol, a thing like ignorant people set in their fields in autumn to frighten dark spirits away – a construction of straw and wood with turnips for eyes and pine cones for teeth. It stared at him for a long time until it changed to become a mask like travelling players used to tell their tales – stuck together with fur and twine.

'What do you want from me?'

The thing said nothing, just watched him, its face bobbing at the edge of the liquid dark like that of a drowned man in black water.

'What do you want from me?'

Terrible hunger consumed Azémar's mind. He needed to eat. He needed to eat!

'You are a wolf.'

The voice made him start. The dark was unyielding. The voice had spoken in Norse. This was not an hallucination but something real and near to him.

'I am a man.'

'You were a man. The wolf stares through your eyes as I have seen him stare before and hope never to see him stare again.'

'There is no wolf in me.'

'Then why do you cleave to that corpse?'

Azémar moved his hands about him. The man he had been lying on was quite cold.

Azémar wept. 'I will not survive this place.'

'You will survive, Fenrisulfr. You will outlive the gods.'

'I feel harm in your voice. You are here to kill me?'

'No. The destiny you carry would not allow it. I cannot find the waters; I cannot find a way to kill you.'

'What waters? What destiny do I carry?'

'To be my killer.'

'Who are you?'

'I am you.'

There was a shimmering, like the moon reflected on water. He blinked and rubbed his eyes, willing them to work. What was it? Skin. A tall man stood close by, a tall man with pale skin and hair of burning red. There was no light other than the man's body. Right next to him, crouching and seemingly oblivious to the vision behind him, was someone else, the one who had been talking.

He peered at the crouching figure. His own face looked back at him but more weathered, thinner by far than he had been before the ordeal in the dungeon.

'You have come looking for her,' said his double, and it was as if a gateway had opened in Azémar's mind. He rememberd how even the glimpse of the lord's daughter riding by had tormented his dreams, how he had struggled with his lust. He recalled other dreams too – a girl with blonde hair by a fire in the snow, a headless body on a beach. The visions seemed so real they were almost memories.

'Go a long way away from this place,' said his double, 'and never come back here, no matter how you are drawn to do so.'

'Kill me here,' said Azémar. 'Kill me here!'

'I cannot.'

'Why not?'

The double sprang at Azémar, putting one hand on his chest to locate him before he went for his neck. Immensely strong fingers squeezed Azémar's windpipe but he had no fear of death. In that place, his body stewing in its own secretions, bitten by rats and fleas, rubbed raw by the rough floor, his mind falling into madness, he welcomed the end. And yet it would not come.

The pale man whose body lit the dark moved his hand in a gesture of calm, and the fingers let go of Azémar's throat. His attacker fell back and sat down. He looked around him with the hopeless gaze of a blind man. Azémar sensed his double couldn't see, despite the glowing figure behind him. Then he was gone, swallowed by the gloom.

The pale figure came forward to cradle Azémar in his arms.

'Who are you? An angel?'

'No. I am of the older earth.'

'A devil then?'

'Men make devils. For what is a devil but an angel of whom men disapprove?'

'Of whom God disapproves. The father of creation cast out the bad angels and they fell to hell, where they became devils.'

The strange man laughed. 'Then I am a devil. But what of you? The father of creation shakes to hear your name.'

'That is blasphemy.'

'It is the truth, Fenrisulfr.'

Azémar knew that myth. Loki had had a son who was a wolf and grew so powerful that the gods tricked and chained him to a rock, where he waits to the final day when he will break his fetters and consume the gods. His father had told such stories; though he had been sincere in his new Christianity the stories of the old land were still dear to him. Azémar had been close to his father. He would see him in heaven.

'I would be with my father now,' he said, 'my holy father and my earthly one.'

'I am here.'

'You are not my father.'

'I am your father and your mother both.'

The knowledge poured in on him, words and visions whispering and flashing in his mind. He had been a foundling. His brothers were all so blond and big, he skinny and dark. A vision entered his mind – a woman, scarred and gaunt with a baby at her breast. His brother – or the boy he had called his brother – lay sick in a longhouse, more likely to die than make the sea journey to a new life in Neustria. The woman was at the door. She could cure the boy but there was a price to pay – they must take the baby she had and raise it. His mother, who had loved her newest son more than all the others put together, had agreed straight away. The child had recovered and, because Azémar had brought such good fortune, they made the effort to have him accepted by the monastery when they arrived in Neustria.

'What is to become of me?' said Azémar.

'My son, you have great things to do. You must drink of the waters.'

'What waters?'

'The waters that the dead god gave his eye to drink. Vision for vision, sight for sight in the waters of wisdom at the centre of the earth.'

'And what will they tell me?'

'I cannot know. Only that you must go there if we are to have any chance at all of getting rid of the old hater.'

'Of who?'

'Old Grimnir, the gallows god, mad King Glapsvithr, the lord of the corpses, Odin.'

'I ...' Azémar felt as if his head lay beneath a crushing stone, that enormous pressure was building within him. The name Odin moved him to fury, to hatred that went far beyond that of a holy man for a pagan devil. He had no idea why. He growled and spat, cried out. Around him the dying men of the Numera seemed to answer his calls, howling and cursing and begging to be free.

Azémar looked up into the eyes of the man who held him, the pale, burning beautiful being who had called him son.

'Father?'

'Yes.'

'Save me,' said Azémar.

'You are such a prodigy among horrors, you do not need me

to save you, Fenrisulfr. Come, before you can drink, you need to eat.'

Blood dripped from the strange fellow's fingers, and Azémar lapped at it, then bit. The skin ripped and more blood flowed. Still the bright, glowing man cradled Azémar, and as he did so, he sang – a song of lovers caught in a story told by a god to please the fates.

The song intoxicated Azémar, filled him with ecstasy, but was it the song in the blood that seemed to draw him on to drink ever more deeply? His own fingers ran down to the man's belly, tearing it open and pulling out the bowels, the liver, the slick wet liver, which he chewed and swallowed with delight.

'Mother. Father. Release me.'

'You are released.'

The song went on as he ate.

And then it stopped, and Azémar realised that, far from lying in the figure's arms, he held something in his own. He let go and it fell limp to the floor.

The beautiful burning figure was gone and beside him was the torn corpse of a man who had died of thirst. A weak light filtered in. The door at the top of the stairs had a small space beneath it and a faint lamplight now shone through.

There rises my sun, he thought. *How soon before it sinks?* The words surprised him. Azémar was a plain man and given to plain speaking. Such thoughts were alien to him.

He moved his feet. The manacles that had restrained him lay empty on the floor. How had that happened? They weren't bent or buckled but the locks had been smashed.

He lay on the ground weeping for a while, asking God to forgive him for what he had done. But strange thoughts sprouted in him now, thoughts no words could contain.

The cries of the prisoners no longer disturbed him. They were ... He searched for a word. *Interesting. Intriguing.* He had a deep desire to investigate them, to go to the stricken and the dying and ... what? He almost laughed as he imagined himself poking the bodies with his nose. He wanted to establish something about them, to discover something. This morbid curiosity was divorced from any moral sense at all and it chilled him.

He crawled forward. He was neither hungry nor thirsty and, after so long with little water and no food, this fact seemed extremely important to him. He remembered the wolfman, the thing that had put its hand around his throat. *That fellow had to have some sort of explanation for this — he would know what was what*. His mind was not his own. His pompous old abbot had used those phrases — 'that fellow', 'what was what' — they were echoes of a previous existence. Words jangled in his mind. *A beggar is a silent preacher, reproaching us for the corruption of wealth. A lazybones who will not work, a cripple cursed by God*. No sense, no reason. Just words.

To his side was a gap where the wall didn't quite meet the floor, a darkness within the darkness. The wolfman had come from there, he was sure. Could he speak to him? He touched his neck. It was painful where the man had grasped him, but he had no fear of him now. Should he leave this place? He thought he could wait behind the door and slip through when it opened.

He wept. He was himself again. *No, no, I cannot escape*. Yet in the next instant he felt strong and lithe, fast as the shadow of a bird. *Yes*, he was a shadow, something defined by what it was not, an expression and a simplification of another, complex thing.

He crawled to the gap at the bottom of the wall. There was something in there, a deepness — he sensed it. He breathed in, drawing a heavy draught of air through his nose. Beneath the prison stink was another smell. Wolf. He was down there, his strange double.

Devils gibbered in his head. What was happening to him? Who was that extraordinary man who had visited him and comforted him? The dark in the crack of the wall held no fear for him. He could smell, he could feel. He rolled into the sightless caves seeking to cool the torment that was raging in his head.

23   Outside the Walls

Loys strode out, surprised at the cold of the sunless streets. Inside the palace was always warm and pleasant, heated by the hot-air hypocaust system beneath the floors. Outside it was freezing. The sky had disappeared completely and the fine ash lay thick on every surface. He had to carry a lamp at midday – not to see so much as to be seen. Fewer people ventured out under the unnatural fog, but those who did moved no more slowly – horses and carriages looming suddenly out of nowhere, clattering past on the cobbles, unmindful of who or what they rode down.

The one business unaffected by the awful weather was that of the soothsayers on the Middle Way. They crowded in the murk under the grand porches and spilled out into the side-streets – dice throwers, palm readers, entrail burners and head feelers. Loys had never seen so many – but he quickly came to the conclusion these people were frauds. For a start, one man he had seen operating as a shoemaker when he first came to the city now sat throwing handfuls of coins into a box and using them to offer predictions. Still, Loys opted to question them in passing, but they wanted money for everything and the explanations they gave of their skills failed to convince. One woman told him he was born into riches, noting his expensive robe, another said he longed for his homeland. Loys thought he could do better than that himself. He asked for charms to help him in his quest for promotion. He was offered all sorts of things – the feet of animals and birds, potions, salves and medallions. Did these things work? He doubted it – they were just tokens sold by charlatans to fools. Loys quickly realised if magicians capable of producing effective magic did exist, he would not find them on the Middle Way.

Magic, though, was not his immediate interest. Rather, it was the beliefs that informed it. The chamberlain had spoken of old cold tides in the city. Loys needed to dip his toe in them to assess how they might have pulled and pushed at people. He spent longer than he had intended outside the palace – a week in all. His strategy was simple. He needed to gather whatever knowledge he could of the city's pagan practices before he made a judgement on the cause of the black sky. This was not a subterfuge; he genuinely did want this information to arm himself in his quest for an answer.

He also wanted to hear rumours about Styliane and the chamberlain. His official robes would silence anyone he questioned, so he returned to the waterfront where he had lived with Beatrice, found the landlord and rented a tiny room. He changed his clothes there, entering wrapped in his big cloak and leaving the same way. The only difference was what he wore underneath – scholar's rags instead of imperial silks.

He used his letter of engagement with its chamberlain's seal to get him outside the city. The guard on the gate made a record of his leaving.

Down towards the water sprawled the Varangian camp, its black banners limp in the cold wet air. It was enormous but not as enormous as the shanty town that spread out from the walls on that side, seemingly as big as the sea that surrounded it on the other. All manner of materials had been used to construct houses here – some stone, some wood, some no more than tents or planks nailed together and propped up into lean-tos. Native Greeks mingled with men of many nations – Arabs and Bulgars, Turks and Moors, even the small, hard horsemen of the Mongolian steppes with their sallow skin and tear-shaped eyes. The camp was full of squabbles and fights. The people were united only by poverty.

Loys gripped the little knife at his belt and felt faintly ridiculous. If these people wanted to set on him, a sword, shield and breastplate wouldn't stop them. The dogs were threat enough, roaming in packs and starved to skeletons. He could not risk wandering in that place alone, so he went to the Varangian camp and hired four men to accompany him with their axes and shields. Loys said his name was Michael, in a bid to put at least a small difficulty in the way of anyone who was trying to discover his business and he offered a daily rate, conspicuously emptying his purse when he paid them. If they wanted more money they would need to keep him safe – robbing him would end the arrangement.

A tall man called Galti took up his offer and brought his brothers. Loys was pleased with them – giants with impressive tattoos and scars. They might be overwhelmed by a mob, but it would be a brave man who attacked first. The Norsemen had no idea what he was doing, had no curiosity and did not speak Greek. They were ideal. He would be conspicuous with his guards but not obviously associated with authority. In his Norman clothes he even passed for another Norseman to anyone who wasn't familiar with the difference between Normans and Vikings.

Loys began by asking for a charm to help him gain promotion. He made it clear he had no money with him but would return should he find such a thing. Loys wore his poverty ostentatiously and visibly, pulling a tear in his trousers, muddying his cloak and – despite the fact it numbed his toes – wearing only his monk's sandals. Plenty of people offered him things, but some were no more than pebbles scratched quickly from the earth, pieces of twig, even.

'Not these,' he said. 'Is there no one here who can call on the old goddess of the city? We are near enough to the walls she blesses.'

There was evidence enough of the worship of Hecate. Her symbol was daubed on walls. At places where three roads – or rather tracks through the debris – met, there were occasional posts, rough things carved with three heads at the top. This too was the goddess's symbol. But who would own up to carving it? And even if anyone did, they could say it was just a post to mark the junction, the faces representing winds or angels.

He asked about the goddess indirectly, but if people knew anything then no one confessed to it or they missed his hints. After the third day anyone following him would have got bored, made their report and gone to buy wine, he thought. So he became a little bolder.

He had located an old man who claimed to have lived in the shanty all his life. 'We make our fortunes by copying great men,' said Loys. 'Tell me, where was the chamberlain Karas born? I wish to offer a prayer of thanks for his success at the place he grew up.'

The old man said he didn't know but knew a man who might. The man who might didn't know either but he said it was possible a neighbour would. The neighbour thought he knew but, when they arrived at the spot, no one there could remember the chamberlain being there at all.

A crowd of children had formed around Loys on his first day in the slum, tugging at his clothes, asking him for money. He shouted at them to go away but they only stood further off, calling to him, offering him women, recommending themselves as excellent and diligent servants. By the third day, they concluded he had no money and was probably a madman. Now they left him largely alone.

Loys stood in the midst of the broken-down shacks, the human stink around him – cooking smells, dirt, urine and worse.

'You're lost, sir?'

It was a small boy. The child was thin and his eyes seemed ridiculously big in his head. He wore a loincloth and his body was red with scabies.

'No.'

'Then can I help you in any way? A woman is easy to find.'

'That's not what I'm looking for.'

'Then what is it?'

'Are you a clever lad?' He had noticed the boy spoke quite well.

'I don't know. My mother says I am useful.'

'Then what will you be when you are older? What will you do?'

'I don't understand.'

'Will you have a profession? Will you be a soldier or a bureaucrat?'

'I can't read, sir. A bureaucrat needs to read.'

'Do you know anyone who can read?'

'I would say you can.'

Loys smiled.

'So you will be a soldier?'

'If I live so long and am strong enough by the time the army will have me. They eat well, those men.'

'But they die too.'

'Here we die but do not eat.'

'You live on this street?'

'Yes.'

'I heard it said the chamberlain of all the empire grew up here.'

'So it's said.'

'So why don't you follow him? Why don't you go to the court and become a servant of the emperor. Be diligent and work hard, and you may rise to that splendour.'

The boy laughed. 'I don't go because I can stay here and get beaten. The city guards would not even let me in.'

'And yet the chamberlain went there.'

'He was blessed by God.'

'By God?'

'By God, sir.' The boy put up his chin, defying Loys to say different.

Loys gave him a coin.

'And only by God?'

The boy put out his hand. Loys gave him another coin.

'Will you give me another if I tell you?' said the boy.

'You've had two; I will not.'

The boy ran away.

Loys shrugged.

Galti laughed. 'These people live like rats.'

'They might say the same of you.'

'I grew up on a farm,' said Galti. 'In winter we sat in the hot spring all day. The Greeks are not clean.'

'No.' Loys had a thought. 'Did you never consider another life, Galti, other than that of a warrior?'

Galti looked at him as though he had sprouted troll ears. 'Not where I come from. The sheep don't always have enough to eat and you get a good crop only every third year if you're lucky.'

'You never thought to come somewhere like here, to study, to be a merchant, to be a bureaucrat?'

'A what?'

'A scribe, a writer.'

Galti laughed. 'The great emperor wants Norsemen for one thing. The same as you do. Our muscle and the swords we carry.'

'You didn't have to follow that life.'

Galti seemed genuinely puzzled. Clearly Loys made no sense to him.

It was the same with the people who lived in the slum, Loys thought. Beyond the wall, in the city, opportunity awaited the diligent man. But here that world was almost unreachable. The children didn't read, they had no manners, and even the cleverest saw no way out beyond the army, were they lucky enough to live long enough to join.

So how had the chamberlain got out? Extraordinary fortune? And why did his younger sister, who he had brought with him and raised out of the mire, despise him so?

'We should go,' said Galti. 'It's getting dark. Well, darker.' It was too: a very fine rain made a veil of the air.

Loys heard a noise from behind a tent. He went to investigate. Sheep. Or rather a sheep suckling a single lamb. A single black lamb. Loys remembered the book he had read. Black lambs were sacrificed to Hecate. He walked through a line of tents and lean-tos. At the top of the hill was another black lamb, this time in a rough wooden cage. He ran down into the valley that dipped by the walls before the long climb up into the hills and the distant trees. Another lamb, tethered. Also black. It was very nearly the full moon. Three days before a ceremony to Hecate would be held. He needed to see where those black lambs were taken.

He returned to the Vikings.

'We need to go,' said Galti, 'it will be dark soon.'

'Yes,' said Loys, 'but I have a service to ask of you.'

'What is it?'

'I need you to find me some smaller guards,' he said.

24   The Price of Power

The shadows were wolves again, their long jaws stretching towards him as he slept. He heard their snuffling and grunting as he lay dream-bound in his bed.

And now the voices, the shrieking and the howling, the sensation of falling, the helpless descent into the blackness that the runes had hollowed in his mind. The bright symbols floated away from him leaving trails of silver as he plunged after them through the shadow world of his sleep.

Where are they, those needful symbols? Where are they? The voice sounded in his head.

'They are in my heart. They are growing here.'

Whose are they, those needful symbols? Whose are they?

'They are mine, for I paid the price for them.'

Who are you?

'I am Karas, who gave the waters what they asked. Who are you?'

Your sister, dead by your treacherous hand.

Her face emerged from the darkness, bloated and bleached by madness, her eyes swollen and puffed like fungal growths, her hair lank and wet as seaweed.

The chamberlain seemed to fall forwards and there was light. The runes were there again, symbols growing inside him, the eight, feeding off him and sustaining him, clasping their tendrils around his heart like a tree curls its roots around a rock.

'I took your life. I took your symbols. They are mine.'

You but borrowed them a little while. Come away to the waters from where they came.

'They are mine, for I paid the price for them.'

Come away, descend as the spirits of the dead descend, travel through the great galleries of darkness.

'I will not give what I paid so dearly to own.'

I am wet with the blood of gods. The vision put forward its hands, red and bloody.

'Why are you here?'

This is the time. This is the needful time. The time of endings. She is calling the wolf. She is calling the wolf to you.

'The goddess will reward me, not punish me. It cannot end, not while these things are mine.'

Listen, the black dogs are barking. The wolf is near. Can you not hear her call?

'Lady of the crossroads, lady of moonlight.' The chamberlain crossed himself, though he uttered a pagan charm.

The moon has been eaten.

'I call on the sun.'

The sun chased away.

'Lady who is three. The snake, the dog and the horse. Protect me here. Jesus, who is three, the father the son and the holy ghost, protect me here.'

Walk to the lower dark and never look back, though you hear the sound of footsteps and the barking of dogs.

'Lady of walls.'

You have broken the walls.

'Lady of gateways.'

You have passed through the gate.

'Lady who returned from death. Christ who returned from death, help me here.'

She is clothed in her funeral jewels and waiting with her dogs, those guardians of the threshold.

'Lady who protects from demons. Christ who cast the demons out.'

You have called the demons in. They that despise the light. You know where they dwell.

'I will not come to you.'

The wolf will follow her. She is near you now.

'Who is she?'

She who is three. The storm, the trap and the wolf maker.

'No!'

The chamberlain sat upright in bed. The lamps in his room were lit, as they were always lit, but they only served to deepen the sense of encroaching darkness all around him.

From a walnut wood box at the side of his bed he took a pierced golden sphere, the size of skull, on a chain. He walked to the centre of the room and swung the ball around his head. The holes in the sphere caught the air and a howl like that of a miserable dog sounded, sour and low. The chamberlain muttered incantations into the night – psalms and spells.

'The Lord is merciful and gracious, slow to anger, and plenteous in mercy. He will not always chide; neither will he keep his anger for ever. He hath not dealt with us after our sins, nor rewarded us according to our iniquities.'

He tried to believe it was true, he would be forgiven, his grave sins would be absolved. But still he could not stop the prayer to the goddess coming.

'Hecate, who triumphed over death, who rose in the black jewels of burial, I invoke you. Hecate, lady of the moon and of the shadows of the moon ... I ...'

He broke down, let the chain slacken and sank to his knees.

'You lifted me up. You raised me high. Maintain me so.'

He stood and put the sphere back in the box, went to the window and looked out into the night. Flat black. No moon, no stars. All eaten by the enveloping cloud that sat over the city.

The chamberlain came back from the window, took up a cloth and dipped it into water in a copper basin to wipe his face. He felt sick. The magic sat uneasily in him. It was moon magic, he thought, Hecate's magic, woman's magic – magic that expressed itself in symbols that shone in his mind, that creaked and groaned like a hangman's rope, that sucked and whispered like the sea, that smelled of spring and rebirth or of autumn and death. He rarely dared to use it but kept it damped down inside him with wine and herbs he got from his doctor. But still the symbols asked things of him. They wanted out. He was sure they had attacked the emperor. They fed on Karas' distress, on his discomfort. The operation that had stopped Karas becoming a man had not made him a woman.

What if the scholar discovered the truth? His men told him Loys was not as incompetent as he had hoped. The chamberlain had concealed even the presence of the wolfman from him. But he would find out. Styliane, who he had brought with him from the slum, who he had protected and favoured with his magic and lifted up as a lady, had a sliver of her family's magic inside her – she was working against him, all the reports said so.

The bond with his sister had severed on her thirteenth birthday. The full moon had risen in the sky and in her mind, and she had begun to suspect him. He let her talk and plot against him, for the sake of the guilt he felt, for the thread that connected him to human feelings of duty and love.

All those years, clinging to sanity, clinging to position and to power. Fighting the pull of the runes inside him; thankful for what they had brought him, fearful of what they would bring. When the rebel had risen up the runes had told him Basileios would fall to the usurper. That would have been the end of everything. So he had sweated and starved for a month and allowed the symbols inside him to travel forth to the rebel and strike him down as he rode forward. Such magic, once released, is not easily contained. The comet had come and now the black skies and the wolf.

Karas sat down on a couch and wiped his face again. The cloth came away with blood on it. A nosebleed. He felt disordered and vulnerable. There had to be a way out. There had to be a means, other than death, by which he could avert the fate that stalked him. He had run from the wolf for too long. Perhaps now it was time to seek it.

He would need a ritual.

'Fetch Isais.'

The runes stirred inside him. He needed to establish some sort of control, to at least sacrifice to the goddess who had set the symbols in his mind. The streets were dark enough and the moon – though invisible – was in the right position. He had to go to the hillside, to be among the people he had come from and to make the observances he hoped would buy him a little peace.

After a while there was a whisper at the door. The chamberlain opened it to the commander of the messengers, plainly dressed in dark soldier's attire.

'Tonight?'

'Yes. Immediately.'

'I will arrange it.'

Isais left.

The chamberlain went to a side room where he kept his clothes, including his campaign gear. It was plain and worn, and no one would think that odd. In the field he emulated the emperor in dressing like a common soldier. He took his sword and checked the folds of his padded jacket. Stuffed into a pocket in the interior was a mask of black cloth – like the Arabs wore in the desert – with no more than slits for eyes. He picked up a tight-fitting desert hood, white to reflect the sun and proof against grit and sand. He pulled his horse cloak around him.

The door opened; there was no knock.

Two men accompanied Isais, again dressed plainly as guards.

'The way is clear,' Isais said.

The chamberlain lowered his eyes in acknowledgement and walked out of his chamber, down to a room where there was a secret staircase that led to the bowels of the palace and from there out through the kitchens to a back door to the outside. They encountered no one, Isais as good as his word. The chamberlain put on the desert hood and stepped out into the street. From here it was two hours to the hillside, so they would have to move fast.

25   A Sacrifice

Galti got Loys what he wanted by the second day of waiting — four good Varangians who were not giants and so didn't stand out among the Greeks. They would never pass for natives of the city close up but, at a distance and in dim light, they'd invite no attention. The deal was done on a promise and an oath in Norse — the Vikings said Loys spoke their tongue so he would know the value of a vow. The Vikings wore their sea cloaks, stained and eaten by salt, and covered their heads against the rain with close-fitting caps or cowls. It was dark and the weather miserable. They would pass well enough, thought Loys.

'Chance of a scrap?' said one — a stocky youth, nearly a man, handsome but for his missing teeth. His name was Vandrad.

'Yes, but we need to be careful,' said Loys. 'We're going to watch one of the Greeks' rituals. I want to kidnap one of them and we may have to follow him back into his camp to do it.'

He quickly made his way up the hill, the men following him. All the black lambs had gone from the camp. Up on the hillside torches floated in the murk — nine or ten ascending in the distance.

'There,' he said.

The men trudged on over the sucking ground. The torches were very faint and Loys had no certainty they belonged to the people he sought. But he recalled what he had read — that the ceremonies of the goddess were often conducted by torch-light. They were planned with strict attention to detail, for fear of invoking the goddess's anger.

The night was black. All perspective was gone: the fires and lamps of the camp seemed to hang in space, glowing like odd moons. One of the Varangians took a torch as he passed a tent and no one came out to complain that he had. Ahead the lights they followed were will-o'-the-wisps. Loys almost laughed to himself. He'd been worried about being recognised; they would be practically invisible in the gloom.

From ahead he heard a keyless grumble: dogs howling and moaning on the hill – a lot of dogs.

Loys lost sight of the torches and began to think they had taken a wrong turn, but a track was under their feet and they stuck to that. It was impossible to judge how far they had gone. Only the ground beneath his feet told Loys he was not moving through a murky ocean and he almost imagined sea serpents looming from the mist, the blind grey monsters of childish nightmares.

The going became steep. They still saw no lights ahead but, denied another reference, they headed towards the sound of the dogs. Then they crested a ridge. Lights, lots of lights. Other torches joined those they had followed, coming up a track from another side of the city, while others still descended out of the night.

'On,' said Loys.

The Varangian nearest smiled at him. 'Nair,' he said.

'What?'

'The world of the dead,' said a voice at his shoulder.

Now they climbed over rocks – big boulders. It took all Loys' concentration not to slip and break an ankle. The howling and grumbling of the dogs became louder, and under it they heard a murmur of conversation. People were assembling.

Loys kept going, the Varangians at his back. Something moved by his side. A small dog was leaping from rock to rock and, in doing so, brushed his hand.

'One torch extinguished. We need twenty-seven; there are twenty-eight,' said a voice. Loys took the Varangian's torch and threw it down into a cleft between the rocks.

'Start!' Another voice, from Loys' right.

'Why are you here?' The voice was strong and commanding and Loys almost felt inclined to answer it.

'To stand at the gateway of death,' forty or fifty unseen speakers replied.

'Why do you stand at the gateway of death?'

'To offer homage to the lady of the gateway.'

'What do you seek for this homage?'

'Blessing and protection from evil.'

'She that is Propulaia.'

'Standing before the gate.'

'She that is Chthonia.'

'Lady of the earth, the lower earth and the dark places of the earth.'

'She that is Apotropaia.'

'Protector and guardian.'

'Accept our sacrifice and hear our prayer.'

A lamb's bleat turned to a shriek. The dogs went wild, barking, baying and howling. Still Loys saw very little beyond the soft glow of the torches.

A chant pulsed through the mist. Loys gripped his knife. The voices surrounded him.

'Up out of darkness and subvert all things
With aimless plans, I will call and you may hear
My holy words since terrible destiny
Is ever subject to you. Thrice bound goddess,
Set free yourself, come raging
Plunged in darkness with sorrows fresh,
Grim-eyed, shrill-screaming.
Come.'

Loys shivered. The chant broke into many separate choruses, gabbling on all sides.

'In my power I hold you.'

'Your thrice-locked door.'

'Her burning hearth, her shadow.'

'One morsel of flesh.'

'Blood of a turtledove.'

'Hair of a virgin cow.'

'The bond of all necessity is sundered
And the sun's light is hidden.'

It was a cacophony. Torches flashed; people stamped and dogs howled.

'We need to capture one of them,' said Loys to the Varangian nearest to him. He needed to ask some questions.

'Our sort of work. Wait until they separate. If one goes off on his own we'll have him.'

'And if he doesn't?'

'We'll have him anyway.'

The ceremony continued, with singing and chanting and invocations to the lady of the moon, she that is three, the lady of the cypress, warden of graves, lady of the yew, filler of graves, lady of the mandrake whose birthplace is the grave.

More flames flared. Loys guessed they were burning branches held up high.

Then there was shouting and moaning and a voice cried out loudly, 'Do not drive these demons on to us, we who have evoked your displeasure. Three black lambs have been sacrificed, as you require, three times nine torches, as you require; the invocations have been observed, the three directions faced and the three names called. Do not abandon us.'

A word came from all around that sounded very much like 'Amen' and the torches began to move away.

'We'll take the last to leave,' said Loys.

'If only to get their light,' said Vandrad. The fog was truly freakish – Loys could see no more than five paces ahead.

The torches filed away, dark figures passing them clambering over the rocks. As careful to conceal their own identity as to demonstrate their lack of curiosity in that of others, none paused to look at the Varangians.

Only one or two torches remained, up near where the ceremony been conducted.

Loys heard voices through the still air.

'We need to open the gate again.'

'Not yet. I stepped through it years ago. That way is a hard one and I will not walk it while there are alternatives.'

'But the comet, the sky, these deaths. You need to look for an answer.'

'I can scarcely hold what I have inside me. You don't know how it costs me – what might be asked.'

'If you went within you might rid yourself of the magic. It is that which causes these abominations to afflict us.'

'I do not know. I do not know.'

'Could the Christians be right? Could this be the end of the world?'

'Or the Norsemen or the Arabs. They both seem to agree a one-eyed god must emerge, and we haven't seen him yet.'

'I'm glad you can joke about it, sir.'

'I don't joke. Who knows what is happening?'

'You have taken from the goddess; now she wants something back.'

'I don't know. The wolfman. What about him?'

Loys edged closer with the Norsemen. One of the voices was high-pitched – a eunuch. *The chamberlain?* He told himself not to be ridiculous. The chamberlain grubbing in the dirt with heathens? *Impossible.* The other voice was familiar to him, he thought. But who? He stumbled on a rock.

'Is there someone there?'

Silence.

'We need to go.'

The torches moved off, but the Varangians had clearly

decided they were in striking distance of their prey. They ran forward. Confusion, shouts.

'Hey! Let me go!'

'Run!'

A torch fell and someone cried out in pain, but the other torch went bobbing across the rocks, down and away. Loys crawled forward. Someone jumped at the limit of his vision – a shadow across the torchlight, no more. Then, leaping from rock to rock through the mist, came a figure. It crashed straight into Loys, knocking him down.

'Who the—'

The man had hold of Loys by the tunic. He wore a desert hood but Loys saw clearly who it was.

'Isias!'

The spymaster said nothing, just drew a knife.

Loys could not say if it was the instant before or the instant after that he thought of the spymaster's threat to Beatrice, thought of the impossible task he had been set and the creeping anxiety about what would happen if he failed, thought of the peril in which he had been forced to put his soul, of the tensions he had felt even before coming to Constantinople as he cast aside his life as a monk to take up one of poverty with his lover, the lady of Rouen.

His life seemed to revolve around that moment on the rocks. Everything he had ever done divided into before and after he took his little knife from his belt and stabbed Isais in the neck. He did it without thought, but when it was done, thought came in on Loys like a wave into a headland.

The spymaster lost his footing and slipped between the rocks, blood pulsing from a terrible wound. He tried to speak, but his voice was a rasp and he lay back on the jagged boulders, kicked twice and died.

Someone came towards him – crawling quick as a cat, though he carried a torch. A Varangian.

'The others are gone. Is this one useful to you?'

Loys was breathless, more with shock than exertion. What had he done? He had killed. He was a murderer.

The Varangian went to the body.

'Dead,' he said, and immediately started looting the corpse, stripping him of his soldier's padded jacket, his boots.

Loys crossed himself and tried to gather his thoughts.

'What now, boss?'

'Where are the others?'

The Varangian gave a couple of sharp whistles and waved the torch. There was a scurrying on the boulders and the other three appeared.

'They got away from us. You run in this gloom and you only break an ankle.'

Vandrad examined the corpse. 'A rich man?'

'Money enough,' said the first Varangian.

'Can you hide him?' asked Loys.

'We'll get him in between these rocks with a bit of effort.'

'Good. Let's do that and get back down.'

Isias was a short man, if a stocky one, and it was not too difficult to push him into a cleft.

Loys forced himself to think logically. *Would the stolen clothes identify the Varangians?* He doubted it. Isias had been dressed as a simple soldier and the Varangians had looted hundreds of such men at Abydos.

'Let's go,' said Loys. 'Who knows who might come looking up here if we stay too long.'

They made their way off the hill, down to the fires of the Varangian camp. Loys would stay there until dawn and then enter when the city gates opened. They reached Vandrad's tent and Loys watched while the men built a fire. His heart was racing and his head ached. Murder. The word resonated in his head like a struck gong. Sin begets sin, so his abbot had said. First fornication, now murder. He stared into the Varangians' fire, trying to anchor his thoughts. He had acted in self-defence, against a heathen too, very likely. But why had Isais been there? He was too prominent, too well known. He ran the spy network; he surely didn't take part in individual operations.

It had all happened so quickly and reason had given way to animal instinct. But another, darker thought was building. If he had captured Isias, could he have allowed him to live? Would he have told the Varangians to cut his throat? Could he have risked letting Isias know he had been spied on, to return to the palace and move against Loys in whatever terrible way he chose? Loys shivered, though he sat near to the fire. He concluded he had done in anger something that cold reason may have commanded, had he time to think about it.

The more he did think, the more worried he became. Isias was the head of the messenger service. It was he who had spoken through the dark rain, he who had called someone else 'sir'. The other person had had a reedy voice. The implications terrified Loys. He couldn't have said for sure it was the chamberlain but he was far from certain it was not.

Could the man who had employed him really be a sorcerer himself? He found the thought very difficult to accept. But Styliane had been plain in her accusations. And what of the wolfman he had mentioned? Who was he?

Loys prayed for forgiveness, promised God he would donate greatly to his churches and slept an uneasy sleep.

It wasn't until he entered the gatehouse on his return to the city that his thoughts cleared and he remembered the guards had a record of his leaving. Clearly, he and Beatrice had to get out of Constantinople and fast.

26 A Wolf Discovered

Loys was woken in his room by the sound of banging on his door. Beatrice retired to the woman's quarters and the servant opened the door. Six soldiers confronted him.

'By order of the chamberlain,' said the officer, a squat hairy man who gave the impression of having been basted in oil, 'I appoint these your guards.'

'I have no need of guards.'

'They will attend you whenever you leave the palace and wait outside your room here when you are at home. Intelligence has revealed there may be a threat to your life. We need to be careful.'

'I can look after myself and it's necessary for me to do delicate and painstaking work. I can't have soldiers tramping around. How do you think I'll ever get anyone to speak to me?'

'The guards will take up their posts now,' said the officer. He turned smartly and the men followed him out of the room. At least they weren't going to actually stand guard at his shoulder.

Beatrice came out from her chamber.

She spoke quietly. 'We're prisoners?'

'Maybe. I don't know.'

Loys had told Beatrice nothing about what had happened outside the city, just that he had made progress towards his goal and she should be ready to leave quickly.

'I'm not a fool, Loys. You tell me we need to depart and suddenly we have an armed guard. Why?'

'Like I said. I think the nearer I get to the truth, the more dangerous I become.'

She held his hand and whispered, 'Then assume we are scrutinised at every moment. Our servant cannot be trusted, nor any messenger or soldier. Everything you say must be said as if the chamberlain stands in the room with us.'

She had made up his mind for him. He wouldn't tell her anything.

'How are you?' he said. 'I've hardly asked.'

'I'm well.'

He drew her to him, hugged her and said, 'I will work out a way to bring us through this. We will overcome our difficulties, I promise.'

Loys' old life was behind him. No looking to God now. He had fornicated. He had killed. If his soul was to be saved he needed to act as God's soldier – become a martyr even – in the pursuit of truth. For himself he could have done it, thrown his life away heroically. But when he thought of Beatrice carrying his unborn child and felt the solidity of his connection to them, he could not.

He had no choice: he needed to make a success of his time in Constantinople, under whatever conditions he found himself. Philosophy, though, was an indulgence he couldn't allow himself. From now on Loys needed to be a man of practicalities, focused on survival. Ironically, that brought him back to seeking the truth. If he identified sorcerers at the heart of the court then he would have done his job. Styliane had come forward as an ally. She might be useful.

Loys was sure the secret of his role in the spymaster's death was as secure as it could be. He had told the Varangians the soldier came from an elite unit, and they should sell his clothes quickly and deny knowledge of his murder. Politics, he had said, could mean their commanders would hand them over to be hanged.

The Vikings hadn't understood what he meant by politics so he had simply asked them to vow not mention the death. They said if he would consider them for future work they were happy to swear. He said he would and they swore. That was enough for Loys, who knew the Norsemen didn't take such oaths lightly.

191

The only evidence against him was he had been outside the walls when Isias died. That proved nothing but it did raise questions. Hence the guards? He may have been followed, but no one could have seen what had happened in that unnatural night.

If it had been the chamberlain out there in the murk, then what? Loys remembered the words he had heard on the hill. Isias had been sure the person to whom he was speaking was in some way responsible for the odd occurrences. The other man, though, had been less certain. And he was the senior.

He felt a powerful urge to simply give up but he knew that was impossible. Even if, as he was starting to suspect, the chamberlain didn't want him to discover anything, then he would still punish him for coming back empty-handed in a pretence of displeasure. What to do? Blame the Varangians. But that would not stop the sky, would not cure the emperor. He had to find the truth and then decide how he would use it.

Beatrice was very near to giving birth now and that filled Loys with dread. Had he imperilled her and the child? For a moment all the normal anxieties of a father whose wife is about to have a baby engulfed him. Would she be all right? Women died in childbirth all the time. He couldn't bear to lose her.

She was at his side, his hands in hers.

'Attention to duty is your best way forward.' She kissed him. 'We will prevail, now get back to work. There is a man who has been trying to see you for the last five days. You might start by interviewing him.'

'Who?'

'Meletios – he's been calling every day since you sent for him.'

Kavallarios Meletios was a chubby minor official of the court responsible for checking prisoners in and out of the Numera. Loys was used to intimidating people by now and the policy had reaped some dividends. He had received no open threats from anyone and even been invited to celebrate certain feast days with some lesser officials of the court. Meletios, however, needed no intimidating. The man all but sobbed as he came through the door.

Loys' servant sat Meletios in front of the desk then left the room. Loys picked up his fan, turned the open end towards Meletios and opened his hands, the sign he was conducting an official interview. They exchanged the tedious formalities of the official greeting and then Loys began.

'You know why—' Loys didn't have time to finish his sentence.

'I have been mentioned, I am aware of that.'

Loys said nothing. One of the effects of his investigation had been to allow all manner of grudge bearers to come to him seeking to make life difficult for their enemies. So Meletios had been mentioned, but it would have been very surprising if he hadn't been. Only great men were exempt from being named because they were exempt from being called.

'I know what people are saying,' he said, 'but it was not me who lost the sorcerer. He was a sorcerer, that's the thing. You can't give a man like that to normal guards without warning. That's how he got away.'

Loys tapped the table and snorted in a way that indicated he didn't think that was much of an excuse. He had no idea what the man was talking about.

'I allocated him four guards,' said Meletios. 'Four! That should be enough for any man. And I guarantee this – he has not escaped. He is down there, somewhere in the old tunnels, and sooner or later he will starve.'

This, thought Loys, was interesting. He decided to remain impassive, to give nothing away. He had to increase the pressure on Meletios, to make him feel blamed.

'Your guards aren't up to much if one man overpowered four of them.'

'Well, he marched into the emperor's tent through an entire army, didn't he? They didn't stop him. I needed warning. I only found out what he'd done by the back door. Thank God I have friends in this palace.'

'This is the sorcerer?'

'Yes, the Varangian.'

That surprised Loys. He had been told the sorcerer was an Arab. Perhaps there was another one. Or perhaps – as seemed more likely – rumour had turned the deranged Norseman into an Arab somewhere between Meliotos and the doorkeeper who had spoken to Loys.

'And what did he do to the emperor?'

'Threatened to kill him.'

'Why?'

'Well, you tell me. He's a wolfman of the wilds – why do they do anything?'

A wolfman? The figure on the hillside had mentioned someone like that and speculated he might have something to do with the strange occurrences. Was that the same person who had attacked the emperor? The chamberlain had simply called him a savage and dismissed the danger he'd posed.

'No, you tell me. I will then judge your blame in this matter.'

'I'm not to blame.'

'The sorcerer escaped somehow. Someone must be.'

Meletios was deathly pale now.

'I am an official, no more, an official who has done his best. I was given an impossible task – to restrain a highly dangerous prisoner without proper warning and—'

'Meletios, we all have difficult tasks.' Loys smiled. 'My task is difficult. Make it easier and I will do my best to make sure you do not suffer for what you have done. Why did the sorcerer go to the emperor?'

'To kill him, I thought. Others say he came to warn him. Look, I shouldn't be telling you this, but I can see the writing on the wall. I know which way this is going and where the blame will be dumped. Me.'

Loys wondered why the chamberlain had not seen fit to inform him a sorcerer had had direct contact with the emperor. How could he dismiss a man who had breached the imperial tent as a mere lunatic?

'Where is the sorcerer now?'

'Well, he hasn't got out of the Numera, I know that much. He'd have to get past four sets of guards to do that, and we might be lax but we're not that lax.'

Loys breathed in. Here was his first solid clue connecting the emperor with dark forces. A sorcerer had confronted the emperor. But the chamberlain had seen fit to play it down. Why? And did he really think Loys wouldn't find out? Perhaps he genuinely believed the sorcerer to be unconnected with the magical attack on the emperor and the darkening of the sky.

'Have you searched for this man?'

'Of course, but he's gone into the lower tunnels. There are so many and the men are too scared to go down there. The chamberlain sent four down but they never came back.'

'And no one's mentioned this?'

'They told us to keep quiet.' The man's eyes widened. 'But you knew all this. I mean, you're the chamberlain's man. I'm not revealing secrets here. It was your office that gave the order.'

Loys said nothing again. He wanted Meletios to feel uncomfortable.

'What happened to the men?'

'I don't know. Those tunnels are winding and full of ghosts. They got lost; the wolfman got them; they're still down there. Who knows? Not my men. Not my problem.'

'It's your problem that you lost the wolfman.'

'Yes.'

'So you can do me a favour.'

'What?'

'You can help me look for him.'

'I haven't got any men who would be willing to do that.'

'Why not?'

'People have seen things in the tunnels.'

'What?'

'Ghosts.'

'Men's fears can conjure phantoms from the dark where

there are none. You will search the tunnels and bring the wolf-man to me within the week.'

'I cannot do that. The chamberlain himself could not make my men do that. He rules according to the law and has no power to command it. The Hetaereian generals wouldn't allow it. That's why we used mercenaries.'

'I will visit tomorrow and you will escort me. Either that or I will have you imprisoned in your own dungeon. Am I clear?'

The man said nothing, just stared.

'Am I clear?'

'You are clear. But you will find it hard to get men to go with you. You could get lost and never be heard of again.'

'It's possible to get lost and never be heard of again just walking out of the palace. Losing a prisoner of the emperor is treason. And you know the penalty for that.'

Meletios swallowed, opened his mouth and let out a loud pant like an exhausted dog.

'If you insist on coming, then I will have no choice but to escort you,' he said.

'Fine, then tomorrow.'

'Yes.'

'And one thing. It is not politic the world knows about this. Do you have the name of a prisoner I could pretend to interview?'

'I've got a thousand of 'em,' said Meletios.

'Good, then put the word about that I'm coming to interview some unfortunate of your prison,' said Loys.

'Yes, lord,' said Meletios, which Loys thought was overdoing it.

Loys moved the fan to dismiss the man. When he had gone, the scholar put his head into his hands.

Beatrice came out from behind the screen. 'You put yourself in great danger.'

He smiled. 'A noble man disdains to show fear. Isn't that what you told me? I have the option to go – I don't have to. It was just the way the questioning went. Do you think it's wise?'

'I think it sounds dangerous. But to do nothing is dangerous too. You must be seen to be making progress so it's necessary and it's politic to look for the truth. Only when you glimpse it can you assess if you need to walk towards it or away. Styliane implied ...'

Her voice trailed away. She didn't have to finish her sentence and it might have been dangerous to do so.

The lady had hinted her brother had something to do with the curse that attended the emperor and the town, even unwillingly. And she had suggested Loys might be vulnerable. So if Loys gained possession of the truth he would at least have either a weapon against the chamberlain or he would know how to construct a convincing lie to please the great man. The figure on the hillside − if that was the chamberlain − had mentioned the wolfman and had clearly been puzzled by him. If Loys could offer an explanation that might raise the chamberlain's respect for him. Did he want the favour of a magician? Well, Loys had killed, hadn't he? Kissing a pagan's sandals was a small sin when held against that.

There were good reasons for a visit to the Numera: it would show he needed to be taken seriously, that things could not be hidden from him. And if he came near the truth ...

'I hope a hunt for the wolfman might see me removed from the investigation,' said Loys. 'The chamberlain doesn't want me to know about him or he would have told me. If it looks as though I might turn up something embarrassing then perhaps he will release me from this task.'

'And then what? Back to the lighthouse quarter?'

Loys shook his head. 'The chamberlain cannot have me fail. That becomes his failure. No, I think that if Styliane ...' He didn't finish, letting a shrug convey what he meant − if Styliane had spoken the truth and the chamberlain was implicated then ... 'He will find a way to have me succeed that causes the least damage to those he values.'

'Or he will have you killed.'

'That would show he couldn't protect me. No. I am beginning

to understand these great men. The point is not to succeed but to please the competing interests around us. A visit to the Numera does all those things. If we find nothing then it will at least signal we are looking in the right area. If we find the wolfman then the chamberlain can only be pleased – he was seeking him himself.'

'Four men are missing.'

'The point is to make a show of visiting. It's better to look and not discover anything. Then we offer a threat but not so strong that anyone must move against us.'

'You're becoming quite the courtier.'

'God gave me brains. I have neglected to use them up until now,' said Loys. 'It's time I put that right.'

'Be careful.' She kissed him.

'You're always telling me to be bold.'

'Be careful while being bold.'

'Very like a woman,' he said.

'And very like a man to seem to be bold while being careful.'

He smiled and kissed her back.

'You have my plan in a nutshell,' he said.

27 Hidden by Darkness

Loys walked over to the Numera. It was dusk, or the time that should have been dusk, but the sky was black, and the only light was from the lamp carried by the two guards who accompanied him and from those of the citizens who moved around the streets.

The fog was almost choking and he could see very little. The prison was invisible from the palace, not eighty paces away. Loys followed the palace wall and then took off at the diagonal across the square. A few steps into the filthy air and the prison loomed like a menacing rock seen from a ship.

As he walked, he kept one hand on the short knife stuffed into his belt. Loys came to the gate of the prison. A group of four women strained at the bars of the gate, shoving through loaves and wine, money and even clothing to the guards. The only way of surviving the Numera was to have friends or relatives on the outside working for you, agitating for your release, bringing in supplies and offering bribes to the guards to take them in. Loys wondered how much of what was intended for the prisoners ever made its way to them.

The gate guarded the front of a small compound leading to the entrance to the prison itself, a black doorway no wider than two men. He went to the gate and leaned through the bars. A guard was relaying news of prisoners to those outside He caught the man's attention with a quick 'Hey,' and he came strolling over.

'Meletios,' said Loys, 'get him here now.'

'Your manners aren't up to much, are they?'

Loys withdrew his cloak to expose the blue silk beneath. The man gave a little whistle of surprise and went back into the prison. Loys stood tapping at the gate with his shoe. Then the fat form of Meletios came out of the dark doorway with two guards, their swords drawn.

Meletios gestured to the gate with his eyes and one of the guards unlocked it.

'Quick!' said Meletios as the gate opened.

His own guards went to come through, along with an old woman who tried to shove in front of them. One of the guards brought her a smart whack with the flat of his sword and she stepped back for a second, allowing him to close the gate.

'We need to come with the quaestor,' said one of Loys' guards.

'No one but Numeri in here, chief, you know the rules,' said Meletios.

Loys' guards protested uselessly. Already Meletios was guiding Loys towards the entrance of the prison. Loys smiled to himself. He'd anticipated having to jolly his guards along in the Numera. Now he wouldn't face that problem.

'If we left that open we'd be overrun,' said Meletios.

'Don't people normally try to get out of prison?' said Loys.

'Plebian idiots,' said Meletios. 'They think they can just walk in here and take their friends out with them. I don't know what they think we're running here.'

'What are you running here? Looks more like an extortion operation than a prison to me,' said Loys.

Meletios bowed his head. 'I have everything ready for you to descend,' he said. 'Mark that I have exerted myself for you.'

Loys swallowed down a 'thank you'. The chamberlain's men expected such indulgences as a right.

He followed Meletios to the dark doorway. Heat and a terrible stench breathed from it. Loys was reminded of a rotten mouth in an ugly face.

They entered through a short corridor. Ahead of him Loys heard music, a high nasal pipe and a drum. Meletios opened an inner door.

It opened into a large vaulted room lit by reed torches, ropes of incense smoke curling in the stale air. A band of musicians played in one corner and a girl danced across the floor. She was very beautiful, dark-haired and dark-eyed, and she wore long scarves of bright silks tied about her body. A man lay in chains on a rich couch of green velvet watching her. She bent backwards and writhed in front of him, casting herself to the floor, rising again and discarding a scarf.

'Can you believe this?' said Meletios. 'Even in here some people need to demonstrate their wealth. This is supposed to be some sort of ceremony.'

'It's the dance of the seven veils, or a version of it,' said Loys.

'What's that?'

'A pagan myth. The goddess Ishtar goes to the underworld to seek wisdom. As she passes through each of the seven gates that lead there she is forced by the gatekeeper to discard an item of clothing until she is naked. She bargains to escape the underworld, taking up her clothes as she goes. When she emerges she is free but must find someone to replace her. She chooses her brother, who has been drunk since she has been gone.'

'Well, she wouldn't be emerging from here if it wasn't for those two,' said Meletios. He nodded to two men who sat in the corner. Loys recognised them as Normans. Her guards, doubtless. He didn't know them, so chances were they wouldn't recognise him.

'You allow prisoners to have private armed guards in here?'

Meletios shrugged. 'We allow anything for the right price.'

'Even to walk free?'

'Depending on the quality of your enemies,' said Meletios.

'So this merchant must have high-quality enemies indeed.'

'Very high.'

Four men came to join them – prison guards.

'Do we need so many?' said Loys.

'Word gets around,' said Meletios, 'I don't like it any more than you do but they were sent over from the palace under imperial seal. Someone doesn't want anything unpleasant happening to you.'

Loys had felt clever losing his guards. He felt less clever now he realised that whoever was watching him was one step ahead.

'Who sent them?'

'Don't know, emperor's seal. Could have been anyone.'

Loys appraised the men. No uniform to speak of.

'Who sent you?'

'Army chief of staff, sir,' said a man at the front, 'we're here for your protection.'

'With four of you we should be all right if I'm attacked by a small nation in here. Let's get it over with, shall we?'

They passed through two more sets of doors, down another tight corridor and out into a wider, darker, danker area, where the roof was supported by tall pillars. Here there was no dancing, just songs from the men who sat chained, calls to Christ and for loved ones.

Someone sang a kontakion in a high, clear voice: 'Though thou didst descend into the grave, O immortal one, yet didst thou destroy the power of Hades, and didst arise as victory.'

'The wolfman's hiding in here?' Loys spoke quietly to Meletios.

'No, in the tunnels below.'

Loys swallowed. This was clearly not the worst horror the prison had to offer. Another door, steps and a smell like a fist in the face.

Melietos took a torch off the wall, seemingly unbothered by the fetid air.

'Down.'

'Here?'

'Still further.'

They descended the steps to a vision from a doom painting – the mouth of hell made real on earth – men lying wasting and dying in irons, too weak to call out, stewing in their own filth.

He was powerless to help these people and that made him angry. He could use his authority to get one released, maybe two, but he couldn't order them all freed. Besides, they were there for a reason. The state would collapse if crimes went unpunished.

'The tunnels are beyond, sir,' said Meletios.

Every sinew in Loys' body seemed to strain to return to the surface. A deep animal repugnance was in him, an instinctive need to withdraw from filth and disease. He steeled himself and followed Meletios over the bodies of the sick and the dead.

The room, an adapted natural cavern, was huge and it led away into denser darkness at its far end. As Meletios's torch revealed more, Loys saw the roof dropped quite quickly. Only a narrow crack in the wall by the floor gave any indication it continued. The crack was nowhere near tall enough to walk through or even crawl. Anyone wanting to go within would have to writhe on their belly and trust they would not get stuck, or that the floor didn't fall away into nothing beyond the limit of the torchlight. Loys picked his way among the bodies to examine it closer.

'That's the way down,' said Meletios, 'that's where the sorcerer went.'

'Why has this never been sealed?' said Loys. 'Can't the prisoners escape this way?'

'To what?'

'To something other than this.'

'They are chained,' said Meletios, 'as you can see. Even if they weren't, that way offers only death. You can get lost, you can fall, or the ghosts of the passages can take you.'

'All the more reason to seal it,' said Loys.

'It was sealed,' said Meletios, 'but God was angry and shook the earth to unblock it. It's said it's a path to hell and I have no wish to explore it.'

Loys had imagined the caves as tall and broad affairs, not like this. Was he going to pursue the wolfman into there?

Meletios saw his hesitation. 'Would you like to go in, sir?'

'Pass me your lamp.'

'Or perhaps you'd like to interview the prisoners.'

'Why?'

'They were here; they may have seen something.'

Be careful. Beatrice's words came back to him.

Meletios watched Loys with mocking eyes. He reckoned he didn't have the stomach for it.

'I will look within. You know the way – lead.'

'I don't know the way,' said Meletios. 'I don't know the way at all. I've never been down there.'

'Perhaps you should have. You've left a dangerous wolfman roaming in there.'

'He's no danger. We have two sets of strong doors between us and him.'

'Go within.'

'Six men died.'

'So now you know they died. You said they might be lost.'

'Lost, dead, it's the same thing here. Will you not speak to the prisoners? One has seen him.'

'Who?'

'The scholar, the monk. Let me find him.'

Meletios raised his torch and peered around.

'He was here, he was. Wait!' Panic was in his voice.

He galumphed to the stairs, jumping over the bodies that obstructed his way, and went up. Very quickly he was back with a guard.

'Where is he?' Meletios was almost hysterical, shouting and gesturing as he pulled the man down the steps.

'We have a number of monks in here.'

'The special prisoner. The lady's prisoner.'

'The Norman Azémar?' said the guard.

Loys felt all the breath leave him.

'Yes, him.'

'He should be here.'

The two men searched through the prisoners, turning them over where they lay, staring into wasted and pale faces.

'What was that name?' said Loys.

Meletios came to him and bent his knee.

'On my life, sir, I speak honestly now and hope you will deal with me kindly. I understand there is a prisoner who you know here. I had hoped for you to discover him so I might win favour with you for bringing you to him and arranging his release. He has gone. That places me in grave danger.'

'Who is this prisoner?'

'Azémar, a Norman. He begged us to contact you when I admitted him. He says he is here to warn you. I—'

'Why didn't you?' A cold fury rose up inside him. Azémar? His friend.

'I was forbidden from doing so. An express order on high imperial authority.'

'What was he doing here? Who ...' Loys was so shocked Azémar was in that awful place his thoughts failed him.

'I am a servant and a jailer; I know nothing of these things.'

'Are you a jailer? You seem scarcely capable of doing anything other than taking bribes. Why didn't you come to me with this information?'

'He remains here by the authority of the chamberlain. His sister put him here and she derives her right from him. I would be as good as dead if I told you about him. If you discovered him, however ...'

Loys was convinced he had been played for a fool by someone. Why was Azémar in this prison? Unless he really had come to warn him about something and had been prevented from doing so. By whose hand? Was Beatrice in danger? *No, Loys, think clearly.* Whoever his enemies were they hadn't struck at him yet. An assassination or an abduction in the emperor's house would cause more trouble than it was worth.

He had to help his friend.

'Forgive me.' Meletios was actually on his knees.

'So where do you think he has gone?'

'There can be only one place, sir,' said Meletios. 'Down

there, in the caves. He's somehow slipped his bonds and tried to escape that way.'

Loys pushed Meletios in the chest and stared into his face.

'That man was my mentor and my friend,' he said, 'and we are going to find him.' He turned to the guards. 'You lot,' he said, 'can at least make yourselves useful.'

28 The Wolf Free

The dark did not frighten Azémar as he crawled through the tunnels because it was not a true darkness.

The touch of the rocks, the far-off sound of water and above all the smell, the smell of the wolfman, brought pictures to his mind, showing him the way forward. This did not strike him as strange, or rather he thought it only slightly odd he had never noticed these senses before.

As he went on it seemed to him he wandered in other caverns, the caverns of the mind. He was there for a purpose, he recalled. In fact he was there for several purposes. He tried to order them. He was in Constantinople. Why? To find lodgings. No. That was his purpose but it was not his main purpose. Why else? To kill someone. No. To save someone. To save someone and to kill someone. The same person. The thought almost struck him as funny. He was in the caves. Why? Because someone had put him there. No. He had gone there himself. Someone else wanted him to leave. Who wanted him to leave? A wolf. A wolf who was not a wolf.

He remembered his youth, running on the riverbank with other boys on a deep green day in summer. He had run that way before, years before, in lives gone by – now he could sense it.

Memories tumbled through his mind, no more intelligible when he tried to understand them than the blot of an ink cup spilled across a page. He remembered a cornfield, the sun on the unripe stems, the sparkle of the river waters and beside him the woman in her black robe with her hair a burning gold. 'Do not seek me,' she had said. Yet he had sought her – he thought he had known her a long time.

In recent years, sleep sent him to strange places. He found

himself by a low peasant house, its turf roof no more than waist-high, watching the woman with the golden hair putting herbs out to dry on the thatch. He wanted to talk to her, to tell her he loved her. But she ran from him — always she ran and he followed, begging her to stop.

All his life he had been happy in the monastery. The food was plentiful, the company good, and he was a natural scholar. His order required obedience, stability and conversion to its way of life. He had no need to convert. He had lived under the rule of the monks since his earliest years.

One day he had been working the fields. The lord rode by and behind him his children. He'd seen her in the distance across the river, the duke's daughter on her grey horse, flanked by warriors. For a moment he glimpsed another life, imagined he was one of those men, destined to marry, to have children and to fight in wars. Then he had gone back to his toil.

His friend Loys had gone, if not to fight then to love, and Azémar had been left with his books, observing the hours of devotion, making the food, cleaning and cooking.

He crawled forward on his belly.

'What have I been? What have I been?'

He sensed water.

Lights flared behind him, lights and voices. He stood, his shadow long on the walls. From somewhere in the tunnels another voice called. A woman. A girl?

There was water in front of him. The water connected him to her. He put his mouth to it and drank.

'This is the stream . . .'

He said the words himself and edged forward into the water. A song came to his lips.

'The water weft that knots in the world well.
Where the dead god took his lore.'

A current tugged him forward. Was the current of this world or of the dream world?

A scream.

'What are you doing? It's him you want!'

'You've made enough mistakes, Meletios!'

'In the name of the chamberlain, I tell you to stop!'

He recognised one of the voices behind him. It seemed to recall something of his old self, before the Numera, before he had eaten of bloody fruits, sucked knowledge from the marrow of men's bones, seen the world as it is, in its stains and its sweats, its smears and its stinks, not as men imagine it to be.

There was another scream and a crash.

'He's got a knife! The bastard has a knife!'

'Where's he gone? Get that torch lit again. You idiot, get a light!'

Frantic voices jabbered down from the upper tunnels, floating on a hot wave of panic, delicious to Azémar as the smell of a cooking pot.

You are near her. Bring her. I will be your salvation. It was a girl's voice, sounding in his mind as clearly as if she'd been standing next to him.

'Who are you?'

One who sits and waits. She who gave the most for lore.

'You are a demon.'

No.

'You are a thing of darkness.'

You are of the dark, of all fears and fancies made.

'Who are you?'

Bring her to me.

'Who?'

There was no answer.

'Get a light! A light!' The voices again.

A cry, a shout of pain brought him jolting back to himself.

He remembered Loys. His friend was just a child when he'd met him, too scared to sleep in the big dormitory, crying in anguish and loneliness. Azémar had told him he'd felt like that too on his first night. Loys was among friends, kind and gentle people who would help him.

'Find him. Here. That's better. There, down the passage, down the passage.' The harsh voices were full of panic.

Azémar spoke: 'I would not be what I am.'

What are you? It was the girl's voice.

'A hunger,' said Azémar.

You are the wolf.

And then he was running towards the lights that flickered from the upper passages, towards the screaming and the stink of fear that drifted down.

Six men, one on the floor dead, one rushing past him, others pursuing.

Azémar didn't think or question. His keen senses put the world into two categories now — foe and everything else. The man plunging into the dark behind him was not his enemy. The others, their sweat sharp with the stress of battle, their hearts pounding out a rhythm of excitement and fear, their knives bright in the lamplight, were the same guards as the men who had dragged him to the dungeon and left him to fester.

He sprang from the shadows unseen and unsuspected, catching both men in his arms, lifting them and slamming them down hard. Then the others attacked. A knife drove at his belly but it seemed slow, like the man was passing it to him rather than trying to kill him. Azémar stepped past the blade to deliver a backhanded blow to the man's throat, crushing his windpipe and sending him choking to the floor.

The next knifeman stabbed at him with a high, downward motion. Azémar caught the knife hand and pulled him forward, driving the man's head into a knee and knocking him cold. Then he span to face the two behind him. They'd regained their feet staggering, groggy, like men on a ship's deck in a gale. Azémar leaped at the nearest, seizing his head and thrusting his teeth into his neck. The man fell back, his head and chest soaked in a burst of blood. The last died more easily, his neck broken with a quick twist.

Azémar sank to his knees, the man's head in his hands.

'I am a hunger,' he said.

You are a hunger, said the voice in his head.

His nails worked back the skin of the chest to expose the flesh beneath and he ate, enraptured by the taste of blood.

'Azémar! Azémar!'

The voice. He recognised it. Who was it?

'It's me, Loys. Leave him! You have starved too long in here. You've gone mad. Leave him!'

Azémar tried to speak. 'I ...' The word seemed like an anchor to his storm-blown thoughts.

'Azémar, please. It's me. Loys.' The man had a torch in his hand.

'Yes. I knew you at Rouen.'

'You knew me? I'm your friend, Azémar. Do you not remember?'

'You were scared and I comforted you.' His voice was distant.

'I have come to save you, to take you from this place. You're not yourself. You need to recover.'

'Yes.'

'Come on. Come with me.'

'The guards will fetter me again.'

'No. I have authority over them. These are not prison guards. They are enemies of mine sent to kill me. Come on. I will get you out. You need proper food and drink and to be clean again.'

'Yes.'

Loys searched the bodies. There was nothing on them.

'How did you find me?'said Azémar.

'We thought we saw you and followed you down.'

'I have not moved.'

'Then it was someone else. Let's get to the surface. Can you find the way?'

Azémar pointed up the passageway.

'To the bad air,' he said, 'and beyond it to the good air. Can't you smell it?'

'No, not here.'

'I can. And other things too, the water and the rock, the blood and the corruption of death. I can smell it all. I can feel it on my skin. I don't know what has become of me. I am not myself.'

'We won't speak of it again. No man can be held responsible for what he does down here. God's light does not shine here.'

'Do his eyes see?'

'The test he set you was too hard. Come on, to the surface. You will return to yourself with care and with affection.'

Loys extended his hand to Azémar, who took it and allowed his friend to pull him to his feet.

'Loys.'

'Yes.'

'Loys.'

Azémar said the word almost as if he didn't understand it. A presence he recognised was at his side, someone who had shown him kindness and to whom he in turn had shown kindness.

'Loys?' That name. He knew it. He had said it for a reason.

'Azémar, my friend, we have you, we have you.'

'Save me,' said Azémar, as a darkness came down upon him and he fainted into Loys' arms.

29 Snake in the Eye's Bargain

Mauger tried to dissuade Arnulf from pursuing his claim of *hölmgang* against Snake in the Eye. The boy was rash; he had been humiliated in front of the camp; too much blood had been spilled already.

Snake in the Eye stood watching the negotiation, his mouth wet with anticipation. He wanted to see Arnulf die and was afraid Mauger — or Ragnar, as he was now known — was on the verge of backing out. He had guessed the man was more than a monk the first time he had seen him. Mauger's way of walking, how he had scanned the buildings from the top of the church steps — not warily, as a field mouse, but boldly, like a hawk. His fighting skills were impressive, but would he use them on Snake in the Eye's behalf? Was he trying to crawl out of what he had promised? 'You will help me with my problem,' Snake in the Eye had said, 'and I will help you with yours with the scholar.'

He needn't have worried. Arnulf wanted vengeance for his son and insisted on his right to ritual combat. He couldn't fight the boy but he could strike his friend and feel someone had paid for the grief he was suffering.

They had gone to it down by the shore on a black morning when the wind whipped in from the ocean and the air was full of grit and sleet. Mauger's sword had caused an intake of breath in the crowd. It was an excellent Frankish weapon, its blade almost blue beneath the shroud of dark clouds.

Arnulf had a spear in his hand and an axe in his belt.

Three shields each were allowed. Snake in the Eye had bought them for Mauger. The Norman held one; the boy held another ready, and a third lay nearby.

Bollason called, 'Go,' and the two men circled each other.

A flash of steel and it was over. Arnulf took two quick steps towards Mauger, who retreated, but when his opponent took a third step, Mauger suddenly advanced, brushing away the spear with his shield and slashing at Arnulf's left calf. The shield offered no protection there and the sword bit flesh, forcing Arnulf to one knee.

Snake in the Eye cheered as Mauger drove a kick into his opponent's face, sending him back into the mud. Mauger stepped forward again, sword high, but Arnulf was unconscious on the cold ground.

'Do I have to finish it?' said Mauger to Bollason.

'Yes!' shouted Snake in the Eye.

Bollason gave the boy a simmering glare. Then his eyes turned back to Mauger. 'No. I declare honour satisfied, his and the boy's.'

Mauger threw his shield to the ground and strode back towards Snake in the Eye.

'Don't cheer for death, boy; it finds us soon enough in times like these. I have performed you a service,' he said, 'now it is time for you to perform me one. You will go to the university and the churches and the palace and you will find this scholar Loys and let me know where he is. Then I'll have to worry about getting to him.'

Snake in the Eye went straight away. It was not too difficult to locate Loys. His second port of call was the Magnaura and, the emperor's medal in his hand, the boy had quickly established Loys worked for the chamberlain in the palace. He lacked the subtlety to disguise his purpose but was lucky enough to pick on someone who was impressed by his medal and willing to talk.

The men on the first gate deferred to his medal and he was allowed through to the school proper. There he questioned the custodian of the door to the Magnaura, a shy man but a proud one, who took the opportunity of the ease he felt talking to a boy to demonstrate the range of his knowledge. The doorkeeper was one of that species of men in lowly jobs who imagine themselves the colleagues and intimates of the more celebrated men they serve. He was eager to show his familiarity with palace and university gossip.

'You've been called by him, then?' he said.

Snake in the Eye said nothing, not quite knowing how to answer.

'No need to be shy about it, boy; he's been examining half the palace and all of the university. He's putting the fear of God into people.'

'I should see him,' said Snake in the Eye.

'Didn't the messenger who summoned you not make it clear he's no longer here? You have to visit him in the palace. Ask at the Room of Nineteen Couches and they'll let you in.'

'Right.'

'Don't be fooled by his foreign looks,' said the custodian, 'not that being foreign means you're automatically stupid but ...' He gave Snake in the Eye an up and down glance and then thought better of expanding his point. 'Look, he's a slippery bastard. Remember that. He's an expert at finding devil worship where there is none, so admit to no amulet, no charm, no number square. He'll use it against you.'

Snake in the Eye smiled, not quite understanding at first.

'He casts curses?'

'No, he studies them and seeks to remove them.'

'What sort of curse?'

'This sky for a start. And many we're not supposed to talk about.'

'How does he do this? He's not doing it very well – the sky is still black.'

'It's an enormous magic,' said the custodian. 'You can't shift that sort of thing overnight; I think even the most rudimentary knowledge of the correct charts and positions of the stars would reveal that. No, he's working towards it, slowly. He'll get there. He's a scholar of the Magnaura. Our men never fail.'

Snake in the Eye touched the hilt of his sword.

'Has he successfully removed curses before?'

'This university attracts the finest brains from throughout the world. Of course he has; it's why he was picked. The word is he was shipped in from the north specifically to solve this problem.'

'Hmm.'

'You are awed,' said the custodian, 'and no wonder. Every day here we see marvels that men from other countries – indeed men from two hundred paces down the Middle Way – have never seen in their lives.'

Snake in the Eye thought about that. He thought about the mechanical tree in which birds sang, the great statues, the amazing mosaic that stretched out under his feet.

'Could this man remove a curse on a person?' he said.

'He could,' said the doorkeeper. 'For do you think the chamberlain would trust him to take the stain of hell from the sky if he could not do such a simple task?'

Snake in the Eye's tongue wet his lips.

'Thank you,' he said. 'I will go to the Room of Nineteen Couches now.'

'Don't apologise if you're late,' said the custodian. 'The guards there don't keep proper records like we do in here. Just tell them he's sent for you and leave it at that.'

Snake in the Eye walked out of the building, his heart pounding. If this man was as good as the custodian said he was he could cure him. Then Snake in the Eye would lead Mauger to him and honour his debt.

He cleared the university grounds at a trot and ran to the palace through the dirty air. He was on his way to his destiny, his future of blood.

30   A Curse Removed

Loys helped Azémar up the stairs of the Numera, his mind numb with shock.

'For pity,' Azémar kept saying, 'help some of the others too. Use your authority to spare them the dark.'

'It will be a close call getting you out of the prison,' said Loys. 'I can't risk any others.'

'God does not see here,' said Azémar. 'He does not see. He is a blind thing fumbling through the night. Can't you smell him? He's here. I can smell him; I can hear him breathing in the tunnels.'

Loys said nothing, just helped his friend on. He was convinced Azémar had become deranged by his ordeal. He had to get him back to a calm and clean place. The palace was ideal, but he had been frightened by the assassins in the tunnels. Who had sent them? The chamberlain? Styliane? The Office of Barbarians? Who knew?

He felt very vulnerable. Loys' discovery of the presence of the wolfman had triggered the attack. There had been threats before but no move against his life. The wolfman sorcerer was the key to whatever was going on, Loys was sure. Beatrice was in the palace; rest and food for Azémar were there. He had to enter the den of his enemies.

What to do? The emperor had insisted on the study. He had initiated the whole thing so he must be interested in seeing it done well, accurately and effectively. He was Loys' only certain ally but he had no way to contact him. He couldn't just run off to find him in the field and put all his suspicions in front of him. Loys was aware he was implicating great men, allies of the emperor. The proof would need to be undeniable before he acted.

Azémar looked around the Numera with terror in his eyes.

'He's here,' he said.

'Who is here, Azémar?'

'The pale fellow, the one who led me to the abomination.'

'Come on, come on.'

Loys had got Azémar as far as the door now. Two guards stared at the men, one holding up his hand. 'Where do you think you're going?' said one, a tall man with a scrappy black beard.

'Out,' said Loys.

'Who is this?'

'A prisoner of the chamberlain. I am the chamberlain's lieutenant and I am removing him.'

'No, you're not, son,' said the tall guard. 'No one leaves here but by the say-so of Meletios.'

Loys swallowed. Meletios was dead in the caves – one of the assassins had done for him. The noise would not have carried to here, past the groans and the screams of the prisoners.

'Your Meletios is under investigation by the chamberlain's office. This man is part of that investigation. Do you want me to report that you are obstructing the chamberlain?'

'He can't leave without official sanction.'

'What is that?'

Loys pointed to a cheap medallion made from a coin on the man's neck.

'Just a necklace.'

'Worn to what purpose?'

The man took a pace back.

'No purpose at all, sir.'

'Because it looks very much like an amulet to me, soldier. It looks to me as though you might have drilled that coin and uttered charms over it in order to protect you from this black sky.'

'Men need some protection,' said the guard.

'That is devilry. And I am the man appointed to root devils out of this city. We will return the prisoner.'

'No!' said Azémar.

'We will return the prisoner but you will report for interrogation to my rooms at the palace tomorrow. What is your name?'

The guard went pale.

'Let him go,' said the other one. 'He's a quaestor appointed by the chamberlain. That gives him a lot of clout.'

The guard with the beard lowered his eyes. 'Go on then,' he said.

'No,' said Loys, 'you come with me. You can lead us out.'

'If I must.'

'You must.'

They passed through the building. The presence of the guard removed further questions and soon a patch of weak daylight appeared at the end of the corridor. Freedom.

'You need to wait for the formalities,' said the guard as he approached the little office at the side of the corridor.

'Handle them yourself,' said Loys and led Azémar out into the courtyard.

The guards there looked twice at his dirty official robes and dithered before the gate.

'Open it,' said Loys. 'Now.'

The guards did as they were told and Loys took Azémar's hand and led him out of the prison. Loys' two palace guards came trotting to meet him with expressions of broad relief.

Azemar stopped, gazing up in wonder at the black skies. 'The world is a prison,' he said, 'with prisons within it. Boxes of darkness, one inside another.'

'Come on.'

They went to the palace, around the back curtain wall to the courtiers' entrance rather than the public reception area of the Room of Nineteen Couches.

Loys was very aware of how dirty his robes had become and of the terrible state of Azémar. He put his cloak around his friend and bundled him on, telling the guard on the palace door to mind his own business when he asked who the beggar was. The man was cowed by the force of Loys' rebuttal and immediately let them through.

Loys had succeeded in his aim of acquiring a terrifying reputation and commanding respect. He hated what he was becoming – a barking, snarling dog who could not even trust his own master.

They made their way through the corridors of the palace to Loys' room. He strode in.

'Servant, bring food and water for our guest. Get them now!'

Only then did he focus on who was in the room. There was the servant; there was Beatrice drinking from a cup, but opposite her on the couch reserved for guests sat a very strange figure. A boy, but not quite a boy. His skin was smooth and his muscles undefined. Despite this he wore an iron breastplate and an empty scabbard on his belt. *Odd.* Weapons had to be handed to the palace guards on entering but most people gave over their swords and scabbards complete. Not this boy. It seemed he was keen to emphasise he normally wore a sword.

'Loys, what's happened? Who is this?' Beatrice was full of concern.

'A friend,' he said, 'my friend Azémar, from home.'

'What's happened to him?'

'Never mind. Bring him a drink, servant, bring him a drink.'

The servant rushed to scoop water from a bowl and Azémar's eyes roamed the room.

'There are snakes here,' he said.

'Only paintings, my friend, only paintings.' Loys had not taken his eyes from the figure on the couch.

'Who is this?' said Loys.

'One of the emperor's men,' said Beatrice. Azémar gulped at the water.

Snake in the Eye stood and bowed. 'Is it the scholar Loys I have the honour of addressing?'

'This is not the right time,' said Loys, gesturing to Azémar.

'I have an important question.' He produced the medal the emperor had given him.

'I've had enough of charms for today,' said Loys.

'It is the emperor's badge of responsibility. It's only given to those he trusts very deeply.'

'Well, good for you,' said Loys, 'but ...' A thought struck him. He was looking for access to the emperor. This boy might be useful.

'I'd be pleased to see you later, or tomorrow,' said Loys, 'but for the moment ...' He gestured to his filthy clothes and then to Azémar.

'I would be seen now,' said Snake in the Eye.

Loys had encountered some odd behaviour in his time in the palace but this was truly strange. The boy seemed almost deranged. Azémar had collapsed on the floor; Beatrice and the servant were bending over him, but the boy acted as though nothing at all was out of the ordinary. His stood with a stiff formality, waiting for Loys' response.

'Let's get Azémar to the bed,' said Loys.

Between them they lifted Azémar up and carried him across the room and into the bedroom at the rear while the boy stood watching them with an expression of intense concentration. He stared at Loys, making him feel uncomfortable.

'The lady must leave the room before we can strip him, sir,' said the servant.

'Don't be an idiot,' said Loys. 'Our families are only one generation out of the longhouse. Do you think she's never seen a man naked before?'

'People will talk.'

'Not if you don't. Now let's get these rags off him. And send for a doctor — can't you see he's wounded?'

The servant bowed and left the room while Loys pulled the filthy clothes from Azémar and Beatrice went to fetch clean water and a towel with which to wash him. He threw the clothes to the floor and they hit it with a wet smack — blood soaked into every fibre. Azémar's whole body too was stained dark red, but he wasn't hurt. Loys found no cuts.

'When can I expect my audience?' said Snake in the Eye.

'I would like to carry report of your fame and skill to our emperor.'

Loys ran his fingers over Azémar's torso and arms, then his legs, searching for wounds. Nothing. His friend had suffered no obvious injury at all.

'Shall I say the emperor's man was rudely received? The wolfman in the emperor's tent received better welcome than I here.'

Now it was Loys' turn to stare.

'You know about the wolfman?'

'I was there when he entered the emperor's tent. I defended the emperor, not like these weakling Greeks.'

Beatrice returned with the servant and the court physician. She was careful not to approach the bed out of respect for the sensibilities of the Greeks.

'Can you handle this?' said Loys. 'I do need to speak to this young man.'

'Yes, Loys,' she said. 'What's going on?'

'This is Azémar. You know, the one I told you about. My friend from the monastery. He's a brilliant man and he has risked a lot to come here for me, I think. We owe it to him to do whatever we can.'

'I'll stay with him.'

'I'll be back as quick as I can.' Loys turned to Snake in the Eye. 'We'll walk,' he said.

'As you wish,' said Snake in the Eye.

They went out of the room and down the corridor to where the window to the garden should have been. It had been boarded up as if for winter owing to the unseasonal weather.

'Do you mind the cold?' said Loys. After his time in the suffocating prison he needed the air.

'I am a mighty man and can endure anything,' said Snake in the Eye.

Loys was beginning to believe he was dealing with a lunatic or at least someone from a very alien culture. But the boy spoke

Greek with a harsh, northern edge to it. He was a Viking, he was sure, as Loys' own father had been.

'Good, then we'll go to the garden.'

They went out into a cloister which looked out on a statue of a satyr. A light rain fell and he imagined the satyr trying to run off. It had more chance of escape than he did.

'You are a northern man?' said Loys in Norse.

'A Varangian, true,' said Snake in the Eye 'We are noted for our fierceness.'

'Indeed,' said Loys. 'I have questions for you, but as you came to me, you clearly have something you want to tell me.'

'You are an expert in removing curses?'

'Yes.' Loys saw no need to correct him. Reputation was everything in the court and epithets such as 'expert' and 'famous' were highly valued.

'The emperor has a curse.'

'That is treason,' said Loys.

'No, it is true,' said Snake in the Eye. 'I heard him say as much.'

'What did he say?'

'That he was cursed. That demons were trying to trick him.'

'This wolfman was one of them?'

'I think so. He tried to trick the emperor, for sure.'

'How?'

'He gave him a sword and told him to kill him.'

'Why would he do that?'

'The wildmen know many things about the gods. He said a wolf was coming for the emperor. It's part of a great magic. I think he must be the wolf because he threatened to kill the emperor if the emperor didn't strike him down.'

'He wanted to die?'

'He said it was the only way to avert what was coming.'

'What was coming?'

'Death in his glory.' Snake in the Eye gave a big smile, like another man might wear on his face hearing he had a favourite meal for dinner.

'And what did the emperor do?'

'He ordered him confined and questioned. He ordered the chamberlain to tell the best scholars to question the wolfman and find out what was happening. I carried the message myself.'

Loys swallowed. He was the newest scholar in the Magnaura, a foreigner, untested and raw. Not the greatest scholar, though the master had named him so. The chamberlain had carried out the letter of the order.

'Do you believe what the wolfman said?'

'We have many stories. Some of them are true and some are not. I have many stories in my family. They are not dissimilar. Perhaps he believes them too much. The holy men spend so long alone their brains curdle.'

'What stories?'

'I only tell my tales in the hope or expectation of reward.'

'What reward do you want?'

'A service from you.'

'I am always ready to help the emperor's men.'

'Then I'll tell you my story.'

Snake in the Eye told the story he had told on the steps of Hagia Sophia, the one the strange traveller had paid a wolf pelt to hear as he travelled with the Varangian army from Kiev. He told how the slave had two sons who were caught in the schemes of the gods, how she had hidden them away but how the woman who bore the howling rune had brought them back together, as she always did, as she always must.

The boys came back to kill and to die, one to be a wolf, one to feed the wolf and give him the sustenance he required to kill the old god Odin in his human form. Odin embraces this fate as it gives the Norns – who the Greeks call the fates – the death they demand in this realm so he might live on in his heaven. The boys were a sacrifice, an eternal sacrifice, part of a story that had played out through history and would play out again and again, until Ragnarok, the twilight of the gods. Then the boys would avoid their fates: brother would not kill brother, and the dread wolf Fenrir, whom the gods had bound, would break free and the old gods would die by his teeth.

'A man told me this story would bring me luck,' said Snake in the Eye.

'Did it?'

'I met a useful fellow through it.'

'This story is common to your people.'

'Parts of it. They know their gods must die. The part about the slave girl and her sons is told in our family. It is passed down from my grandfather, I think.'

Loys took this in. The wolfman may have approached the emperor believing this tale to be true, believing he was a part of that destiny in some way. The chamberlain's concealment of the wolfman alone marked him as important.

But the sky, the death of the rebel. How did that fit in? He would dearly love to have interviewed this wolfman.

'He can speak, the wolfman?'

'Yes. He is a Varangian but not of our army.'

'I would like to find him.'

'Is he not in the prison?'

'He has escaped to the lower tunnels.'

'He could be found,' said Snake in the Eye.

'How?'

'You need the right trackers. Our Vikings are rare wolf hunters. You should hire a few and take them down there. They'd flush him out.'

'Perhaps.'

'If you want to, send for me at the Varangian camp. I am a terror to my enemies and will gladly escort you to the depths. I have men I can bring with me. One of them is a mighty man indeed. Ragnar, of the far north, newly come to the camp, the one who fought Arnulf in *hölmgang*. He would find your wolf.'

'I'll remember that,' said Loys.

'I have given you a service,' said Snake in the Eye, 'now will you repay it?'

'What do you want?'

'How do you remove an enchantment of ...' He couldn't finish the sentence.

'What? Impotence?' Loys almost laughed. The boy had coloured to his boots.

'Like that, yes. Not that, but like it.'

'Of what then?'

The boy rocked back and forth, staring at the satyr as if he thought it might say what he could not.

'It's not manly for me to admit it.'

'What are the effects of this enchantment?'

'It is a battle fetter, so my father said, bestowed by Odin. The best and bravest warriors he wants for his own and afflicts them on the field of conflict so they cannot move, cannot fight or defend themselves. This is the fetter. I have a fetter on me.'

Loys smiled. 'Not everything is an enchantment. Those who God made gentle cannot be unmade and reformed.'

'I was not born gentle,' said Snake in the Eye with a conviction that Loys found unpleasantly convincing. 'I have a wolf inside me but he cannot get out.'

'Perhaps he is content to stay where he is.'

Snake in the Eye clenched his fist and for a moment Loys thought the boy was going to hit him.

Loys put up his hands. 'I cannot help you. I have never heard of this condition before.'

'Then what of other afflictions? How do you remove a curse of the smallpox or of bad luck?'

'The way to salvation of all sorts is through Christ,' said Loys. 'If you meddle with devils then devils will meddle with you. What is it you wear at your neck?'

'A gift from my father, and to him from his father. It is a magical stone.'

'What magic does it hold?'

'Luck and defence from witches.'

'To put your faith in such things is to put your faith in demons,' said Loys.

'It is a gift. A birthright. I cannot relinquish it.'

'Then you have had my advice and rejected it,' said Loys. 'When you turn to Christ you will find all enchantments fall away. Magic, true magic, has no power against true faith.'

'Then what of the emperor,' said Snake in the Eye, 'and the powerful men who fear this sky? What of this city under a curse of black heavens? It has built the greatest houses to your God the world has ever seen and yet it labours under this. Fimbulwinter. Fimbulwinter!'

'What is Fimbulwinter?'

'The barren and frozen time before Ragnarok, the twilight of the gods. The end of the gods is happening here, so the men say, and the city will fall when it does.'

Loys thought deeply. *Enchantment could not touch the true man of faith. Christ drives out all demons.* Yet the emperor was afflicted; the chamberlain had indicated he was suffering too. He tried to recall precedents of truly holy men who had been plagued by demons. Job, who God had set Satan upon? But demons always failed before the power of God. James 2:19 was the obvious reference: 'Thou believest that there is one God; thou doest well: the devils also believe, and tremble.'

He considered the boy's medallion, the one marking him as a servant of the emperor. This strange boy could be a useful source of information. It would not hurt for it to be known Loys had direct contact with the emperor's man, though he couldn't have too close an association with a pagan. That was permissible for the emperor because no one would question him. For Loys it was a more perilous course. If he brought the boy to Jesus it would look very good for him. He knew how to appeal to these people. The Norsemen in Rouen were impressed not by learning or cleverness but by gold, weapons and fine buildings.

'You have a distressing and intriguing malady,' said Loys. 'It's not right a warrior should suffer so. Boy, I tell you this. While you put your faith in idols, you will never be cured. Look at your people in their huts and their hovels. Even your

227

greatest lords live less grandly than the merchants of the Middle Way here. Look at the church of Hagia Sofia. Did Odin ever raise something so magnificent? Look at the riches of our emperor and priests, the triumphs of our armies. When the rebel fell at Abydos it was God who struck him down, for God hates rebels – rebellion is Lucifer's sin. Relinquish your idol and come to Christ.'

'Bollason and his army do well enough following Odin.'

'They will never be allowed into the city, never allowed to serve the emperor as they might, if they persist in idolatry. You are an ambitious man. Give up the stone and your troubles will end.'

Snake in the Eye put his hand up to the pendant. He tried to remove it, or rather his hand lifted the stone and then put it down again.

'I have never taken it off,' he said, 'or only for a moment when the leather rots and the cord breaks. I think it bad luck to cut it away. It has been off my neck twice since I was a child and not for long. It is a blessing against magic, so all my kinsmen have said.'

'Yet you consider yourself afflicted by a curse.'

Snake in the Eye cast down his head. The light in the garden was dropping, the quick dusk of the grey skies. Loys glanced back towards his chamber. He needed to get to Azémar.

'I will cut it free – if you like,' said Loys.

The boy said nothing, just stood with bowed head.

Loys drew the boy's knife from his belt. 'Here,' he said. 'I will set you free.'

The boy tensed for an instant, as if he would resist.

'I'm tired,' said Snake in the Eye. 'I'm tired of the scorn and my own cowardice. I'm tired of not being a man. Why should other fellows get fame and glory while I stand fettered and mocked, unable to prove myself? If Jesus can give me release, if he can make me a killer, then I will follow him.'

Loys was tired too. It wasn't important this man understood Christ; it was just important he honoured him. The messages of the Bible could be imparted by others with more patience and more time.

'You must be baptised,' said Loys. 'And be sure to tell the emperor it was me who brought you to God. Here, you are free.' He cut the cord at the boy's neck and took the pebble.

Snake in the Eye stood tall and stretched out his arms like a man who had been a long time sitting. 'I feel no different,' he said.

'Then go to the cathedral and pray,' said Loys. 'Ask for forgiveness for your pagan ways. Seek baptism there.' Loys went to leave but Snake in the Eye took his arm.

'What is baptism?'

'They will wash you of your sins, wash you of all curses. Only then will you know if you are the victim of an enchantment or ...'

Snake in the Eye pointed up into the filthy clouds.

'You should wash the sky,' he said.

'I wish I could.'

'I would wash the streets in blood,' said Snake in the Eye.

'Perhaps when you become a man you will feel differently,' said Loys.

Snake in the Eye stared directly at him. 'When I become a man, I will do it,' he said.

Loys was suddenly scared by this odd young man. 'I have to go back to my friends.'

'Give me my stone.'

'You abandon paganism, you abandon this,' said Loys. 'Don't go forward to Christ looking back to Satan.'

Snake in the Eye rocked on his feet for a moment.

'I would thank you, scholar. If my curse lifts then you may ask a service of me.'

'I may do that,' said Loys.

'Come to the Varangian camp. I am Snake in the Eye. My fame is great there. I will find you your tracker.'

He leaned on the rail of the garden. The boy seemed about to faint.

'Are you all right?'

'I am not feeling well,' said Snake in the Eye, 'are there birds in the garden?'

'There are no birds.'

'Then what are those things floating up there. You're mistaken, scholar, they are birds. You should look up from your books and see the world sometime.'

'I'm going to leave you now,' said Loys, 'because I have the emperor's work to do.'

Snake in the Eye seemed not to hear him.

At another time Loys might have laughed at the boy's odd behaviour and gone back to Beatrice to tell her the emperor was employing lunatics. He was too concerned for Azémar. He headed inside, out of the garden. As he reached the door, the boy called after him.

'I'll go to the church!'

'You do that.'

Loys found the physician gone, Azémar sleeping on the bed and Beatrice sitting on the couch watching him. Loys put the pebble down on his desk. It had a crude etched image of a wolf's head on it. *These people are obsessed with wolves.*

'How is he?'

'He drank, though he wouldn't eat.' Beatrice pursed her lips, deeply troubled. Loys embraced her. He didn't have to ask her what was wrong – the state of Azémar was enough to disturb anyone.

'Well, he's had a terrible ordeal. Maybe he just needs rest.'

'Yes. And you need a wash. Get out of your clothes.' Beatrice was talking to Loys but her eyes did not leave Azémar.

'I only have the one set.'

'I can send for some more, sir,' said the servant.

'That would be kind,' said Loys.

Something made him look harder at his servant. For some reason he hadn't quite registered what an odd fellow he was – extraordinarily tall with skin the colour of ivory and bright red hair that stood up in a shock. He had noticed these things before but they had seemed unremarkable. Now the true strangeness of the fellow struck him.

Then the feeling passed; the man was gone from the room, and Beatrice was at his side.

Loys went to his friend. He had certainly suffered badly. The starvation he'd endured in the Numera had shrunk the flesh of his face, leaving it bloodless and lean. His lips were drawn back as he slept and his teeth seemed very white and prominent.

'He is so much changed,' said Loys. 'I hate to see him like this. He is a brother to me. You are the only secret I never shared with him.'

'Why?'

'He would have told me not to risk everything on a fancy.'

'Am I a fancy?'

'No. You are everything, and besides you the world is a fancy.'

'I know him,' said Beatrice.

'Very likely. He worked the fields around your father's hall. Though he is a scholar. His toil was a symbol of dedication rather than a full-time occupation.'

'Fine ladies do not look too long at such men.' She smiled, trying to keep her manner light. 'Or so the Frankish maid my father bought to teach me manners told me.'

'They do in my experience.'

'Of course they do. That is not where I have seen him.'

'Where have you seen him?'

'I don't know,' said Beatrice, but she did. From the place where the moon made a silver road of the river, by the edge of the wood where unseen shapes snuffled and blundered, from the little wall that bore tiny lights upon it, lights that seemed so easily blown out, so in need of shielding and protection. He had come from her nightmares.

31 Lord of Slaughter

Snake in the Eye left the palace, picking up his sword at the Room of Nineteen Couches. He walked down the steps and around the Numera towards the towering church of Hagia Sophia.

His debt to Mauger could wait. He felt very odd, half drunk, and had the great desire to test his sword arm. Figures moved through the gloom ahead of him. This was the time to see if the scholar had truly removed his curse. He felt no different. His aggression was still like a lump stuck in his throat, something he needed to vomit forth.

He would try, he thought. An alley curled through some houses at the end of the Middle Way. It seemed a good place to wait for a discreet kill – dark as a cellar. His victim would provide the light. He had no lamp to guide him so he went in trailing one hand on the wall, the other in front of his face in case he walked into something. Nothing. Then a light.

Someone came down the alley carrying a lamp. Two boys, around ten years old, slaves of some sort by their dress.

'Foul night,' said one, nodding as he came by.

Snake in the Eye nodded back. When the boys had their backs to him he put his hand to his sword. No, he couldn't draw it. The light they carried shrank. Snake in the Eye was at the rear of some warehouses which supplied the markets. There were no doors and the place stank of piss, shit and rubbish blown in from the Bull Market. Four paces to his right was an even tighter alley between two buildings – not even an alley. The warehouses leaned and sagged so much even a relatively small person like Snake in the Eye had to wriggle his way in. He did so.

After ten minutes another lamp. This time a soldier. He set

the lamp on the ground not six paces from where Snake in the Eye was hiding and took a heavy piss. Snake in the Eye's hand tightened on the sword. *Relax, relax.* He remembered what the warriors at Birka had told him when he asked for tips.

He loosened his grip on the weapon and reapplied his hand. He brought the sword free.

'Who's there?'

The Greek let down his soldier's skirt and wheeled around. This was what Snake in the Eye had dreamed of.

'Only me.'

He stepped forward, his sword catching the glow of the lamp.

'You've picked the wrong man to rob, kid,' said the Greek. His speech was slurred and it was clear he was slightly drunk. 'You've—'

Snake in the Eye was on him, swinging his sword high and hard towards the soldier's head.

The man caught Snake in the Eye's sword arm at the wrist and drove a kick into his guts. The boy crashed back into a wall, his sword flying from his hand. The man drew his own sword and smacked Snake in the Eye hard on the head with the flat of his blade.

'You're lucky you find me in a good mood, you little shit,' he said. 'If you were a man I'd have put this through you by now.' He sank another heavy kick into Snake in the Eye's balls. The boy rolled forward into the dirt, coughing and retching. 'Take that as a lesson,' the soldier said, 'and I'll take your weapon as a forfeit.' He walked across to pick up Snake in the Eye's sword.

The boy lay on the ground feeling very peculiar. His agony seemed to take him to a very strange place. He saw himself by a river, walking. He had walked by the river before, he thought, though he could not recall exactly when. A penny moon hung in the branches of the trees and made the water a shining path.

He said a name under his breath.

'Bifrost.' Was he there – in front of the shimmering bridge that led the way to Asgard, the home of the gods?

The remains of a wall were by the river, a broken-down overgrown thing, almost hidden by ivy. There was a niche in the wall and inside it something glowed. What was it? A candle or a tiny lamp? A flame of some sort. He couldn't quite see it clearly. He had a powerful urge to extinguish it. In his vision he spat on his fingers and put his hand forward to snuff it out. He seemed to fall into darkness, his eyes closing, consciousness fading.

Another lamp was by him. He sat upright to inspect it. It was the same lamp the soldier in the alley had carried. Ten paces from Snake in the Eye lay the body of the man, still holding Snake in the Eye's sword. No one else was nearby, no one at all. Snake in the Eye remembered the flame in the garden of his mind and laughed. The scholar had been as good as his word. Snake in the Eye had accepted Christ and the snake in his heart was free. He went to the body and touched it. It was freezing cold.

Snake in the Eye giggled. He was cured, more than cured. He had killed his opponent without touching him. He took up his sword. It would have been preferable to kill him with a weapon. He hacked at the body a couple of times. Then he had an idea. He rolled the man onto his front and straightened his neck, took a pace back and leaped at him, swinging the sword down at his neck. He missed his aim slightly, catching the back of the skull. He was fascinated to see how the sword stuck. He put his foot on the head and levered the sword free. Then he tried again. Another miss, this time hacking into the flesh of the shoulder. The third time Snake in the Eye was more accurate. He made a good wound in the neck. Two or three more cuts and the head would come away. He hacked and hacked again. Finally the head fell from the shoulders.

Snake in the Eye sheathed his weapon and picked the head up by the hair.

'Well,' he said, 'not so sure of yourself now. Am I still a boy to be laughed at and scorned? Wag your little tongue.'

He put his fingers into the mouth and padded at the tongue. He did not throw the head aside but carried it with him proudly, a trophy that proved his battle prowess. He had done as the scholar said and surrendered the stone and reaped a marvellous reward. He must follow through on the rest of the advice.

He headed up the alley to Hagia Sophia, which rose above him like one of the monsters of the Greeks, gazing down with its many fiery eyes. Around him the people of the city sped with their lamps through the cold wet streets. No one paid him any notice, and even if they had, they could scarcely have seen him in the gloom. He sensed their living souls. He inhabited two realities, one in the black Byzantine night, the other somewhere stranger, where he moved on a river past a broken-down wall, watching lights flicker and gutter in the moonlight, knowing he only had to snuff out a flame to snuff out a life.

He reached the entrance to the church, and ran up under its great arch. The door was open for prayer. Snake in the Eye went within. The night church burned to the light of a thousand tiny candles, hummed to the muttered prayers of worshippers. His thoughts seemed things of light, mingling with light, the candles of the church's interior and the candles of his mind almost indistinguishable. So many people in the church, so many candles. And he, what was he? A wind to them.

The priest in his great beard sang out a prayer.

'What night falls on me,
what dark and moonless madness
of wild desire, this lust for sin?
Take my spring of tears
thou who drawest water from the clouds,
bend to me, to the sighing of my heart,

Thou who bendest down the heavens
in thy secret incarnation ...'

'I am a killer,' said Snake in the Eye. He spoke in his own
tongue, in Norse.

No one turned.

'I am a killer!'

He shouted it as loudly as he could. The priest didn't pause
in his recitation.

'... dawned the light of knowledge upon the earth.
For by your birth those who adored stars
were taught by a star
to worship you.'

The rhythm of the man's voice was intoxicating to Snake
in the Eye. The light of the candles was like the water of a
beautiful sunlit lake on which he floated. A hand was on his
arm. A soldier.

'What in the name of God are you doing with that?' he said,
pointing to the bloody head Snake in the Eye held in his left
hand.

Snake in the Eye's heart pounded, the rhythm exciting him
so much he did a little dance. The light was taking shape, or
rather shapes. Glittering and shining symbols hung in the air,
floated, light suspended by light. He sang out,

'Alone I sat when the old one sought me,
The terror of gods that gazed in my eyes:
"What have you to ask? Why come you hither?
Odin, I know where your eye is hidden."'

The soldier put his hand on Snake in the Eye's shoulder.

'You've got some questions to answer, son.'

'Am I not battle bold?' said Snake in the Eye.

Another soldier had him by the other arm but still Snake in

the Eye did not let go of the head. He saw the soldiers by his side but he sensed their truer selves too, little lights burning in a garden, an offering to fate. What offering? The same offering fate always demands. Death. They must die so the gods would live. The gods had not given life to humanity. They had given death, to save themselves. The Norns, the strange women who sit weaving out the fates of men by the roots of the world tree, demand death. So the gods had created men to die in their place.

'Get out!'

'He's a Varangian, and he's killed a Greek! Cut him down here.'

'Not in the house of God; drag him outside to do it.'

One of the men drew a sword.

'Is this God's house?' said Snake in the Eye in Greek.

'Yes, barbarian!'

'Then it is my house.'

They pulled him towards the door but he was somewhere else too – a garden by a river where candles were lodged in niches in the wall, so many that the wall seemed made of fire. In his vision he put forward his hand and snuffed two out – he knew just which ones to choose. The guards at his side fell dead.

'This is my house!' shouted Snake in the Eye. 'And it is a house of the dead!'

His mind was a vortex: he felt the ice winds of the north, the hot breath of the Caspian desert, the summer storms of Birka, their raindrops warm and full.

He released them in the garden of his mind, sending them as a gale against the wall of candles.

In Hagia Sophia, the Church of Holy Wisdom, centre of the faith of the great Roman empire, dedicated to Logos – Jesus as the revealer of the invisible God – the song of the priest stopped and the congregation fell as one to the floor. Snake in the Eye stooped and took a beaded cross from around a dead man's neck. Then he walked forward over the ranks of corpses, towards the altar, under the light of its glowing gold. He put the head of the Greek upon it and spoke to it.

'How shall I have my baptism now?' said the boy. Then the light swamped his thoughts and he collapsed too.

32   A Face From the Past

'I am fettered, I am pinioned and I am bound. My mouth is propped open with a cruel spar and the voices of my tormentors mock me.'

Azémar felt the thin cords binding him to the rock, heard the keening and wailing of his own voice, writhed with the agony of his mouth. He strained against his bonds but they would not break, would not come free. His mind was full of murder, to tear and kill those who had tricked him, tied him and humiliated him.

'My friend.'

Azémar opened his eyes. The sensation of being tied was gone, the terrible pain in his mouth too. Above him was a face he recognised. Loys.

He tried to speak but found himself coughing.

'Relax, my friend, you've undergone a terrible ordeal.'

'You rescued me.'

Loys put his hand on Azémar's arm. 'Yes.'

Azémar opened his arms and Loys leaned forward to hug him. 'You were always my protector, Azémar, and it's good to repay the favour. Do you need water?'

'Yes.'

Loys brought a bowl up to his lips and Azémar sipped at it. 'We have food here.'

A plate of cold meat and bread was on the table next to him.

'I'm not hungry, Loys.'

'Well, perhaps you will be later.'

Loys smiled at his friend and then said, 'I am bound to ask, Azémar. Why are you here?'

'I ...'

As he began to speak Beatrice came into the room. Azémar watched her.

'You're up,' she said.

'Yes.'

'Has he been looking after you?'

'Very well.'

Azémar's heart kicked. It was her, he knew, the lady he had seen all those years ago, going past on her little grey horse, her hair brighter than the corn in the sunlight.

He had steeled himself to meet her because his whole up-bringing and education had taught him to regard her as a temptress and a whore. It was her fault Loys had abandoned his vows, her fault an assassin had been sent to kill him. But he could not bring himself to blame her.

Neither could he look at her for long, she conjured such odd emotions in him. It was not lust, nor anything like it. She was beautiful but beauty was a snare he had learned to avoid. This was a deeper longing. He saw all the possibilities that had been denied to him as a monk: home, hearth, children. The longing went beyond the comforts a wife would have brought. He could not name the feeling, nor fully summon it to the front of his mind. He just knew when he looked at her he thought of those empty hills that rose above his monastery, of the wide featureless blue ocean on which he had travelled to Constantinople, of the call of the wolf in the night. Loneliness? Perhaps. Or something like it.

'You came a long way to suffer so,' said Beatrice.

Azémar lay back, dizzy. He'd caught the suspicion in her voice.

'I came to warn you,' he said. 'Your father has dispatched assassins. He intends to kill Loys and bring you home.'

'How does he know we are here?'

'Your sister.'

'She betrayed me?'

'Your father was going to burn the monastery unless some-one told him where you had gone.'

'She could have lied.'

'She's a young girl,' said Azémar. 'She thinks it a sin to lie.'

'We have enough problems here without worrying about that,' said Loys. 'Anyway the palace is well defended. He'll send one of his clottish northerners.'

'What makes you so sure?'

'The duke looks to the future in many things, but when it comes to war, he likes the men of the old country, isn't that so?'

'Yes,' said Beatrice. She squeezed his hand. 'Do you know how many come for us?'

Azémar took another sip of water. The sensation of it made him remember its lack in the Numera. Memories spumed – the thing that had tried to kill him, the pale figure who had stood beside him, comforting and caressing him, the meat, the meat he had eaten in a place even God didn't see. He shuddered and said, 'No.' He didn't want to have to explain how he had come to Constantinople to Loys. A flush came over him, like he'd drunk too much the night before. The lie seemed to dry Azémar's mouth and he drank some more.

'So you came alone?'

'I sailed as soon as I heard your father was looking for you.'

Azémar put down the bowl and leaned back on the bed. Why had he lied? This was the opportunity he had waited for, to alert his friend. He could have given Mauger's name, described him, put the palace guards on alert, but he had not. Why?

Because the man had very likely been captured and put in the Numera or even killed. Such a warrior would not be taken without a fight, and perhaps the only way to subdue him was to kill him. He didn't want to alarm his friend or raise pointless questions.

Beatrice came to the side of the bed.

'Were you ever at the duke's court?' she said.

'Never, lady. I have spent most of my life in the monastery and its fields.'

Azémar spoke the truth, though his thoughts terrified him. He knew her. Yes, he knew her, but not from the world – from his dreams and from the nightmares of the Numera.

'I'm sure I know you,' she said.

'I have seen you riding by,' he said, 'but from a distance. You would not recognise my face.' He couldn't meet her eyes.

'Do you recognise me?'

'I know you only from afar.'

Loys put his hand on Beatrice's arm. 'Let's not trouble Azémar too much. He's come a long way and suffered a lot for us.'

Azémar closed his eyes. He didn't want to see the girl any more. He knew who she was - the one from his dreams who had told him she loved him, had always loved him. She was the girl in the fields, the one who had haunted his sleep in his monk's cell, the one he remembered, though not like any other memory. It was a memory he had been born with, something he had carried with him all his life.

He needed to wait until his thoughts cleared, until he worked out what had happened to him in the Numera. He had killed, he had eaten things no Christian man should eat and now he had a wildfire in his head.

There was a knock at the door.

'The quaestor is engaged in the service of the chamberlain,' said the servant, giving the official reply to indicate visitors were not welcome.

The door opened anyway. It was a captain of the messenger service, with three men.

Loys' fingers closed on the little knife on the plate of cold meats.

'Quaestor,' said the officer, 'you need to come now.'

'For what?'

'Sorcery in the most holy place. A demon has come to the Church of Holy Wisdom.'

'What sort of demon?'

'The sort that leaves five hundred dead,' said the officer. 'It seems your mission to protect the people of this city has had the opposite of its intended effect. You have some explaining to do, Quaestor, so I'd get yourself down to the church now if I was you.'

'Look after Azémar,' said Loys to Beatrice. 'You have the eunuch as your chaperone.' He picked up the little knife with his back turned to the messengers and put it into his belt. Then he took up his cloak and strode from the room.

33 Awakening

Snake in the Eye opened his eyes and wondered where he was. He was in a room with five other beds in it – two of them occupied. One contained a fat man who lay motionless with a cloth across his forehead, the other a youth of around sixteen with a splinted leg propped up by cushions. The youth wrote on some parchment which rested on a small table he'd positioned over his thighs. On it was a candle, the only light in the room.

The young man smiled at him. 'You're awake at last. Thank goodness, I could do with the company.'

Snake in the Eye felt for the pebble at his neck. Only the cross. The strange sensations he'd experienced in the church were quieter now but their resonance was still in his mind.

Memories came back to him. He'd been in a garden with a girl. There had been lights and then the lights had gone out. What had happened? He was alive. Was he a hero? He had killed many people – yes now he recalled it – and that meant he really was a hero.

'Where am I?'

'In the hospital of the Church of Holy Wisdom. You are the only survivor of the evil that happened tonight. Well, the only well-dressed survivor, anyway. They wouldn't want to risk picking up someone who couldn't pay.'

A story ran through Snake in the Eye's mind. It was the one the traveller who had visited him in his camp had asked for – and given a fine pelt for. He couldn't remember all of it now, only the end.

He was giggling as if drunk. 'The old gods, those ancient savages will die.' The story began again inside his head: *There are three women – the Norns* ...

He tried to stop the pitter-patter of the words, to concentrate on finding out where he was and what he was doing there, but the words blustered through his mind loud as rain tearing against a tent. And – whoa! – there were the runes, forming of candlelight, symbols that rattled like carts, that blew like the wind and shone like the sun, bellowed like bulls and sprouted like seeds.

'Where is my sword?'

'I don't know. I should have thought you'd have had enough of—'

'I want my sword!'

'Well, really. I don't know. I suggest you ask the nurses. Please speak to me no more as you're obviously well below my rank.'

'Please be quiet,' said the man with the cloth over his forehead. 'I am dying of a nervous fever brought on by these strange skies and I must not be frightened or alarmed.'

Snake in the Eye smirked and grinned as the runes shimmered and chimed. They led him to the wall in the dark crevices of his mind. The men's lives seemed like little flickering candles. He almost saw them, so strongly did he picture them. He let them take his attention, their cosy little flames filling up his thoughts. And then he no longer wished them to burn. He wanted them to go out. They did and the men spoke no more.

The gods in their schemes ... There was more of the story to tell, scraping away in his head like a trapped rat.

He got up, light-headed, though he wasn't hungry. He looked at his clothes. He was in a long tunic in plain brown cloth, in the Byzantine style. His boots were at the side of the bed. He put them on and walked out of the room, leaving the corpses behind him.

He came into a larger space beneath a dome where people lay all around on beds and matressess. These were of a lower station to the men he had just left in the room.

At his feet was a mosaic – a depiction of a woman drawing a bow, a crescent moon above her head.

He offers the sacrifice to the fates.

A doctor – a short man with a Greek beard – came wandering towards him. He wore a robe similar to Snake in the Eye's but in dark blue.

'You're awake.'

'Where is my sword?'

'We have good care of it.'

'I'd like it now.'

'I think you need to rest a little. How long have you been awake?'

'Where is my sword?'

Snake in the Eye grabbed a hank of the man's tunic at the chest.

'You're not in a fit state to leave,' said the doctor.

Eternally reborn, eternally sacrificed.

'I am a warrior of the north, no soft southern man am I. Get me my sword.'

His tone was insistent enough for the doctor to give in. 'Follow me.'

Snake in the Eye was led through a series of arches, through ranks of sick people. The place seemed ready to overflow. Few bore signs of injury but many sat weeping on the floor, some calling out that the final day was upon them and Christ was returning to his kingdom.

'You'll excuse the crush,' said the doctor. 'The sky has convinced men they are sick.'

Snake in the Eye followed him to a door.

'Wait.'

The doctor went inside and after a few minutes returned with Snake in the Eye's purse and sword. Snake in the Eye snatched them up.

'We've deducted your bill from your purse,' said the doctor but Snake in the Eye was already on his way outside.

He emerged onto a high hill overlooking the city. Was it night or day? He couldn't tell. The sky was dark but with a strange metalled glow, not night or day but something between. Below him like a huge pale serpent was the long arched bridge, the water road. To his left was the massive dome of the great church.

The gods in their schemes ...

The tale seemed like a fly buzzing through his head, and to sit and tell it seemed to be the best way of getting it out. He would wander the streets and find an audience for his story. Perhaps he would kill the audience when he'd finished it. It would be a fine tale to hear as your last. If only he could recall it. The story was annoyingly incomplete in his mind, the words he remembered like the top of a mountain glimpsed through mist. In moments the mist would clear, revealing glimpses of the bulk beneath.

'And Loki loved her, and knew death in one lifetime was a small price to pay ...'

Death in one lifetime. Such a small price. Behind him he heard someone wailing, calling on God to take them and spare them such misery. He looked back at the hospital. If he let his thoughts drift, the building became insubstantial, unreal. More solid by far seemed the runes, bright like floating light, that turned in the air around him. He could feel them, one like an ice wind, another like a bristle of thorns, a third like a drowning current enticing him to unseen depths. They had always been in him, he knew, and the curse had kept them from him. He put out his hand as if to touch them and he saw the garden by the riverbank, the wall full of candles.

He thought to blow them out. But not everyone who asked for the gift of death would receive it. He would not kill cowards, only brave and worthy opponents like the faith-strong worshippers in the church. Yes, he wanted more like that. He took out his sword. First he would test himself in the old way. He longed to feel his enemy's life blood spurting over his sword hand, to look closely into the man's face as he died. There would be time enough to blow out candles. He needed a more feeling murder first, a death of blood, of hot, expiring breath, of terrified eyes and grasping hands. After that he would begin to get even with the Roman soldiers – Greeks as they truly were. He'd seen the look the Hetaereian guard had given him when he'd left the emperor's tent. The man would pay for his scorn, him and all his friends. He would leave them dead in piles.

Snake in the Eye walked down the hill towards the city. He sensed the lives of its inhabitants spread out before him like twenty thousand fireflies flickering in the dark, the wavering lights of their mortal existence as real to him as those of home and hearth.

34 House of the Dead

Loys entered the great church. The night was dark and candles had been lit, intensifying the gold of the altar, turning the air to umber and the pillars to the shining trunks of magical trees.

A carpet of dead – men, women and even some children – sprawled on the floor. Monks moved among them, intoning prayers.

'Any alive?' he called.

'None,' said a monk.

Loys drew in a breath and touched the hand of a merchant who lay facing the altar, gaudy in his yellow silks. Freezing. Loys sat down on a bench. His mind was utterly blank before this scene of devastation.

'Your explanation?'

It was the messenger service captain, a thin man with the face of an angry rat.

'You're the security service; let's have yours.' He responded by reflex rather than thought, his long inquisition having made aggression a habit when dealing with Byzantine officials.

'You are charged with the protection of the empire from magical attack. Doesn't look like you're doing a very good job from where I'm standing.'

'You're charged with the protection of the empire from everything. Don't make this my fault.'

Loys was ashamed to be squabbling in such a way in front of so many dead but he wasn't going to let this bastard stick the blame on him. His mind was full of strategies about how he could claim to have warned this might happen. He crossed himself. What was he becoming? *Think of the dead, Loys, and how this happened, not of watching your own back.*

His hand felt the outline of someting inside the little bag he wore at his neck. He realised he hadn't discarded that pagan stone.

'Well, it's your job to have an idea,' said the captain. 'The chamberlain will be on his way in a minute so I'd start thinking of something if I were you, because I think he's going to want to hear it. Personally, I'd also like to know what you were doing at the Varangian camp last week.'

'I will consider all possibilities,' said Loys, giving the man a hard look that implied he might be the first to be investigated, 'but first let's attend to the matter in hand.'

Styliane's accusations, what he had heard on the hill, even the chamberlain's own words when he had commissioned him, telling him his mission was to safeguard 'great men', all pointed in one dizzying direction. Some sort of sorcery had taken place and the chamberlain – or someone very close to him – had lost control of it.

Loys walked through the bodies. So many gone at a stroke. *Could it be some natural phenomenon?* It had happened in God's house so the worshippers must have provoked his wrath. No diabolic power could hold sway here.

Dead faces stared back at him, like an accusing mob. He had failed to find out what was happening, failed even to make an inroad, and this was the price. Loys felt entirely inadequate to the task. Surely there were greater powers at work here than could be faced down with questions and study. He had to try to explain this, but how?

Trumpets sounded, a drum beat and a voice cried out, 'Stand back in the name of the emperor for the chamberlain Karas.'

Loys crossed himself and instinctively knelt to pray. 'God deliver me. God deliver me an answer. Deliver Beatrice and deliver the people of the city.'

Three files of soldiers dressed in the chamberlain's blue cloaks marched into the great church, fanning out before the corpses, followed by the huge eunuchs he had seen on his first day with their golden whips. Finally the chamberlain appeared, dressed in his ceremonial array of breastplate, short blue cloak, skirt of leather straps and sapphire diadem on his head. At his belt he wore a fine sword and in his hand he carried a black cane inlaid with ivory. The message to the people was clear. A threat was in the city and the authorities were responding.

Loys prostrated himself, his eyes fixed on the flagstones. He heard the reedy voice questioning the messenger captain.

'When?'

'We were alerted an hour ago, Parakoimememos.'

'Answer my question.'

'We think perhaps two hours ago.'

'Any survivors?'

'One. He has been taken to the hospital.'

'Do you not think you should be interviewing him?'

'He is still unconscious, lord.'

'Tell the doctors to wake him. If they can't they'll answer to me.'

Loys was aware he was shaking.

'Scholar.'

Loys looked up. The chamberlain gestured towards him with his cane.

'Lord?'

'Stand up.'

Loys did as he was told. The chamberlain was thinner than he recalled, and his face was white with powder. The ranks of soldiers stood at attention. These were disciplined troops but they fidgeted and shifted on their feet, fear and bewilderment in their eyes.

'Your verdict on this?'

Loys didn't know what to say. He had no idea. He couldn't accuse the second most powerful man in the empire to his face, but he had to give the chamberlain something.

'My investigations,' he said, 'have uncovered devil work going on here in the city, which we must eliminate as quickly as possible. The northerners worship demons. They are causing the problems here.'

'The northerners? We should have them eliminated,' said the chamberlain. The eunuch seemed deeply shaken. He kept wetting his lips with his tongue and his eyes roamed the church.

'I don't think it can be the Varangians,' said Loys, 'but other northerners.' The Varangians were pagans, true enough, but Loys wanted no blood on his hands if he could help it.

'Which others?'

'I have yet to identify them,' said Loys, 'I have yet—'

The chamberlain jabbed a finger at him. 'This is no time for trifling. I read men and I read you like a psalter on a chain. I am not your dog, scholar, so do not think to throw me a scrap and dismiss me.'

Loys bowed again. It was time to show he had advanced his studies in some way, that he was to be taken seriously.

'I need to speak to the wolfman,' said Loys.

The chamberlain was impassive. 'I would have thought he would have been the first person you sought to interview.' He gave no sign he had concealed the wolfman's existence and Loys knew better than to mention it.

'He had escaped before I came to do so.'

'What do you think an interview with him will reveal?'

'There is a story his people hold to be true – that of the coming of the end of their gods. They think it is happening here. There is a well in which their god gave his eye for wisdom. The well offers insight but asks a great price for its gifts. The god is coming here in the form of a man to die.'

'The Arabs too say a one-eyed man will herald the end of the world.' The chamberlain seemed lost in thought for a second. 'There is so much lore, so much ...'

'I have checked the events against the text of Revelation and there is a ...' Loys searched for the right word '... a correspondence.'

The chamberlain crossed himself.

'This northern demon, how is it coming here to die?'

'At the teeth of a wolf.'

'What? What wolf?' The chamberlain took a pace towards Loys and for a heartbeat the scholar thought he might strike him with his cane.

'I don't know. The wolfman? The sky? They have a myth about a wolf who eats the sun.'

The chamberlain scanned the bodies. Sweat cut dark lines in the powder on his face.

'You are telling me the lies they believe are true?'

'No. I am saying they open themselves up as a channel for demons. Their gods are clearly demons in disguise. We need to find the sorcerer who has summoned them and eliminate him.'

'Go and find the survivor of this,' said the chamberlain, 'and ask him what happened here. I have had enough of keeping you and your northern slut in finery for no result. An explanation and an end to this in a week's time or you will be going to the Numera and she will be going back to her father.'

Loys bowed.

'I have your authority to search the Numera for the wolfman? My evidence indicates he is the key to this.'

'You do not. You have bungled this matter so far and I was right to think I couldn't trust such an important task to you.'

'We should purge the soothsayers to be sure,' said the messenger captain.

'No!' said Loys.

'The time for half-measures is over,' said the chamberlain. 'Do it, and quickly. Do not chide me with your eyes, scholar. This is your doing. If you worked more efficiently none of this would need to be done.'

The messenger captain bowed. 'We will begin immediately, lord. Allow my men to search the Numera for the wolfman. I can have forty troops in there before the next night bell.'

'Leave him,' said the chamberlain. 'You've wasted enough time already. Now, scholar, do as I tell you and find this survivor. The rest of you, clear up this mess. All bodies to be buried or put into the sea before tomorrow at dusk. If you can call it dusk.'

Loys bowed and the chamberlain swept from the great church, his troops clattering out behind him.

35 The Moon on the Water

'You said I should come here at this hour if I needed you.'

Beatrice knelt in the little chapel, lowering herself carefully. She felt so hot, so heavy and so tired with the baby. She desperately wanted to give birth so she could just walk without wheezing again. Everything had been so new and difficult since she arrived in Constantinople she had hardly had the time to think of the danger she was in simply by being an expectant mother. Plenty of women died in childbirth. The care at the palace was excellent but still women died, and regularly. She put it from her mind. Azémar had disturbed her too greatly for her to dwell too long on that.

The chapel was the Lady Styliane's private space for worship but the guards had been told to admit Beatrice.

The lady knelt beside her in front of the candles on the little altar and an image of Christ preaching.

'What is it you want?'

Beatrice was no fool and realised that by going behind Loys' back to this woman she was taking a great risk. Lady Styliane had said she herself knew 'a little' of magic and pagan practices, which Beatrice recognised as a coded invitation to talk about these things.

'My husband is greatly burdened by his task of office.'

'It is no surprise. The waters of this court seem still to the outsider but they teem with dangerous currents.'

'Quite so. But there has been a development.'

Could she trust the lady? She had no one else to turn to. The Church? The priests of this place were strange and did not speak her language, and anyway she had always needed to be dragged to church by her maid. It was not her instinct to confide in holy men but in other ladies.

'What sort of development?'

'Someone has come looking for us.'

'You are under my protection, and in the palace no one can harm you.'

'I just need your advice. Your husband made a study of demons.'

'He wrote a book on them before he died.'

'Is it possible a demon can come out of hell to walk the earth as a man?'

'Demons are full of tricks. I think it might be.'

'I have dreams. I have always had dreams, and they concern something that is looking for me. In the dream it is a wolf but it is also a man at the same time.'

'Half man, half wolf?'

'No, not exactly. It appears as a wolf but in the dream I know it to be a man, or it appears as a man but he has a violence in his eyes that tells me he is a wolf.'

'This is the development?'

'No. My husband's friend came here to warn us of an assassin stalking us. The friend was cruelly imprisoned. I had never seen this man before he came here but I know him. He is the one from my dreams. He is a wolf and a man at the same time.'

'Your husband released the scholar Azémar from prison as a quaestor conducting an investigation. I have no power to put him back in there.'

'It was you who imprisoned him?'

'Yes.'

'Why?'

' "Why?" is not a question guests of the palace address to great ladies.' Her face was stern in the candlelight.

'You are angry he has been released?'

Again the lady said nothing. Beatrice needed to confide in her.

'I left my home to get away from him. I had a fever that nearly cost me my life, and in it I saw him, in terrible dreams. I wonder if Loys' investigation into these magical abuses hasn't called him forth by error.'

'When one gazes into hell, hell gazes back at you,' said Styliane.

'Exactly,' said Beatrice, 'so is it possible hell regards Loys as an enemy and is moving to stop him?'

'I thought this man was his friend. He has done nothing to hurt him so far.'

'Demons are in no hurry, so my nursemaid told me.'

The lady thought for a moment.

'My brother's choice of your husband seemed at first to me to be a political one.'

'In what way?'

'He is a foreigner and an outsider. Difficult for a man like that to make any progress here. Lady Beatrice, your life is under many threats; to add one more would seem only a small matter.'

'I don't understand you, lady.'

'If I confide in you and you betray my trust − to anyone, including your husband − then you will not live to see the dawn, should it ever come under this black sky.'

'I am trustworthy.'

'I find it interesting my brother chose your husband. I find it interesting this man you perceive to be a wolf has come.'

'He is working for your brother too?'

'There are greater bonds in the world than those of money, or of duty or of kin.'

'I don't understand.'

'The wolf is important to my brother. It's something he spoke of many times when we were growing up. Is it possible there is a magical bond between my brother and your wolf-man?'

'How so?'

'Well, there's the question. It might be useful, given you seem central to all this, to ask some questions of you, to explore why this man has troubled your dreams.'

'Any there are, I will answer gladly.'

'It is not easy, though it could be done tonight if you are willing.'

'What done?'

'What do you believe of God?'

'In one God, the father almighty, maker of heaven and earth, of all things visible and invisible. I believe in our Lord Jesus Christ, the only begotten son of God—'

Styliane put up her hand. 'Spare me the creed. In God, Jesus his son and the holy spirit?'

'Yes.'

'Do you find it possible to believe God was worshipped in this way for many years before Christ?'

'No, because Christ was born one thousand years ago. He could not have been worshipped in that way before.'

'Perhaps the Bible is only one telling of a much longer story. It is not so much about people and things – how Jesus was sent by Pilate to die – but of the fundamental nature of eternal God. How the divine nature is threefold, how God suffers for his power.'

'I am not a philosopher, lady.'

Lady Styliane raised an eyebrow. 'But you know sacrilege when you hear it?'

Beatrice bowed her head. 'I only want an answer to why I feel such dread when I look at the man my husband has rescued.'

Lady Styliane put her hand on Beatrice's.

'I am willing to help you. I have examined that man before. I saw him coming here too. It is no surprise to me he is free. Imprisonment was only ever a temporary measure. What to do? What to do?'

'How did you see him coming here? In dreams?'

'In something like them. It is possible to choose to dream if you know the way. When I was brought to this palace I was three years old – a child of the slums. I was raised correctly and in the ways of Christ. There are other ways and ideas here.

My brother arranged for me to be adopted by a noble family, but perhaps the chamberlain, arranger of fates, was himself arranged. I was taken in by one of the city's oldest families. They were Christian people but their slaves had been with the family for generations. They had come from Egypt years before and kept some old traditions in secret. I was raised to understand the things my mother would have taught me, had she lived.'

'Your mother the sorceress?'

'Hardly. Just a woman of insight who kept the old ways, from what I'm told. I heard the rumours about our family. When I came of age my family's maid took me to the hillside and under the sickle moon she showed me the rites I had been denied by my adoption.'

Beatrice crossed herself.

'So it is you who is in league with devils?'

'No. I believe in Christ, who died for our sins but I know God cannot be limited to one form or one expression. So I know too he walks with the moon as his lamp in the form of Hecate, goddess of the gateways, lighting the way to the lands of the dead, lighting the way from the lands of the dead.'

Beatrice made to get up but Styliane stopped her with a gesture.

'Remember my warning, Lady Beatrice. It was not a joke. This sky, these deaths, are nothing to do with me. I only fore-saw calamity. Your father's court must have had fortune tellers and seers visit for your amusement. Think of me, then, as like them. I saw this fellow who comes to you before he arrived. I had him captured and interrogated and I visited him. I tried a rite of divination but I could not go through with it. I saw only death around him and, like you, I was terrified.'

'So why did you not kill him?'

'Because he has the protection of a mighty god, or a demon. He cannot be trifled with without extreme peril to those who move against him. It was not clear, the vision was not clear. I put him into a dungeon so I could have time to think. Your husband released him. This only confirms what I thought. Something is protecting him.'

'What?'

'We could find out. Or endeavour to.'

'How?'

'Let me perform the rite with you. Let us both explore your dreams. I will go with you there. I will see what you see.'

'That is sorcery.'

'Think of it as prayer. I will not ask you to pray to any devil or goddess. Pray to Christ. Ask him for his guidance. Do so with me, tonight, when the hidden moon is full and the labyrinth that leads us to truth is bathed in a light no cloud can obscure. There are paths we can walk that may lead to an understanding of this man of dread. We can go together to the gardens of heaven where Christ walks in his many forms.'

'It will imperil my soul.'

'No. Could you go there unless Christ wished it? Could you stand before the face of the creator if he didn't wish you to? Come, my dear, have more faith in God.'

Beatrice thought of the man in her chambers. Her husband had called him friend, but she remembered the carnivorous smile that lay upon his face as he slept, the horrific dreams that had consumed her in her fever, that strange shape that seemed to writhe and slink and howl in her heart.

'I will go with you,' she said.

'Then follow.'

The lady extended her hand to help Beatrice to her feet and led her out of the little chapel, down a corridor. They turned left past another guard and walked through more corridors decorated with forest scenes. They were empty of people. Everywhere else in the palace eyes followed you. Here, in Styliane's quarters, they did not.

Eventually they came to a plainer corridor and then to a door where a guard stood. Styliane simply lifted her finger and pointed to the door. He went through it and closed it behind him. The draught of cold air told Beatrice it led outside.

On pegs on the wall hung three dark cloaks. Styliane passed Beatrice one and put another on herself, pulling up the hood.

'We wait for a while,' said Styliane.

'Gladly.' Beatrice leaned against the wall, trying to get her breath. 'What are we waiting for?' she said.

'Transport,' said Styliane.

'I cannot ride a horse.'

'A boat, not a horse.'

The women stood silently in the corridor. Shortly, the door opened again and the guard came back through, saying nothing, just resuming his post. Styliane stepped through the door followed by Beatrice.

A long damp jetty ran down to a gate. The night was dark and they had only the light of a small lamp to guide them. Beatrice's ears and her nose, though, told her where she was – by the sea. They went down through the cold air to the gate. The bolt was stiff and Styliane struggled to pull it back. Beatrice could not think what secret would make a great lady of the court struggle at a gate like a common guard.

When the gate was open, Styliane pointed away from the palace. Beatrice peered into the night. Two lights hung in space. The smaller light moved. It took a while for her eyes to work out what she was seeing, but then Beatrice realised it belonged to the promised boat. They went down to a small beach, Styliane bowing three times as she passed through the gate.

Beatrice found the gesture very disquieting, with its pagan overtones, but she had made up her mind – she would not turn back. If Styliane wished her harm or wanted her dead then she had no need to go to such elaborate lengths. She felt the baby inside her, kicking. She put her hand to her belly.

'Not yet, child. You must wait until we've done what we need to do.'

The boat was small – no more than a fishing vessel, though well built and sturdy. A middle-aged man and a youth, slaves by their dress, waited beside it.

'We can cross?' Styliane spoke to the older man.

'The lighthouse is visible from here and the palace has enough lights to guide us on the return. We can cross.'

The boy helped both women in, the man climbing in to sit at the oars.

'Strange times, lady,' said the oarsman.

'Indeed,' said Styliane.

'Should she be here in that condition?'

'It's a needful time.'

Beatrice was struck by the familiarity with which Styliane treated these people, allowing their questions without reminding them of their place. There was no distance between them; she adopted no superior air. Beatrice's father would have warned her such an attitude would lead to trouble with the servants. Her father, Rouen and the court. That life seemed so far behind her.

They went on through the water, the lights of the palace fading behind them, their own lamp and the bigger light in front of them the only breaks in the darkness.

'I'm like Charon,' said the oarsman. 'Do I get a coin?'

'What?' said Beatrice.

'The boatman on the river of the dead,' said Styliane. 'The old Greeks said that we cross from this life to the next across a river and Charon rows.'

Beatrice could not appreciate the humour and kept her eyes on the growing light in front of her.

'What is that?'

'Leander's Tower,' said Styliane. 'A lighthouse.'

'Why are we going there?'

'For light,' said Styliane.

Beatrice was cold and huddled into her cloak. Soon a large tower with a burning beacon loomed from the fog. The tower was a straightforward round structure in stone with an open roof for the fire platform. A large sheet of polished metal had been positioned behind it to improve its effectiveness as a beacon.

The boat bumped against a rough quay. Two men from the shore helped moor the boat but then disappeared back inside the building.

The youth helped Styliane and Beatrice ashore and then passed Styliane the lamp. She took it and went inside the tower, Beatrice close behind.

A crude ladder led up to an internal platform. Again, Styliane led the way. Beatrice was convinced she couldn't climb the ladder but found a way, turned half sideways. Desperation overcame her exhaustion and caution. From the platform another ladder went up onto the roof. Could she make it? She had to. She climbed.

She reached the top and looked out over the sea. Even with the light of the brazier she could see hardly anything beyond the roof itself. The fog was thick. Beatrice glanced behind her and gasped. An old slave woman, dressed all in black, turned around and it was as if she was appearing from nothing, her dark features shining in the light of the beacon.

'This is Arrudiya,' said Styliane. 'She raised me.'

The woman cast down her eyes but not with deference, Beatrice thought. There was defiance or truculence in her expression.

The brazier was very hot and Beatrice moved away from it.

'Now?' said Styliane.

'When the fire has died a little,' said Arrudiya. 'The moon is still climbing.'

'How does she know that?' said Beatrice.

'I can feel it,' said Arrudiya.

'Why is she here?' said Beatrice.

'Because God sees things in threes,' said Styliane, 'and God is three.'

'Moon, earth and underworld,' said Arrudiya, 'past, present, future. Father, son, spirit; virgin, mother, crone.'

Beatrice didn't want to hear any more. She sat, waiting for the brazier's light to weaken. It didn't take long, and soon it was reduced to glowing coals, a tight cluster of light buried in the great darkness.

Eventually the old woman came to her. She poured something from a flask onto her hands and anointed Beatrice's eyes.

'Water from a shipwreck,' she said.

She took out another flask and put it to Beatrice's lips.

'Drink,' she said.

Beatrice did as she was asked. The drink was honey water but with a bitter musty taste behind it.

'What is this?'

'Kykeon, as our forebears drank,' said the woman, 'made with Syrian rue.'

Then the two other women sat down around the fire, equidistant from each other and Beatrice, and intoned in a low drone:

'Wherefore they call you Hecate, many-named, air-cleaving, night-shining, triple-sounding, triple-headed, triple-voiced, triple-faced, triple-necked, and goddess of the three ways, who holds untiring flaming fire in baskets three, you who protect the spacious world at night, before whom demons quake in fear and the gods immortal tremble. Subduer and subdued, mankind's subduer, and force-subduer; chaos, too. Hail, Goddess.'

Beatrice hated the invocation. She concentrated on prayer, on calling Christ to protect her, to save her soul. But she did not move; she wanted revelation.

The old woman threw a handful of something onto the coals and they flared. 'I burn for you this spice, goddess of harbours, who roams the mountains, goddess of crossroads, nether and nocturnal, and infernal goddess of dark, quiet and frightful one.'

Beatrice found she was repeatedly crossing herself.

'You who have your meal amid graves, night, darkness, chaos deep and wide, hard to escape are you. You are torment, justice and destroyer. Serpent-girded, who drinks blood, who brings death; destructor, who feasts on hearts.'

Beatrice coughed and fell forward on to her hands. Her nose was streaming and her throat was dry.

'Flesh eater, who devours those dead untimely, and you who make grief resound and spread madness, come to my sacrifices, and now for me do you fulfil this matter. Shall we speak about the things not to be spoken of? Shall we divulge the things not to be divulged? Shall we pronounce the things not to be pronounced?'

The fire was suddenly bright again and Beatrice tried to get up, but her body seemed fixed to the floor.

'Grant us revelation,' continued the chant, 'open our eyes and chase away the night, wandering lady, bright Selene.'

The moon had come out from behind a cloud, full and bright – much brighter than it had ever been, she thought – as if it resented its long time cloaked in black and was redoubling its light in joy at its release.

When she looked back down again, she was no longer on the rooftop. She was in the place by the river she went to in her dreams but not on the path by the wall; she was in the deep wood beside it. Styliane and Arrudiya sat on the ground next to her, each holding a small candle. Something crashed and bumped in the woods. A creature, she thought. A weird sense between hearing and touch, not quite either, had sprung up in her and the presence of the creature seemed hot and snuffling, as if hot and snuffling were the same thing.

'How do I find my answer? How do I find his purpose?'

Styliane and Arrudiya gave no reply, just sat staring ahead.

Beatrice had a very strong urge to get out of those woods. The blundering thing wasn't the only presence in there. She stood. She saw nothing but trees and darkness; the moon was caught in the branches, her own hands glowing pale in its light. She walked forward, pushing away branches and briars. Something was behind her. She turned. Nothing. She wanted to get onto the path, to go to those little candles in the wall and see they still burned. That was unaccountably very important to her.

Ahead the river shone like a silver road. She headed for it, her clothes tearing on the brambles, her skin scratched and cut by thorns.

She heard rustling in the woods behind her. She pulled and tugged her way forward, the baby heavy inside her even in the dreamworld.

You are going to the well. The voice was in her ear, more a whisper of the trees than anything human.

'I will resist my fate.'

You are fate. Say your name, Verthani.

'I do not know that name.'

> *Three wise girls come from the hall beneath the tree.*
> *One is called Urdr, Fated so men call her;*
> *Another Becoming, Verthani is her name;*
> *Skuld – Must Be – is the third. Together*
> *They carve on tablets of wood the fate of men.*

Something stirred inside her and it was not the baby. *That symbol.* It crawled and writhed, gnawed at her like a wolf in her guts.

She made the path. Footsteps were coming the other way. It was a boy, a youth – the one who had visited Loys in their chamber.

He was walking towards the candle wall but he stopped when he saw her.

'You are here, lady,' he said, gesturing to the wall. 'Shall I snuff you out?'

All around the boy, like things glimpsed at the end of a dream, half-seen, coming into existence, fading and returning like sleep spectres, symbols shone and span. She recognised them – Norse runes of the sort some of her father's men liked to carve though these were things of air and light and fire and darkness, not designs in wood.

'Who are you?'

'I don't know. I know what I do here but I don't know who I am.'

'You are the one who came to my husband in our chambers.'

'Yes, Snake in the Eye. That is certainly one of my names, though I begin to suspect I have others.'

'How so?'

'There are things inside me, living things. They woke up when I turned to Christ. I am baptised now. They bathed me in the waters and then I baptised myself again in the priest's blood to be doubly holy. Am I not holy?'

'I am here to seek answers. Who is the man my husband took from the Numera? What is the meaning of the black sky? And the deaths?'

'Three questions. A suitable number for a god. I only know one answer.'

'What is it?'

'The deaths have no meaning. I find them pleasing, that is all.'

'You are their cause?'

'Yes. I come here in my fancies and I blow out the lights. Men die. I see four here, one little one for your child. There are others with you?'

'Yes.'

'Reveal them to me.'

'They are in the wood.'

'Who?'

'Two women. They brought me here.'

'I don't suppose I need to see them to kill them. Here!' He leaned into the wall and blew out one of the candles. Then he put his hand to his ear. 'Heard no one fall. I'll blow out another and you listen. Unless it's you who falls, of course. I wonder if I kill the baby whether it'll kill you. Hmmm.'

Beatrice took a pace back. The boy was mad, she was convinced. He shaped his lips to blow out another candle and the thing inside her, the jagged, barbed shape that crawled and slunk, began to howl, a dreadful keening note like a funeral lament.

'What is that?' said Snake in the Eye.

Beatrice had always fought it down. She knew now what she had done by that river, what had caused her fever. She had heard the rune howling and gone to the wall, tried to extinguish the candle that represented her life so she would no longer hear the call of the dread symbol. She had not managed it and had succumbed to fever and illness and dementia. Beatrice had tried to die but could not. That was before Loys, before love, and, faced by this awful boy, she wanted to live.

She no longer fought down the rune; she embraced it, opening her mind like a great sluice on a dam to allow what she had kept locked away to come bursting forth. The rune screamed and howled, raging like a cornered wolf. The trees stirred but not with the wind. Something was out there.

Snake in the Eye stared transfixed by the remaining candles in the wall. A low seething growl rumbled from the woods, a pure animal voice of threat that speaks to ancient fears and commands complete attention in a heartbeat.

There from the trees came Azémar, but it was not Azémar. Beatrice saw a man, but the idea in her mind was that of a wolf. Then she saw it, a great grizzled black thing, its eyes a shining green, its voice low with threat.

Snake in the Eye pointed at the wall. 'There is no light here for the wolf,' he said. 'If you have drawn it here, lady, I do bid you send it away or I can snuff out your lamp as easily as any of the others.'

'I am no one's to command,' said the wolf and its voice was like an avalanche.

Snake in the Eye backed away down the path, retreating from the wall.

'Go,' said the wolf who was Azémar and – Beatrice had one of those strange ideas that only exist in dreams – several other people too.

'I could fight you,' said Snake in the Eye. 'I—'

The wolf sprang at the boy, knocking him to the ground, roaring into his face, his lips pulled back over his great teeth.

'I am not free,' said the wolf, 'and you are not yet whole.'

'I am a man as good as any.'

'You will find the waters. You will find the well. You will pass over the bridge of light to find a place where you will die a meaningful death.'

The wolf released the boy and backed away from Beatrice.

'Who are you?' said Beatrice to the wolf.

'Your killer,' said the wolf, 'time and again through many lives.'

'Am I to die?'

'I am bound, fettered and bound.'

'You are free, sir.'

'I send forth my mind to travel the nine worlds. Release me from the rock where the slaughter gods bound me and release yourself from your eternal suffering.'

'Who are you?'

'Ask rather, who are you, lady?'

'Then who am I?'

> 'Of many births
> the Norns must be,
> Nor one in race they were;
> Some to gods, others
> to elves are kin,
> And Dvalin's daughters some.'

'Don't talk in riddles. Who am I?'

'A dream of a god. A dream of one greater than the gods. You spin the fates of men and gods. '

'I am a woman, born of a woman, and I will die a woman.'

'You lead me to my fate and only you can keep me from it.'

'How should I help you?'

'Release me. At the well and from there to beyond the bridge of light.'

'Lady Beatrice!'

Behind her was Styliane, her eyes wide with fear.

Images rushed in on Beatrice — she saw herself as she had

been before, in lives past. She was a country girl by a low hut, drying herbs on its roof in the sun; she was a lady dressed in man's armour, fleeing beneath spring skies; she was something she did not understand, someone who had once carried the bright chiming symbols she had seen around that murderous boy by the river, a woman walking in a wood holding the hand of a man who she had known in lives before and would know in lives again. Azémar, the wolf, her killer.

'Lady, come away from this place. We should not have come here.' Styliane tugged at her, trying to pull her away.

She heard the snarl of the wolf and its voice, low and furious.

'She is mine in lives past, present and future, and I will never let you take her!'

'Azémar, no!' said Beatrice, but it was too late. The wolf rounded on Styliane, Beatrice leaped to protect her, and the world went dark.

On the platform of the lighthouse tower Beatrice came back to herself. Her two companions lay flat; the coals of the fire burned dim. The moon had gone and the night was black again, the only light from the dim beacon.

She stood and had to put a hand to the wall for balance. Her head swam. She retched and stood panting for a while. She went to Arrudiya. The woman was dead, cold already. Styliane was warm and breathing but Beatrice couldn't rouse her.

She sat down and sobbed. What was happening to her? Then she regained control. Styliane needed help. Beatrice leaned over the parapet of the tower. The boat still bobbed by the quay. She went to the top of the ladder and shouted down, 'Get up here now. The lady needs your help.'

The slaves hurried up as Beatrice leaned on the wall for support, looking across at the night lights of Constantinople. She had seen enough in the dream to convince her Azémar was a demon. When she got back to the palace, she would cut his throat.

36   Twice Hidden

Guards bearing torches and swords marched under the black sky down the broad avenue. Loys tore ahead of them with his lamp down the Middle Way to warn the soothsayers of the purge. He shook them awake from their places in porches and alleys, screaming at them to get up and run. The wild women and fortune tellers, the casters of bones and the penny wizards cursed him and told him to leave them alone until they saw the soldiers coming. Then they fled for the city gates.

Next Loys ran to the hospital, the chamberlain's words haunting him: *We're running out of time.*

The chamberlain clearly believed the strange happenings had a purpose and, more than that, that they were building towards something. Loys thought too of those words that had come to him when he had spoken to Snake in the Eye. *Thou believest that there is one God; thou doest well: the devils also believe, and tremble.*

God's protection had not worked in the church. Loys shivered. What if this was not a visitation from the devil but from God, chiding his flock for their sins? What did the Bible say – the Book of Revelation? First would come a rider on a white horse. He would come as a king and a conqueror. Well, Basileios fitted that description, though so did many warrior kings throughout history. Then would come War on a red horse. There had been plenty of war. Next Famine on his black horse. Such cold could not be good for the crops. Finally Death would ride in on his pale horse. The souls of the martyrs would cry out for vengeance beneath the altar. The faces of the corpses in Hagia Sophia loomed in his mind.

Loys told himself to calm down. Such imaginings swept the common people occasionally, when a storm or a flood would have them crying that the time of tribulation had started, that Christ was coming back to his kingdom. The abbot had always counselled folk not to read too much into natural things. Every famine, pestilence or drought could not presage the end of the world. Loys had to stick to the task at hand. If Christ was returning, what better way for the Lord to find him than engaged in the pursuit of demons?

The same clear head needed to be applied to his assessment of the chamberlain. Could he really suspect him? Yes, he had seemed flustered, desperate almost but very likely the emperor would want answers as to why his people were collapsing in the aisles of his greatest church, and if the chamberlain couldn't provide them, he was as vulnerable as anyone. And then there was Styliane. She opposed her brother and she had told Loys quite clearly the chamberlain had employed diabolical forces to secure his position. But could she be trusted?

Loys reached the hospital and went inside. It was busy as a marketplace, full to bursting. The patients had heard what had happened at the church and they wept and wailed. He found a doctor and enquired about the survivor. The man didn't know what Loys was talking about but directed him to the admissions clerk, who found the doctor he needed.

'What did he look like?'

'A Varangian. He was a boy,' said the doctor.

Loys recalled the boy who had come to see him. Not him, surely? He had told him to go to the church to seek baptism. Hagia Sophia was the nearest church to the palace.

'Did he say anything to you?'

'Just that he wanted his sword and he wanted to be baptised,' said the doctor.

That did sound like the youth.

'Did he speak to anyone else?'

'We put him in a separate room. There were only two other patients in it.'

'I need to speak to them.'

'It's the middle of the night.'

'I need to speak to them.'

The doctor shrugged and led Loys through the hospital, stepping around whole families who were huddled together as if sheltering from a storm. They went down a corridor to a closed door. The doctor knocked and, receiving no reply, went in.

A young man lay across a bed, an older man face up on his, a towel over his head.

'Rouse them,' said Loys.

'I—'

'I am the chamberlain's man and we are on business vital to the state. Rouse them.'

The doctor bent and shook the young man by the shoulder. 'Sir, could you ...' He stopped, wet his finger and put it beneath the young man's nose. He crossed himself. 'He's dead!'

Loys crouched to examine the body. He touched its hand. Freezing cold, like the corpses in the church.

The doctor went to the older man. 'Dead too! My God, that boy's of a very powerful family, they'll have my blood, oh my God!'

'The boy who was here,' said Loys, 'what did he look like? I need more detail.'

The doctor paced back and forth. 'I don't know, a Varangian. Still a child, though dressed in war gear. We have a hospital full of sick and those who imagine themselves sick under this sky. I have my doctors trying to establish what killed the people in Hagia Sophia. I cannot recall what one child among hundreds who come here looks like! What are we going to do about these two bodies? I'm not taking the blame, that's for sure.' A commotion sounded in the corridor, cries for help, people urging others to hurry.

'What?' The doctor went out of the room to see what was happening. When he returned he looked very troubled.

'More trouble on the Middle Way. More dead,' he said.

'The soothsayers?' said Loys.

'Yes, but Hetaerian guards too. There are a hundred dead down there.'

Loys ran out of the hospital and hard back down the hill, almost tumbling he ran so fast. He needed to find the strange boy. The boy had been going to the church; he had been at the hospital; he could tell him what had happened.

Panic gripped the streets. Lamps cut bright lines across the dark. Families on carts pulled by donkeys rolled by, wailing and screaming. Some ran, others carried the weak and the sick. The Middle Way was strewn with corpses. Dogs had caught the people's fear and bayed into the black night.

Loys saw soldiers joining the rout to the gates. He ran back towards the palace, breathless, shoving through the fleeing crowds. In the unnatural night, carrying their lamps or torches, they reminded Loys of that smaller procession that had climbed the hill outside the walls to sacrifice its lambs to the city's old goddess. Was this her doing? Was this the light-hating demon who had been worshipped here for years, come to reap its payment of blood? Hecate, burst from hell to torment the people for their sins?

Loys needed to speak to the wolfman, whatever the chamberlain said. The emperor himself had wanted him interviewed. The wolfman had said his death could end the trouble and the emperor had not believed him. Loys had to get down into the tunnels beneath the Numera but he couldn't go alone. The Varangians had helped him before; he could seek their help again. He couldn't reach their camp by the main gate along the Middle Way – too many people were pressing to get out that way.

The military gates, though, would be easier – they were habitually barred and not open to the public. He could bluff his way through. Loys strode up the hill towards the great Theodesian Wall. Away from the Middle Way the city was quieter. Not everyone had decided to flee – perhaps only those who had seen the horror or who had been frightened by the attack on the soothsayers. Others remained inside, doors bolted, some houses quite dark, others lit — people not knowing which to fear the most, the dark or the attention a lamp might bring. The light was very dim and Loys realised he would need a lamp of his own before long.

Reaching the wall, he ran alongside it until he arrived at the gatehouse. The inner gates were closed — strong wooden doors confronting him as he approached. A few frightened-looking poor families huddled by the gate, waiting for their chance to get out. Loys guessed the rich had too much to lose to flee, demon or no demon.

'Chamberlain's man! Chamberlain's man!' he shouted up at the towers.

A man appeared at the battlements. 'What do you want?'

'I need to get outside the walls.'

'No one leaves tonight. Orders. Not until the sorcery has been defeated.'

'That's what I'm trying to do. Mark my robes and shoes. I am Quaestor Loys and I demand you open this gate.'

There was silence for a while and then the little door set into the gates opened.

Three men came through, spears levelled. 'No one but the quaestor!' shouted a burly soldier, and Loys went inside. The people begged and pleaded but no one pushed forward to test the soldiers' resolve.

A soldier led Loys by lamplight to the outer gates, which had no small door and were locked.

'Is all this security necessary?' said Loys.

'With the Varangians camped where they are we're taking no chances,' said the soldier. Still, the gates were secured with only one relatively small bar of wood — the great trunks that would hold them shut in a siege lay to one side, ropes around them ready to be swung into position should they be needed. The gates were immensely thick, and Loys knew no enemy had managed to breach the city's walls for years. Some of the watchtowers had supplies for three years and their own water sources. The city would not fall easily, if at all.

The soldier pulled the heavy gate back a fraction and gestured to Loys to go through.

'Your lamp,' said Loys.

'Well bring it back; we've only got a few,' said the soldier.

'I will.'

The gate let him out at the top of the Varangian camp. He could afford to waste no time and he plunged straight in, calling out as he did in Norse, 'The emperor Basileios seeks good men to help his servant! The emperor Basileios seeks good men to help his servant!'

He approached a fire and men stood to greet him.

'I am the scholar Michael and I seek help from the Varangians as I did some nights ago.' Loys thought it best to stick to his disguise, to avoid needless explanations.

'I don't know you, friend,' said a voice, 'but any employment we can find we will take.'

Loys brought the lamp up to the man's face.

'I'm looking for a tracker,' he said. 'Do you know where I can find a man called Ragnar, who fought for the boy Snake in the Eye?'

'I do,' said the man at the fire. 'That is a fellow whose fame is great among us. Wait until morning and I will lead you to him.'

'I need him now.'

'What will you give?'

Loys caught the threat in the man's voice. Suddenly the realisation of just how vulnerable he was came over him. It was one thing to travel as a poor scholar seeming to offer more reward as an employer than a victim, another to come as an imperial bureaucrat. The silks the chamberlain had given him alone would be enough to spur many men to murder.

'My thanks and that of my friends. Vandrad is one of them,' said Loys.

The man laughed. 'No need to be afraid, scholar. We need all the friends we can get in your city. Come, share our fire. I'll send my boy for Vandrad and for Ragnar. They are warlike men you seek, and no mistake.'

'Have you seen Snake in the Eye?'

The man glanced down momentarily. 'I have not.'

Loys sat down by the fire, arranging his cloak under him to stop his robes getting wet. He was among wild people but they were potentially friendlier than those in the palace. The Norsemen didn't conspire and plot behind a man's back. If they disliked him, they'd just cut his throat openly and honestly.

'You sent for me.'

Loys had drifted off, numb with the shock of the day's events and with tiredness.

A man was at his side, his white hair cut short in the brutal Norman style, though he was no Norman. This man addressed him in Norse, had tattoos of dragons and wolves curling around his arms and neck and bore himself like a Viking. There was no courtesy in his demeanour, no hint of courtly manners. Loys had seen his sort enough in Rouen to know their rough ways should not always be mistaken for unfriendliness. His father had been such a man until, by effort and practice, he had shaped himself into a Norman merchant rather than a Norse pirate.

Vandrad and the three others approached through the fire-light.

'Michael!' said Vandrad. 'Michael who is soft-spoken but can act like a man when he chooses.'

'Too long to be a nickname,' said another.

'Give me time – I'm working on it,' said Vandrad.

Loys acknowledged the men, feeling safer for their presence.

'I have heard of you, Ragnar,' said Loys in his slow and careful Norse, 'and I hear you are a hunter.'

'I am.'

'I need you to find someone for me.'

'I have work already,' said Mauger.

'I can pay you.'

'My pay is honour,' said Mauger, 'and the service of my lord.'

'I am an official of the chamberlain of Constantinople, a quaestor charged with investigating the cause of this black sky and the deaths that grip this city.'

'A title means nothing. How do they measure your worth?'

'Look at my fine robes. Know I have the ear of the chamberlain himself. Know I dwell in fine rooms in the palace. In there I live better than barbarian kings. I have a scroll of office and the gates of the city open at my command. Men fear me.'

Loys was aware he was speaking to a barbarian so he couched his worth in ways the man could understand – gold, accommodation, the right to move freely.

Mauger looked hard at Loys. 'You could get me into the palace?'

'Yes. Why would you want to go?'

The big Viking thought for a couple of seconds.

'They say they have metal trees there and that golden birds sit in their branches.'

'This is true.'

'I would see the marvels of the inmost palace,' said Mauger.

'I could arrange it if you help me find the man I seek.' Loys couldn't believe this man's simplicity. However, hadn't he himself thrilled to see the fountains and the singing trees? He had to remind himself he was only separated by a generation from men exactly like Ragnar.

'Where shall I seek him?'

'He is in the dungeons of the city. He has gone to the caves beneath.'

'He is an escaped prisoner?'

'Of a sort.'

Mauger tapped the hilt of his sword. 'And your Greeks cannot find him?'

'Or don't want to.' Loys was surprised at the words that came out of his mouth. Had the chamberlain really sought the wolfman? Or had he sent his men in there to die?

'Is the mission dangerous?' said Vandrad.

'Yes. The man has killed several Greeks.'

'Then fame could come of it,' said Vandrad.

'I believe the emperor would be grateful,' said Loys.

'We need to impress him,' said Vandrad. 'He's kept us sat here freezing our arses to the mud for too long. He needs a reminder of our worth.'

'I can find your man,' said Mauger, 'if you can get me into the palace safely. They may not welcome a northern man there.'

'No one will dare move against you under my protection,' said Loys.

Mauger said that was good enough for him. 'But one thing, friend. How do you know of my fame? And how do you know our tongue?'

'I am a scholar and know many languages. As for you, the emperor's translator Snake in the Eye mentioned you,' said Loys. 'He said you were a useful man.'

'I am that,' said Mauger. 'Give me a second to collect a water skin and some food and I will be with you.'

'Be quick,' said Loys. 'Strange things are happening in the city, and the longer we wait the worse they will be. And here,' he gave him a coin, 'buy some food for me.'

At least Beatrice was in the palace, though he knew she would be worried for him. He would send a message with a boy when he got into the city, he decided. If the messenger wasn't allowed in, that would be a good sign. She would be safe behind the spears of the Hetaereia. There was no indication the deaths were going to come to the palace. What could he do to protect her anyway? Press on, on his present course, try to find the answers the chamberlain – or the emperor – demanded.

The walls of the city were almost invisible in the wet air. Lamps hung on them, and it would have been easy to imagine them floating spirits or avenging angels. He would find the wolfman and stop the madness. If anyone was up to the job, these hardy northerners were. He would take whatever reward was going and retire to live among the olive groves on the rich earth of an island, where he and Beatrice would be safe from the predations of the world. He imagined the bright blue light on the ocean, the dark soil of the land. But before light, darkness. He squeezed the hilt of his knife and readied himself for the caves of the Numera.

37 The Uses of Love

The city was falling to anarchy. The chamberlain looked out
from a high tower of the palace. To the north-west, high up
on the seventh hill, some buildings flared with flame, bright
against the night. A gatehouse too was burning.

Were his own men in revolt? Or had the Varangians tricked
their way in? He feared the Varangians because he knew they
were keen to displace his own Hetaereians. He called in a
messenger and dispatched a Hetaereiarch with a squadron of
city guard up to the burning gate. The man was white with
fear. How many of them would obey? The messenger said the
dead lay in piles on Middle Way and there was news of more
strange happenings across the city.

The runes that moaned and hissed inside the chamberalin
seemed in tumult, unquiet and fretful like sheep in a pen at
the howl of a wolf. He was to blame for this chaos, he was
sure.

He gestured to his servant to bring him a bowl of water from
the stand. The chamberlain lifted it to his lips and tried to take
a drink but he couldn't. His stomach was tight, his throat too.
He put the water down, feeling sick, leaning against the wall
for support. A bright berry of blood burst onto the tiles at his
feet. He put his hand to his nose. More blood.

'A cloth, a cloth!'

The servant quickly found one and the chamberlain dabbed
at his nose.

Still more blood.

He called up a magical symbol in his mind, allowed it to shape
his thoughts. The symbol had many names, he knew. Today it
seemed to murmur to him in the language of the northerners.
Mannaz had always brought him insight before, shaped his

decisions, allowed him to second-guess his enemies. Now, though, the symbol was trying to leave him. It was almost as if it was preoccupied with something else. It reminded him of a difficult horse, the sort convinced predators lurk behind every unfamiliar feature and which pays greater attention to its fears than it does to its rider. It seemed much more a living thing than an idea or a vision; he could feel its shape coiling through his mind like a serpent, pulling and tugging to be free.

In the aftermath of his murders it had seemed so easy to command the runes. Symbols was too weak a word for these beings. They were more than just the scribbles of the Norsemen. Were they truly demons in a strange form?

He tried a further symbol, willing it to obey. Othala – again the name in Norse. Were the runes trying to tell him something? He put his hand out, as if to touch the symbol, to use it as he had once used it to secure influence for his family and friends, to bring Styliane to the court and have her adopted by a rich family, to blind people to his sorceries and love of the old religion. It seemed to shy away from him.

He finally stopped the blood from his nose. More shouting, more sounds of torment out in the city. More deaths. He could not see what was causing them. He had performed the rite of divination, mixed dead man's blood with myrrh and bay leaves to spread as a tincture on his eyes. He had said the words to command the goddess:

> 'By the sound of the barking dog, I call on you.
> By the hanged who are holy to you,
> By those who have died in war,
> By this blood, violently taken,
> I call on you to grant me revelation.'

The runes inside him had moaned and shifted but nothing had come, no insight into the terrible events. Was this the end of the world? Was this Hecate's victory over the realms of light?

The chamberlain called on one more rune, the one that burned like a single torch. It was shrouded now, as if seen through mist or the gritty black drizzle that had fallen since the comet had been seen. He tried to concentrate, to make it clearer, but he knew the symbols would not be commanded. They were things that appeared in dreams, in the moment between waking and sleeping, things of the threshold between the physical and the supernatural world. Or rather, they would be commanded, depending on the sacrifices he was willing to make. He remembered his mother's words: *Nothing is won without effort.*

'No.'

It was as if he spoke to the rune, answering a suggestion it had made. But the rune had made no suggestion, given no insight. The chamberlain spoke to himself.

He had thought he had raised Styliane up out of a sense of guilt, as a sign he was not entirely without pity or decent feeling. She was his sister and he felt guilty he had robbed her of any family but himself, and in the days when the magic in him had been easier to use, he had worked to help her.

He saw more. The magic had known what it needed. Shock. He was a man, a poor vessel for such powers. His castration had helped tie the magic to him, but the bonds that had been formed between him and the symbols in the blood light of the well needed renewing. He had let them wither, preferring the comfortable life to sacrifice.

He *had* sacrificed, of course – the black lambs and the goats and sheep his goddess demanded – but the magic could not be sustained by such meagre offerings. He knew what it wanted – pain, revulsion, a horror to shake the sanity from its everyday existence, to jettison the mind's clutter and leave it free to understand the fundamental relations of the universe as expressed in the runes he had taken from the waters to plant in his head.

Something moved at the edge of his vision. He wheeled about, searching for it, but there was nothing there. He sensed a presence, though – bitter and angry. His dead sister. Was her spirit doing this? Could her anger enable her to break the bonds of death? She was a priestess of Hecate, goddess of the dead. She had died at the most holy place, where the three waters met. Had the goddess granted her the right to return? Was she sending the symbols mad inside him, loosening his control, letting them pull from him to kill and cause chaos in the city?

He sensed this to be true. He had gained control and insight once, power even. If he was to regain it, he needed a sacrifice equivalent to his first.

Styliane. He had kept her there, his one connection to a life of love, of tenderness and familial feeling. He had bound himself to the runes in the well once and done great things. He needed to be bound again.

Across the city lights flickered, buildings burned, people screamed. What had he unleashed? He mouthed the words of the dedication to Hecate.

> Goddess of depths eternal,
> Goddess of darkness,
> Come to my sacrifices.
> I am burning for you some dreadful incense –
> Goat's fat dappled, filth and blood,
> The heart of one untimely dead.
> Your greatest mystery, goddess
> Who opens the bars to the lands of the dead,
> Who makes light useless and plunges the world
> Into premature night.

He'd thought the words were just an acknowledgement of the goddess's power, not a description of something that might actually happen.

Again, a movement, a thickening of the air in his lungs.

'You're here, aren't you, Elai? Sister?' said the chamberlain out loud.

A dog howled in the distance.

'Well,' he said, 'you need disturb yourself no more on my account.' He dabbed the cloth against his nose.

'I shall come to visit you,' he said.

Far off on the walls, someone cried out in anguish. He heard distant voices, the screams of battle. Just visible, a mass of torches streamed through one of the lower gates – not the one that burned. Norsemen.

He guessed what had happened. Death in the streets, civil disorder, the incident with the wolfman. It had all become too much for the emperor. Reports had reached him in the east. He had sent his seal and ordered a gate opened to allow the Varangians to do as they had requested – replace the Hetaereian guard. That would not be accomplished without a fight.

It was a move against him. Basileios had trusted the chamberlain with everything, freeing himself up for his campaigns, but if the chamberlain could not keep order or subdue the magic assaulting the city then he would destroy his power by removing his loyal Hetaereia and replacing them with foreigners. It would have been obvious to the chamberlain had he not been so preoccupied with magic. The threat spurred him to action.

'Get me messengers here now,' he said to his servant, 'and send in the new master of post.' The servant left the room, leaving the chamberlain alone. He put his head into his hands and said, into nothing, 'This is not the end time. I will endure. Whatever it takes, I will endure.'

38 Revelation

The dark again and the damp again and the sounds of torment and the stink of men rotting alive in their shackles.

The Numera had multiplied its horrors since Loys last visited. The messenger service had filled the prison with anyone at all who was suspected of sorcery, anyone who had ever had a seditious thought and anyone with whom they had a score to settle, which was a multitude.

So many had been crammed in they had run out of manacles, and on the bottom level men had even ventured – or blundered – into the lower caves in search of space to uncoil their cramped limbs. They did not go far down. The tunnels were too tight, too jagged and dark for anyone to risk going into them without a light, a rope and pegs to mark the way out.

Loys and the Varangians had to shove, push, bully and threaten their way to the caves. Vandrad and his fellows cracked a few heads, and though the prisoners vastly outnumbered the northerners, no one attacked them. These men, thought Loys, had lost their will. The party pressed through the last of the prisoners and clambered up a rockfall. From here it was a belly crawl into the bigger caverns beyond, Loys knew.

'You can't keep people like this,' said Vandrad. 'Kill them as a man kills his enemies or let them go. There can be no glory in this death.'

Loys knew the messenger service wasn't seeking glory. They wanted power, to terrify their enemies.

'It's a sacrifice,' said Loys, 'made by fear to fear.'

'I know that I hung on that wind-racked tree, pledged to Odin, myself to myself,' said Vandrad.

'I was talking about human evil, not your pagan idol,' said Loys.

'Odin is human evil. Odin is fear,' said another Varangian, 'and he sacrificed himself to himself as your god Christ did.'

Loys couldn't be bothered to argue with the man. He was too keen to get into the tunnels and away from the mob of dying men at his back.

'Let's press on,' said Loys. 'I want this wolfman taken alive.'

'Might not be possible,' said Mauger.

'I pay double for a living wildman,' said Loys.

'You mean you will show me the fountains of the palace twice?' said Mauger.

Loys almost laughed. He had forgotten that Ragnar – as he knew the northerner – was alone in not working for pay.

'If you catch him I'll bath you myself in one,' said Loys.

Loys led the way, holding the lamp before him. He knew it was important to appear brave to the northerners. The first section was incredibly tight and he had to wriggle his way in. He was glad he had employed smaller men.

He emerged on top of another pile of rubble, looking out on the broad cave where Azémar had taken on the messengers. Things had moved so quickly since then he hardly had time to think about how strange it was that his friend had struck down so many enemies after his long ordeal. Perhaps Azémar feared being sent back to the prison. Men could fight like wolves when they were afraid, Loys had often heard it said.

Loys' mouth was already dry with dust as he lowered himself onto the cavern floor. He took up his lamp. The bodies of the Greeks Azémar had killed were still there. He tried not to look at them.

Vandrad came bumping down and then the rest behind him. Six men now in the cave. Loys couldn't help thinking eight men had already died in there, to his knowledge. Never mind, he had to go on. The wolfman had the answers he wanted, Loys was sure.

Here the passage was tall enough for them to walk without

stooping. They went on, their progress somewhat hampered by the uneven floor, but in the next cavern great slabs of rock protruded precariously from the ceiling. Loys and his men had to sidle around them. No one dared touch them for fear of triggering a collapse. The way was obvious at first, but as they descended other possible routes emerged. A black crack in the floor made Mauger pause and wet his finger to detect the movement of air. Another fissure, halfway up a wall, bore signs of dried blood just inside it. Mauger again licked his finger but this time rubbed it on the rock and tasted it. He climbed a little way up inside but came back to report the route was blocked by a decayed corpse. No one had been up there in years.

They went further down the biggest tunnel until a rockfall barred their progress. 'What now?' said Loys. 'There were other tunnels – should we try them?'

Mauger glanced at him to silence him. The northerner spent a long time padding about on the rocks. Then he climbed the rockfall and began clawing away rocks at the top.

'Careful,' said Vandrad. 'You don't want this down on us.'

'No chance of that,' said Mauger. 'These rocks are loose.'

After some time only Mauger's feet were visible, and he had to wriggle to pass out the rocks he was removing. Then his feet disappeared.

'Pass me through a lamp,' said his voice.

Loys climbed up with a lamp and squeezed in himself. Mauger took the lamp and Loys crawled through. He was in a cavern quite unlike the ones above. This was damp, the walls shiny with moisture. The floor was more even too, with fewer loose rocks, and smooth, the rock rippled in layers as if it had lain on the bed of a river.

The Vikings came through to join them.

'Those men above would dearly love to know this place existed,' said Vandrad. 'You could live licking the water off these walls.'

'It would be impossible to find in the dark,' said Mauger.

'How did you know the rocks were loose?' said Loys.

'I didn't know,' said Mauger; 'they just looked wrong. The ones that had fallen lay differently. The ones on top had been placed there.'

'Someone's trying to cover his trail,' said a Varangian.

'Let's hope so,' said Mauger. 'Nothing makes a man easier to follow.'

'I'll leave a mark on the rock to help us on our return,' said Vandrad. He scratched at the wall with his knife.

'What's that?' said Loys.

'Thor's hammer.'

'You don't need a sky god down here,' said Mauger. 'Best call on Odin – he finds people's way in the dark.'

Loys glanced at the Norseman. He wore a rough wooden cross at his neck but here, underground, in the old dark earth, he reverted to his heathen ways.

'Then Odin,' said Vandrad. He carved a strange symbol of three interlocking triangles on the wall. Loys was too concerned to get in and out of the tunnels to reproach him for his idolatry, but the symbol sparked his scholar's curiosity, despite his unease.

'What is that?'

'The dead god's necklace,' said Vandrad. 'A hanging knot.'

'Three in one,' said Mauger.

'Three what?' said Loys.

'Never bothered to ask,' said Mauger. The Vikings seemed to think this was a great joke. Mauger saw he had embarrassed the scholar and said, 'It is a way of showing he is not a straightforward god. He's many things to many men.'

'Most gods are,' said Loys, surprising himself with his cynicism. He offered an inward prayer as an apology.

'Not Thor,' said a Varangian. 'He's a smack round the head to many men.'

'Well,' said Vandrad, 'let's find old wolfboy and honour him in a way that god would like.'

Mauger held up his hand. 'Silence from now on in,' he said.

'If he's anywhere he's down here. He'll know we're coming no matter what we do – the lamps will give us away – but let's try to keep the warning to a minimum. When we find him we'll try to take him alive. That might be possible – he's been a long time down here with no food so he could be weak. However, I've encountered sorcerers like this before. They're tricky bastards and hard ones too, some of them. If it gets too tough let's make sure it's him who dies and not one of us.'

Grim nods, a couple of muttered words of agreement and the men went on, Mauger first. The passage quickly became very steep and then narrower and steeper still. It split into two tunnels, both dropping. Mauger threw a pebble into one. A long pause and then a splash. In the other tunnel the pebble rattled down. That one then.

The descent was precipitous and there was no way to hold a lamp. Instead Vandrad waited at the top of the shaft with a light. When all the others were down, Mauger lit a lamp at the bottom, then Vandrad extinguished his and climbed down. A long low tunnel stretched away in front of them. They crawled along it until what Loys had feared happened – the tunnel dipped into water.

Mauger tapped Loys on the shoulder and beckoned him forward. Loys crawled around the Viking.

'Someone has been through here,' said Mauger in a low voice, 'both ways. Look.'

In the flickering light Loys saw a muddy hand print on a rock near the water.

'So?'

'We can go through. Or try,' said Mauger.

'It's a brave man who will go first,' said Loys.

'That's you,' said Mauger. 'You are the one who most needs this wolfman. You can take this risk.'

'The crawl could be any length,' said Loys.

'We will tie a rope about you. If you fear you're starting to drown give three sharp tugs on it and we'll pull you back.'

'And if I make the other side?'

'Just draw the rope through. Can you find a way to keep your tinder dry?'

'I have a box,' said Loys.

It was his one valuable possession – a small box in worked pearwood, so tight-fitting it was proof against damp weather. Would it keep the tinder dry underwater? Perhaps.

'Go through, and if you can light your lamp then give five tugs on the rope,' said Mauger. 'If you can't we'll need to turn back.'

Loys prepared himself, checking his bag – his bread and cheese were going to get soaked so he quickly ate the bread. His lamp and the spare would likely be all right – their wicks were soaked in oil. The tinderbox was in God's care. He put his knife in his belt.

'Are you ready?'

Loys shrugged. He tied the rope around one leg – Mauger said he would get stuck if he put it around his waist. Then he took three big breaths and crawled down into the water. It was horribly cold and drove all the breath from him as he went in. He floundered and gasped, gulping in water. In four heartbeats he had returned to the surface, spluttering and coughing.

The Vikings greeted him with contempt in their stares. He lay panting on the floor, the men silent around him. When he had recovered, he tried again. This time he went under properly. Panic gripped him once more but he fought it down and clawed his way on. He floated up. White light flashed in his eyes as he banged his head on the ceiling. He flipped onto his back, pulling himself along by gripping the uneven rock above him. He desperately needed to breathe. He couldn't go on. Panic was overwhelming him. He gave three sharp pulls on the rope with his foot but it was slack. He had to continue. Finally he could feel no ceiling above him and he kicked up, not knowing if he had reached the end of the tunnel or just some drowned chimney of rock that led nowhere. He didn't know if he had reached air but he had no choice: he had to breathe in.

He gulped air into his lungs, casting about with his arms for dry land. Then the rope tightened and he was pulled back under. The Vikings clearly thought they had detected a signal and were pulling him back. He plunged back under the water, thrashing and scrambling to get purchase on the bank but it was no good, they were hauling him backwards. Horror made him find his knife and he slashed himself free of the rope.

He surfaced again and his hand hit something. He kicked towards it and felt around. Yes, dry rock. He carefully pulled himself out of the pool, wary of hitting his head if the ceiling was low. It wasn't.

The dark was terrifying. Loys imagined the massive weight of rock above him, bearing down like a giant's hand ready to crush him. He breathed in deeply, trying to summon up his courage. He reached into his bag. He had to be careful not to soak the tinder, so he put the box down carefully. Then he squeezed dry the wick of the lamp and made sure it was soaked in oil. He found his flint and tinder, struck – and screamed.

No more than an arm's length away crouched the cadaverous figure of the wolfman. Even in the brief instant of the flint flash he saw he was filthy and nearly starved, indeed like a wolf, or a corpse come back to life to answer a sorcerer's call. His cheeks were hollow, his eyes dark pits and his body sinewy, terribly lean.

'You've returned.'

The words were in Norse. Loys heard only the voice. Once again he could see nothing. He backed into the wall, desperate to hide from that horrible man.

'You were with my brother.' The voice was just as near.

Loys held his knife out, praying his eyes would adjust to the dark. They did not. There was no light, none at all.

'Calm yourself,' said the wolfman. 'I have no reason to kill you. Why are you here? I took steps to make sure I was not followed.'

'I'm looking for you,' said Loys. No profit in lying.

'For what reason?'

'This sky, the deaths, the emperor's affliction ...'

'What deaths?'

'In the streets above people are dying all at one time, falling to lie cold on the ground where a moment before they stood living as you and I live.'

'He is coming,' said the wolfman.

'Who? Christ?'

'Does it matter to give the god a name? He who hung on the tree, wounded by the spear, chilled by the stars and blinded by the moon. The god who is three, he is coming here.'

'A demon then?'

'Who is the one who killed the guards, the one you took from here?'

'He is a monk of the Norman lands, as am I.'

'How do you know him?'

'He was my friend. He came here to save me.'

'From what?"

'Assassins sent to kill me.'

'And why are you so important?'

'I am a scholar. Loys of the Abbey of Rouen. I ran away with the lord's daughter.'

'He is not coming to help or to kill you,' said the wolfman; 'he comes for a purpose that he might hide even from himself.'

'What purpose?'

'He is instrumental in everything you see, the sky, the deaths. He is a killer.'

'Who would he kill?'

'A god, the one who is here now. Odin, present in the three tiers of runes, Odin, king of the dead.'

'How do you know this? It's superstition, it's ...'

'There is a woman.'

'I don't understand.'

'You must have had a woman with you. The Norns have said he will come to find her.'

'There are many women in the palace.'

'She will be haunted by dreams. She will have seen him. Seen me. On a path by a river under moonlight, she will have seen us.'

Loys crossed himself.

'There is such a woman. Why does he seek her?'

'He comes for her blood too. He is murder, he is massacre and obliteration. He is the slaughter beast. '

'This is my friend. I know him. He would not kill anyone.'

'Your friend, what is his name?'

'Azémar.'

'This monk tore apart four guards in the tunnel. Explain that.'

'He was afraid for his life. Men gain great strength in such circumstances.'

'Some more than others. I stood next to him while he crawled to the corpses, like my brothers the wolves. I saw how the flesh filled him and made him new. He broke his manacles to be free.'

'This is not true.'

'How else does a man who has been locked under the earth for a month find the strength to perform such feats? I recognised him.'

'How do you know all this?'

'I have sweated and frozen in dark places. I have walked to the edge of the lands of the gods and looked within, and I have stood while those who know more than me have suffered and screamed for lore.'

'You are a sorcerer.'

'No. I am a man, but a man the gods notice and sometimes reward.'

'What is to happen to the woman, the one who sees the wolf?'

'She draws him to her, and she is drawn to the god. She finds the god; the wolf finds her.'

'And then?'

'The god has his reward. Death in this life so he may live in the realms eternal.'

'What happens to the woman?'

'She dies.'

Loys' silence told the wolfman what he needed to know.

'She is dear to you?'

'She is my wife.'

'Then you have a part in this too.'

'I don't believe you.'

'The wolf is my brother.'

Loys remembered the story Snake in the Eye had told him – how two brothers were caught in the destiny of the gods, how one would kill the other and take on the power to kill a god. But still he didn't believe the wolfman.

'No.'

'You have your flint?'

'Yes.'

'Strike.'

Loys struck, and in the flash he saw the tinderbox and the lamp. A couple more strikes and he had them in his hand. He lit the lamp. The wolfman's face was haggard, scarred and gaunt, but it was also, unmistakably, that of Azémar. He remembered what his friend had said: *I found my double down there in the dark.* The lamp shook in his hand.

'How can I protect my wife?' said Loys.

'By helping me,' said the wolfman. 'I have no great desire to die by the hand of my brother. I want to thwart the god's aims.'

'How can you do that?'

'I need to go behind the water, to the well of wisdom, where I can drink to discover what needs to be done. I had thought my own death would be enough.' The wolfman gestured behind him to an expanse of water, glittering golden in the light of the lamp. 'The well is beyond that.'

Loys looked into the wolfman's face, the face of his friend Azémar. He was inclined to believe him. The wolfman's eerie resemblance to Azémar gave credence to the idea that he was his brother. Beatrice, Beatrice. The idea that she was ensnared by these magical afflictions, that she might even be a target of dark powers, made him want to throw off the weight of rock above him and take her in his arms. He'd seen what Azémar had done to those men down there in the dark, his killing and his feeding. He could believe him to be a wolf. And Loys had brought him to the palace, put him next to Beatrice in her own chamber.

'Can he be saved too?' said Loys.

'I don't know. The answer is at the well.'

Loys felt desperation like a knife in his belly – he would do anything to remove it.

'I will help you,' said Loys. A gasp behind him and the white head of Mauger appeared from the water. 'And so will my men. What is your name?'

'Call me Elifr,' said the wolfman

'I am Loys.'

Mauger hauled himself into the tunnel.

39 Killers

The odours that woke him were the odours of death. Corpses lay all around, very near. There was a smell of burning too. Azémar sat up in his bed and touched his chest. It was wet with drool. His sleep had been troubled. She had been in his dreams again, Beatrice, the lady. He had committed two treacheries while he slept – one against the Church and his vows of celibacy and one against his friend.

The dream felt so real. He had been in a forest in autumn, the ground thick with leaves of red, russet and gold. They seemed so brilliant that he imagined some dwarf in his cave cutting each leaf from fine metal before puffing it into the sky to be caught by the wind and blown to the forest floor. The trees were far from bare, though, and the dying sun turned their leaves to cold fire. She was next to him and he was naked on the ground.

'Wake up,' she said. 'I have washed the wolf away.'

Azémar sat up, embraced her and lay with her on the leafy ground.

'Who are these fellows?' he asked her. Around him, ragged men lay dead as the leaves.

'Their light is gone,' she said. 'I took it so they would not harm us.'

Awake and in the palace, Azémar told himself he had dreamed, though it did not seem like a dream but a memory – because it didn't stop when he woke. He remembered the forest, the little house where they had prepared for the winter. He remembered how his appetite had driven him from his bed to go snuffling through the moonlight to the bodies of the ragged men.

Azémar was sure he had been deranged by his stay in the

Numera. He had seen demons there – the pale fellow, the wolf-man. Had one crawled into his mind to drive him mad?

She came into the room, unchaperoned, not even the servant beside her. Beatrice tried not to stare at him but couldn't stop herself. There was no friendliness in her eyes.

'Good morning, lady.'

'It is afternoon by the bells.'

'Then good afternoon.'

Her wariness seemed almost enticing, like bread cooking in the monastery's ovens.

Beatrice stood very still for a while. Then she lowered herself onto a couch and said, 'Sir, you trouble me.'

'Why so?'

'I trouble you too, I can see it.'

'I am unused to the presence of lone women. I ...'

'It is more than that.'

Again a silence.

'Yes, it is,' he said.

'Then what?'

Could he tell her? He would sound mad. Yet he had a powerful urge to do so. The palace seemed alive to him, so many smells – cooking, sweat, the mould of clothes, the make-up of the courtiers, the leather of the soldiers' tunics – and beyond those a scent like he smelled on Beatrice but sharper, with a tinge of smoke, a bitter undercurrent that set his tongue tingling as if he had licked a lemon.

'Lady, you must forgive me. I have undergone a terrible ordeal. I have been kept in a foul dungeon, denied light, denied food, given only water. It may be some time before I am myself again.'

'Say what you have to say.'

'I cannot.'

'Then I will say it for you. I know you, sir. It is only because you are my husband's friend and you have helped him in the past that I sit here now. My soul longs to run from you, and I tell you plainly I am afraid of you.'

Azémar bowed his head. 'Why fear me, lady?'

'You know, I sense it. In my dreams, since I was a girl, I have walked in a strange place. A riverbank under the moon. I have never been there, but I visit it so regularly when I am sleeping that it's almost as familiar as my home. In my dream I am looking for something and something is looking for me. There is a man and he follows me.'

Azémar crossed himself. 'In my dream there is a lady and I follow her.'

Beatrice stood up. 'You mean me harm!'

'No, lady, no.'

'You will harm me. When I turn to confront the man, to ask him why he follows me, then he is no longer a man.'

'What is he?'

'He is a wolf. I have seen what he does with his nails and his teeth. A lady of this palace lies unwaking on her bed because of him.'

'How so?'

'She came with me to that place, that riverbank, and the wolf attacked her.'

'Came with you? How could she come with you in your dreams?'

'The women of this city have arts you cannot guess at, Azémar.'

'Sorcery?'

'I don't know what to call it. I just know I have seen you and I have seen what you are capable of.'

'I am a gentle man and I would never harm anyone.'

'But you have been to the river?'

'Yes.'

'So what does it mean?'

'The devil sends many things to test us.'

'This is not the work of the devil,' said Beatrice. Her voice was low, though she felt like screaming.

'Then what?'

'Tell me.'

'I saw you in the fields,' said Azémar. 'I am a man and you are a beautiful woman. I thought you had just entered my dreams in the way women do. It's a sin to think of you so deeply that you appear to me when I am sleeping, but no more.'

'And then?'

'In the Numera, far from God's eyes. A man came to me and I saw you again. This time it was not a dream. It was real.'

'Were you in the forest, where the dead men lay?'

'I was.'

'You went to them, and I asked you to come away, to leave them and be free of your hungers.'

'Yes. I looked for you in many places. Below the earth, in caves and tunnels. I have hunted you through my dreams.'

'A wolf hunts me.'

'In that prison a man came to me, or more than a man, a demon, and called me wolf.'

Their eyes met. Azémar had the powerful urge to embrace her, to tell her he loved her and that he had come so far to find her. But he did not. She was married to his friend. He was a monk.

'So what are we to make of this?'

'We are to make nothing,' said Beatrice. 'It's clearly an affliction of demons, of which this city seems to have many.'

Again the cold night air drifting beneath the doorway, a smell of the newly dead. If Beatrice noticed these things, she showed no sign. Azémar had to swallow. He wiped drool from his chin. His stomach grumbled, empty.

'My abbot told me not to put too much store in natural phenomena. These skies may be sent by God, by the devil, or they may be simply some rare weather.'

'And the dead?'

'What dead?'

Beatrice told him of the reports of deaths in the churches, of deaths in the streets, people cold to the touch almost as they hit the floor. 'Loys is supposed to find what is causing this. He has to provide a spell to stop it.'

'A rare sort of heresy for the state to demand.'

'This state is full of heretics, and worse, I suspect.'

'Lay the case before me,' said Azémar. 'I am Loys' equal in study and two men may make clear what remains obscure to one.'

So Beatrice told him everything she knew – from the coming of the comet to the death of the rebel, the darkening of the sky, the weakness of the emperor and now the many sudden deaths that were afflicting the city.

'A wildman came to the emperor on the night of the victory, predicting death and calamity. Loys seeks to find him,' said Beatrice.

'In the city?'

'Below the Numera. He was there but he escaped to the lower tunnels.'

'I have seen him,' said Azémar.

Her fear was something he could taste, pungent and harsh but pleasing for all that, like a hot spice. All his life his instinct would have been to offer her words of reassurance, to calm her; now her fear seemed almost beautiful. Once the world had been shrouded in night. Now it had come to glorious day and he saw clearly for the first time in his life. He heard the beating of her heart, smelled the sweetness of the sweat of stress upon her, noticed the tenseness of her muscles as if she was ready to run. There was a palpable hostility to her.

'What did he say?'

Azémar remembered the wolfman, his strange double, the pale fellow and the smothering dark.

'He told me to go far away from here,' he said.

Beatrice put her hand to her throat. 'He thinks you have something to do with this!'

'I don't know. Lady, I was in the dark a long time. I was . . .'

Azémar couldn't finish his sentence. The smell on the breeze was becoming too much for him. It reminded him of salt beef but with many more colours to its flavour. Words no longer seemed to fit into his mind.

Someone knocked hard at the door and Beatrice started and involuntarily crossed herself.

'I ...'

'What?'

'War and death. Here ...' The monk stumbled over his words.

'Speak clearly, Azémar.'

He took her hand. 'The city is under attack,' he said. 'The Varangians are through the gates. I smell their sweat. I smell their fires. The palace will be locked down.'

Beatrice pulled free of him. 'I will not stay here with you!'

'Lady,' said Azémar, 'I will defend you.'

'When I look at you my heart is full of dread.'

'Do not fear me, do not ...'

He held up his hand. It felt strange to him – his fingers longer and more powerful, a power that wanted using. He itched to test those fingers, to feel them crush and tear. He ran his tongue along his teeth and tasted blood. The taste made him clamp shut his jaw and suck at his teeth. Something nagged between two of them. Without minding the presence of the lady he pushed a fingernail into the space and pulled the thing out and examined it. It had the texture of chicken skin. He couldn't tell what it was but he had the urge to pop it back into his mouth and swallow it down.

He stretched out his neck. Even in the dim light, the colours seemed to burst upon him. Outside he heard cries in the distance; so enticing – the screams of men, curses, prayers, the names of women, mothers, wives and daughters said on dying breaths. He didn't care. The lady was there and his only desire was to be near her.

Then he saw the knife. She had taken it from beneath her robe.

'What is that for, lady?'

'I took it from the woman you attacked on the riverbank. She has no need of it now she cannot open her eyes.'

'Lady, be careful what you do.'

'I would kill you. I know what we have been to each other. I remember it as if it happened this morning. You have followed me from beyond the veil of death but I do not want you, Azémar – Jehan – Vali. I do not want you.'

She didn't know where she got the names from but they came naturally to her lips.

She raised the knife but couldn't make herself attack him.

'Leave,' said Beatrice. 'Go from here.'

Tears poured down her face.

'Why?'

'Because you come from my nightmares, but you have taken flesh and revealed all my dreams as much more than fancies or the terrors of the dark. I remember you and I know what I did to escape you. I called down fevers and tried to die. I immersed myself in the love of a man to spite the will of fate. I have something in my heart and it is calling out for you, but I do not want you.' She hardly knew what she said; she seemed to be speaking from a place deep within herself, as if she had kept all this knowledge locked inside a dungeon and now its gates were burst open, her prisoner thoughts coming blinking into the day.

'Can you not hear? Death is in the streets here. Let me protect you.'

'Go or I will kill you.'

Azémar stood up. 'My soul feels as though it is on the edge of an abyss,' he said, 'and you are a darkness into which I will fall.'

Footsteps hammered down the corridor and voices shouted out:

'They're already at the palace!'

'How did they get inside the city walls?'

'The emperor has betrayed us.'

A voice was clearly audible through the door. 'This is it, boys. They're not coming here to plunder; they're here to stay. They mean to take our ancient right as protectors of this place. The emperor's cut us adrift because of all these deaths. There's no half-measures. We kill them and live, or we die. We won't be thrown aside by the emperor to live as vagabonds!'

'We're outnumbered, we'll never beat them.'

'We won't with that attitude.'

'We're going to die. Well, I'll die happy.'

The door flew open and three of the Hetaereian guard burst into the room. They didn't pause to say a word; one went straight for Beatrice, grabbing her by the hair, the other was already freeing his cock from his beneath his military skirt. Another charged for Azémar, his sword high to hack the monk down.

Beatrice stabbed at her attacker, but he caught her wrist and punched her hard in the face, knocking her to the ground and the knife out of her grip. Hands mauled her, ripping away her robes, pawing at her body. She only thought of the baby – to defend it, to keep it from harm.

Azémar didn't think, just responded to the threat as an animal responds. He saw his hand strike the sword from the Greek's grip, sending it clattering to the floor. The itch he'd had in his fingers was satisfied as he drove them into the man's eyes and cheeks. He was surprised, intrigued even, by how easy it was to tear off his attacker's face.

He ripped and bit, sating his curiosity. What would happen if he bit through a neck; what would it feel like to plunge his fingers into a belly and rip out the guts? When the men stopped moving, how easy would it be to reach in and tear out a tongue, to bite into it as if it were a blood-gorged lamprey?

He saw Beatrice pulling her blood-wet robes about her. The fight had disordered his mind. A lady was with him. Should he offer her something from his table to eat? An eye? Some sweet liver?

The lady took up a sword and at first he thought she would strike him. But she ran from the room in great wide strides, weighed down by the baby inside her. Azémar breathed in, the odour of the blood filling his mind. He should follow her. He would follow her later; her trail would be clear. First, he would eat.

40 Glory

Snake in the Eye wandered down the Middle Way. The fighting around him was fierce, though it seemed almost an irrelevance to him. He was hot with the fear of the wolf he'd met in his dream.

He'd been by the silver river under the light of the big moon, wandering by the wall that held the candles that were the lives of men. The runes had showed him the way through the labyrinth of his mind. He had seen someone there, he couldn't remember who, but someone he wanted very much to kill. But the wolf had moved against him, the wolf that snuffled and snarled beyond his vision. It had no candle in the wall; it was not a thing of light. No, it was an enemy of light, an eater, a devourer. Its hunger was so intense it was like a smell the thing exuded, potent as musk. Snake in the Eye did not like the way the creature made him feel. He cringed from it when he should have longed to fight it, and he was loath to look inside himself again, to go to that wall by the river where he was a god who could snuff out men's lives.

The battle made him dizzy. He found it difficult to understand what was going on. Tiny details seemed incredibly important. A gout of blood bloomed on the head of a fallen Varangian like a rose in a girl's hair. He noticed the dancing, to-and-fro movements of warriors as they clashed shields, retreated and came on again, the billowing blue robes and scarlet cloaks of the Greeks. *What was happening?* The best thing, the thing he had wanted for so long. *Battle*, so beautiful in its flashing silvers, its reds and its whites, vivid even under the muted sun. The sun. He glanced up. A pale disc like a god's shield. It must have been noon – the sun was not visible at any other time.

Snake in the Eye had his sword drawn and had picked up a fallen shield. He willed himself into the fight, forcing himself to find the aggression he had felt his whole life before that creature had come hot-mouthed through the mind's night for him.

Three Varangians circled in a stand-off with four Greeks in front of the Bull Market. The wispy mist made it seem like a scene from beneath the sea. Snake in the Eye had heard the tales of Atlantis and now imagined himself there – the buildings looming through silty water, weapons flashing from the murk like quick fish.

A Greek came running at him. Snake in the Eye caught his spear on his shield, stepped in and stabbed down. His blade missed the man's thigh but took him in the shin. The Greek stumbled, and Snake in the Eye kicked his remaining leg out from under him. The man rolled, but Snake in the Eye dropped on him, smothering his spear with his shield and driving the tip of his sword through his chest. That felt better.

A flash of scarlet. Bollason backed into view whirling and cursing, isolated, surrounded by five Greeks. Now four as the Viking's strange curved sword cut through a helmet to send a soldier spinning to the cobbles. Snake in the Eye sheathed his sword, picked up the spear and charged. The man he skewered had not seen him coming and Snake in the Eye ran him straight through, battering into one of his fellows and knocking him sideways too. The Greek never had time to regain his balance. Bollason's sword moved so quickly it seemed he had three hands and three weapons in them. Three men dead, two left. Bollason kicked one in the centre of the chest, sending him sprawling, then ducked to a crouch as a Greek sword snicked over his head. Bollason dropped his own sword and picked his attacker up, one arm driven up between the legs, the other seizing his tunic. The Greek was lifted high into the air and then smashed head first into the ground. Bollason regained his sword and the remaining Greek ran.

'Well done,' said Bollason to Snake in the Eye. 'So you can fight after all. Stay by me, I may need you.'

Snake in the Eye felt a jolt of energy go through him as he heard the Viking's words. He had been honoured, and by such a man as Bollason. Often had he dreamed of such a thing.

'Let's have some slaughter!' said Snake in the Eye.

'We will that!' said Bollason. He took his horn and blew a great blast.

Vikings came running to him bearing torches. There was a clatter like a hundred sticks rattling against a fence. As if time had slowed, Snake in the Eye saw an arrow bounce off his shield and up to slice away part of his ear. He put his hand up. Blood. Arrows lay all over the cobbles but no one had been hit.

He laughed. Things were getting better and better. No man could look at his wound and not know how he got it.

The rest of the Vikings dived for the cover of the side-streets but Snake in the Eye walked forward, trying to find the archers in the fog.

'I am Snake in the Eye, son of Ljot, son of Thiörek, of the berserker clan of Thetlief. You ladies don't bother me with your pins!'

Another volley of arrows, directed towards where the Vikings had abandoned their torches. The archers couldn't see properly, they were just aiming at the flames. Snake in the Eye ducked behind his shield. He was small enough for it to cover his whole body, and though two arrowheads smacked through the wood, many missed and none hit him. He saw movement ahead of him, screamed and charged. More arrows, but the archers were panicking. Some reached for axes and spears, some ran, some shot. Snake in the Eye weaved and ducked as he charged blind, his big shield in front of his face. More arrows punched through it but again none touched him. The other northerners, emboldened by Snake in the Eye's charge, leaped forward too. At five paces the remaining Greeks' courage broke as one and they ran. Snake in the Eye took a bowman with a looping blow from his sword. The other Vikings came screaming past him as Snake in the Eye put his hands up to the heavens and threw back his head like a farmer welcoming the rain that breaks the drought.

He was delirious with happiness. As he discarded his arrow-heavy shield he looked for more opponents. Women ran across the street behind him – a big group of them doubtless fleeing the Norsemen. Or running to them, thought Snake in the Eye. Sluts. His cock hardened and his head was dizzy as if he had stood up too quickly.

'I am a man and a mighty one,' he said. Then laughed again. His voice was hoarse, like a dog speaking. Finally he was becoming a man.

He turned to follow Bollason, and as he did, something seemed to wheel around him. The runes, all in an orbit – eight of them. Not eight – or rather eight not as a number on its own, but as part of something greater. Part of twenty-four. That number seemed very important to him. Twenty-four. Eight and eight and eight.

He ran down the street towards the palace. There he could have his fun. The woman, the one Mauger wanted, was there. And the scholar, the one who had cured his curse. What to do? He had vowed to lead Mauger to the scholar but he had vowed to reward the scholar too. He could do both. Could he fuck the scholar's wife and then reward him? Snake in the Eye had killed three men that day with sword and spear – not by sorcery. Of course he could. The palace doors were barred and the Varnagians had no siege equipment, so they were left with just beating at them.

The ground shook under Snake in the Eye's feet. Was it his imagination? An earthquake? Snake in the Eye had heard of them but never experienced one. No, not an earthquake; something that seemed to come from the same place as the silver river. It was a tremor from the dreamworld.

For a moment the street faded away. He was standing on the branch of a huge white tree that stretched above him into a sky of stars. Stars were below him too, shining like ice crystals in the sun, and below them was a well fed by three rivers who were also women. The strangeness of the thought struck him, but when he looked again both ideas — river and woman — were in his head as he saw the shining streams flowing from the roots of the tree. Were they rivers? Or were they three long skiens of cloth that extended from the spindles in the hands of the women who sat at the base of the tree? How could he see them so clearly if they were so far away? How could he not identify them as women or rivers or lengths of cloth if he could see them so clearly?

One of the rivers twisted to flow upwards towards where he was, the glittering waters reaching for him. He put out his hands and the water burst over them, turning his body with the force of its flow.

He understood where he needed to go — to the roots of the tree which stretched up here at the centre of the world. Something was down there for him. He saw a symbol in his mind — the dead god's necklace, three triangles locked inside each other — and he understood, as he understood the rivers were really women who were really rivers that were skeins that were woman-rivers, that he was one of those triangles. There were not three below him, nor even two. There was one, and it wanted the others to join it.

His head cleared. He was in the street again, people running for their lives, Greeks and Varangians battling. He fell to his knees. Something called to him from beneath the ground. He needed to answer it. He tried to work his fingers into the cobbles, as if he could burrow his way into the earth.

More cries ahead. He followed the sounds. The shouts of anger and the clash of steel upon steel were like sparks of light flashing in the fog, calling him on. A strange oily smell drifted by and something flared in the soupy air, a flash of fire.

The Numera's gates lay wide open. Vikings huddled either side of the doorway but couldn't get in. The entrance was very narrow and the Hetaereia within had shields, long spears and a siphon of Greek fire. The burned bodies of four men lay in the short passageway that led into the building. As he watched, flames spewed forth as if from the mouth of a volcano, keeping the Varangians away from the entrance.

Snake in the Eye walked through the gates. He needed his courage, not to charge the door but to go where he needed to go – to the place where the wolf was waiting, the garden by the river where the moon was on the river and the river was a bridge of light. Even as he allowed himself to fall into that place he heard snuffling at the edges of his thoughts, the wolf slavering and creeping through the recesses of his mind.

The Vikings discussed what to do.

'Starve them out!'

'Bollason wants this place taken now – he says it's important.'

'If we all charge together we can't *all* get burned.'

'No, you're right. Some of us will get shot and others speared.'

'We need a berserker.'

'They'd cook him. There's no chance.'

'I will go in,' said Snake in the Eye. The men didn't even acknowledge he was there.

'We can get some bowmen.'

'They'd have to go into the passage to shoot, it'd be suicide.'

'My name is death!' Snake in the Eye screamed at the top of his voice.

A wiry Viking waved him away.

'You're a boy and a weakling and have proved yourself to be so. The women and kids are plundering the markets, join them and find us some meat. I'll want a good stew when this is over.'

'I will take the door.'

'Go home.'

'No, let him.' A big gruff man pointed an axe at Snake in the Eye. 'I am Arnulf's kin. This boy wronged us. If he wants to go to his death then we should not stand in his way.'

310

Another man laughed. 'Looks like it's your own meat you'll be stewing, boy.'

Snake in the Eye ignored him. 'I am ready.' He had on his iron breastplate; his sword was in one hand, an axe in the other. *What a warrior I must seem to these men.*

The Vikings were divided into two groups, sheltering from the flame on either side of the passage.

Snake in the Eye stepped forward. By the light of the torch used to ignite the siphon, he saw the blackened faces of two Greek guards peering out at him. The men shouted nothing, issued no threat, but Snake in the Eye knew he would only have a couple more steps before the plunger was depressed on the siphon and a stream of clinging oily flame shot towards him. He was yet to get inside the building but he felt sure the fire would reach him if he took another pace.

There were other flames, smaller lights dancing and flickering on a riverbank wall only he could see. The guttural grunting was in his ears, but he would have time enough at the wall to do what he needed to do and run.

Many little flames flickered, but he only wanted two. He took one and snuffed it out in his fingers. The man on the siphon dropped and the nozzle of the apparatus dipped towards the ground, dripping oil. Snake in the Eye snuffed out another flame. The man with the torch collapsed and the whole apparatus ignited.

Flame erupted with a low roar from the entrance like the belch of a dragon. Snake in the Eye staggered backwards, his hair and eyebrows singeing. Inside the guards screamed and howled, burning. Snake in the Eye strode through the doorway and cut a man down as he came running down the corridor like a fire giant, his head ablaze.

'I am death!' he shouted. 'I am death!'

He stepped around the fallen corpse and charged into the prison, jumping over burning bodies and hacking at those who still lived, men more occupied with the flames that engulfed them than defending themselves. Other guards were arriving from the rest of the prison but the Greeks retreated as fast as they had come before the mob of Varangians pouring in behind Snake in the Eye in a howling rush. The Greeks dived through the inner door and slammed it shut.

'Am I not a man?' shouted Snake in the Eye. 'Am I not a hero?'

He saw so many lights in front of him on the wall, lights for the prisoners, lights for the guards, lights even for a piper and a dancing girl who cowered in the corner.

Snake in the Eye smiled at the girl. 'I have no need for entertainment today,' he said. Then he scraped his hand across the wall in his mind, knocking all the little candles to the floor.

41   Captured

Beatrice waddled in to Styliane's chambers. The baby was terribly heavy, like trying to carry a sack of coal, but she could not let that concern her. The guards had abandoned the doors and no one stopped to question her or demand she indulge in some exhausting formality. As she passed the little chapel, she saw two guards dead on the floor. Had the Varangians got in this far already? On to Styliane's rooms. More dead men — four of them in the scarlet livery of Styliane's personal bodyguards.

She stepped over the bodies and into the splendid chambers. Styliane's bedroom was empty but a fight had clearly taken place in it. Three dead guards of Styliane's retinue and two in the chamberlain's blue. Three ladies-in-waiting were hiding behind a bed.

'What happened?' Beatrice was almost breathless from running.

'The chamberlain took her.'

'Where?'

'I don't know. I don't know.'

Beatrice hurried out. Men rushed everywhere and she kept a grip on her little knife in case one should attack her. The Varangians were outside, screaming and howling threats to burn down the palace.

She ran to the chamberlain's rooms. No guard tried to stop her as she threw open the door to his chambers. The first room contained four big chests, one with a lock. He had his secrets, that man, and she was determined not to pass up the chance to discover some of them. She took a heavy candlestick and smashed off the lock. It came away at the hasp, the rivets pulling free of the wood. Inside was a bullroarer on a chain, five books, some soldiers' clothes and a desert hood.

She picked up one of the books. It was written in Greek, full of charts and tables − *A True and Faithful Record of the Magical Practices of the Ancients − The Key of Solomon*. She picked up another. *Night Works*. This was written in Latin and the vellum was relatively new − scored by crossings out and corrections, clearly some sort of notebook. She turned a page − a chapter heading: 'On Sacrifice'. There were sketches and drawings of the positions of the stars, a list of items offered 'at the crossroads' and a comment on their efficacy.

Beatrice was under no illusions about what she was reading. This was as damning a document as could be imagined. But the chamberlain had left it behind. How desperate was he? What did he intend to do?

'Oh God!' A man screamed in the passage outside, metal scraped on metal. A fight. She looked around the chamber. A door on the opposite side. She took the book and headed towards it, but as she put out her hand to open the door it crashed open and she leaped back.

A Varangian stood in the doorway − a tall bloody man with wild eyes. She turned to run but one was behind her. *They were everywhere!* She was sure she was going to die. She thought of Loys, of the future they would never have, of the children they would never raise and the peace they would never know. She was a Christian woman and would not let these pagans defile her without a fight. She raised her knife but a big hand grabbed her wrist and twisted it up behind her back. She gave a cry and dropped the weapon. The man siezed her hair with his other hand, jerking her head back.

The Varangian in front of her pointed at her with his sword. He was gaudy in appearance, as so many of the northern men were − dressed from head to foot in bright red, as if soaked in blood. 'This one?'

'This one.'

She couldn't see who spoke but it was a female voice.

'Is she going to make it where we need to go? She looks ready to drop.'

'She will make it. It's foreseen.'

'Now?'

'Have you taken the Numera?'

'It can't be long before we do.'

'Then get her over there. We have no time. Put everything into capturing it.'

'The entrance is very narrow. One man can defend it for a week.'

'If one can defend it, one can attack it. You wanted your time to die for me, Bolli – this could be it. Take the prison. You are a hero to men. If you can't do it no one can.'

'We will take it.'

The man holding Beatrice's hair released his grip a little and the big red Viking stepped aside. In front of her now was a small red-haired woman, old but quite beautiful. Her face, though, bore a terrible scar on one side.

The woman spoke to her in Norse: 'I'm sorry.' Then she addressed the Viking holding Beatrice. 'Bring her with us. Don't let her go.'

'Yes, Vala.' And Beatrice was shoved through the door.

42 The Old Way

Five men waded ashore from a boat beached behind the Varangian camp – three in the green uniform of messengers, one in the purple robes of a minor court official and one – a tall pale fellow with a shock of red hair – in the orange of a palace servant. Two carried a stretcher to which was tied the body of a woman. To anyone watching – had anyone been watching – they would have looked like a funeral party. One of the stretcher bearers also had a shovel on his back and a small pick at his belt, and the red-haired servant carried a length of rope. But the woman was not dead: once they were ashore, the red-haired man poured water from a flask onto a cloth and wet her lips with it, squeezing a little of the moisture into her mouth.

The weak sun was dying, and the moon, a faint gleaming disc behind the smoky clouds, had risen, full but pale, like a penny seen through murky water.

The men said nothing but pressed on up the hill. Two ran slightly ahead with spears before them. The spearmen were large and frightening in appearance – one a huge Greek with a shiny beard, the other a black man with a fearful glare and a big sword at his belt.

The Varangian camp was almost deserted. The northerners' women and children had gone with the warriors into the city, even taking their livestock and their dogs.

The chamberlain hurried through the darkening air, a torch in his hand, a bag at his side. They went up the hill into the shanty town. It was sparsely populated – its inhabitants had followed the Varangians in, looking to pick up what spoils they could – so the men hurried through what was effectively a huge rubbish tip.

The steeper climb up into the hills was harder on those

carrying Styliane, and at points the men swapped duties on the stretcher. Only the chamberlain didn't take a turn – it wouldn't have occurred to him to offer and the men would have only held him in contempt if he had. Nobles handed out the orders; they didn't fetch or carry.

Down in the city they could see, even through the mist, that a substantial fire had started. No one commented; they just made their way up onto the first hill and into the boulder field. Here flies were thick in the air and the odour of rot drifted in. The chamberlain guessed Isais was among the rocks some-where, causing as much of a stink in death as he had in life.

Progress was slow. The chamberlain went ahead. Once he would have hopped over those rocks, now he had to tread more carefully, picking his way and at points supporting him-self on his hands. He was getting old, he felt it. The symbols, the bright living shapes that burned in his head, which coiled like ivy around his heart, which seemed to prick at his skin like thorns or chill him like ice, they were pulling away from him. He could not reach out to take one down, like a fruit from a tree, and send it to kill a rebel charging at the head of an army, to banish a black sky or remove the curse of death from his streets. Not yet, until steps were taken to regain control.

'Here?' The man with the shovel – a Greek, thin, tough and small – pointed to a gap between the rocks.

'It'll take time to find,' said the chamberlain. 'Wait.'

He picked about among the rocks for a while. The chamber-lain knew exactly what he was looking for – three rocks leaning into each other, a hole beneath. He'd drawn it to the attention of the Church as soon as he'd entered Constantinople and they had ordered the hole stopped up to prevent heathen practices. The chamberlain found Isais first, a pennant of flies rising up from the corpse as he approached. He didn't bother to look at him – the body wasn't where the hole had been. Eventually he spotted the three goddesses, the three big stones.

'Here,' he said.

The little Greek squeezed into the space with his spade.

He dug for a while. 'The pick.' It was passed down, and the man chipped and levered at the rock barring the hole. 'We're in luck,' he said. 'They've used earth and not cement. Small rocks too. If they'd used a big one we'd have been here ten times as long.'

'Did none of the priestesses think to open it?' It was the big black man who spoke.

'No. My mother did not emerge, and it was taken as a sign of the goddess's displeasure. I had it blocked as a precaution.'

'If the goddess is angry it is wise to be cautious,' said the black man.

'All caution is gone,' said the red-haired servant. For the first time the chamberlain considered him. He had simply ordered him to help when he had found him in the palace, the other servants having fled or hidden from the assault of the Varangians. He was the servant he had placed to spy on Loys and Beatrice – the one who never seemed to give a report but whom he had never thought to question. He was an odd-looking fellow. Very likely a northerner himself but smooth and polished as his countrymen were rough. *Never mind. Concentrate on the task at hand.*

He had remembered the servant as a tall man, but now he seemed quite small. That was a good thing – he would be able to help underground with Styliane.

The little man was throwing out rocks now and the others stood back.

'Aha!' The sound of a kick, then falling earth and 'We're through!'

'Is it big enough to get her down there?'

'Only one way to find out.'

The chamberlain turned to the big men, his bodyguards. 'You can't follow in here,' he said. 'Go back to the city and kill some Varangians.'

'Will we meet you at the palace?'

'Perhaps,' said the chamberlain. 'It's dangerous work I'm undertaking.'

'How will we know if you're successful?'

'You will know. The Varangians will fall, the sky will clear and death will leave our streets.'

'If you fail?'

'Then look for other employment.'

The big men stepped back and watched as the red-haired northerner and the Greek manoeuvred Styliane down. She had to be brought back out and the entrance dug out further before they could get her through. Eventually, though, she disappeared into the earth. The chamberlain lit a lamp and passed it down. Then he went in himself. He had worried he wouldn't remember the route, but it was as if a door had opened to a cellar in his mind and all its contents were there for him to examine.

Even if he hadn't recalled, the runes, those symbols of his ancestors the Lucari, would have guided him. The chamberlain couldn't use them, couldn't touch them, but he could feel them pulling him into the depths like a tugging on his skin. Styliane was not as difficult to move as he'd feared. In fact, she went through the quickest, her stretcher dragged by the rope through the low sections, carried where it was easier to stand. The damp reassured him he was on the right track, stonebound faces looming from the rock, shadows like the tongues of hungry wolves lapping at his ankles, snapping at his hands. It was all as he recalled.

They took no rest. He was possessed with the need to get to the well and the two servants were hardier than his sister and mother had been. When the northerner took a handful of water from a stream, the chamberlain knew he was near.

'A good sign,' he said. 'These streams feed the well.'

'And all the worlds besides,' said the pale northerner. He let the water fall through his fingers without drinking it.

'You're not thirsty?' said the Greek, who scooped up a big handful himself.

'Not for these waters,' said the northerner. 'These are the waters of wisdom and knowledge. I would prefer those of

319

your Lethe, Ameles Potamos, whose taste makes all men lose their memories. The power of forgetting seems a higher gift than that of knowing,' he said.

'Those waters are not here,' said the chamberlain.

'How do you know? If you had drunk from them you would not remember.'

'I have been here before.' Why was he, the chamberlain, arguing with a servant?

'You are right: it was not the forgetful waters of Lethe, the daughter of strife, sister of toil and murder, from which you drank, but of deeper and more dangerous streams.'

'What do you know of this place?'

'Only the price it asks to drink its waters.'

'What price?'

'Not gold nor silver nor jewels nor cattle,
Just lovers' bones and the old death rattle.'

This man disconcerted the chamberlain greatly. He had seen him before, he was sure. Not in the palace but in some other place. He recalled him like he recalled the wolf of his dreams, like he recalled Elai. He couldn't quite focus on what the man said. He understood his words when he heard them but their meaning would not stick in his mind.

'What's that ahead?' The Greek spoke.

The chamberlain lifted the lamp and peered through the darkness.

'It's where we're going,' he said. 'Where everything is won or lost.'

Ahead of him, away down the tunnel, was a blood-red glow.

43 A Necessary Rage

Mauger drew his sword as he stood up from the water.

'No need for that,' said Loys. 'We have spoken.'

Vandrad's head popped up from the flooded passage behind Mauger. The first northerner didn't pause in his advance, just strode towards Loys. Only at the last instant did Loys realise Mauger wasn't coming for the wolfman but for him.

'Ragnar! What? Have I offended you?' He leaped back.

Mauger was in no hurry, walking after him slowly but determinedly.

'There is no way out of here,' he said. 'Bow down, thief. Bow down, oathbreaker, and accept the justice of your lord.'

'What are you on about? Get away from me.'

'Ragnar, the scholar's paying our wages, have you forgotten?' said Vandrad, now climbing out of the water.

Loys ducked behind the wolfman and Mauger paused, assessing the situation.

'I have no fight with you, friend,' he said. 'It's the man behind you I seek.'

'What's got into you, Ragnar?' said Loys.

'I am not Ragnar and you are not Michael. I am Mauger, sworn vassal of Duke Richard, who was Bengeirr, of the lands of Neustria called Norman. You are the scholar Loys who has stolen away the lord's daughter and whose head I am charged to fetch.'

'Can't let you do that, old chum,' said Vandrad. He had his sword free. The head of another Viking emerged from the pool. 'This man owes me money, money I'll never get if you give him a trim.'

'I'll give you double what he pays.'

'No. I swore.' He pointed with his sword to the Viking

emerging from the pool. 'He swore. There can be no debate.'

The third Viking came up in the water.

Mauger said nothing, just leaped at Vandrad. The Viking got his sword up to block but it snapped clean in two.

'Shit,' said Vandrad and went for his knife, but Mauger brought his sword around again and cut deep into his neck. Vandrad dropped, his fingers clutching at a big wound.

'Whoa!' The other Viking had his seax free – a big, long sturdy knife. The next one, emerging from the water, pulled out an axe.

The man with the seax aimed a cut at Mauger but was too slow. Mauger took a step back, the swipe missed and he smashed a backhanded blow into the side of his opponent's head, caving in the skull at the temple with a noise like an axe chopping wood and dropping him flat.

Loys drew his knife. He was determined to defend himself but he was a scholar not a warrior. He felt as if his legs had turned to stalagmites like those coming up from the floor. He could not make himself move. The wolfman, however, could.

It was all so quick.

Mauger hit the floor, the wolfman on top of him. The axe-man hacked at them both, swiping at the men as they writhed and rolled. Once he connected with Mauger's back, but the axehead bounced off the mail and a sword flashed out of the melee to cut him down at the knee.

The two men broke and stood facing each other. Mauger's arm was wet with blood and his cheek was torn half away.

'Give me the scholar,' said Mauger. 'In fact, I don't even want all of him, just give me his head.'

Loys backed towards the pool. The wolfman raved, hissed and spat, his lips wet with blood, his hands too.

He gave an terrible scream and jumped – not towards Mauger but at Loys, driving him into the water, pushing him down into the freezing darkness.

Loys was helpless against the wolfman's strength, pulled through the water like a frog taken by a pike. He tried to cry out, but his mouth filled with water. The wolfman forced him down – down and forward. He was being pushed under a great bulge in the rock, shoved on into darkness. Loys heard nothing, could see nothing. He tried not to breathe in, but he was choking.

Mauger advanced into the water up to his neck. The Norseman was not an impetuous man and he knew it was time for cold thinking. He couldn't risk going any further. It was one thing to negotiate a short waterlogged passage in mail, sure someone had been through before you, quite another to plunge headlong into unknown darkness. He would need to take a flint, dry tinder, a lamp and a rope to pull himself back. He'd also need to be prepared for instant attack, should he make it through to the other side. It was not the work of a moment to prepare for all that. He considered the situation. Had the wolfman drowned the scholar? Had they gone through to another chamber? The wolfman and the scholar had seemed to be talking as reasonable men when he'd come through. He had to assume they had become allies.

The axeman screamed and writhed on the shore, his leg nearly severed at the knee.

Mauger waded back. He killed the Viking with the man's own axe. He didn't want to risk damage to his sword if he didn't have to and he didn't want to kill an honest warrior but the last man had to die. It would have brought a blood feud if he'd survived to tell the tale of what had happened. Down in the caves he was just one more victim of the dark. Mauger touched his cheek. The wound was bad but he'd had worse. He could feel the cut was only to the skin, the muscle beneath was intact. It was bleeding badly so he took the lamp and poured some hot oil over it. It was agony but the bleeding stopped. He sat and recovered for a little while. Then he climbed out of his mail. He glanced at the black water. He was going in to find them.

44 A Thinking Beast

The Varangians had got into the palace. Its doors had not been built to withstand a siege – if an enemy had got over the Theodosian Wall, then over the remains of the Walls of Constantine inside the city, a reinforced door wouldn't have held them back. The doors were designed to keep out the common people, not invading armies, and the Varangians had eventually broken them in with their axes and hammers.

Azémar finished feeding and stood. He was torpid, gorged and wanted to sleep. The blood tide that had risen to engulf his thoughts when he had killed the guards began to recede. The realisation came to him that the bodies on the floor, the human wreckage of ripped torsos and flesh-stripped limbs, had belonged to people. He knew he should have wept to see such a mess, but he didn't. He wasn't interested in it any more but then he was not hungry.

The Lady Beatrice. He needed to go to her.

He went out of the room. All the lamps had been removed in the passageway as a precaution against the attackers using them to burn down the palace and it was very dark. It didn't matter to Azémar.

The fighting was somewhere close. He smelled the sweat of fear, the stress leaking out of the men in the smell of their saliva, their piss and their shit. It meant little to him. He had fed.

He breathed in again and he could smell Beatrice, her distinct scent in its many registers, rosewater, sweat, silk. Memories burst in his mind. Beeswax for the candles unlit in the church when he had first met her, mint her mother had showed her how to grind in the kitchen when he had first met her, the smell of the hot wheat as he'd worked his scythe to bring in the harvest when he'd first met her. The ridiculousness of the thought struck him. He couldn't have first met her three times.

He followed her scent through the corridors of the palace. More shouting ahead.

Two Varangians. They eyed the fine robe Loys had lent him.

'Hand that over, friend. We don't want to risk damaging it by killing you.'

'It's covered in blood, Kolli.'

'We can wash that out easy enough.'

Azémar didn't understand them at all. Or rather he understood them in a new way. He felt their animosity, sensed their complacency. He knew, in a way words could not describe, that the living processes of their bodies had relaxed when they had seen him.

'I am looking for a lady.' Azémar found the Norse of his forefathers.

'We're all looking for one of those.'

'I've been without her for a very long time.'

'And we've been without one for a very long time.'

'You were with a whore this afternoon,' the other Viking spoke to his friend.

'That's a long time by my reckoning. The robe. We're not here to gabble.'

What were they saying?

They didn't understand the urgency of him seeing Beatrice, that was clearly the problem.

'I need ... I am dizzy.' Azémar fought to regain control of his thoughts. He remembered a lesson at Rouen given by a great scholar monk from the east.

'I have been taught understanding by the use of the Porphyrian Tree,' said Azémar. He had abandoned Norse. It didn't have the words he needed and he returned to his scholar's Greek.

'What are you on about? Speak Norse or I'll talk to you in a language all men can understand.'

'The tree by which we organise our logic. The supreme genus is substance, all scholars agree,' Azémar continued in Greek.

'Strip it off him. He's a madman.'

'The differentiae are material and immaterial. The subordinate genera are body and living. These are the topmost part of the trunk.'

The Varangians strode towards him.

'You descend the trunk to find the proximate genera of animal. Beneath that we cannot accept this teaching for that is a pagan lie and contrary to holy teaching.'

One of them had hold of him and pulled at his robe.

'By Sif's tits, he's a guard. He's built like a horse. He must be some sort of berserker. That's why he's raving.'

The man backed away.

'The differentiae below animal are rational and irrational. Below animal, they include the category of man. As a species of thinking beast. I cannot . . .'

The sounds of battle drifted in from all over the palace. The second Varangian pushed past his comrade.

'I don't care if he's built like Blind Hod; I'm having the robe.'

'Substance, material and immaterial, body, living and dead, animal, rational and irrational. Man. Below the species is the individual. Where is God? Where is God in this?'

The Varangian wrenched off Azémar's robe.

Azémar looked down at himself. He wore only a pair of light leggings and was bare-chested.

'I'll have those as well,' said the Varangian. 'Take them off and I might let you live.'

'Here is God. Who told thee that thou wast naked? Hast thou eaten of the tree, whereof I commanded thee that thou shouldest not eat?'

Something was burning.

Azémar's head cleared for a moment. He felt ridiculous half-dressed in such a fine palace. He smelled the smoke, saw the axe the Varangian with the red beard bore, the dagger the one who had taken his robe had drawn. There was still something he didn't quite understand about this situation. He spoke in Norse: 'I can't be naked. The tree of knowledge brought us shame. We know. Now we know.'

'Well know this.' The man with the dagger lunged.

Azémar only realised what had happened an instant later. The men lay on the floor. He couldn't make sense of why they were there. He trembled. There was an odd low gurgling noise and he realised it was his own voice. He was snarling, sitting on top of a body with one arm torn from its socket. The other body lay a few paces away. The man had tried to run, he recalled, but now he was bent double, the wrong way.

Men in the corridor, screaming, fighting. A Greek fell with a short spear clean through him. A huge man with a bushy blond beard came howling towards Azémar. He stood. *Where is Beatrice?* These people were in his way. They weren't going to help him. Animosity engulfed him like a lava flow.

The big Viking didn't even get the time to swing his axe as Azémar smashed him down. Azémar stepped past him and into the man who ran in behind. He swung him from his feet and banged his head into the wall. *Slaughter beast, god killer, slaverer and slayer.* The words went through his mind like comets across a black sky. He had a name, he knew, but what was it?

More men died, torn and ripped, broken and dismembered. They thrust things at him, sharp things, slow things. He was so strong. He tore free of the fight and ran. The night air hit him as he spilled out of the palace door and into the street. His nose and mouth stung and he recognised the taste of the big white flakes in the air. Ash.

Through the clinging fog he heard something. Not a voice, not an animal cry but something resonating deeper within him, an emanation of something older than sound. It called to him. He pictured a sign, a jagged slash with a line through it.

His skin rose into bumps as he heard it howl. He understood it, knew what it said.

'I am here, where are you?' It was the lady, she was calling to him, or rather something inside her was.

He looked back at the palace but then turned away from the fight with its delicious scents of murder and battle. He was summoned and he could not resist.

Azémar threw back his head and shouted, 'I am here! Where are you?' But his voice was the howl of a wolf.

45 The Bloody Waters

Air! A hand pulled him out of the water. It was flat dark, no glimpse of light. He lay gasping on cold rock.

'We are through. Those men were sent by the gods, but they did not serve the gods' purpose. Who was the white-haired one?'

'His name is Ragnar.'

'He followed you?'

'He was sent to kill me, I think.'

'I have seen him before.'

'Where?'

'In a past life. I have fought him before. He is a powerful enemy. Did he have the sword?'

'What sword?'

'The one that is curved. Like a sickle moon.'

'I saw no such sword.'

'It will come, along with the stone.'

'What stone?'

'A magical stone. The Wolfstone.'

Loys was so shaken he didn't even think of the stone in his bag.

'What is happening?'

'A god is coming. His symbol is the three hanging knots; his presence is in the runes. When twenty-four are in one person, he is here, and the wolf will come to kill him.'

'You have meddled with devils,' said Loys.

He longed to see. He took the bag from around his neck and felt inside, pulling out the flint, the lamp and the oil-soaked cloth. Very carefully he tore off a strip of the cloth. He placed it near the flint, which he struck against the iron. Quickly he had a spark, which he blew to a small flame. Now he could light the lamp.

The chamber was almost a sphere, just big enough to stand in. Loys was sitting on a shelf of rock with the wolfman beside him.

'What now?' said Loys.

'This is the world city. It is a flowering of the magical forces of the well. This is where the world tree draws its water. We're on our way to that well.'

'And if the god you're seeking doesn't come?'

'He will come. The god is in three forms. He is one of them. The Vala's vision revealed it. Beneath the comet, at that battle, the god who sleeps with the head at his feet. It was a sign – as Odin drank the waters of the well, next to the headless Mimir so the god would be found. He should have killed me when I asked.'

'I thought you sought to kill him.'

'He cannot be killed.'

'I think Basileios can kill all the world if he so chooses. But he is far away.'

'He will come.'

'How can you avoid your fate?'

'At the well. I will receive insight.'

'How do you know where it is?'

'I can hear it.'

'What can you hear?'

'The runes. There are runes within it. They are calling to others.'

He stood and climbed to the top of the chamber. A small tunnel led away, scarcely wider than his shoulders. The wolfman wriggled in. Loys had no alternative but to follow, pushing the lamp before him. It was not even a crawl. He went forward like a snake, writhing on his belly, progressing by tiny increments. He had a terrible feeling of claustrophobia, a desire to breathe freely without the tunnel pressing in on his ribcage. He would have lacked the courage to go on if the wolfman had not been before him. Pulling himself through, using only his fingertips at points because his arms were so restricted, he found it very difficult to see, his head forced down by the narrowness of the tunnel. He moved the lamp on, fighting down panic.

He had to go on, for Beatrice. He didn't accept what the wolfman was telling him but it was clear there was demonic involvement. If Beatrice was caught up in this, he needed to get her out of it. That gave him strength.

His knees were raw, his elbows too. He went on, moving the lamp a little, snaking forward, resting, moving the lamp. The darkness around him seemed so tight, like a great hand that could reach out at any moment and snuff out his little light.

Ahead of him, a light wavered. The lamp was taken from him. The wolfman signalled for Loys to be silent then helped him out. They were in another small cave, but this one was half flooded from a waterfall that tumbled down from a tunnel that entered near the ceiling.

The water poured away down another low tunnel. In there was the light, not quite torchlight but a soft and constant red. The wolfman climbed down through the stream, his movements inaudible beneath the trickling of the water.

Loys strained to listen. There were voices. A mumble of words, a drone.

'In the sacred waters where the three streams meet,
Goddess who is three in one,
Goddess of the night and of the dark of the night,
Here by the waters
I pay the price of lore.'

He recognised the voice now. It was unquestionably that of the chamberlain.

Suddenly the voice faltered. Above him a skittle-skattle sound of someone bumping down the stream bed, a cough and a curse. Someone else was coming.

46   A Girl Weaving

In the cave's pool sat a dead girl. Elai knew she was dead by the coldness of her hands, her absence of breath. The ritual of herbs and meditations had worked, and she had gone to the threshold of where she needed to be.

In those three streams were the fates of all men. In that pool waters entwined, eddied and knotted to weave the skein of human destiny. Three faces of the goddess Hecate, three fates, three Norns – the name of those women came so naturally to her – three streams whose flow not even the gods could resist.

But *he* had tried to resist. What was his name? Odin. Her mother had said the name and though it was strange to her, the syllables seemed to resonate in her bones. Her ancestors had followed that grim fellow, the waters told her.

She put her hand above her to touch the stream that flowed into the pool.

She said its name. Uthr. *What was.* To her right another stream trickled down. She said its name. Verthani. *What is.* A third entered in front of her under the surface of the water – she could feel its flow. She said its name. Skuld. *What must be.* The language was strange to her but completely comprehensible. Not the Greek her mother used to worship the goddess. Older, far older. She thought of Odoacer, who had taken his wolf warriors to Rome, who had made the emperor kneel. Had he spoken that way, her mighty ancestor?

Her fingers played in the flow of the unseen stream. It wound and twisted in her hands. Its movement fascinated her. On impulse she went to where the stream left the pool, put her fingers into its sucking flow. It was so seductive. It did not feel like water at all, but rather like an endless length of beautiful thread, soft and pliable, moving through her hands.

A rhyme came into her mind.

> *Thence come the women*
> *strong in wisdom,*
> *Three to the dark waters*
> *down beneath the tree.*
> *Uthr is one named,*
> *Verthani the next,*
> *and Skuld the third.*
> *Mightily wove they*
> *the web of fate,*
> *While Bralund's towns*
> *were trembling all.*
> *And there the golden*
> *threads they wove.*
> *And in the moon's hall*
> *fast they made them,*
> *The wyrd of men and gods.*

One of those names resonated above the others: Skuld. *What must be.*

'That is my name,' she said into the ghost light of the rocks. 'Something is owed here.' Her voice came back to her as the dead echo of the small chamber.

The well had asked for her death and that of her mother. It had showed her clearly what was her fate, and that of so many others if she was too weak to make the sacrifice.

Death, eternally, again and again, agony and torture, denial and madness. Some things were in the water, bright shining things, and she wanted pick them up, as if her soul was a shrine to be decked with candles and trinkets.

What were these things? Shapes, symbols, *runes*. That was the word. What did these runes do? They held the universe together. They were the connections between things – the things that allowed sense and reason. They were understanding – the foundations and the structure of the sane mind. But they were not meant to be seen, not meant to be touched and used. The ability to do that was the key to magic and to madness.

'We have tired of the tale the god has to tell.'

The god had intended to set his runes inside her, to drag her to his death. Did he think he could cheat her, blind her and control her? The water flowed around her and she fell in on herself. She was not sitting in a pool of water. She sat in a pool of thoughts, of visions and memories, a stream of words, fears, hopes and disappointments running out of it over her fingers into blackness. She could manipulate it, change its course.

She saw the remaining symbols in the water, keening for their sisters. Her death, her self-sacrifice, had trapped the runes in the pool but not all of them. Some had gone away, fearing their fate, each one a fragment of a god.

Where had they gone? Did it matter? She would call to them and they would come back, to be released by death, back to be trapped in the pool. Then the eternal dumbshow would stop.

The god had not reckoned with her magic. He had asked for her mother's death and for that of her brother but he hadn't understood who she was. He knew only she was a magical creature, not who she truly was – a Norn, one of the three sisters who spin the fates of all humanity. She laughed as she realised what had happened. The god had mistaken her for an incarnation of himself, an empty vessel into which he could pour his runes. She was to die for him after the runes had assembled within her. But she had pre-empted him and gone to death before he could fill her with his magic. It had not occurred to him she could manifest herself in the realm of men too. As Odin began to claim her for his own, to put the runes within her, to inhabit her flesh and offer that flesh to the wolf so he might live, suffer and die, she had done what he had not thought possible. She reached out into the stream, twisted the current through her fingers, felt it as a multitude of threads and drawn out those she recognised as belonging to her brother.

The threads trembled with the deep currents of his ambition, the hot flow of his jealousies, and she had weaved them together into a skein of murder. He had killed her and thwarted the dead god's will.

'Odin,' she said, 'you could not live in me. I am stronger than you and my magic cannot be gainsayed. Here by these dark waters that feed the tree on which all worlds grow, I will have what I am owed.'

How many had he tried to set inside her? Twenty-four in their orbits of eight – twenty-four, a magic number, a god's number. When twenty-four runes came to life inside any human, then the old god was present and ready to face his little fate on earth so he might avoid his bigger one in eternal time.

He had tried to make her his sacrifice, as he had done to her sisters in times past. Sisters? Did she mean Styliane? No. Others – sisters bound to her eternally.

Where were they? Uthr. Verthani. The strangeness of those words struck her. *Have they taken flesh as I have?* Where were these thoughts coming from? From the water. She saw the god's wake, a trail of blood dripping throughout human history. *He should pay the price for that.*

> *The raven's wing is black*
> *Scarlet stains the snow's white field.*

The dirge-voice was in her head. She didn't like it. She didn't like *him*, the one who was speaking. *Are you here for your sacrifice?* She'd known him a long time, longer than she remembered. The dead god. Odin, Hecate, Mercury – that many-formed fellow. He was near. She saw a hill, grey in a raw dawn, and on it a tree where men dangled and choked from hanging ropes, their legs doing the dead god's dance. She saw the gold of kings thrown into waters rich with loam, holy slaves bound and drowned, around their necks the dead god's symbol – the sticky, tricky triple knot.

Then she saw him, near her in the water in the blood glow of the rocks – his bloated corpse face, the black rope at his neck, his good eye staring at her, the other torn and ragged. He chanted a dissonant song:

> 'Under the gallows tree they worship me;
> By the moon they call me;
> Triple-knotted, triple-faced, triple-looking.
> Three times I suffered to sacrifice
> Myself unto myself. In the branches
> Of that terrible tree.'

She heard mad bursts of poetry:

> 'It is said, you went
> with dainty steps in the city,
> and knocked at houses as a vala.
> In the likeness of a fortune teller
> You went among people.
> Now that, I think, betokens a base nature.'

The words seemed to have a great power. They fell as earth to bury her, and she stretched out her hands to shovel them away. She heard a drum, its beat toiling and slow above her. The god's will was bound by cold irons to eternal death, and she knew what he offered. Death, again and again, spreading like a stain across the light of the world.

'Lady,' said the god, 'it seems to me I know your name. I mistook you for someone.'

'For who?'

'For myself.'

His mind roamed over hers, a sensation of cold fingers on her face, a desperate pulling and upending of things within her, as if her soul was a house and he a miser searching for a coin within it.

'You know me, old one. As I know you. Maddener. Frenzied
One. All Father. All Hater.'

'I know you.'

'What is my name?'

'I dare not say it.'

'My name is Skuld.'

'Have you fallen to the world of breath?'

'Did you think I would let you travel here unwatched?'

'I have a bargain with you.'

'Only for as long as you can honour it.'

'I will honour it. By the runes that I am, I will honour it.'

A great white tree stretched out to the stars above her. In
the pool the symbols sparkled like shipwrecked treasure in the
tales of children.

'You play the fates falsely, Odin, made us share in your
deaths, weave strange magics and sacrifice ourselves to ourselves. Now see what I weave for you.'

She held up her hand. Crimson threads flowed from it,
streaming out towards the god, entangling his pale body, pulling her towards him.

He stretched out his hands, snapping the threads, and
images appeared: a starved girl-child lying broken in a cave, a
blonde-haired woman covered in blood and screaming, a wolf
guzzling on her entrails.

The god's voice spoke:

> 'These are the gifts I have given you:
> Death for life, life for death.
> I have bowed to your will.
> For you I have suffered agonies deep and long.'

Elai heard herself speak: 'Can you not hear how he howls
for your blood? The wolf strains against the bonds with which
you tied him.'

Each sinew, each curve of the muscles of the corpse god's
pale and wounded torso seemed no more than the twist of a

rune; the tattoos that stained the flesh of his body, his arms and his face were runes too. The god was the runes. He had promised to die for her – that was the destiny in the stream that played through her fingers – but he had killed her, in her many and various forms. She saw herself as she had been – a sorcerer in an animal mask looking out over a cold sea, a wolf-man in his skins, many other things, male and female over many lives, trying to bring the god to his destiny of death. He had torn her, tricked her and broken her heart, left her as a dead girl in the water – Odin, that ancient killer.

'You have played me basely, lord. For this you will pay what you owe.'

The god spoke:

> 'I took a fetter and the fetter was called Thin,
> And I bound the wolf to a rock called Scream,
> The human rock, the living flesh, where I tied myself,
> So he might tear and I might die to please the Norns,
> Spinners of the fates of men and gods.'

Elai replied, 'Your destiny is to die. See the skein I have woven.'

'If I am torn in this middle earth then you must honour your vow.'

'You will not be torn,' said Skuld. 'I have trapped your runes within this pool. They cannot come to the flesh.'

'Sixteen I pulled from the waters and threw them to the stars to be be born in men.'

'Eight I kept here; sixteen shall return.'

'I will pull them from the waters.'

'You poured yourself into cracked cups. I will draw them here to die. Here I shall hold them while the wolf is freed to slay you. Such is your destiny as was woven when the world began.'

'I am master of magic. You, the fates, are bound to my will,' said the god.

'Then we will stay and fight a while, you and I.'

'I think that a good way to spend my days. I will call my servants.'

'And I will call mine.'

'Men will sing of how Odin sat and battled his wits against a Norn's.'

'They have sung already; the outcome is known.'

'At Uthr's well does Odin sit
But the wolf comes slinking soon.'

'On your own you cannot match me. I will have my death here. My bargain will be fulfilled.'

'I am not alone. My sisters will come.'

In the face of the dead god the girl saw fear.

Her hands were in the magic pool, turning and directing the flow of the stream, weaving the water and the destinies of men and gods. The god sought to distract her from her work. It became cold in the chamber and it seemed to her she had wandered onto a moor locked in fog where spectres roamed. She was entombed in a sandy grave, the bones of dead men all around her. She flew over battlefields hearing the screams of the dead, seeing their tormented faces and knowing that with a turn of the threads in her hands she could save them from their fate.

'I am fate and destiny,' she said.

'I am lord of the fallen. King of the dead.'

'I am the maker of the dead. The weft of life and death runs through my hands.'

'You shall not prevail.'

She twisted the threads pulling in her brother in her hands, twisted those that brought the rune bearers to the pool. The mad god battled to stop her. He sent visions to make her forget her weaving, mad-eyed ghosts that tried to tear her hands away from her thread. All the time he stared ahead, his eye fixed upon nothing, grunting and snuffling, looking for the howling rune, the one that would draw the wolf and bring about his earthly death. So they sat for a long time – the suicidal god and the girl who sought to bring him death – working to opposing ends that only the mad and the magical could understand.

47 Brother and Sister

He'd sensed her from almost his first step into the caves. The chamberlain knew she was waiting, in those tunnels, waiting for him. Behind the footfalls of the men who carried Styliane he heard another movement, faster, a patter of steps like those of a child.

When he held up his hand to tell his men to pause, the steps had gone, just the tight silence of the caves remained.

The way was easy for him to remember. He could not forget it, he had trod it so often in his dreams. Though the tunnel split, though many routes offered themselves, he knew which one to choose. The one he had travelled before. The others stretched away like ignored possibilities – things he could have done, other roads to other lives in which he had not been a murderer, not been this vessel for magic, cracked and damaged as it was.

The runes keened and sighed as he descended, gleaming and moving like bright fish in dark water.

Karas.

He heard her voice in his mind.

Karas.

The chamberlain crossed himself – a gesture of habit rather than faith.

He had loved Styliane as he had loved his other sister, loved his mother. The well had given him great things for one sacrifice, it would give him great things for another. He had protected Styliane, used his magic to raise her high, been careful to love her, no matter how much she opposed him. Because of that care and love she was appropriate as a sacrifice. The well required gifts that were hard to give. His eyes were wet when he looked at her, the runes jangling madness through his head as they pulled away from him, tumbling down into the dark as if drawn by invisible threads.

He checked her. She was still unconscious. *Why?* He found that disquieting. Something to do with the deaths that had swept the town? She'd been to the island, his spies told him. What had happened there? He would find out in the waters of the well. He would give and he would receive. Then he would banish the city's affliction and return to his former life. He hoped he would grieve. He had not grieved for his mother or Elai until his grip on the runes began to fade. Grieving, however, was human — a connection to the mundane world and sanity where magic was a tool rather than ... *What?* He could not put it into words. An ache behind the eyes, an inability to think or to reason, something that made shadows into spectres, reaching out to drag you from your bed at midnight, to consume you and turn you to darkness too.

Now the little stream dropped before him. He remembered his mother bumping down, the lamp in front of her, her arse soaked. A glimpse of the boy who would have found that funny came back to him.

A rune had lit up in him that day, a brilliant shining rune. But it had cast a shadow, something created by light but of the darkness.

'Are you all right, sir?'

The little Greek watched him. The chamberlain realised his cheeks were wet with tears.

'Go on. It's not far now. When we reach the place you can return. I won't need you from there.'

The man held up his lamp and looked closely at the chamberlain.

'You're bleeding. Your nose.'

The chamberlain touched his upper lip. A big gout of blood on his fingers, black in the torchlight.

'Go on,' he said. Lights swam at the edge of his vision and he thought he might faint.

The men slid down the smooth rock of the stream bed, one

going in front of Styliane's stretcher, the other behind. The chamberlain followed. Down again and he saw the glow of the rocks. His men hesitated.

'It is a natural thing, I believe,' said the chamberlain. 'I have looked into it and such things are not unknown to miners. There's no need for you to be afraid.'

The Greek said he couldn't believe that to be so.

'Get her into the pool and then you can go. Take her off the stretcher.' He carefully set his lamp in a nook in the rock.

The chamberlain crawled past them down the passage. Here was the cave, the little crucible where his life had been renewed, the water blood in the red light. He drew in breath.

Something spread out in the water – a cold weed. Hair. There were bodies in there. In what state, after years in cold water? The horror would be useful to him, he thought, to jolt him from his everyday consciousness to where he could find and work the runes.

He lowered himself into the pool, gasping with the shock of the cold water that squeezed the breath from him. The men lowered Styliane. The chamberlain focused intently on her as she came into the pool, grasping her about the waist, pulling her to him, not wanting to see what was in the water next to him. His men all but ran away back up the passage. He recalled the words of the spell he had researched. His mother had not been alive to teach it to him, nor would she have done, he being a boy, but he had paid the price the merchants had asked for the ancient papyri. He had none of the herbs or mushrooms his mother had used in her ritual but he sensed he would not need them. The lamp guttered in the chamber; the light of the rocks breathed, as if they were living things. Around him he saw the runes. This was where they wanted to be. They had fought to return here, and he had followed them into the earth to win them again. He began the incantation.

'Here in the drowning water,
By the names of those who died violently,

343

By the names of those untimely dead,
Hecate, lady of the crossroads, lady of night,
Who feeds on filth, grim-eyed, dreadful girl-child
Girt with the entrails of the dead, luckless men, unlucky
  women,
By their violent deaths I summon you.
Cthonic lady, I call you by your drowned attendants,
  entombed spirits,
Night-locked sins and submerged dreams,
The awful waters of the Styx, streams of Lethe,
Hades' Acherousian pool. Hecate, night's witch,
Answer me, guide me. Shine, moon's witch, illuminate.
Send your phantoms to guide me.'

Nothing. The water was extremely cold; colder than he remembered. Three women in the water, two dead. Three aspects
of the goddess, three ways to look, three streams trickling in.
He pushed Styliane's head under the water. He wept. Even
though Styliane hated him, she was a connection to what he
had been before. A rubbish-tip-crawling boy, a street child,
hungry and poor. But Elai and his mother, they had loved
him. Now they were dead. A light shone in the darkness, giving shape to the gloom, his shape – his shadow.

He pulled Styliane's head up out of the water. He couldn't
do it. He couldn't finally sever his connection to his family,
to mundanity, to a world governed not by demented symbols
but by thirst and hunger, love and death.

He repeated the incantation, the cold numbing his mind.
Again and again he chanted until he couldn't tell if he spoke
the words any more or if they had a life of their own – bird
words flapping against the walls of the cavern, rat words
scuttling around the rocks, star words burning like comets,
the cave like the vault of heaven. *Eight runes. No, not eight.
More. Sixteen.* Two orbits of eight, shining and revolving like
little planets about the chamber. He feared them. They were
in a dance with themselves, oblivious to him. What would it

take to control them? Styliane was his key. All it required was courage. So many runes. He had only ever seen eight. Who else was there?

A voice, as much in his head as in his ears: *The lord of corpses. The lady of corpses. He who, a corpse, lies among corpses. She who, a corpse, lies among corpses.*

'Elai? Sister?'

It is me, Karas.

'Elai, forgive me.'

The chamberlain wept, holding Styliane, pale and cold, in the water.

The voice spoke again:

> *Luckless women, confined in this place,*
> *May bring success to him who is beset*
> *With torments. You who have left the light,*
> *Unlucky ones, bring success to him*
> *Who is distressed at heart because of her.*
> *Unholy and ungodly, bring the sacrifice,*
> *The woman racked with torments. Bring her.*

He recognised it as a spell – he'd read it, he was sure, or someone had revealed it to him. One of the old goddesses' spells. For what, though?

'Elai, I am sorry.'

You must give again.

'I will give.'

Not her.

'What?'

You must give what I gave.

'I took your life.'

You were my instrument. I had the will to give my death to the waters. Do you?

'I cannot. I lack that strength.'

Strength to kill but not to die. The well sets its price very high for such as you, Karas.

'I have brought her. The only one I love and cherish. She is all that connects me to the world.'

You have brought yourself. You cannot walk forward to lore looking back to life.

The chamberlain's thoughts spilled from his mouth like grain from a split sack: 'I have only ever wanted the glittering palaces, the silk and the satin, to command men and be a lord of earthly powers. Magic was for me just a means to an end.'

He saw the treasure room at the palace, the ships of the navy arrayed and awaiting his word to sail, the towers of the great city shining in the bright morning, the order of battle at Abydos, spears that seemed to gleam for him, swords drawn to do his will, even the emperor beneath his sway. What tents there had been, blood-crimson and royal purple like brilliant flowers under the morning light. What slaughter he had made. For glory, for achievement's sake – so when men spoke of him they would marvel at the reach of his hand.

He had not wanted to be a god. He had wanted to be a king. And to be a king he had taken a little of a god's power and thought to shape it to his own.

You are a means to the ends of magic. The old god tried to put his runes in me, but I hid them in you. I went to cross the bridge of light but he barred me entrance. I brought you back, Karas. I saw the scholar's worth. Now all the needed are coming. I have sent for them, Karas. Prepare to receive them properly as the dead man you will surely be.

'I will not die!'

You took the dead god's runes and became part of a god yourself. Now you must unite with him in death. Your pain can end the story of agony. We can destroy the god, Karas; we can cease to exist. How sweet will that be?

'I am a man, not a god.'

He pushed Styliane towards the shelf of rock, brushing against something he could not bear to look at. He lifted her out of the water and set her on the shelf.

'I am capable of kindness and compassion. I am not cruel like a god.'

You have been cruel.

'You made me cruel! Your magic, your runes.'

It was only a spark to the tinder of your soul. Join me in death, Karas, join me in death because one is coming who is greater than death. Walk across the bridge of light.

'I will not die. I will not die! Elai! Elai!'

His sister's voice faded. In its place, coming from the tunnel, was the sound of someone splashing towards him through the stream.

A voice spoke, almost sang, in Norse, though he didn't understand a word.

The runes around him shivered and moaned. There were no longer sixteen; there were twenty-four. He didn't know what to do. He wanted to run from this cold awful place with its corpses, its ghosts that whispered inducements to suicide.

The chamberlain tried to lever himself out of the water, but he was frozen and his arms shook in great spasms as they took his weight.

Someone spoke to him in Norse – a boy. He thought he recognised him. Yes, he had brought the emperor's instruction to begin the investigation.

'I don't understand you,' said the chamberlain in Greek.

'Well, you're a fine fellow to be taking a bath down here, my lord,' said Snake in the Eye in Greek. 'Let me lend you a scrubbing brush.' He threw something into the pool. The chamberlain caught a glimpse as it splashed into the water. It was the head of the little Greek who had helped him down. The red-haired man had gone.

'Help me out!'

Snake in the Eye put his hand to the glowing rock, captivated

'Oh, I don't think I shall,' he said. 'These waters are singing a song, can't you hear it?'

'I hear the runes.'

'Yes, and do you know what they want?'

The chamberlain swallowed. His teeth chattered with the cold.

'Death.'

'Yes, they do,' said Snake in the Eye, 'which is lucky, because here I am.'

The runes in the cavern began to hum and shake, and what seemed like a wave of excitement rushed from them like, thought the chamberlain, the roar of a crowd greeting a favourite charioteer.

48 No Way Back

I am on my way to death. Loys, where are you? I cannot die without saying goodbye. Where are you? Come to me. Don't come to me — these people are killers. Run, Loys. I've brought you to this. If I'd never smiled at you I would never have been here and you would be in the monastery, safe and warm.

Beatrice was dragged, bound at the hands, through the dark of the Numera. The effort was excruciating, and she cried out for them to go more slowly, that if she fell and killed her baby it would be her death too. Her legs were so weak, she was so heavy, so ungainly with the burden of her belly among these hateful men. The northerners pressed on. They were grim-faced dirty savages, she thought. She'd seen their like at her father's court, but there they had been out of place, hesitant, fearful of offending a lord whose customs and ways were unfamiliar to them. Here they were at home, marching through the darkness, torches blazing, swords drawn and spears before them.

So much slaughter, so many dead. Corpses everywhere, from the burned and blackened men at the entrance to the prison, to the prisoners dead in their irons, to butchered and beaten guards. Beatrice had been heavily sick on the way in and even some of the Vikings retched. The street level of the prison held no one alive. Bodies lay torn by ragged wounds, hands severed, heads smashed in. One man had a broken spear through his chest — someone had clearly tried and failed to get it out of his body. Stranger though were the men who sat dead but unmarked in their irons, the dancing girl who clung to a fat old pimp, both wide-eyed, pale and dead, as if killed by fear.

Beatrice did not wonder people died that way here. Her

father had said of all the tools he had at his disposal to govern, nothing worked as well as terror – King Fear, he called it. If there was such a ruler, this was his palace.

They came to a door. That too had been burned away – the invaders clearly improvising to make up for their lack of siege equipment. Down, through more silent galleries of the dead, the torchlight bright on harsh faces, the terrible woman who had ordered Beatrice taken at her side. Somehow the men, full of grim purpose, hostile and rough, were easier to bear than her. Beatrice glanced at the scar on the woman's face – no worse a deformity than on any beggar on the church steps on a Sunday, but something about it frightened her. It seemed like the expression of an internal agony, like a blister that had bubbled to the surface from some heart-deep fire.

'Where, Vala?'

'Down, down. He is here. Look around you. He is here.'

Beatrice was pulled on, through doorways, down stairs. She retched and staggered. Against herself, she wept. 'My baby. My baby!' Screams and shouts from below. A Viking walked towards them out of the gloom.

'You're late to the fight, lads. We've had some slaughter here tonight.'

'How do we get below?' The big one, the one in the red tunic and trousers, was curt, ill-tempered.

'Along there and down. They're all dead. The Greeks must have killed them all rather than let us collect their ransoms, though how I can't see.'

They pushed on through another doorway and Beatrice saw steps descending into a huge room. As she was pulled down she cried out – the torches of the Vikings revealed a slaughter-house. Hundreds of men lay dead on the floor, their bodies copper in the torchlight, like the fallen leaves of a hideous autumn.

'This is hell,' she said. Clad only in rags, the corpses were in various states of emaciation. Some were little more than skeletons, bones showing through the skin, others were merely thin; some were decomposing, others newly dead. Even the warriors with her murmured at the sight.

'Down again.' It was the woman who spoke.

Beatrice now had to be carried by one of the Vikings. Her strength had gone. He picked her up in his arms as if she was a baby herself and walked her across that terrible floor. She tried to blank her mind, closed her eyes and breathed through her mouth to avoid the stench.

'Here, it is as was revealed.' The woman's voice again.

Beatrice felt herself lowered to the floor and opened her eyes. A darkness gaped at the foot of the wall.

'Not in there. Not in there!' said Beatrice.

What were they doing with her? Did they plan to entomb her? She was quite convinced they were all mad.

'Lady!' The big red Viking shook her and stared into her face, speaking Norse slowly so she understood. 'I will go first. We will not leave you alone in this place.'

'Am I to die?'

'We're all to die one day.'

He lay flat on the floor and crawled within. One of his men followed him in. Another gestured to her that it was her turn. She had no choice, and whatever was in that hole could not be as bad as the charnel house she was standing in. But how to get in? She had to lie on her side, holding her belly. The man behind her pushed and the one already in the tunnel pulled at her arms. 'Be careful, be careful!' It was agony, as if they'd tear her arms from their sockets and crush the child inside her. The woman came in after her, then the other men.

They were in a long tunnel stretching away into darkness.

'Why am I here?' Beatrice wanted to weep but she wouldn't give the savages the satisfaction. Her legs cramped and her vision blurred. She needed to lie down but there was nowhere to lie. She had to go on, so she went on.

No one replied to her question; they just pressed on, sometimes carrying her, sometimes making her walk, sometimes making her crawl. *Loys. Loys, where are you?* She thought of her happy times with him – the woods near Rouen, kissing him in the wet dawn, the cold of his cheek against hers, watching the sun rise and pull the mist from the grass, the smell of the earth and the feel of his body next to hers as they walked in the morning light.

'Why am I here?'

'You have dreams?' It was the woman.

'We all have dreams!' Her anger came bursting out of her but she checked herself. She depended on this woman and the Vikings, if she was ever to get out of this place.

The woman spoke and her voice was soft. 'The wolf. He is coming for you.'

'I have seen him, yes.'

'So we will see if he can be stopped. You are a lure to him.'

'I would rather have a million nightmares than experience this reality.'

'You know they are more than nightmares. You see reality. In here –' she tapped Beatrice on the head '– when you are sleeping. You go to the river and he comes looking for you.'

'Yes.'

'He must not find you.'

'No one will ever find me down here.'

'He will.'

'Are you bringing me to him?'

'No. I am trying to save you. If not now then in times and lives to come.'

'That is sacrilege.'

The woman took her by the shoulders. 'Look at me,' she said. 'I have lived to see men born, grow old and die, though I have never aged. I have been the mother to a god's sons, again and again. I tire of seeing the same boys born, knowing they only exist to satisfy a god's need for sacrifice. Sacrilege, maybe. Truth, yes.'

Beatrice took a pace backwards. The woman scared her and Beatrice was convinced she was mad.

'What do you intend to do to me?'

'At the waters we will see. You need courage.'

'I have none.'

'Then you need endurance. The rope will provide your courage.' She touched Beatrice's bound hands then turned to the Vikings. 'Keep going. Soon the way will become harder.'

'If it's open,' said one of the men.

'It will be open.'

'The one on the hill wasn't open and you foresaw that.'

'This is the way we are destined to come. The Norns have woven our thread,' said the woman.

Down and further down into the dark. The court slippers Beatrice wore were completely inadequate and quickly fell to pieces, but there was no respite for her bleeding feet.

'This is ridiculous,' she said. 'I can't escape. Why am I tied?'

They said nothing, but when they came to the tighter crawls untied her. Beatrice shuddered at the start of those breathless squeezes and several times panic took her as the lamplight was obscured for a moment and darkness came down. Her belly was so big and she instinctively sought to protect it. She was a small woman, which was lucky. Bollason had to remove all his clothing and crawl through naked. At one point his men had to tie his hands and pull him through. He made no complaint, just stood up smiling, filthy and obscenely nude at the other end.

'Don't think of one of your women while you're in there, Bolli. If you get a hard-on we'll never get you out,' said a Viking. They all seemed to find this hilarious.

Splashing and shouting ahead. Flints sparked, lamps lit. Bollason picked up his sword, not bothering to dress. Beatrice had not noticed the sword before – a curious curved thing. She had never seen its like. Bollason hurried forward into the dark, two men behind him, one with a lamp.

Beatrice heard a shout. 'Ragnar's here! He's hurt!'

The rest of Vikings ran down the passage, the woman following. There was no thought of tying Beatrice now – they knew they were too far in – but like a lost ship she followed any light.

The tunnel dipped and then widened. To her left a broad pool of water spread out into darkness, the reflections of the lamps shimmering like buried treasure among its pillars. On the floor lay a man, tall, lean, white-haired. She put her hand to her mouth when she saw him. He had arrived at her father's court only days before she left. He was a cousin of Lord Richard and, it was said, the fiercest warrior who had ever sprung from the north. He had come for only one reason. To take her home and – she knew her father – to kill Loys. Mauger was his name.

Was he dead? Had God blessed her? No. He was coming out of a stupor. One of the Vikings brought him water from the pool.

'You are a great warrior, Ragnar,' Bollason was saying, 'and to honour you I shall not let you die. Give him the drink.'

A Viking put a horn to Mauger's lips. Mauger whispered something.

'He's raving,' said the Viking.

'He spared me,' said Mauger. 'He spared me.'

'Who?'

'The boy, for the service I did him.'

'Which boy?'

'Snake in the Eye.'

Bollason took the horn himself and put it back to Mauger's lips.

'That is an odd fellow. I have seen him too cowardly to strike another youth who called him womanly. Yet I have seen him charge the Greeks, a hero in every appearance.'

'My life is a flame. He blew upon it and knocked me down.'

'Troll work!' said Bollason.

'Seid magic,' said the woman with the scarred face. 'If the boy spared Ragnar and left him like this then we need look no further for the source of the deaths that have been stalking the city.'

'We will kill him and win great honour with the emperor!' said a Viking Beatrice had heard called Gregnir.

'That may be,' said the woman, 'or it may not. We must get to the waters.'

Mauger came back to himself.

'They've gone through those waters,' he said. 'The way is not easy. I have tried it.'

'Beneath the pool?' said the woman.

'Yes.'

'It is as was foreseen. Bolli, this will test even your courage.'

'What do I need to do?'

'Go under there and emerge the other side.'

'If there is another side,' said Gregnir.

'There is,' said the woman.

'I cannot go in there!' Beatrice couldn't control herself. She heard her voice echoing off the cavern walls. Mauger glanced up at her, a faint smile of recognition on his face.

'You can and you will,' said the woman. 'Bolli, you will take the rope. If you make it to the other side you can pull the rest of us through. It will be easier for those who go second.'

Mauger sat like a troll in the torchlight, his gaze unmoving upon her. *What choice? The waters or here with him.*

'You said "they" had gone beneath the waters,' said the woman.

'Yes, Vala, a wolfman and the scholar Loys too,' said Mauger.

'You are looking to kill the wolfman?'

'No, lady, the scholar.' His gaze never left Beatrice. She leaped forward to strike at him, but Gregnir caught her.

'He's talking about my husband. Half my fortune to the man who strikes him down.'

'You have no fortune, lady,' said Mauger. 'Your father will pay no dowry for you now.'

'If you help us we will give her to you,' said the vala.

'No!' said Beatrice. No one answered.

'I will pay a man to stay here with the lady while I fetch the scholar,' said Mauger.

'Not possible,' said Bollason. 'She must come with us. If

your scholar is on the other side then you will have both your quarries together.'

Mauger kept staring at Beatrice. 'I won't let any harm come to her,' he said.

'What harm comes to any of us is in the lap of the Norns,' said Bollason. 'You are a mighty man, Ragnar, and a bold killer. But so am I. Widows curse my name from the shores of Britannia to the Caliphate. You know my fame.'

Beatrice shivered. She recognised what was happening. Her father had done his best to take on French ways when he arrived in Neustria, but in an argument or a fight he went back to being the Viking he had been. His language would become elevated, more ornate in a clear message to his enemy – 'I am preparing to write myself into a saga. This is how heroes talk.'

'I do,' said Mauger, 'though I should like to test your worth.'

Bollason raised his sword but the old woman stilled him with a glance.

'The way out is sealed,' she said to Mauger. 'Three hundred men guard the Numera now, and in the unlikely event you could cut down Bolli, you would not escape them. Nor me.'

Mauger looked into the woman's ruined eye and bowed his head. 'You are a vala and a great troll worker, I can see,' he said.

'The work we do here is for no earthly lord,' she said. The sorceress too spoke in a self-consciously high manner. She was honouring Mauger, Beatrice understood, but at the same time emphasising her own position as someone who demanded respect. 'Our destinies are set. The girl goes beyond here to the well. That is foreseen.'

Nothing was said for a while but it seemed Mauger had accepted he could not challenge the woman's plan. Bollason spoke: 'Give me a rope.' I will go first. Tie the girl and she can go through bound if she's going to become hysterical. Put one of those dead men's helmets on her head. You have tinder for the lamps?'

'Yes, lord.'

'He is a killer!' Beatrice pointed at Mauger.

'The Norns weave out our fate, girl,' said Bollason. 'Accept yours once you see you cannot influence it. Better to go smiling to hard places than cowering like a child.'

He waded out into the water, only his sword on its belt about him, a helmet on his head. He paused as the water reached his waist.

'Cold?' said Gregnir.

'It's like a bath compared to Eithafjord,' said Bollason and waded on.

Beatrice was prodded into the water with the butt of an axe, the Vikings following. The water was freezing and she cried out but Mauger's hand at her back pushed her on.

Where the ceiling of the cave met the water Bollason turned. 'Here?'

'The wolfman went through a little to the left,' said Mauger.

'Then wish me luck, boys,' said Bollason. He took three sharp breaths and dived under. It was quiet for a very long time. And then ...

'He's tugging the rope,' said Gregnir. 'He's through!'

'The lady goes first,' said the woman they'd called the vala. 'You have a helmet for your head and try to go on your back and push away from the ceiling with your hands. It'll be easier without breath in your chest, but you won't believe me. You'll have to discover it for yourself.'

They looped the rope to bind Beatrice's hands, Gregnir grabbing the end to stop it being pulled all the way through.

'If I lose my child then I will die and all your efforts to bring me here will come to nothing!'

'You will not lose it,' said the vala. 'Your destiny lies deeper than this.'

From away in the caverns, up towards the surface a howl chilled the air.

'Be quick,' said the vala.

Beatrice turned back to Mauger. 'You have come to find my husband?' she said.

'Yes, lady.'

'Well, so have I,' she said.

One of the Vikings gave two good tugs on the rope to tell Bollason they were ready; Beatrice took a big gulp of air and was pulled forward into the water. The cold clamped down on her terror for an instant as she was tugged under as if someone had placed icy bands of steel about her head and chest. Thought was impossible. The pull forward suddenly ceased and the rope went slack. She tried to cry out but the water forced its fingers into her throat, choking her, freezing the words inside her and she slipped into blackness.

49 Death by Water

Loys listened to the boy speaking. He was mad, the scholar was convinced. They had thought it was Mauger and had quickly taken to a side passage to hide, dimming their light. Only the lamp ahead and the glow of the rocks provided any vision now.

It was not Mauger, but the boy, wandering along as if he was out for a stroll on a sunny day. He mumbled to himself in Norse as he went.

'Speak more of your stories to me. Do not run ahead so. How shall I fight this wolf? Not to fight? I am a warrior and must always fight.' He became angry. 'I run from him by the riverbank because I have no weapons to face a wolf. Give me a spear, sharp and cruel; give me a sword to cut him or a hammer to crush him. I will offer him blood all right, I'll offer him his own. Here, wolf, I make a sacrifice of yourself to yourself. See how your hungers fare on your own flesh. Do not run from me, my friends; come back, let me touch you again. Send me to that place again and I will face him. He took me by surprise before. I am not a coward. Do not think me a coward. My destiny is death in battle. I am death. Do you not see the corpses I made for you? I have made a city of the dead for you. Come back. Hey, bright symbols, come back. I will build you houses of bones. Ho, what's here and who's here?'

Loys heard another voice, this time speaking Greek: 'Help me!'

He glanced at the wolfman, scarcely visible in the dim light. The wolfman squeezed Loys' arm – partly to restrain him, partly, thought Loys, as a gesture of reassurance.

'He is Odin!' whispered the wolfman. 'It was he who was in the tent with the head of the rebel at his feet!'

'Will you go to him to die?' Loys didn't want that at all. The wolfman was his protector.

'He would need the sword.'

The voices again, now both speaking Greek.

'This pool is a drowning pool. It whispers to me.' That was the boy, Loys was sure.

'Save yourself and save me. She has called us here.' The voice sounded very strained.

'For what reason?'

'For death. There is a mad ghost in these caverns and she is hungry for your blood.' This was accompanied by coughing and retching.

'I am a man, not a boy. I am no coward and will face the ghost. I am likely a famous ghost killer and a god of death. Remain a while in the water, sir; it suits my temper to see you there.'

'Can you not feel? Can you not understand? You bring the runes with you. You are a killer, true, but you are a fragment of a death god. She will have us united. The runes are slipping from you. Can you not feel it? I can feel it.'

'I would have more of these pretty symbols. I cannot yet fathom their use but they take me to a place where I snuff out men's lives. Take me there again, symbols.'

'Let me out of the water; I will freeze. Let me out.'

'Remain a while yet, sir, please.'

'How old are you, boy?

'Fifteen years, so my father said. I killed my mother when I was born.'

'And not yet a man. Are you cut?'

'No man would dare cut me.'

'Then you have been held that way by luck or by enchantment. Listen to your voice. You are changing. No man can hold the runes, no man.'

'You are a brave man to tell me that. I can hold them, true enough.'

'She will kill you. She will kill me. Death is here. He's talking to her. Can't you hear him whispering?'

'I can hear only you whining.'

The men continued arguing as the wolfman whispered to Loys: 'Who is that?'

'Who?'

'The man in the water.'

'The man is the chamberlain. The boy is called Snake in the Eye. He is a Varangian.'

'You know him?'

'He came to me for a cure for an enchantment.'

'What cure?'

'He said he could not kill.'

'What did you do for him?'

'Nothing. I told him to come to Christ and give up his savage thoughts.'

A splash from the submerged passage. Loys thought he would crush the handle on his knife, he held it so tight.

The voices at the pool stopped. Snake in the Eye came running up past them, no lantern to guide him, he was just a shadow in the dim light.

'Get the man out of the water,' said the wolfman. Then he was gone after the boy, a silent shadow himself.

Loys slithered down the smooth rock bed of the stream to the edge of the well.

The chamberlain was trying to get out but he was shivering violently and could not make his hands grip the ledge of the pool. On a shelf of rock next to him lay the Lady Styliane. Loys put out his hand but the man didn't have the strength to reach up and take it.

'She's here. She's taken them back. She means me to die.' His speech was slurred and slow.

Loys lay down and grabbed him, but the eunuch was far too heavy to pull out that way. *How to get the chamberlain out of the water?* If he rescued him he would have his gratitude and all the benefits that brought.

Loys got his hands under the chamberlain's arms and pulled hard. He didn't budge. He shook as if his flesh was trying to writhe free of his bones.

'She wants a death, for sure she wants a death. He wants a death. He is she as she always was he. Death begetting, mother and father of death,' Snake in the Eye spoke from the passage.

The chamberlain grabbed Loys' arm.

'That's right, come on, try to lever yourself up.'

But the chamberlain didn't drag himself up, he pulled Loys down and forward into the freezing pool.

Loys took in great mouthfuls of water. The chamberlain's arms wrapped around him, pressing him down into darkness. Fighting for air, grabbing at the chamberlain, forcing him down in the chest-deep water, Loys pushed himself up. The two men staggered through the water, falling, rising, fighting and falling again. Loys heard screams and shouting behind him, saw snatches of light before those arms forced him down again.

The chamberlain was exhausted by his time in the water, and whatever strength he'd suddenly found deserted him just as quickly. One moment he was powerful, almost irresistible, the next his energy had faded as rapidly as a flow of a stream cut off by a sluice gate. The chamberlain's hands continued to claw at him, but his eyes were frightened. He clung to the scholar for support now.

'Help me,' he said. 'The magic has deserted me. I am alone here and she means me to die. I took my power from here years ago and now she wants it repaid.'

Loys remembered how he had been used – played false and set up by the chamberlain. He could not trust the man, and now he knew his secret the chamberlain was a peril to him. Anger fuelled him. A verse from the Bible went through his mind: 'till thou return unto the ground; for out of it wast thou taken: for dust thou art, and unto dust shalt thou return'.

Isais was dead. Loys was a murderer already.

He shoved the chamberlain down and held him. He put up

no resistance and drowned easily, his hands on Loys' hands, gentle almost as if the chamberlain was thanking him. Around Loys the light of the rocks seemed to suck and breathe as he waited for the chamberlain to die. A year ago he could not have killed but he had been transformed. By what? By love and the defence of his love. He released the chamberlain and the body floated face down.

He waded to the ledge nearest him, at the far end of the pool from the entrance. Something was around his hands, like weed. Hair. Long hair. He couldn't look down, he just washed the hair from his hand and pulled himself up. As he did so a sharp pain bit his leg as something dug into his flesh. The stone he had taken from Snake in the Eye was still in his little bag on its cord. He sat for a moment to regain his strength. *Where was the wolfman?* Without him he would never get out of the caves. He had to find him.

The woman's voice was in his head but it made no sense. *A rock called Scream, a rope called Thin.* What did it mean? He reached into his bag to cast the stone away but he didn't. He examined it. A wolf's head crudely scratched upon it, just a pebble tied in an elaborate knot on a thong of leather. The voice gabbled like a market trader. *A rock called Scream, a rope called Thin. A rock called Scream, a rope called Thin.* Something told him to put the stone around his neck. *No, that is devilry.* The insane shrieking of the childish voice jumbled all his senses, threw his thoughts into disorder. He would do anything to make it stop. Instinctively he knew the stone would help him. He tied it about his neck clumsily, his fingers at first unable to make the knot. In the end he managed it and the voice fell silent. As soon as it was quiet he was tempted to take it off again. He did not. He tucked it into his robe so no one could see the pagan symbol. He was ashamed of it, but the stone comforted him.

He heard a scream and he recognised the voice at once. 'Beatrice!' he shouted.

At the entrance to the tunnel, he saw someone move,

someone with a head as white as a deathcap in the lamplight. Mauger was crouching at the edge of the water, a cruel curved sword in his hand.

50 Mighty Killer

The wolfman watched as Snake in the Eye walked through the dancing shadows towards the man who had emerged from the water of the tunnel, his sword drawn. It was the big Viking, naked save for a sword belt. The moonsword! Elifr would have recognised it anywhere. He wanted to spring forward, to insist the boy killed him with it. But the big Viking was there and he had the sword. Elifr opted to sit and wait, to see what unfolded.

Snake in the Eye approached Bollason boldly.

'Hello, Bollason!' Snake in the Eye's voice was like that of a man greeting a friend on a fine morning rather than a warrior meeting another in such uncertain circumstances.

Even the battle-worn Bollason gave a start when he heard the boy's voice.

'Snake in the Eye,' he said.

'That's a poor greeting, my friend,' said Snake in the Eye. 'Do you not welcome your leader and your god?'

Bollason kept his eyes fixed on Snake in the Eye. 'What are you doing here?'

'Need gods explain their purposes to mortals? Do we, who ride shooting stars across the void of heaven and whose enemies suffer numberless griefs, require to give reasons to men?'

'Still mad and incapable of sense,' said Bollason. 'Light a lamp – the light here is dim and I have work to do.' The wolfman caught the wariness in Bollason's voice.

'You paid me the service of allowing me *hölmgang*,' said Snake in the Eye. 'I shall repay you by lighting your lamp. That's how gods work.'

He took a bronze lamp from Bollason's small bag, shook,

rubbed the moisture from the oil-soaked cloth and quickly kindled a flame.

'I have work to do here,' said Bollason.

'Don't let me stop you,' said Snake in the Eye.

'Put down your sword,' said Bollason. 'We are friends here.'

'We are,' said Snake in the Eye. He sheathed his weapon.

Bollason gave a couple of tugs on the rope. Then he began to pull hard.

'I think I saw you by some waters before,' said Snake in the Eye.

Bollason said nothing, just kept pulling.

'I know your name. This is not your well. You have a well, though – it's near here, or is it the same well? Are all wells the same well? Is that your secret?' said Snake in the Eye.

Bollason carried on pulling.

'I took your head. When I gave my eye for wisdom, I took your head. You advise me and speak truths in my ear. I took your head when I gave my eye!'

'You have two eyes now, boy,' said Bollason.

'I'm not a boy!'

Snake in the Eye snatched up Bollason's sword and struck at the side of his head. The warrior had anticipated the blow and ducked, the sword sparking into the wall. Bollason dropped the rope and dived at Snake in the Eye, driving him to the floor of the tunnel.

'Who are you? Who are you, old man?' the scholar Loys cried out from down in the pool.

Snake in the Eye gave a great sigh as all the wind went out of him, and Bollason froze, lying unmoving on top of him.

'There they are, all the pretty candles,' said Snake in the Eye.

Bollason was quite still. Snake in the Eye wriggled from beneath him.

'You don't look right with a head on your shoulders, old Mimir, my friend,' he said.

He stood and took out his own sword. Then he hacked off

Bollason's head. He gave the neck five or six good blows but still the head was not severed. The boy snorted in frustration.

'If you were a better corpse, your head would come off more easily,' he said. 'Your head's meant to be off. It doesn't look right any other way.'

He walked to the rope that emerged from the water and looked at it as if he didn't quite know what it was. Then he began tugging on it, singing out in a high voice,

'Oh I am the fisherman,
And fish are what I catch.
Big ones, little ones, fat ones, thin ones,
In fish I have no match!'

Four or five pulls and a woman came almost lifeless from the water, her hands bound to the rope. It was all Elifr could do to keep silent. It was her – the one who had tormented his dreams, the one he had vowed never to meet because he knew he had loved her too strongly and that their love was cursed by the gods. His head pounded, his vision blurred. He wanted her so much but he couldn't go to her. That way death came into his kingdom and the cycle of misery began again.

'Now I know you too,' said Snake in the Eye. 'Lady, we have met before. Well, it's time for us to meet again.'

He pulled her onto the dry ground. The woman was face down, vomiting water, sucking in air in great rasps. Snake in the Eye turned her onto her back and hitched up her skirts. Then he undid his trousers and stepped out of them.

'I think this,' he said, 'will prove once and for all I really am a man. And all my friends, my silver, shining friends, here to see me in my glory.'

He paused for a second.

'This candle I see is not yours. Why do I not see you, woman? Two candles. Perhaps I should snuff them and see what corpses I find planted in this rich earth.'

The rope started coiling back through the water.

'But wait,' said Snake in the Eye. 'It seems I may have other fish to catch!'

The wolfman gave a shiver. He knew who the boy was, knew who killed without touching, knew who carried Mimir's head for wisdom and had given his eye at the well. Odin, the dead god. Come to the earth to die, as the prophecy had foreseen. He'd been so near to being free of his destiny in the emperor's tent.

Every instinct told him to attack but, though Elifr had lived as an animal, he was not an animal. The woman was there. If he allowed himself to be killed by the god, what would happen to her? She would be saved in eternal time, perhaps killed in this incarnation. But seeing her alive, so vulnerable, he feared for her and his resolve left him. He needed to defend her. But how, against a god? A ritual was impossible now in the waters, he needed more time.

Again the howl, fear given sound. There must have been another entrance, and the wolf was in. The god's story was unfolding.

Elifr knew he didn't have long. The wolf's destiny was to kill him, the last stage in a magical conversion that would empower him to kill the god. He had to get the woman away. He mouthed her names as he'd known her before. Adisla, Aelis. What was she called this time? It didn't matter. It was up to him to save her. *How?* Hide and then ask the well's guidance when he had the chance.

Snake in the Eye was pulling at the rope, singing all the time.

> 'O lady, rage at the ocean,
> The storm-torn fields of grey.
> But the ocean, it is heedless
> Of anything you might say.
> Your tears sit like diamonds
> Upon your cheeks so pale and fair,
> And the spray it sits and sparkles

A rainbow in your hair.
Your son is son of a father,
Dead and lost to the sea,
So lady, rage at the ocean
Then turn your eyes to me.'

With one final tug a shape emerged from the water that sealed the passage, a flash of white. A head.

A man stood up with a great cough. He bore a large wound on his cheek. The wolfman saw he was nearly as afflicted as the woman who lay half-naked and gasping on the floor, but he was a warrior and instantly mastered himself.

'Ragnar, my fine killer!' shouted Snake in the Eye. 'I have spared your life once, but even for the service you did me you cannot expect such indulgen—'

There was the sound of steel on leather, a heavy exhalation and Snake in the Eye sat down. Mauger's sword had gone straight through him. The boy grasped at the hilt as if he was afraid it would be taken from him.

'I've had enough of your talk,' said Mauger. 'Speak to that.'

He bent to the lady and pulled down her skirts, checking to see if she was breathing.

'You know the penalty for this offence,' he said to Snake in the Eye.

The warrior picked up Bollason's strange curved sword, which lay on the floor next to the dead man's head. He weighed it in his hand for a second, and the wolfman knew he was about to cut off the youth's head. Snake in the Eye sat glassy-eyed, gazing up at the man like a child listening to a story.

'Ahh!' A shout from behind Elifr. The wolfman glanced left from his hiding place. The scholar. The white-haired warrior forgot about the dying boy and ran down the passage towards the sound.

Again the howl – no echo, just forcing its way through the dead air of the caverns, flat and toneless. Was the boy the god? He had to die at the teeth of the wolf, yet the warrior had put a sword clean through him. The wolfman needed to get away from the woman. The wolf was coming for her, and if Elifr fled then he wouldn't die as part of the magical transformation that would bring the wolf god to earth.

But he couldn't leave her stricken on the cave floor.

Elifr ran to her. From up the passage, towards the well, he heard the warrior bellowing, screaming for Loys to show himself. The scholar had hidden in the dark. The woman was breathing. He held her to him to warm her with his body heat.

He wept as he did so.

'I've tried to stay away,' he said, 'but the fates are weaving for us and they bind us too closely. Come on, wake up. You must run from him.'

Snake in the Eye still sat, impaled on Mauger's sword, clutching the hilt. He kicked Elifr's leg to get his attention.

'Now no one can doubt me, for I have a mighty wound,' he said. 'I ask you, sorcerer, could you live with a wound like this? I tell you, you could not.'

Elifr picked the woman up, saying nothing. He had no idea where to go or what to do. His original plan seemed best – go to the waters, perform a ritual and see if the well would talk to him – but he needed to get the woman somewhere dry and warm. There was no such place here. He headed towards the well.

'There are many candles here for snuffing,' shouted Snake in the Eye. Again the howl. 'I cannot go to the wall if he is here – he'll see me. Let me stand. Let no one doubt me – let me stand!'

Elifr pulled the woman down the little stream. Only then did he see what was happening at the well. Loys clung to one side, cowering from the warrior. The warrior was not in the pool; he crouched at the entrance, looking around him in wonder.

'Who's here?' said Mauger. 'Who is speaking to me?' Bollason's sword was in his hand.

Elifr heard the voice in his head, a woman whispering,

singing and muttering. *He is here, he is here.* The voice was very clear.

'Show yourself, woman. Ghosts won't protect you, scholar.'

The woman in the wolfman's arms began to stir. She opened her eyes.

'Set me down,' she said. 'Can you hear her?'

'I can hear her. Who is she?'

Beatrice was shivering and he was reluctant to put her down, but she wriggled out of his arms onto the floor.

'She is the voice of the waters. She is my sister. I must go to her. Get away from me, Azémar – this place is death to you.' She crawled towards the pool.

'I am not Azémar.'

Her eyes scanned the cavern as if trying to make sense of what she saw.

'Where is Loys? Where is my Loys?'

'Here, Beatrice. Run. Flee this place.' Loys stayed back in the water, fearful of Mauger. Beatrice cried out and slid down to the pool's edge, oblivious to the warrior beside her, the cruel sword in his hand.

'Who are you and and who is this old fellow?' she said. 'I do not like his looks. He has a noose at his neck.' Beatrice's eyes were wide, staring into nothing. 'Why am I pursued by foul wonders? What is this thing writhing and howling in my breast?'

'Beatrice! Beatrice!' shouted Loys, but she showed no sign of hearing him.

His shout seemed to wake the warrior from his stupor and he jumped into the water. Loys tried to scramble up towards where Styliane lay but he was too cold and too scared.

The warrior stood in the pool, the water up to his chest. 'Who is it? Who is calling me? You, child?' He pointed his sword directly in front of him, staring into space.

Someone scrambled down the stream towards the well. It was the vala.

She came to Elifr and hugged him. He felt her warmth.

'Mother,' said Elifr. 'So the fate is inescapable.'

'Yes,' said the vala, 'as we foresaw. This is the price of wisdom, Elifr. It is no great thing. '

'I feared this day above all others.'

'The skein is spun,' she said. 'There is nothing to stand in your way. Better to suffer now for an instant than to face torture in eternal time. This is the appointed place.'

'I had thought to offer myself to the waters.'

Again the howl shook the cavern.

'He is here for you. Your certain death unless you act on what was revealed. My name is Uthr. I am a Norn and a spinner of fates, the waters whisper it. I need to go across the bridge of light.'

Tears came into the wolfman's eyes, his face long in the glow of the rocks. 'Then go.'

They waded out to the furthest part of the well, forty paces in under the low roof.

The howl was close now.

The wolfman held her and kissed her. Then he pushed her beneath the water.

51   The Norns

'Three have come.'

'Future, present and past – virgin, mother and crone.'

'The Norns are at the water, weaving the fate of men and gods.'

'The Norns are at the well of fate. It took me so long to find and bring my sisters. It cost so much.'

Who was speaking? Women. The dead girl? Beatrice was one of them, she sensed it.

'The wolf is coming.'

'The god is nearly here.'

'What is required?'

'What is ever required?'

'Death of the most dear.'

'Death of the most dear.'

'You will not have my baby!' Beatrice cradled her belly. 'Loys?' He came to her, wading warily past the warrior, who seemed oblivious to him.

'High prices are paid at the well of fate.'

'Odin gave his eye; what will you give?'

'What will you give to hear the oracle speak?'

A clatter and a groan from the entrance to the pool and the boy Snake in the Eye came skittering down. The sword was still in him but in his hand he carried Bollason's head.

He wriggled down and sat on the shelf beside her.

'Well, here's a pretty thing,' he said. 'Do you not see how the runes come to me? See them in their orbits, eight and eight. Yet eight go missing. Why, they are sitting in the waters. How shall they come to me?'

On the other side of the pool sat the girl, arms around her knees on a shelf above the water. She was young and pale in the ghost light. Next to her sat an old man – one-eyed, his skin stained dark, a rope tight at his neck, his beard and hair a dirty white straggle. He too stared down into the well, his good eye wide, full of madness, his other just a decayed socket. In his hand he had a spear – a blackened, burned shard of wood, but wicked sharp – and he held it as if in deep concentration, like a fisherman waiting on a bank. At Rouen, in the Rouvray forest, she'd seen a body dug from a bog by peat cutters. The old man reminded her of that. He chilled her to the core.

The howl again, nearer and louder.

The man stirred. She had the sense he wasn't seeing what she saw – he hardly seemed to notice her. His movements were slow, almost torpid, and she remembered how she had felt in her trance on the beacon tower. Was he even there? Or was he some sort of apparition, as the girl seemed to be?

The girl knows what to do; she will lead the way.

Loys pulled himself out of the water, his body convulsing with the cold. He went to Beatrice and she opened her arms to him. He held her tight, trying to make his trembling jaw say some words of comfort. Inside her something keened and moaned. That symbol, the one that said 'wolf trap'.

That terrible boy, that half-man Snake in the Eye, was talking to her. Her cold-numbed brain hardly registered what he said. Death, death, he was talking about death. He put out his hand to Loys and made a little blowing motion. Loys didn't pay any attention and the boy looked puzzled.

The howl came from the top of the stream and Beatrice turned to see the wolf.

It was Azémar, though he was terribly changed, his eyes flickering green gems in the lamplight, his body twisted and misshaped like an exhumed root, his muscles tight, so tight they seemed to contort him. He held one shoulder high, the other low; his hands were talons, his jaw long, full of teeth as big as boar's tusks, and his tongue lolled from his head, black with blood.

Snake in the Eye's eyes widened with fear.

'I don't wish to have any conversation with this fellow,' he said and jumped into the water. The splash seemed to wake Mauger. He stared at his sword as if trying to work out what it was for.

Azémar – or the thing he'd become – spoke: 'What is happening to me? I've come for you. All these lives I've come for you; don't turn me away now. Aelis, Adisla, Beatrice, don't turn me away.'

'I do not belong to you, Azémar.'

'Do you not recall the light on the hills? Do you not remember what we vowed on the mountainside? I am yours, returned. I am yours.'

'I remember now,' said Beatrice. 'I remember, pain and suffering and a love that died on the teeth of a wolf.'

'I do not want this,' said Azémar, 'but I cannot leave you. I am driven by things I cannot control. I have eaten. I have been consumed. A wolf's eye watches me.' He seemed tormented by his words and jumped out over the water, to cling to the side of the cavern, his great talons seizing the rock.

'Do not let that thing near me!' shouted Snake in the Eye. 'He wants something from me, for sure.'

The story you told to the pale god.

Tell it now.

The girl's voice was in Beatrice's head.

Snake in the Eye answered it. 'What story?

Of the god who dies to please the fates.

'I know you, girl.' Snake in the Eye had terror in his eyes.

You have always known me.

Snake in the Eye babbled, seeming to talk to no one: 'There seem so few to slaughter here. I cannot go near the candle wall while he is in front of me.' He pointed to Azémar.

The wolf Fenrir stands here, the god killer, seething and growling in his hungers. Someone else lies at the threshold, as befits her goddess. Her fate is unseen and undecided. Her skein is not yet woven, her death knot untied.

'*The Norn Verthani is here, mistress of the present, caller of

the wolf, holder of the howling rune, mother. The wolf will kill
her. Her destiny is foreseen. The Norn Skuld is here, the future,
her fingers weaving in unseen currents, dead and so deathless.
The crone Norn is here. Uthr. The past, immortal, for ever. She
who rules the domain to which heroes fall. Men call her Memory
and they call her Hel. We are three and he is three.'

'Who?' Snake in the Eye cast his eyes about him, desperate
to find the source of the voice.

He waits unbodied in the waters, eight and eight and eight.
Gods and men are drawn by the Norns, each to play his part.

'What of Loys?' said Beatrice.

One person can still die.

'He can't because I can't see him,' said Snake in the Eye.
'Those that can be killed have been killed.'

He is hiding from fate, as you hid.

'What is his fate?' said Beatrice.

To die so you might shake free of your destiny of torment. The
skein is woven, the threads of fate entangle him.

'I would die a thousand times before I let him come to harm!'
said Beatrice.

He must die. The well has revealed it. The future is being spun.

As the ghost girl spoke again the white-haired warrior suddenly remembered what his sword was for. He came rushing
at Loys through the water, but Azémar sprang off the rocks
and knocked the sword aside.

'For all that has happened, he is my friend,' he said, his
horrid tongue lolling from his saw-toothed jaws.

A voice from somewhere, a shrieking rhyme. It was not the
voice of the girl. It was stranger, deeper. At first Loys thought
it came from the bloody waters of the well but he realised it
was the wolfman, his voice changed, different.

'She saw wading there through harsh waters
Men who foreswore oaths and murders
And one who covets another's beloved.
There the snake sucks

On the corpses of the fallen
And the wolf tore men – would you know yet more?'

Azémar's great teeth ground at the warrior's ear, his tongue slavering at his neck.

'I have had my fill of murder,' said Azémar, his voice like a rain-swollen door on flagstones. 'I am a holy man and seek only peace. Do not provoke me.'

Mauger did what he had been trained to do since his earliest years. He struck at the wolf, cutting a huge slice out of its flank. The thing screamed terribly as the curved sword bit into its flesh, but it seized Mauger's arm, tore it from its socket and threw it, still holding the sword, back up the stream.

Mauger's remaining hand sought the wolf's wound to tear it open, but he was too weak and too slow. The wolf picked him up and smashed him on the rocks. Then he leaped upon him and began tearing at his flesh.

Loys felt something warm on his fingers. He put up his hand. Blood. Not his own. Beatrice slumped against him. Azémar had knocked Mauger's sword into her and she had an ugly wound in her side.

'Help her! Help her!'

Elifr began to speak as if entranced: 'We have struggled for nothing. Is the wheel turning again? Then the dead god will come and offer his sacrifice and the Norns will be bound to take it.'

'No!' shouted Loys. 'No!'

'Again and again will she suffer and die? All tenderness denied her, her life washed away on the blood tide.' Elifr's eyes were blank as he cradled the corpse of his mother under the water, and it was as if the words were not his own.

'I will not let this happen!' Loys tried to staunch the wound but the blood would not stop.

Azémar gulped and tore, his face grotesquely distorted, his wolf eyes green in the lamplight.

Elifr worked his ritual, muttering and whispering as he held the vala down.

> 'The wolf shall be the bane of Odin
> When the gods to destruction ride.
> The wolf shall be the bane of Odin
> When the gods to destruction ride.'

Azémar looked up from his feeding, his body like a wax effigy left too long in the sun. His eyes narrowed when he saw the wolfman.

Elifr gave a great cry and let go of the corpse in his arms. He leaped towards Loys, grabbing at his leg. 'If you want to save her take off the stone,' he said. 'Take off the stone! The waters have shown me. Take off the stone!'

'Why?'

'To die. The god is coming.'

Loys' hands were wet with Beatrice's blood.

Azémar rose to his full height. He was huge – a head above even the tallest man, horribly muscled, his head a patchwork of flesh and hair but unmistakably that of a wolf. Still he fed on the body, gripping the torso in one hand, biting at it as if it was a hunk of bread.

Loys' mind was numbed by the terror of the wolf-thing, by the sight of Beatrice, wounded and bleeding.

'Take off the stone,' said Elifr.

'What are you going to do?'

'Take you across the bridge of light.'

'Why me?'

'Because you have no place in the god's story. You are not divine nor cursed nor monstrous. You are a man and your skein is still unwoven.'

Beatrice lay dying and he could not imagine his life without her. Loys took off the stone and Elifr dragged him down into the water.

52   The Blood-Rooted Tree

Loys fell, fell through water, fell through air, through darkness pricked with light, through a tree made of light, caught in threads of light.

Above him the pool stretched up like a shaft, a glimmering disc of silver at its top, the threads that suspended him spinning down from three points.

'I am falling.'

'You are falling.'

As he'd removed the stone, a tide had swept over him – of water, yes, but of voices and of images, strange emotions of fear, anger, love and hate. New words formed in his mind to describe new ways of feeling. One was like a purr – he could hardly say it, but it reminded him of a cat in the monastery at Rouen that the abbot had joked he was sure sniggered behind his back. Then another feeling like the tight-stomached, dry-throated sensation a warrior has the instant before battle begins.Yet another – a stolid sadness, a resentment, the way an old man resents his body.

Falling, falling, falling still.

'Where am I?'

'At the well of fate, where the Norns weave the skeins of men.'

Next to him was a girl no more than thirteen years old, her flesh pale and her eyes eaten. Bubbles were coming out of his mouth and Loys realised that, in some strange way, they must be underwater. He was falling, but he was falling upwards.

He had been at the base of a great tree and now he span up through its roots that stretched out like the feet of mountains – massive, more like things of stone than wood.

Things flashed past him in the dark, faces of light, creatures of light.

He was tumbling but up, towards the stars that spread above like the lights of a great army. Up through branches and leaves, and everywhere the light, pouring out of him, pouring out of the god who flew beside him.

A noise was in his ears, a crashing and breaking of branches. A great thump drove all the wind from him. He was on a strange riverbank. The river flowed beside a path and a broken wall.

'What boat is this?' It was a longship which seemed constructed of thousands of tiny petals, pale as bone.

At the prow of the ship stood a man, tall with a shock of red hair. Loys was sure he had seen him at the palace. Here he was not dressed for court. His head was smeared in blood and his body wrapped in a cloak of white hawk feathers.

'This is Naglfar,' said the girl.

'What is it?'

'A ship.'

He nodded to the tall man.

'Who is he?'

'A god. Lord of lies. Enemy of death.'

'How can a liar be an enemy of death? Lies breed death.'

'How can you be mortal unless you lie to yourself? Somehow you all think you will live forever,' said the god, turning to face Loys.

'Go with us,' said the girl.

'To where?'

'Death's kingdom.'

'To do what?'

'You will see.'

Loys' mind felt a wide and beautiful thing, horizon deep and shot with stars. He let the dead girl lead him on board the ship, along a gangplank.

'What is this boat made of?'

'The nails of dead men,' said the god. 'And dead men to row.'

A Viking crew was at the oars, their eyes the eyes of the dead.

A woman sat leaning against the mast – she was red-haired and beautiful but with a terrible scar across the side of her face, the chamberlain was there too. He sat huddled in the stern of the boat, vacant-eyed, seeming mindblown.

'Is this a ship of the drowned?' said Loys.

'Are you drowned?' said the god.

'I am in the waters of the well, I think.'

'What city sits above that well?'

'Constantinople.'

'What goddess rules that city?'

'Hecate.'

'Ruler of what domains?'

'Of gateways and thresholds, of the moon and the night,' said Loys.

'So you are at the threshold,' said the god.

'The waters seek death.'

'Men who say so presume more than the gods. The waters seek the offer of death. They do not always accept it.'

'What are these woods? You are the angel Michael,' said the chamberlain. 'This is Jordan and I have fallen to the foot of the tree of life that Enoch saw.'

'My name here is not Michael,' said the god.

'What is it?'

'I have a name for every mood.'

'What is your mood today?'

'As black as ever was.'

'What is the name that suits it?'

'Loki,' said the god.

The moon was bright, but in the distance were dark clouds, flashing with fire from below. The river seemed very strange too – a glittering road of white light.

'I know you,' said Loys. 'You are a devil and this is hell.'

'You fell here with me. What does that make you?'

'One of the damned.'

'Justly?'

'I do not know. To be damned is to be justly damned, for it is God who damns.'

'I tell you it was unjustly. What did you do but love a woman, a woman marked for death by a darker spirit than mine?'

'The woman is not here,' said Loys. 'That is how I know this is hell. I saw her dying. I ...' He couldn't control himself and put his hands to his face to shield his tears.

'I'm sorry,' he said. 'Men do not weep.'

'Oh, they do,' said Loki. 'They weep and they mewl and they ask for their mothers as the blood bubbles at their throat. Their tears drown all pretence of heroism and they see at the last how sweet it would have been to spend a life at the plough or the nets, and they see the fellows they have killed are men just like them. How petty pride seems with a spear in your belly.'

The boat was moving. Bollason took an oar, Vandrad another, other Vikings too — the men who had taken him to the Numera.

'The slaughtered sons are coming back to the carrion god, ravenous for his blood. We must cross the bridge of light,' said Loki.

The longship glided down the river under the metal moon.

'I am dead,' said Loys. 'Without her I want only death. Oblivion.'

'My word, you don't ask much, do you? Oblivion — whose lure is deeper than rubies and gold, to be as unmindful as a stone — the gods grant that rich prize to so few who ask.'

'I ask,' said Loys.

'I know,' said Loki. 'Your task here is to seek death. King Death.'

He could not tell how long they had been sailing. A long time, it seemed. A week? Many years? Under the moonlight his hands were strangely beautiful, delicately wrought. *God's work*, he said to himself. *God's work*.

The boat was slowing and approaching the bank. The night was windless, and the trees stood shining in the moonlight, as still as if the smiths of the emperor's court had made them from silver to stand in the palace courtyard. The longship grounded by the broken wall, Bollason jumping ashore to tie a mooring rope around a stump.

'Alight,' said the god, 'for a light, a light from which old grim guts cannot hide.'

Loys stepped onto the riverbank. The night was cool but not unpleasant, and the woods were fragrant, noisy with insects and the calls of owls.

In the wall he saw a single little lamp burning, others beside it dead and cold. He went to it. The flame seemed weak. He touched it and saw her – Beatrice in the frosty woods, her horse steaming in the dawn sun, Beatrice naked in the bed next to him, standing by the prow of the merchant ship that had brought them to Constantinople, the blue waters of the Aegean turning her eyes to turquoise. The warmth of the flame was like the warmth of her touch, the sound of the wind in the woods like the sound of her voice and the moon hung above him, like God's eye, judging his worthiness to call her his wife.

'The dead do not wait,' said the pale god from the ship. 'Make the needful action, that necessary gesture.'

Loys took another lamp from the wall. It was wet so he dried the wick on his tunic and upended it so oil ran onto the wick. Then he lit it off the flame of the single burning lamp. It flared, guttered and finally caught.

'This is my lamp,' said Loys, standing back from the wall.

'Yet you will not use it to see your way.'

'What will I use it for?'

'What is a lamp ever used for? To banish darkness.'

Carrying his lamp carefully, Loys climbed back onto the ship, which pulled away from the bank and glided forward again. At first he thought they were bound for Constantinople, for the sky ahead seemed to bubble with black clouds and fires flashed and flickered in the far distance.

The shore disappeared. The white of the moonlit river faded as red, gold and blue replaced it, three separate streams of light playing beneath the keel of the ship, shooting rays from its spars and sails. Loys put out his hands to watch the beams stream from his fingers.

'Where are we?'

'Bifrost.'

'What is that?'

'The bridge between the realm of men and the realm of gods. The rainbow in its colours three.'

'We can sail across a bridge?'

'Is it less marvellous that you could walk across light?'

'The women at the well spun light.'

'They spin everything. We are an expression only of their spinning.'

'Where are we going?'

'To the lands of death. To the Dark of Moon plain.'

'Who are these who travel beside us?'

Loys was aware of other shapes in the streams of light. Men? Spirits? Demons? He couldn't tell. Some seemed like giants with burning heads, some like corpses with eaten-away faces and rotted eyes, some like misshapen men, stooping and running, some like giant women. Demons all, he was sure.

'The enemies of death. They follow you and your light.'

'I do not want followers like these.'

'The world hears too much of wanting. There is no choice here. Only destiny.'

'Where shall I go?'

'Where you are fated to go.'

The streams of light intensified until Loys had to shield his eyes to see. A great roar, screaming and a smell of burning. Loys fell to the deck of the ship, cradling his little lamp as he did. The light around him was intense and even with his eyes tight shut he saw red on the inside of his eyelids. The roaring

384

grew louder and louder, and he recognised it for the sound of battle – the monstrous smithy sound of steel on steel, thumps and crashes along with the stink of earth and fire. The longship smashed into solid ground, and Loys was thrown out, the impact as he landed driving all breath from him. A taste of ash and grit was in his mouth. Miraculously the little lamp he'd carried from the wall was still in his hands.

When he opened his eyes he saw its light still burned, but the world was wild.

53   The Fenris Wolf

He lay in the mouth of a great cave in a hillside. Below him was a starlit plain. In the far distance a gigantic city, its walls even greater than those of Constantinople, burned like a night sun. The fierce fire reddened the clouds above it, as if the sky was a beast with a wound in its side. Closer to him, Bollason and some Vikings fought a huge red-bearded man who swung a terrible war hammer. Bollason was fast for a big man, and danced, ducked and thrust as the hammer thundered above his head, around him, past him, never quite touching him. Elsewhere a twisted figure, the one-eyed fellow he'd seen in the well, his body stained and tattooed, his one eye mad with battle lust, a spear in his hand, thrust at enemies three times his size who attempted to pluck him from his horse. The horse! It had eight legs and kicked and bit at the giants as its rider thrust with his spear. One of the giants was engulfed by flame but fought as though it was no bother to him at all, another bore a terrible sword and cut at the rider but could not hit him. Loys realised the rider and the man with the hammer were not simply trying to defeat their opponents, they were trying to get at him.

He became aware of a deep animal stink behind him.

Just inside the cave was what he first took for a pile of rubble, but his eyes only took a moment to adjust. It was not a heap of stones but an animal, an immense wolf as long as five men from nose to tail and so bulky its side rose to twice Loys' height. The wolf was tied with fine threads almost like spider silk, which cut and marked its flesh. It strained against the threads as if in a delirium, its green eyes vacant, its tongue lolling. A stream of drool dripped from its mouth, which was propped open by a good thick sword. It was bound to a huge black rock that reached up into the cave, a terrible thing. The wolf had rubbed a big sore into its side and its blood glittered in the light of the burning city.

Beside Loys was the woman with the burned face, the one he'd seen drowned at the well.

'The threads,' she said. 'Burn through the threads.'

'How are you here?'

'I found a way to die. Now burn through the threads.'

'Why?'

'So the story will end. So the cycle of agony will end. Your lover will be free of what has hunted her all those years. Free of the past – of me, for that is what I am.'

'Those men down the hill will kill me.'

'They are gods and they will fight there forever unless you release the wolf or step out of the cave.'

'Then I might stay here for ever.'

'Then your lover will die.'

'My lover is dead.'

'I think so. She will die again and again, as horribly, if you do not act.'

Loys sensed the woman spoke the truth. It didn't matter. Beatrice was dead. He wanted only one thing.

'If I die here, properly, do I go to darkness?'

'Yes.'

'If I fail to act?'

'You stay here for ever.'

'I could welcome the gods or walk to them, for them to slaughter me.'

'Fail to release the wolf and the gods will welcome you. They will build you a palace in Asgard, where you can live out eternity without her.'

He was overwhelmed by the firelit dark, the smell of the wolf, the beast's low keening and rasping, the feel of the stones beneath his feet. He sat down.

'Burn the threads. Remove the sword. Free the wolf. It is your destiny.'

His little lamp still burned after his terrible journey through the rainbow light.

'Is it my death?'

'Yes. Be quick. The rock to which it is tied banishes all magic but in the other eight worlds his mind roams free. The wolf will not know you are coming to help him and could still kill you at the well.'

'And then?'

'Your lover lives again, to die again in agony.'

Loys walked to where the wolf heaved and panted. Its eyes moved as it watched him approach. As he advanced, the wolf drew back its lips in a growl and Loys shook in fear. The beast's voice groaned like the protests of a ship's timbers in a storm, its eyes were full of ancient hatred.

He thought of Beatrice. No particular memory came to him, just her smiling at him. Could he live with that memory in this gloomy place for ever? In a palace, on a plain? Anywhere? No. He couldn't.

He considered climbing around the back of the wolf, to burn the rope where it was secured to the rock, but he wasn't sure he would be able to carry the lamp. He couldn't hurt the wolf with the flame, he knew, not properly. He went between its bound back legs to its belly. So many threads crossed its body he didn't know where to begin. He just held the flame to the nearest thread and, of necessity, to the animal's skin.

As the wolf's flesh burned the animal snarled and spluttered, its great head straining at Loys. The threads were burning too, blackening and snapping one after the other. He watched the flame catch and grow bigger as it fed off the threads. The animal howled and growled. More threads blackened, thinned and snapped, and suddenly the great wolf could move.

The wolf lunged at him. Its head jerked back, still held by some of the remaining threads and it howled with a note that Loys thought might plunge him into madness as it bit down on the sword that kept its jaws apart. How soon would it be, he wondered, before the animal broke completely free, got rid of its sword and tore him to pieces.

He glanced at the woman next to him.

'Hurry,' she said.

'What about you?'

'I am dead. I have no lamp to burn.'

'Use this one.'

'I will not touch it.'

Loys reapplied the flame and the animal strained against the threads as the little lamp burned its skin. More threads burned and parted. More. The animal's head swung round, swiping the air next to Loys' head. Its breath was like a blow, and Loys reeled back. The wolf was still not loose but it tore at its remaining bonds with its claws.

Loys became aware of someone else in the cave. In the shadows at the corner of his eye crouched an old man. He was thin but terribly muscular, his skin stained black like aged leather, a rope around his throat, one eye staring at Loys, the other just a slit. In one hand he bore a long spear fashioned from a piece of burned wood.

Loys knew him. He could not mistake him. He was the man on the eight-legged horse. But down the hill, the same man still fought the giants. He was a god, in many places at the same time, thought Loys.

'King Death,' he said.

The wolf's snarls grated throughout the cave, its teeth tore at its bonds. Still it could not break free, the threads were so tight it would have to bite away its own flesh to be rid of them.

'He is not here,' said the woman with the scar to Loys. 'He is fighting the giants. That rock is called Scream and it denies all magic, even his. This is the nearest he can send his mind. Do not approach him and he cannot hurt you.'

The man cleared a few rocks away and scratched something in the sand. A rune like an angular r. To Loys it seemed to sparkle with water, to shift like the rain on a hillside.

'What does it mean?'

'You don't know, so that means you are safe. Stay where you are.'

'And you?'

The woman stood almost next to the rune, gazing down into it.

'I . . .'

Her body twitched and shook and she stepped forward to stand beside the god. Her head lolled to the side, her shoulders sagged and her feet went onto tiptoe as if she was being hanged with an invisible rope. The old man stood and extended his spear at arm's length, prodding the woman in the back.

She spoke, her voice strangled: 'There is still time. The giants will die and we will come here. There is still time. No! No! The god speaks through me; it is not me.' The woman had her hands at her neck, as if to pull something away.

'Time for what?' asked Loys.

'For life and for death.' Her voice had gone down an octave. It was now that of an old man – deep, full of spite.

'What life, what death?'

'Her life, your death.'

'My wife is gone.'

'I am King Death. She is not gone unless I will it.'

'Then do not will it.'

'You have done me great harm.'

'I sought only death.'

'Do not pay to bring her from the well!' It was the woman's usual voice again, terribly hoarse and strangled.

'What is the price?'

'Die on the teeth of the wolf before he is free,' the god spoke through her again. 'He last ate when the world was young. We will retie him while he feeds on you.' The woman twisted and fought with whatever encircled her neck.

'Why not throw the woman to the wolf?' said Loys. 'She is a sorceress and has brought this thing on herself.'

'She is part divine.' The woman spoke, but Loys knew it

390

was the twisted figure of the spear god who commanded her voice. 'It is dishonourable to kill her in this place.'

'Not me?'

'You are a man and an intruder here. Yours is the necessary sacrifice. Yours is the death I require to work my magic.'

'If I don't do it then you will die.'

'If that is what honour requires. We could have killed the wolf instead of binding him, but honour said no. We raised him and cannot stain the fields of Asgard with the blood of a guest. Better to die than be dishonoured. You come here bearing fire, as the prophecy foresaw; you have tried to free the wolf, as the prophecy foresaw. You are my enemy and I demand your death.'

The wolf lunged towards Loys but its jaws snapped short of him. It was still held by the threads binding its back legs.

'I want more,' said Loys.

'What more?'

'She must not be alone. Make sure she gets back to her father. All I believed in has been shaken today, and it grieves me to bargain with demons, but give her a protector; let her live and prosper.'

'I will.'

'Do you swear it?'

'It is my oath.'

'No! No!' the woman screamed. Now she was flung to the ground by the invisible force. She crawled towards the snarling wolf, out of the reach of the god's magic.

The wolf's paws tore at its back legs in a frenzy, its voice like the scrape of a ship grounding. Loys realised the beast could not claw the final strands free. It snapped and twisted, writhing in frustration and agony.

'Your oath?'

The god said nothing, just held out his hand. Loys was sure he was going to die so feared nothing. He stepped towards the god and put his hand in his.

It was as if he had taken a blow to the stomach, the feeling someone dozing in front of a fire gets as they suddenly snap back into consciousness from the edge of sleep. Images went flashing through Loys' mind — a vast sky of stars, a high tree, a man hung upon it pierced by a spear, his eye a raw wound. Loys felt a weight to the air — air more like water, as if he had to struggle through it to move. Cold water, dark water, black water. He saw what the god had suffered, his thirst, his agony, but he saw more. He saw heroes who carried the god's symbols, the raven or the triple knot, cast down and stabbed, he saw them crying out to the god for help, but women or ravens, or something between ravens and women, swept down on them, carrying them away. He knew they were the god's servants and he knew the god's names. Odin and Bolverkr — the evil-worker. Ginnarr — the deceiver. Grimnir — the masked one. Skollvaldr — ruler of treachery. He could not trust the oath.

He let go of the god's hand. Back down the slope the weird horseman still battled the giants, but two huge bodies lay dead and the others were giving ground.

He took his little lamp and walked towards the wolf, where the god could not send his mind.

54 Stronger than Death

We are three. A voice spoke in Beatrice's mind.

The wound in her side hurt badly. She tried to get up, to help Loys but her injury was too severe. She wept in frustration and pain.

The tattooed savage, Azémar's double, stood chanting in the pool, holding someone beneath the water, the wolf-thing tore at Mauger's flesh and the boy splashed in the water calling out, 'Why here's the answer; there are runes aplenty here.'

You are the only. The existing. The now. A voice in her head. Her own? No, a girl's. A name came to her. *Elai,* and another name too. *Skuld.*

'What was?' Beatrice didn't know where the words came from but she knew she spoke them.

I release it.

'What will be?' said Beatrice.

I do not fear it. This is the well, the well of wyrd. The well where destinies are spun. For some life, for others death.

'Is that skein spun?'

You are spinning it.

'Where is Loys?'

He will die for you. Long ago the magic was set, burning in the back of the minds of strange sisters in dark places like this, burning in your mind – this is how you will escape the god. Put your blood into the waters to see. It is your blood that lets you see.

Beatrice clasped to the wound in her side. Her hands were soaked with blood. She knew what to do. She dipped her right hand into the stream.

What have you given? She couldn't tell who asked the question. It was almost as if she asked it of herself.

'I have given my lover and my blood,' she said.

Then see.

Beatrice saw the black hillside: she saw the battle between Bollason's Vikings and the giants and the two gods, she saw Snake in the Eye dodging and ducking the swipes of the great hammer; she saw her sister Uthr, she with the burned face, lying fallen on the ground and Loys staring up at the great bulk of the snarling wolf, who tore and snapped at his bonds.

She understood it all – how the god had brushed her sister aside. The woman with the burned face was the past. But other women might prove more difficult for him to beat. The gods had had Beatrice in their grip, had cursed and doomed her, but no more. Here she was her own mistress. She did not think of the past, so many lives spent in agony. She did not think of the future – so many more lives to be tortured and denied. She thought of that instant and her love for Loys.

'I would go to him.'

What would you give? It was her own voice in her head now but she knew it was the well speaking to her.

'My life.'

More is required.

'What more?'

Snake in the Eye, who had been splashing in the waters as if searching for a lost coin, suddenly looked up. 'I can go to the wall,' he said, 'and what little flame is this? A baby! These waters seem to want it snuffed, for sure!'

'No!' said Beatrice. The blood on her hands streamed out from her fingers through the water of the well, threads of crimson spinning towards Snake in the Eye to ensnare him. The boy fell back into the water, at the same time reaching forward his hand as if to snuff out a candle. A great spasm shot through her belly. A warm flow spread over her legs and she doubled up.

'Get into the well!' screamed Snake in the Eye. 'Get into the well! The waters want your blood and they want the blood of your child. Get into the water! That will put the wolf off my scent.'

He came splashing towards her and pulled at her legs so she slipped into the pool. Then he held her down.

As Beatrice's blood seeped into the water it became a river of light, and she twisted the light into a cascade of colour that streamed down into the depths of the well, swirled up through the leaves of the starry tree and out, to meet the light beyond.

Outside the cave, Beatrice appeared, the pale girl beside her, their hands linked. Loys could not get to the wolf's remaining bonds, as it thrashed from side to side, turning and twisting and threatening to crush him with its bulk.

The woman spoke, the one with the burned face, but she was fading, her presence more difficult to register. She was there, and then only the idea of her was there, and then there was nothing. The last of her was her words.

'Take the sword from its mouth. It will tear its final bonds if you take out the sword.'

But Loys only had eyes for his wife.

'You are dead, Beatrice,' said Loys.

'I think so.'

'I must go to the wolf, to protect you in eternal time.'

The pale girl was at his side. Something was in her hands, like thread, like blood in water, like light. She was spinning it through her fingers and it flowed out from them, engulfing Loys.

'This is your fate. No more the torn and murdered, no more the tears of separation and death,' said the girl. 'Die for her peace; die so we might be released from this torment forever.'

The gods had killed the Vikings and the giants and came screaming up the hill. The wolf was held by only a few threads, though the sword still blocked its mouth.

'I cannot get to the threads. The wolf will knock me aside.'

The girl spoke: 'Then tear out the sword.'

The gods were running now, the red-haired man with the hammer. The one-eyed man with the noose about his neck galloped up on his eight-legged horse, the projection of his mind that had lurked at the cave's entrance now gone.

Loys looked at the sword and knew he would die if he ripped it free.

The animal strained forward, its hot jaws an arm's length from Loys. He only had to reach forward and take it.

'She will be born again?'

'Again and again.'

'Loys, save yourself. It's not too late. The waters tell me so. You can live.'

Beatrice went to the girl and pulled the streams from her hands, struggling for control of them, the woven blood, the blood light, the life light, streaming over Loys at one instant, past him the next.

Loys spoke to the girl. 'I am human,' he said, 'not eternal. You are the fates, so you say. So you take care of the destiny of these demons. You ask me to end the rule of devils by freeing Satan. I will not do it. I would like to see my wife again.'

'Take the wolf!'

The girl gave a great scream as Beatrice tore at the threads in her hands. Then she fell down and was gone.

The gods ran past Loys, leaping onto the wolf, holding it down, grabbing threads to tie it again. The animal strained forward towards Loys, the great head slamming into the ground an arm's length from him. He could still remove the sword if he chose.

The bonds that still bound the wolf were long ones – long enough for the head of the animal to emerge from the mouth of the cave, to the limit of where the strange drowned god had worked his magic. And then Loys' eyes met the green eyes of the wolf and he was transfixed. The ground seemed to swirl beneath his feet, he saw the stars spin in a great vortex above him. The wolf's agonies were his agonies, the wolf's struggle his struggles, and a seething animosity bubbled within him, hate raw and angry. It had put its mind into his mind, casting itself into his skin.

He was the wolf. There was no difference between them. He saw the gods for what they were – his bitter enemies. He would tear off his bonds, rip them apart and suck on their blood.

Ragnarok – the word burned into his mind like the sound of a branding iron into water. The twilight of the gods. That was his purpose, what he was for.

But then the god with the hammer beat at the wolf's skull, the one-eyed man tying its paws with threads, the strange spirits – half-raven, half-women, things only glimpsed in flashes and flutters – were all around, dragging the wolf back into the cave.

Loys wanted to follow it, to do what he had failed to do, pull out the sword and free the animal, free himself.

'Loys.' Beatrice was beside him. She took his hand and kissed him.

'We will meet again,' she said, 'in eternal time. Look for me. Find me.'

'I will never abandon you.'

'You once held me to life,' she said; 'now I release you to it.'

She let go of his hand, and he flew up through the strands of light, through the rainbow glimmer; he saw the ship of dead men's nails beneath him, felt the rush of the wind through the branches of the tree of light. Then he was back in the cave of the well.

55 Child of Blood

Elifr saw Snake in the Eye pull Beatrice into the pool and push her under, but held fast to his task and what the well had told him to do. He could not go to her. The wolfman had to see the ritual through, had to give the scholar time to do what he needed to do. He couldn't even shout to Snake in the Eye to stop, but kept up his mumbled chant, leaving part of his mind on that shore where he waited for Loys, part in the chamber.

Loys had struggled at first but then he had become calm and was easy to hold. Elifr held him still, looking up at the wolf. A great gash ran along its torso all the way up to its chest. Its head lolled and it panted heavily.

'Come on, come on!' Elifr spoke to Loys. 'Do what is necessary. Do what you have to.'

The wolf was now on its side in the water, its head below the surface. It was still. As he peered through the dead light of the glowing rocks he saw something like a coil of pale rope spill from the animal's belly. The white-haired warrior had done for it. Had it died before the god? Snake in the Eye was still alive. Elifr felt weak with elation. It was done, the act was done, the wolf was dead and the god still lived in Middle Earth.

The scholar was coming, flowing back like light trapped in light, like a shining fish lifted in a net of light. Elifr took his hand, brought his consciousness fully back to the chamber, and the scholar came spluttering to the surface of the pool. Elifr pulled him towards the nearest place he could leave him with his head above the water. He dragged him across the haunches of the great wolf, lifted him up onto the body and then turned to Snake in the Eye. The boy let go of Beatrice and faced Elifr.

'All my friends come back to me!' he said. 'All the pretty runes dancing for my pleasure!'

Elifr leaped on the boy, knocking him back, his hands around his head, one thumb in an eye. Snake in the Eye fell back into the water as the wolfman tore at him, but then Elifr went limp and his grip loosened. The boy stood up, one eye a bloody mess, but his face wild with elation.

'They're here! The runes that kill and slaughter. I am lord of death! Lord of slaughter! I am Odin made flesh on earth and the wolf my enemy lies dead!'

'You have killed her,' said Loys.

Snake in the Eye watched as Loys licked the blood from his fingers.

'I have. And I will kill you. But there is no candle on the wall for you, sir. Pray, tell me who you are. Hurry now, I have a world to slaughter.'

Loys bent down into the water and picked up something bright and curved and wicked. Bollason's sword. He waded towards the boy.

'Why do my runes back away from you? Why do they not chime? Who are you, sir? I ask you again.'

'I am a wolf,' said Loys, and he cut off the boy's head. Snake in the Eye collapsed at the knees, his unburdened neck a blood fountain, his head toppling into the water behind him. Then the light, the bright and burning light, bleached all vision away.

Loys had the impression of symbols flashing past him, signs that were more than signs, things that seemed to express the fundamental nature of humanity, of gods, of animals, of weather and of things stranger and more incomprehensible than any of them.

The runes flew through the tunnels, some falling back into the water, some alighting on the shelf where Styliane lay, others shrieking down into the lightless caves.

Loys blinked his eyes back to usefulness and waded on, throwing the sword up into the passageway and pulling

Beatrice up from the water. He felt strong as he lifted her.

He got her to dry ground and held her. She was not breathing. He felt for her heart. There was a faint beat, but then it stopped.

'Don't go,' he said. 'Remember, I hold you to life. I hold you to life.'

But she was gone and he could do nothing but hug her to him. The lamp finally guttered and died and with it the glow of the rocks. He sat in the dark, listening to his own breathing, cold and waiting to die. The darkness was not true darkness, he realised, or rather some new sense was in him. The rocks had a flavour to them and he could smell the currents of air that drifted down from the surface, taste the smoky sky of Constantinople. He didn't feel tired at all. In fact, he felt quite well, despite his ordeal.

'I have been to dark places and brought back bright things.' A voice behind him. Styliane. He heard her splashing through the pool.

'How can you find me?'

'I see you and I see who you are, what you have become. I have entered the story too.'

'I have become nothing.'

'The wolf put his eyes on you. He's in you now. Just as these signs are in me. There are three here in the darkness beside me. One for each facet of the goddess. I wonder where the others went.'

'What are the runes?'

'Magic. Earned in sacrifice at the well.'

'What did you give?'

Styliane took Loys' hand and put it to her face. On one side he felt the orb of her eye below her lid. On the other was a swollen ruin.

'That,' she said, 'and all my happiness. I saw my sister in the well. She is still here, I think, but she has failed. She is mad now and our future is in her grip.'

'How so?'

'You and I will always find each other, scholar. The gods bind us together.'

Loys didn't want to think about the implications of what she was telling him.

'Can you help my wife?'

'No, but you will find her again. She will be reborn. That has always been her fate. It always will be, until you can find a way to stop it.'

'Reincarnation is a heresy.'

'But for her you know it to be be true.'

Loys said nothing but he felt very deeply Styliane was right. A sense had come over him when the wolf put its eyes on him — a sense of old time, of lives before, of the future stretching out.

'The child, will it live?'

'Perhaps there is no need for it to die. It still lives. These bright symbols can bring it forth.'

Loys thought for a second he had lost consciousness. He saw himself lying on a grassy bank by a river, warmed by the sun. The smell of meadow grass was in his nose, the buzz of bees in his ears. Beatrice was at his side, beautiful. And then he was somewhere else — a high place, by a fire, looking out over a wide valley. She was with him again and he never wanted to be anywhere else.

But then the dark, the tunnel and the damp.

Something mewled. A child. Styliane pushed it into his arms and he felt its warm life against the coldness of his chest.

'The blood waters have made it plain. He tried to kill it. Snake in the Eye didn't know his purpose here; he was the god in his madness but the baby was the sacrifice that would have let her live. She died defending her child.'

Loys could say nothing, just sat weeping and holding the baby.

Styliane pushed something else into his hand. A stone on a leather thong.

'Take this,' she said. 'It will let you live as you would want to.'

Loys touched its shape in the darkness and knew what it was.

'This is pagan magic.'

'It is your salvation.'

Loys did not put it on, but he didn't cast it aside either.

'Can you stand?' said Styliane.

'I think so. But we can't find our way out of here without light.'

'We can,' said Styliane. 'The way is clear to me. Here, a third gift for what you have done.' She put the sword into his hand.

'Then lead,' said Loys. The scent of the outside drifted down very strongly. The mosses and minerals of the rocks each had their unique smell, and he could distinguish the deeper-lying odours from those of the surface. A thick odour of blood was all around – on Beatrice, on him, on the child. The baby clung to him and cried.

He found his wife in the darkness and kissed her.

'If you come back,' he said, 'I will find you. We will not let demons or even death thwart us. Love is stronger than death. You will come back.' He squeezed her hand and kissed it for the last time.

He could not get her out, would not visit that place again. This would be her grave. He prayed:

'In company with Christ,
who died and now lives,
may she rejoice in your kingdom,
where all our tears are wiped away.
Unite us together again in one family,
to sing your praise for ever and ever.'

Then he followed Styliane. She went up through the tunnels, back the way her mother, sister and brother had come all those years before. Loys cradled the baby, the sword under his arm, the stone in his hand. They came out into the open air on the hill with the boulders, where Loys kissed his daughter, the child of blood, and looked down on the great city of Constantinople shining under brightening skies.

Acknowledgements

Thanks to:

Professor Judith Herrin, whose wonderful book *Byzantium: The Surprising Life of a Medieval Empire* formed the basis of my research and who graciously took time to answer some of my questions. Needless to say, any historical inaccuracies in *Lord of Slaughter* are down to me, not her.

Michele Howe for being a first reader and for her perceptive comments.

Praise for *Wolfsangel*:

'Genuinely strange, eerie, evocative. A classic'
Adam Roberts

'M.D. Lachlan's fantasy debut has all the essential elements of a rollicking historical fantasy: action aplenty, vivid description and strong characterisation. The most powerful and original fantasy I have read for some time' *Interzone*

'*Wolfsangel* truly has the epic and bloodthirsty feel of Norse saga' *Waterstones Book Quarterly*

'By Odin, this could be the fantasy-adventure for you!'
Daily Mail

'A fantasy debut that really is a cracker' *Falcata Times*

'What sets it apart as great, rather than merely good, is its ambition. Intermingled with the earthly concerns of Vali and Feilig are disturbing, otherworldly encounters with Gods and monsters alike which truly elevate the scope and imaginative prowess of Lachlan's outstanding first fantasy' *The Speculative Scotsman*

'A strong opening novel in the sequence, and has a dark, bloody-minded tone that makes it feel like something genuinely "different"' *Wertzone*

'This is a cracking read, a good page turner . . . well written and fast paced' *SFF World.com*

'Fantasy addicts will enjoy every page' *Total Sci Fi*

'The strength of *Wolfsangel* lies in Lachlan's superlative storytelling skill. He evokes the frozen wastes of the Viking kings. We feel the biting cold, see the bleak wilderness, hear the myths of the Gods. Despite the oftentimes dark aspect of the novel, it is anchored by a warm heart and it is this that kept me reading long into the night. I can't wait for the next in this series. M.D. Lachlan has penned a winner' *Fantasyliterature.com*

Also by M.D. Lachlan from Gollancz

Wolfsangel
Fenrir
Lord of Slaughter